scenario for a sequel. Fans of medieval adventure, murder mysteries, and romance will all find something to like here, and readers will eagerly await the continuation of this engrossing saga.'

School Library Journal

'Mystery lovers will be delighted ... This may be cause for comparison with *Game of Thrones*; Prince Jared is sure to face plenty of political intrigue in the volumes ahead.'

VOYA

'A complex mix of infidelity, betrayals, political intrigue, and a hint of romance ... the period atmosphere and adventure that provide *Game of Thrones*-inspired drama ... will draw medieval buffs and fantasy fans.'

...ulletin

Also by Justin Somper

Allies and Assassins

ALLIES & ASSASSINS

A CONSPIRACY OF PRINCES

JUSTIN SOMPER

www.atombooks.net

ATOM

First published in Great Britain in 2015 by Atom

A CIP catalogue record for this book
is available from the British Library.

ISBN 978-1-907411-88-5

Typeset in Melior by M Rules
Printed and bound in Great Britain by
Clays Ltd, St Ives plc

Papers used by Atom are from well-managed forests
and other responsible sources.

MIX
Paper from
responsible sources
FSC
www.fsc.org   FSC® C104740

For Arthur Angus-Hill

PROLOGUE

The palace grounds were packed tight with spectators, like crated apples after harvest. Men, women and children jostled against each other, anxious for a good view of the stage. Public executions always attracted a large crowd, not least because they had become a rarity in Archenfield.

There had never been a more eagerly anticipated execution than the one scheduled at the chiming of the Poet's Bell. Today, the Executioner's blade would lay claim to the head of the assassin of Prince Anders, the person who had taken the burgeoning dream of Archenfield and hacked it to pieces. This was no stranger, no avowed enemy, but one of the Prince's most trusted advisors. His name was Logan Wilde, the Poet. Wilde's betrayal had made a mockery of everything the Princedom stood for. Now order needed to be restored. This vital undertaking would begin with the sight of Logan Wilde's head being severed from his body.

Two weeks earlier, the grounds beneath the palace balcony had been filled with people reeling with grief, hanging desperately upon the words of their new ruler. Prince Jared had addressed them from the very same ivy-covered balcony, after the death of his brother. Today, the crowd was still grieving the loss of Prince Anders but now, stirred into that well of grief, was something else – something more primal. A hunger. At last, the Blood Price was about to be paid.

The Woodsman – Jonas Drummond – had built a scaffold so that the beheading would take place in full view of the crowd. As with all the Woodsman's constructions, the scaffold was more elegant than was perhaps strictly necessary. Jonas, along with most of the other members of the Twelve, stood on the raised platform in front of the expectant audience. The message could not have been clearer if it had been drafted by the renegade Poet himself: 'Today, we exorcise our demons. Today we achieve catharsis. Today, the dream of Archenfield begins anew.'

Excited whispers whipped through the crowd as soberly dressed figures emerged from the palace doorway. It was the new ruler himself, sixteen-year-old Prince Jared. He walked sombrely towards the scaffold, flanked on one side by his younger brother, Prince Edvin, and on the other by Axel Blaxland, the Prince's cousin and Captain of the Guard. The new Prince had yet to be crowned and Jared's head was bare, his unruly dark hair striking out in various directions. But though Jared was unquestionably young, he had grown considerably in stature in the past two weeks. Despite the near-fatal wounds he had sustained at the Poet's hand, he walked with confidence; only the occasional, slight wince would have alerted a vigilant onlooker to the bloodstained dressings and angry wounds lurking beneath his shirt. His dark eyes took in the crowd with warmth and understanding. There were cheers for him; he did not smile as he received them, but simply lifted his hand for a brief moment.

The next person to climb up on to the scaffold was the

Priest, Father Simeon. He moved with something of a swagger, his dark robes skimming the straw that had been strewn across the wooden floor. Was Father Simeon relishing this occasion and gladly anticipating the beheading of Archenfield's number-one enemy? Though Father Simeon was another member of the Twelve, today he remained separate from the rest. If the victim required spiritual succour in his final moments on earth, the Priest would need to be close at hand.

Now everyone was in place, bar the two key protagonists of the unfolding drama, and the hushed reverence now gave way to lusty shouts: 'Bring out the prisoner!' 'Bring out the Poet!' 'Death to the assassin!' This last chant instantly established itself as the most popular and what began as an unruly outpouring of noise swiftly evolved into a chilling, communal cry: 'Death to the assassin! Death to the assassin!'

The shouts became louder still as two hooded figures emerged from the palace. The first was carrying a twin-headed axe, its two blades glinting in the late September sun; the second man's wrists were bound in chains. They walked in perfect synchrony.

As the Executioner stopped centre-stage and drew down his hood, the crowd roared its approval. Morgan Booth did not hold back his smile. He knew what the crowd had come for, knew that the several hundred people ranked before him represented every last man, woman, child and babe in Archenfield – all united in one desire. And Morgan, with his twinkling eyes, sharp beard and trusty axe, was going to give them exactly what they craved.

The Executioner began by drawing back the prisoner's hood and the crowd was granted its first sight of the renegade Poet. He had been incarcerated for only a week but still he looked drained. He extended his manacled hands towards the Executioner who, having set down his axe, loosened the chains about the prisoner's wrists. The length of chain slipped down on to the straw, where it lay curled like a dormant snake.

The Poet's hands trembled momentarily. Then he managed to compose himself. Logan Wilde reached into the pocket of his burlap trousers and produced a single coin. He held it up to show the crowd; it glimmered in the sunlight. He delivered the coin into the waiting palm of the Executioner. Then he spoke, in a voice sweet and strong, which carried out across the balcony and through the crowd. 'I forgive you for what you are about to do,' Wilde told the Executioner.

Booth nodded, and the crowd fell silent.

Father Simeon stepped forward, demonstrating his availability to the victim. Logan shook his head. The Priest's face was briefly etched with disappointment, his role in the spectacle fatally diminished. But he nodded, and drew back again.

The victim dropped to his knees and rested his handsome head on the Executioner's block.

'Death to the assassin!' The raging crowd took up the chant once more as the Executioner lifted his twin-headed axe. 'Death to the assassin! Death to the assassin!'

Logan's eyes were turned towards the crowd. If this was unintentional, it was too late now to turn his head in the other direction. In those final moments, he would see the livid hatred in the onlookers' eyes.

The Executioner swung his axe and sliced cleanly through the fibrous tissues of Wilde's neck. The assassin's head thumped to the floor and rolled across the straw, coming to a stop at the feet of the Priest.

Moving swiftly, the Executioner set down his axe. There was one final, important part of the ritual to observe. Morgan Booth reached down to retrieve the Poet's severed head.

Brushing off the stalks of straw stuck to the ball of skin, bone and ligament, the Executioner held aloft the trophy of flesh. The crowd roared its approval, and the palace grounds pulsated with a tribal energy.

The Blood Price had been paid.

ONE

THE BLACK PALACE OF PADDENBURG

Lydia Wilde bolted upright. Where was she? Her eyes focused and traced the familiar outline of her closet, the drape of heavy curtains. She was safely in her bedchamber. She raised a hand to her forehead and felt the slick of perspiration and the heat there. It had spread through her entire body, and her chemise was soaked through. She pushed back the heavy bed-covers and stepped down on to the floor.

She felt giddy and unsure of her reality. Had she actually witnessed her brother's execution or had it just been a vivid dream?

Lydia reached for the black-glass carafe on the bedside cabinet and, not bothering to decant the water into its matching glass, raised it to her lips and swallowed thirstily. Only then did she feel her heartbeat slow, the heat begin to dissipate.

I'm here in the royal bedchamber in the Black Palace of Paddenburg, she told herself. It was only a nightmare. The same nightmare that stalks me every single night. Logan is safe. And I will hold him in my arms again soon.

She set the carafe back down on the cabinet and turned to see if her sudden movements had roused Prince Henning from his slumber, but there was no familiar rise and fall of bedcovers on the other side of the bed. Lydia was alone in the royal bedchamber. She felt grateful for that. It was better Henning didn't see her in such a state. But where had he gone to, and what was he doing, at such an early hour? Had his torturous insomnia got the better of him once again?

She ran a hand through her short bob of hair. It was still a shock to feel cool air along the nape of her neck, but Henning had desired her hair to be cropped like this. She remembered him sitting across from her, that first time, watching intently as her lady's maid had taken merciless scissors to Lydia's long tresses. As the twin blades had moved across one another, their brutal scrape had sent a shiver down the length of Lydia's spine. 'Short enough, Your Infinite Highness?' the maid had asked Prince Henning – no care for Lydia, who might as well have been a yew hedge. Each time, the Prince had given a small, silent shake of his head. And in answer, another inch of her beautiful black hair had tumbled to the rug below, dead as an autumn leaf. Lydia had never felt more naked in her life.

Shivering at the memory, she paced towards one of the pairs of heavy brocade curtains which shielded each of the bedchamber's seven windows and drew them back, conscious that her palms were still slick with sweat. Next, she turned her attention to the thick wooden shutters. Henning couldn't even contemplate sleep without the room being as dark as the grave. It would have been Lydia's preference to keep the curtains parted and the shutters on their hinges, in order to be woken softly, sensuously, by the first rays of the morning sun but, from the time she had first arrived in Prince Henning's bedchamber, she had been made aware that this – along with

2

certain other matters of personal taste – was not up for discussion or compromise.

The shutters open, Lydia unlatched the window and felt the air on her face, neck and shoulders. She leaned forward, grateful for its cool caress, and gazed down on the intricate formal gardens to the rear of the palace. Even from this bird's eye view, the mazes remained as resistant to comprehension as the twists and turns in Prince Henning's and his brother Prince Ven's sinuous minds.

Suddenly – almost as if her thinking of the two Princes had summoned them on to the stage-set below – she saw two flashes of white, moving within the contours of the dark green maze. Then, close by one of the white flashes, a burst of silver. Henning and Ven, stripped bare to the waist, swords in hand, were stalking each other through the Grand Maze. It was a favourite game of theirs, though to call it a game was to diminish the seriousness with which each Prince approached the challenge.

One of the white flashes suddenly moved: Ven was running. True to form, he had good instincts – he was close upon his brother. She wondered if he could hear his brother's heavy breath on the other side of the perfectly tended hedge. She saw the glint of light on Ven's sword; she thought of the maid's scissors. A fresh shiver snaked down her spine. As Ven closed in to claim his victory, she turned away.

Lydia was sitting at a chair by the window – washed, perfumed and dressed in a silk robe patterned with peacocks – when the door was flung open and Henning strode into the room. His eyes were wild and there were cuts all across his pale chest and muscled arms. The stink of sweat emanating from him spoke not only of his recent labours but of the copious amounts of wine he had imbibed the night before.

His lips settled on hers and then he ran his fingers slowly, possessively, through her hair. Stepping back, he stood proudly over her, fists on his hips.

'These games you play,' she said. 'One day, you'll go too far.'

He laughed. 'Don't you want to know who won?'

'I'm guessing it was you,' she said.

'Of course it was me! He thought he had me, but that was just what I wanted him to believe.' Henning ran his fingers along the nape of her neck – it felt like a spider scurrying across her flesh.

Henning leaned down until his face was level with hers. Lydia's nostrils flared at the tang of his sweat. 'Does anything matter to you more than winning?' she asked.

He laughed. 'Lydia, my precious Lydia. There's nothing more important than winning. Don't pretend you don't agree.'

She shrugged.

'The higher the stakes, the sweeter the victory.' He folded his arms across his grime- and sweat-streaked chest. 'You of all people know that.' Now he reached out for her pale hand and placed it on his blood-nicked left pectoral. She could feel, beneath the thin veil of his skin, the wild thumping of his heart. Instinctively, she began to withdraw her hand, but he brought across his own and trapped hers, pressing her flesh against his. 'Winning is the only thing that makes us feel alive,' he rasped. 'It's what binds you and I together. It is the star that steers us towards our future.'

Lydia smiled awkwardly and drew away her hand, wiping it dry on her silk robe. 'You stink like a wild boar. For goodness' sake, go and take a bath!'

'I've been looking all over the palace for you,' Lydia said later that morning, as she approached Henning at the periphery of the royal aviary.

No answer.

She stepped closer but not too close. The door to one of the aviary's enclosures was open; the one belonging to Prince Ven's much-prized golden eagle. Ven was inside, communing with his beloved creature. The eagle was sitting on a steel facsimile of a branch, its vast wings extended as he stroked the bird with his bare fingers.

Lydia felt a shudder course through her. She'd heard the Princes' stories about how this eagle had plucked out the eyes of one unfortunate steward and employed its claws to scratch the face of another, scarring him beyond all recognition. In Lydia's view, the bird should be destroyed rather than cherished. But she knew that this was not an argument worth voicing: it would only serve to widen the gulf between herself and Prince Ven, which, in turn, would not play well for her relationship with Henning.

'Come on!' Ven turned to face Henning with a smile.

Ven was strikingly good-looking – far more handsome than his older brother. Where Henning's face was inclined to be red and puffy, Ven's was all sharp lines and skin the colour of freshly drawn milk; where Henning's hair was tufty at best, and thinning over his crown, Ven's was sleek and black, like the wings of a raven. But there were reasons she had chosen Henning, she reminded herself. His looks, or lack of them, were of little consequence.

She watched now as Ven beckoned his brother into the enclosure. Her first instinct was to cry out to Henning, to warn him to be careful. But she bit her lip, watching fearfully as Henning entered the cage.

He was carrying a neat scroll of parchment. Intrigued, she dared to step a pace closer. Ven reached out and passed a small, tubular container to Henning, all the time talking soothingly to his monstrous bird.

Henning opened the tube and carefully inserted the scroll.

Lydia saw that there was a clip at one end of the canister, and Ven now used it to attach the tube to a ring which circled the eagle's left leg.

Henning retreated from the enclosure with Ven following, the giant eagle resting on his leather-clad forearm. Frozen to the spot, Lydia realised how strong Ven must be to carry the bird without so much as a flinch or a tremble.

Outside the enclosure, the bird extended its vast wings once more. Ven was holding the eagle on a thin, leather rein, which he held gently in his fist. As a new coldness ran through her, he let the rein drop from his hand. The bird was released.

'Fly!' Ven cried. 'Carry our missive across the borders!'

The bird soared into the air. Lydia let out a small cry as it climbed quickly to the height of a kite-string's length above them.

Only then did she dare to move closer to the two Princes. 'What was that note?' she asked.

Ven did not respond. He was standing rapt, his head thrown back, eyes brimming with purpose as he watched the flight of his precious eagle over the dark roof of the palace.

Henning turned to meet Lydia's gaze.

'What have you done?' she asked.

Henning smiled, his eyes dancing with light. 'Something,' he told her, 'that will change everything.'

Now Ven turned his own gaze towards her. In spite of the crucial physical differences between himself and his brother, their eyes were the same – cold and hard and black as obsidian, as if the Princes themselves had been hewn from the same rock as their forbidding palace. In Ven's case, the hardness of his eyes was balanced by the somewhat feminine set of his lips. These now broke into a soft smile as he opened them to speak.

'First Archenfield,' he said. 'Then the rest of the Thousand Territories.'

To Jared, Prince of All Archenfield,

Your Princedom is irredeemably weakened. Paddenburg is ready to take over full control. You have seven days to surrender your lands and people to us.

If you fail to submit by sunset on the seventh day, our armies will break through your borders.

Should anything happen to Logan Wilde during this time, we will know about it and our armies will arrive even sooner.

Enjoy your coronation and the fact that yours will be the shortest reign of any Prince in the history of Archenfield.

Yours in ambition and anticipation,

Prince Ven and Prince Henning of Paddenburg

SEVEN DAYS UNTIL
INVASION ...

TWO

THE COUNCIL CHAMBER, PALACE OF ARCHENFIELD

'We have three options.' Axel Blaxland's voice held the attention of each man and woman gathered within the Council Chamber. 'One, we surrender. Two, we fight. Three, we seek alliances from our neighbour states.'

Prince Jared couldn't help but envy the easy authority in his cousin's voice. In the brief time that had elapsed since Jared had summoned his Captain of the Guard to show him the note – swiftly christened the Paddenburg Ultimatum – Axel's response had been unflinching. Such gravitas was a needling reminder of the disparity in experience between the Prince and his cousin. Jared was a sixteen-year-old boy who had inherited the throne on his brother's assassination; his cousin was ten years his senior, with far greater experience of political disputes and war itself. Whilst Axel had fought alongside Prince Goran and Prince Anders on the battlefield, Jared and his younger brother Edvin had remained cosseted at the palace, playing games of war,

11

where the worst bloodshed had been a scraped knee or elbow.

Jared wished he could summon even a smidgen of Axel's composure to combat the whirling sense of vertigo that had become horribly familiar to him these past weeks. The new state of emergency had arrived so hard on the heels of the previous crisis of his brother's murder that there hadn't been time even to draw breath. It felt like a capricious twist of fate – but these were not two isolated incidents. The crazed rulers of Paddenburg had been the architects of the royal assassination plot, and now it was becoming clear that that had been only an opening gambit in their attempt to take control of Archenfield.

The ultimatum, with its biblical deadline, had made that explicit.

Jared glanced at the sombre faces clustered around the Prince's Table, each member of the Twelve in his or her designated position. The new Prince drew some comfort from the knowledge that this table, hewn long ago from a centuries-old oak, had endured many such crises; other rulers had sat in his position since the infancy of the Princedom, well before the intricate letters had been carved into the wood and filled with molten metal to spell out his title: 'The Prince'. Other princes had summoned meetings with different men and women, predecessors to the twelve that he had gathered here today. Other princes had stared into the eye of the storm, held their nerve and navigated the way to peace. He had to remember this.

'Surrender is not an option.' The words came not from one of those seated at the Prince's Table itself but from the nearby dais, where Jared's mother, Queen Elin, sat alongside Prince Edvin. It was Elin who had spoken, her voice clear and sharp as crystal.

Jared sensed that she had offered her words in order to fill the void created by his silence. He turned to meet her imperious, harshly beautiful face. 'Of course we cannot surrender!' He was surprised by the force of his own voice. 'But if we forge weighty enough alliances, then surely Paddenburg's army will be forced to retreat? There might be no need for us to fight.'

His fleeting relief at having taken control was undercut by the slow shake of his cousin's head. 'I'm afraid that is a naïve thought,' Axel told him. 'Paddenburg will attack, whatever alliances we have in place. The lunatic Princes have not come this far to back off without tasting the blood of Archenfield on their cannibal tongues.'

Jared frowned. Had it been necessary for Axel to underline his inexperience in front of the Twelve by branding his comment 'naïve'? Not for the first time he questioned his decision to elect Axel as his Edling, or heir. Only it hadn't been *his* choice, had it? He had wanted Edvin for the role. It had been Queen Elin who had told him in no uncertain terms to choose Axel. He was still smarting from the memory of that manipulation as his mother resumed speaking.

'You are wrong, nephew. Of course a new alliance will make a difference. Do not forget that our timely agreement with Woodlark brought an end to the war with Eronesia. Prince Anders married Silva to save our Princedom. If the soldiers of Woodlark hadn't helped our diminished forces to drive Eronesia back across the border, Archenfield would have fallen. Woodlark, and its own alliance with Malytor to the east, made Archenfield strong.'

'Whatever else we do, we must make ready to defend our borders.' Axel's glance ranged over the assembly. 'But I'm not saying I disagree with the principle of securing alliances. Far from it.'

'It's good to know you don't feel my every thought to be naïve,' Jared said sourly. Immediately, he regretted it. It sounded petty, even to his own ears.

'If we're bandying about words like "naïve",' said Kai Jagger, the Huntsman, 'I'm not sure what hope we truly have of securing even one alliance within the seven days before Paddenburg invades.'

'Assuming they actually wait seven days!' Emelie Sharp, the Beekeeper cut in. 'If the accepted thinking is that they *are* crazy, why would we take anything they say at face value?'

Lucas Curzon, the Groom, now entered the fray: 'Emelie is right. We cannot trust this enemy. In destroying the Woodlark alliance, Paddenburg has succeeded in making us weak again. It has been less than two years since the war with Eronesia ended. We're still reeling from the loss of life that the prolonged fighting cost us. We simply don't have the manpower to defend ourselves against a new threat.'

Jared was frustrated to hear this from Lucas, of all people. 'Surely you're not suggesting that we just give up?'

Lucas nodded sadly. 'It gives me no satisfaction to say this, Prince Jared, but if we fight, we will lose.'

'I refuse to accept Archenfield's defeat so quickly,' Jared countered. 'We must fortify our border settlements *and* seek a fresh alliance.'

On the dais, his mother nodded encouragingly.

'Assuming we do pursue one or more strategic alliances,' the Huntsman resumed, 'then who should undertake this mission?'

His question had been directed at Prince Jared, but it was Axel who responded. 'Ordinarily, a task of such magnitude would fall to the Prince himself.'

Kai nodded. 'Or, in his stead, the Captain of the Guard.' He paused, smiling. 'Or perhaps the Edling.'

The implication behind the Huntsman's words wasn't lost on any of those in the room, least of all Prince Jared. He *was* too inexperienced to broker the all-important alliances; Axel would do a much better job.

Jared found himself responding before anyone else could. 'I should go. I am the Prince.'

Kai nodded, respectfully. 'You are our Prince and the ruler of Archenfield, Jared. But in these exceptional circumstances, the Prince should not depart the Princedom.'

'The Huntsman speaks the truth.' A fresh interjection from Queen Elin. Jared met his mother's eyes with a grimace. Was even she intent upon undermining him?

'Axel should go.' Jonas Drummond, the Woodsman, drew Jared's attention back to the Prince's Table.

At Jonas's side, Morgan Booth shook his head. 'We need Axel here,' the Executioner said, his muscled arms folded on the table. 'We need Axel in charge of what little army we have left.'

A chuckle came from across the other side of the table. All eyes turned swiftly from the Executioner to the Priest. 'It would seem, Axel,' Father Simeon observed, 'that you are quite indispensable on both sides of the gates. Congratulations to you!'

Axel shrugged off the Priest's mischievous compliment.

'Well, what about Prince Jared?' Emelie butted in again. Her eyes were bright with conviction. 'Why exactly can't he go?'

Queen Elin did not miss a beat. 'Even if he had recovered sufficiently from the traitor's attack, it is not appropriate for the Prince to leave the Princedom or his subjects in a time of crisis. Prince Jared must remain here, to lead Archenfield through whatever turmoil lies ahead. He is our nation's figure-head and a beacon of continuity.'

15

'Rather more than a mere figurehead, I trust,' Jared said. No one responded. Had they all lost confidence in him entirely?

Vera Webb, the Cook, cleared her throat with a phlegmy rattle – a sure sign she was about to take the floor. 'If neither Prince Jared nor Axel is able to venture beyond the gates to seek these vital alliances, then *who* can we send?'

There was silence in the chamber. Then a crystal voice rang out once more. 'I will go,' Queen Elin announced, rising to her feet.

'No!' Jared and Axel cried in unison.

Elin pursed her lips and remained standing, poised and as unyielding as a royal statue.

'Why not?' Elias Peck, the Physician, spoke now. 'Why wouldn't we ask Queen Elin to undertake such an important mission? She is a senior member of the royal family, who carries with her the experience of many years and countless other crises. She is a respected figure, both at home and abroad. She is known to all the leaders we would wish to approach. As such, I think we would struggle to find anyone better qualified to seek out these alliances.'

'There is truth in your words.' Nova Chastain, the Falconer, took up the baton. 'But we should remember keenly the current animosity between Archenfield and Woodlark.' Her voice was low. 'I intend no disrespect, but Queen Elin proved unable to save the alliance with Queen Francesca of Wood-lark.'

'And I, in turn, intend no disrespect,' Queen Elin rejoined, 'when I observe that your affair with my oldest son, Nova, all but wrecked that alliance beyond repair.'

The Queen's words sent shockwaves around the chamber, reminding everyone that Nova had conducted an illicit rela-tionship with Prince Anders throughout his marriage to Silva, daughter of Queen Francesca and Prince Willem of Woodlark.

Jared thought of Silva, whose lifeless body had been fished from the frigid waters of the river days after Anders's assassination. Silva's corpse was now reunited with the royal family of Woodlark, who still laboured under the misapprehension that the grief-stricken widow had taken her own life. In truth, it had been the deranged Poet who had murdered her, at the behest of his masters in Paddenburg.

It had all been part of a plan to send Archenfield spiralling into chaos, and it had proved highly successful.

'We can't lay the blame for our broken alliance with Nova,' Jared said, 'when the true culprit sits in our Dungeons.' He thought of the disgraced Poet and the reference to him within the Paddenburg Ultimatum: '... *should anything happen to Logan Wilde ... we will know about it and our armies will arrive even sooner*.' The Blood Price had underpinned the justice system of Archenfield since the Princedom's very beginnings. Everything had a value – from the loss of a limb to the loss of a life. Yet Jared could not even extract the Blood Price from the assassin of the Prince and his Consort; Paddenburg had succeeded in rendering him impotent in this respect.

Axel interjected. 'Logan Wilde, for all his deeds and posturing, is only the puppet of the Princes of Paddenburg. They are the true culprits of these unspeakable crimes. Let no one forget that, even for an instant.'

Murmurs of assent came from around the Prince's Table.

It was Lucas Curzon who spoke next. 'Queen Elin will need a team to accompany her beyond the borders.'

'I'll go,' Morgan Booth offered, raising his hand.

'Of course you will,' said Emelie Sharp, not quite under her breath.

Prince Jared frowned, aware of the sordid whispers concerning his mother and the Executioner. He set his hands on the table and was, for once, grateful for the distraction of Axel's voice.

'Securing an alliance is a long shot. We must do what we can to protect our border for as long as we can. I will put together an inventory from the armoury and assess exactly how many trained fighters we have to send to protect the outlying settlements. Lucas, we'll need armoured horses. I want to know numbers and how soon you can be ready to deploy them. Elias, field hospitals will need to be erected a safe distance from the front line. I expect a plan on my desk by tomorrow morning. The rugged terrain in the south is our greatest natural defence. It will funnel any invaders into our path and slow the advance of however large an army. But if we follow this line of thinking, both the settlements of Grenofen and Inderwick would be in the immediate line of fire and need bolstering.'

'You are all talking as if this is decided,' Prince Jared said. 'Shouldn't I be the one to choose our strategy?' He glanced up and saw Hal Harness, the Bodyguard, watching him closely. He realised that Hal was the only one of the Twelve who had not yet spoken; it was not unusual for Hal to keep his own counsel. He heard Axel's voice once more at his side. 'Cast your emotions aside, Cousin Jared—'

'*Prince* Jared,' he cut in, angrily. 'We are in the Council Chamber now. Please accord me the respect of my formal title, not my familial one.'

'Of course, Prince Jared,' Axel resumed, calm as ever. 'I'm sorry to cause unintended offence. I just want you to see that this is actually a very sound idea.'

'Thank you, Axel.' The unflinching voice from the dais once more. Jared glanced across at his mother, her hands now resting on her narrow hips. 'Perhaps it is worth reminding everyone that I have crossed the borders many times before.'

As fresh voices resumed around him, Jared lost track of the individual cut and thrust of the debate – all he heard was babble. The members of the Twelve – his own mother too – might as well be speaking a foreign language. And in a way, he supposed, they were: they spoke the language of experience. He was their ruler, and his place at the ancient table was demarcated by the glinting words, 'The Prince', while this time tomorrow would see his formal coronation. But, as he glanced around the table, he suspected that even the placement of a crown on his head would do little to increase his grasp on authority.

I am their leader, he thought, as the voices grew in strength around him. But I may as well be invisible.

THREE

THE GARDENS, PALACE OF ARCHENFIELD

What the Prince needed most was sleep. After the fresh traumas inflicted by the dying day, and all that awaited him on the other side of sunrise, he should have been in his bed. Instead, he was trudging around the palace gardens with his trusty wolfhound, Hedd, close by his side. Jared's boots were caked in earth, his mind whirling with thoughts of the Paddenburg Ultimatum.

The handwritten message had been only a few lines long, but it had been written in a hand as elegant as its import was vicious.

Prince Jared had held the terrible note in his own hands and experienced a strange sensation, as though the parchment had been burning the pads of his fingers. It would certainly not have been beyond the twisted minds of Henning and Ven to soak their missive with poison or even to summon a supernatural power to taint it with a curse, but the burning had ultimately faded and Jared had been forced to accept that it was the words alone that had imbued the note with its horrible power.

It might as well have been dispatched from Hell as from the Black Palace of Paddenburg.

Jared slowed his pace, aware that his heart was racing once more. The taunting words of the note refused to leave his head; instead, they repeated and repeated there.

Your Princedom is irredeemably weakened. Paddenburg is ready to take over full control. You have seven days to surrender your lands and people to us.

Seven days. It was no time – no more than a breath, a heartbeat, in the history of Archenfield. The first seven days of Jared's reign had been packed with incident, beginning with the discovery of his brother's body and swiftly followed by the arrest and execution of the supposed assassin, then a second murder – that of the Prince's pregnant Consort – and then a fresh assassination attempt, mercifully, miraculously, unsuccessful, on the Falconer and, at last, the unmasking of the true assassin, who had plunged a dagger perilously close to Jared's own heart.

It had taken the next seven days of his reign to plant his feet solidly upon the palace grounds and allow himself to say, 'All these horrors are behind us now. The assassin is under lock and key. Our wounds are healing . . . ' When he spoke of healing wounds, he meant not only the painful knitting together of the fibres in his punctured chest and the equally torturous realignment of the fractures in the Falconer's spine, following her flight from the top of her tower, but also those deeper wounds that had been inflicted upon the court and the Princedom at large.

And now this fresh assault, the very day before his coronation . . .

Enjoy your coronation and the fact that yours will be the shortest reign of any prince in the history of Archenfield.

He was to be denied even the illusion of hope in the first

faltering steps of his reign – it was scarcely worth the effort currently employed by the steward tasked with polishing the Prince's Crown for the morrow.

Jared paused from his circuit. He smiled to note Hedd instinctively halting his own movement. Stroking the hound affectionately under his chin – just where he liked it – Jared glanced up. They were not alone in the palace gardens. The Prince was rarely, if ever, alone these days. Hal Harness stood at a respectful distance, lighting a fresh cigarette and affecting to be casually enjoying this taking of the night air. Jared lifted a hand to acknowledge Hal. He knew that the Bodyguard must be as needful of sleep as he was, but when the Prince could not sleep, neither could Hal.

Hal lifted his own hand in salute, then let his arm fall, sheltering his smoke from a gust of autumnal breeze.

Jared sank on to a seat at the end of the gardens – Hedd slumping down at his feet – and gazed back at the palace. Darkness had long since laid claim to the Princedom and this night was painted in a deep, vivid blue, the crenellated outline of the palace buildings seeming somehow fringed in gold against its cerulean backdrop. It was a deceptively peaceful sight.

But even this illusory peace was suddenly cut through: dogs began barking at the edge of the garden. Hedd was immediately alert, racing off towards the melee. Hal too leaped upright, dagger drawn, swiftly joining his comrades who had come out to investigate.

Jared rose to his feet, his heart pumping anew. What fresh disaster did the barking announce? As the dogs' warning fell away, Jared made out voices, initially raised, but then softer – in the midst of the curt voices of Hal and his guards was that of a girl. Jared nodded to himself. Even before Hal brought her over to him, he knew exactly who it was.

'Asta Peck!' Jared declared, smiling. He noted that close upon Asta's heels was Hedd. The wolfhound had taken the same instant liking to the Physician's apprentice that the Prince had.

Asta returned his smile, though she seemed embarrassed at the commotion her arrival in the palace gardens had provoked. The guards were by now moving away, back to the palace, and she cast them a pained glance. 'I'm sorry,' she said, to both Jared and Hal. 'I should have thought before I wandered up here at this hour.'

Jared shook his head, grateful to see the one person in his immediate sphere he thought of as a true friend. 'What brings you up here at this time of night?'

'I couldn't sleep,' she said. 'And, Your Highness, somehow I *knew* that you were feeling the same. I even had an image of you, sitting right here on this bench. How strange . . .'

'It's a pity you didn't picture the guards and the dogs while you were at it,' Hal cut in. 'Your jugular was moments away from becoming intimately acquainted with the wrong end of my dagger.'

'I think you've made your point,' Jared told Hal. 'Asta, since you've made it through the barricades, won't you join Hedd and I on a walk around the gardens? Hal, perhaps you will grant us as much privacy as you feel prudent, and treat yourself to another cigarette?'

Hal nodded. 'Of course, Your Highness.'

Asta waited until the Bodyguard was out of earshot. 'All right,' she said. 'Uncle Elias told me about the Paddenburg Ultimatum but then clammed up, as per usual. What's going on? How are you feeling about all this? What happens next?'

Jared couldn't help but smile at the volley of questions. 'Where do I begin?'

'Begin at the beginning, Uncle Elias would say.' Asta lifted her right hand. 'It's a sizeable garden you have here, Prince Jared. A walk around its perimeter should give us ample opportunity to tackle this new situation from multiple angles.'

Jared nodded, feeling another flood of relief that she had, miraculously, come to find him. He was half tempted to offer her his arm, but something held him back from making such a gesture of intimacy. He felt an easy closeness to Asta, bordering on something more, but, with everything that was going on, now was hardly the time to introduce another complication.

Thoughts turning in his head, Jared lingered on the spot as Asta began walking ahead. Realising that she had left him behind, she turned and looked back at him. 'Is there a problem?' she asked.

'No.' Jared shook his head and strode out, accompanied by Hedd, to make good the distance between them.

'So what do you think?' Jared asked, as he finished recounting his version of the meeting of the Twelve.

Asta's bright eyes met his. 'It's obvious, isn't it? You should go on this mission yourself.'

Her words sent a shiver up his spine. 'So you agree then? I should go because I am the Prince?'

She shook her head. 'No, you should go because you *want* to go. The fact that you are the Prince is neither here nor there ... except that it enables you to call the shots!'

Jared's brow furrowed. Everything seemed so uncomplicated to her. He wished he could see things with the same level of clarity.

'Look,' she said. 'You have talked, very eloquently, about feeling in control, and then suddenly feeling that that control is being wrested from you – whether by Axel or by your mother or even by Emelie, with her acid tongue! But, in reality, you have ultimate control here. It's only when you forget that that you allow others to step in and undermine you. Even then, I'm not sure they do so intentionally. They may simply be trying to help—'

Something in Asta's words struck Jared to his core. 'You think I hesitate too much,' he said. 'Don't you?'

'Actually, no.' She shook her head sharply. 'I completely understand why you need to take a moment to process what is going on and consider how you should respond. You want to make the right decisions. You're new to this but even if you weren't, you have been faced – since that day when we all learned of Prince Anders's assassination – with a sustained series of challenges and pressure. We hoped there might be some brief respite, but now the stakes have only increased. Truly, it's as if you are being tested by some higher power, like in an old folk tale or in one of Father Simeon's parables.'

He nodded. Her words resonated with him, not only in his head but in his heart and gut. Just hearing Asta's acknowledgement of what he was contending with brought some relief.

'All I'm saying,' she continued, 'is that when you do hesitate, for very valid reasons, you allow others to swoop in and seize control. And I think that rocks your confidence, perhaps more than it should. You start to question whether you really are the one who holds the reins of power, whether you *should* be the one holding the reins. But those are not questions you need to ask. You *are* Prince of All Archenfield. Your brother chose you, with – if I can speak plainly – uncharacteristic wisdom for the role. And you have already proved to all of us that you are more than worthy of the job.'

'I have?'

She paused. 'Look within yourself for the answer. You might be surprised and pleased with what you find.'

Finding himself blushing, Jared shook his head. 'How did you get to be so wise, Asta Peck?' he asked, as he reached for Hedd's chin once more.

She shrugged. 'I think I must have been cursed at an early age.'

'Why cursed, rather than blessed?' he asked curiously.

'Because I ask too many questions. You know that. I can't help it. My brain just keeps turning things over and over and, before I know it, I'm in all kinds of—'

'Deep water?' he suggested, with a grin – thinking of her decision to jump into the freezing river to test her theories regarding Silva's death.

'I'm never going to live that down, am I?'

'Not until you do something even more spectacular. Which, personally, I'm confident you will.'

She nodded. 'It's a distinct possibility.'

Jared fell silent for a moment, and then he spoke: 'If I do go on this mission, Asta, would you come with me?' His eyes met hers.

For the first time, Asta's confidence seemed to waver. She glanced up, as if searching for her answer in the constellations above. 'I'm not sure what use I'd be.'

'You would keep me sane,' he told her. 'You have a remarkable knack for that. You are my antidote to everyone else in court.'

Her brow furrowed. 'They're not all against you, you know.'

'Oh, I know . . .'

'Do you? Really?' She looked at him keenly. 'You have to give them time to adjust, Jared. They are so used to your brother. They're unsettled too – not *by* you, but by these significant shifts in circumstance. The spinning of the wheel of fate . . .'

He smiled.

'Did I say something amusing?' Asta enquired.

He shook his head.

'What, then?'

'You called me Jared.'

Her eyes narrowed. 'It is your name.'

'Yes, but—'

'Oh, I see!' Asta looked at him, startled.

'In the days of my ancestors, they'd lock you up in the Dungeons for a week for a slip like that.'

'I'm sorry,' she said. 'I didn't mean to offend—'

'I'm only teasing you,' he said, reaching out for her hand. 'Asta, I like it when you call me by my name.' He squeezed her hand. 'It reminds me that there is more to me than my title.'

'There is much more to you,' she agreed. She could feel the blood rushing to her cheeks at his touch. 'I think we are all just beginning to understand how much more to you there is.'

Her words, her unswerving belief in him, touched Jared deeply. He stood there, in the midst of the palace gardens, holding her hand, reluctant to let it go. Only a hair's breadth separated them. If he dared to kiss her, he was fairly sure she would not recoil. Her eyes gazed into his for what felt like an eternity. He could picture himself leaning just a fraction closer . . .

'I should go,' he said, letting go of her hand. 'I need to think all this through,' he blustered. 'Thank you, Asta. Thank you for coming to find me and for your advice. As usual, you have helped me to see things with much greater clarity.'

A stray gust of wind ruffled her flame-coloured hair and she lifted a hand to brush the strands away from her eyes. She glanced over his shoulder in the direction of Hal, then turned back towards him. 'You are much better at this than you realise,' she assured him.

Did she mean being the Prince, or something more personal? Before he could ask, she had given him a nonchalant salute, and turned away to navigate her way back to her home in the Village of the Twelve.

'I'm depending on you to call off the dogs,' she called back to him, over her shoulder.

'Depend on it,' he said. 'It's the very least I can do for you.'

FOUR

THE QUEEN'S QUARTERS, PALACE OF ARCHENFIELD

The first of Queen Elin's rooms – designated as her office and parlour – was host to a flurry of activity, even at this late hour. Several large packing cases lay open on the floor. Two of the Queen's handmaids were carefully folding clothes and laying them in the open cases. Another had been tasked with packing the Queen's jewels in a smaller trunk. Meanwhile, two more of the Queen's servants moved busily back and forth between this room and those beyond, ferrying out more clothes, jewellery and other items for Elin's imminent departure. Jared could hear his mother's sharp voice in the other chamber, issuing a stream of commands.

Weaving his way between the harried maids, he entered the second of his mother's rooms. There, he found Elin, sitting on a chaise, turning over in her hands a jewelled casket. At her feet, arrayed on the fine carpet, was an assemblage of treasures.

'Sidse!' Elin summoned back one of her maids and placed the casket into her hands. 'Yes, we will take this but it needs a good polish.'

'Very good, Your Majesty!' The maid nodded to the Queen and took the casket off to be cleaned.

'You're still up then, Mother?' Jared said.

'Very observant, my darling,' Elin said, her eyes remaining on the diverse display of gold, silver and jewel-encrusted objects laid out before her. 'Yes, I am still up. There is so much to get organised ahead of my trip.'

'You look like you are getting ready to flee the country,' Jared observed, kneeling down to retrieve an intricate jade carving of a ship. Its five green sails were as thin and delicate as spring leaves, its rigging no thicker than the threads of a spider's web.

'You can have that if you like,' she said. 'It was a gift from the Prince of Baltiska – *not* Prince Ciprian, obviously, but his father, I seem to recall.' She glanced across, her mouth twisted into a tight smile. 'I can't very well re-gift him his father's heirloom and expect to secure an alliance on that basis, can I?'

Jared set the carving back down carefully and, rising to his feet, pulled across a chair to sit directly opposite his mother. 'So this is your plan, is it?' he enquired. 'To travel out with a caravan of treasures to bribe and barter your way into alliances?'

'That's something of an over-simplification.' Elin ran her fingers meditatively along the fine silk covering of her chaise. 'One doesn't, on the whole, bribe one's fellow royals, though Prince Rohan loves anything a touch flashy – that gold pineapple thingy over there, for instance, is very much to his taste – or lack thereof.' She smiled. 'But no, Jared, these gifts are only to oil the wheels. They will not form part of the central negotiations.'

'I see,' Jared said, keeping his tone as level as possible. 'And how many horses and how big an entourage are you planning to take on this journey of yours, in order to transport all these treasures and your not insubstantial wardrobe?'

Elin looked at him, unmoved. 'I'll leave Axel to work out the logistics, my sweet. My job is simply to pack the bare essentials for my trip.'

Jared couldn't help but smile. It wasn't only his mother's notion of the 'bare essentials', but also the thought of the many maids currently hard at work cleaning, sorting and packing while Elin assessed the worth of her precious treasures.

'I see you find this amusing,' Elin observed, reaching down and scooping up an intricately painted egg. She held the fragile ornament up to the light. 'It's no more than a trinket, really, is it? No, I think we can certainly categorise this as Not Wanted on the Voyage.'

Jared nodded, imagining how best to break his news to her: 'Actually, Mother – the thing Not Wanted on the Voyage, is *you ...*' *Yes, because that would go down very well.*

She rolled the egg thoughtfully between the blossom-pale palms of her hands. 'Darling, I don't mean to be rude – it *is* always a delight to receive a visit from you.' She leaned forward, her dark eyebrows raised. 'But I am, in point of fact, rather busy.'

He smiled pleasantly at his mother. 'I appreciate that. What I have to say will take only a few moments of your time.'

'You're going on the mission yourself?' Axel exclaimed, leaning back in his chair.

'That's right,' Jared said, standing before the Captain of the Guard's desk in the centre of his office.

'Dare I enquire if Queen Elin has been informed of this change in plans?'

Jared nodded. 'I told her myself, on my way here to see you.'

Axel arched an eyebrow. 'And how, pray, did she take the news?'

Jared grimaced. 'Let's just say it's probably a good thing that I shall shortly be out of her immediate range for a few days.'

'Oh, Jared,' Axel said, light dancing in his eyes. 'You haven't forgotten, have you, that it's your coronation tomorrow? It really would be most ... unfortunate if Queen Elin decided to boycott such an important event.'

'She'll be there,' Jared assured him. 'However angry she is with me now – and the word "incandescent" springs to mind – she won't be able to keep away. She'll be there, front and centre, to see you place the crown on my head.'

Axel's eyes met his. 'I cannot tell you how much I am looking forward to it. With all that's happened, and all there is to come, we need moments like these. I wonder who it was who established the tradition that the Edling places the crown on the Prince's head?'

Jared shrugged. They both knew well enough that Axel would far rather the crown was placed on his own head. Jared couldn't help but wonder if, in the brief time during which Axel would have the crown in his possession before the ceremony, he would try it on for size. He shook his head. Of course he would. Blocking out the unwanted image, Jared reached into his pocket. 'I've drawn up a list of who I have chosen to accompany me on my mission.' He passed the folded piece of parchment to Axel, who took it and unfolded it, setting the small sheet of creamy paper in the centre of his vast wooden desk.

Hal Harness
Kai Jagger

'It's not exactly a list, Jared! There are only two names here,' Axel observed, glancing up.

Jared nodded. 'Three of us will be quite sufficient. And only three horses.'

'Is that even sufficient to carry all your necessities?'

Prince Jared folded his arms. 'In marked contrast to my mother, I'm not planning on riding out with the entire contents of the royal vaults.'

'With one horse apiece, you'll be able to take little more than a change of clothes.'

Jared nodded again. 'That and a few basic provisions are all I intend to take. I do not plan to be away for very long. And I don't see any necessity to employ the treasures of Archenfield to "oil the wheels" of negotiation, as my mother so poetically puts it.'

'You don't?' Axel enquired, his voice guarded.

Jared shook his head. 'I will sit down, ruler to ruler, and make a plain argument for the alliances.'

Axel gave a quick nod. 'I see. Time to tear up convention and do things a little differently, eh?'

'Something like that,' Jared agreed. 'Though, of course, I would welcome your advice on where to go and what case to put before each court.' He smiled, enjoying the feeling of control. 'I would be a fool not to draw on your experience.'

For a moment, Axel said nothing and Jared wondered if his words had come out just a bit too sardonically. If so, he might have shot himself in the foot: the truth was, he genuinely did need and want the benefit of his cousin's advice.

Still saying nothing, Axel rose to his feet and crossed the room. Was he going to offer Jared a drink? The last thing he needed at this point in the proceedings was a stinging glass of aquavit. But no, Axel had come to a standstill before a map of Archenfield and its neighbouring territories. He turned and glanced impatiently over his shoulder. Jared realised that he was supposed to go over and join him.

'Here *we* are,' Axel said, planting his forefinger on the map so that it obliterated the *E* and *N* of ARCHENFIELD. His finger travelled downwards. 'And here's the bastard Princedom of Paddenburg in the south, bordering our old friends in Woodlark.' His finger moved eastwards to Francesca's territory, resting there for a moment, then tapping the stretch of water that, for the most part, bordered the two lands.

Removing his finger, he placed it back down on the Princedom immediately north of Archenfield. 'And here's the warmonger Eronesia and' – his finger skated east again – 'its erstwhile ally, Schloss.' Axel turned to meet Jared's eyes. 'Frankly, you can forget about alliances with any of these territories.'

Jared frowned – so far, he wasn't finding Axel's briefing very motivating.

'You need to focus your attention here,' Axel said, moving his finger to the right of Schloss. 'Here you have the three smaller territories of' – his finger continued to travel as he spoke each name in turn – 'Baltiska, Rednow and Larsson.' He tapped the map again. 'These are the courts you need to visit, to plead your cases with Ciprian, Rohan and Séverin.'

Jared's eyes narrowed upon the three Princedoms under discussion. 'They all share the same river with us ... and with Woodlark.'

'Good observation,' Axel said, nodding. 'And if you're asking my advice, I would offer them an alliance of the four river territories.' He turned and stepped away, leaving Jared staring at the map. 'These three smaller Princedoms have the most to lose from the expansionist ambitions of the bigger territories – whether it is Paddenburg or Woodlark pushing out from the south, or Eronesia and Schloss from the west.

Archenfield is almost twice the size of each of the three and it would certainly play well for you to remind them of this. You can even play up our own fears if you wish. If Archenfield were to be conquered, then Baltiska would become vulnerable next, whether from Paddenburg or from a renewed alliance between Eronesia and Schloss.' He returned to Jared's side, the stench of aquavit on his breath. 'Either way, if *we* fall, then the whole house of cards begins to collapse.'

Jared nodded, both fearful of Axel's words – as sour as the scent on his tongue – but also exhilarated at the challenge. It was just as Asta had said: his confidence was returning. 'So I should begin in Baltiska and work my way east?'

Axel cleared his throat. 'I wouldn't if I were you. Prince Ciprian is a loose cannon. You'd be better advised to start with Rohan in Rednow, and entreat his help with his two neighbours. We've been on good terms with Rohan for the most part, so I'd be surprised if he didn't play ball. You'll enjoy his palace too, I think – it's nothing at all like ours, but still rather wonderful.'

Jared turned. He could see the pleasure Axel took in knowing things that he did not. But those tables could be turned just as easily.

'I will take your advice and entreat Prince Rohan. But, before him, my first port of call will be Woodlark.'

Axel, who had just taken a fresh sip of liquor, spat it out on the floor. 'You have got to be joking! Don't waste your precious time throwing yourself to the lioness Francesca!'

'I appreciate your opinion,' Jared continued, satisfied that his news had unsettled Axel, as he'd hoped it might, 'but I intend to petition Queen Francesca to reinstate our former alliance.' He returned his glance to the map. 'Woodlark is such a large, strategically positioned territory that I cannot resign myself to letting go of the possibility of a renewed alliance.'

Axel shook his head. 'I think you're mad, but I know of old that when a Wynyard man makes up his mind, it's not worth the time or pain to try to change it.' He paced back towards his desk. 'Let's revisit this list of yours again.' Jared turned as Axel lifted his scant note. 'Kai Jagger. Well, of course you'd want the Huntsman at your side to defend you from man and beast and, if you should be away for longer than you intend, to provide food.'

Jared nodded. There had never been any question in his mind that he'd take Kai with him.

'Hal Harness,' Axel continued. 'Yes, yes, of course you'd have to take your Bodyguard. You know you can trust Hal in any situation.' He glanced up at Jared thoughtfully. 'But, if I might make a suggestion, take a second guard. Bram Gentle would be my recommendation. He's a gangly youth but vicious as a baited bear when he needs to be.'

Jared hesitated. He had wanted to keep the numbers as small as possible, but perhaps one extra member of the guard wasn't a bad idea. 'I'll talk to Hal about him,' he agreed.

Axel nodded agreeably. 'You know, cousin, I half expected to see another name on this list of yours.'

'You did?'

'Yes.' Axel's lips curved up into a smile. 'Asta Peck.'

'Ah,' Jared said, returning the smile. 'Asta. Well, yes, I did want to talk to you about Asta. I've had some interesting thoughts about her.'

'I'm sure you have, cousin,' Axel said, his eyes dancing with light once more. 'I'm sure you have.'

SIX DAYS UNTIL
INVASION . . .

FIVE

THE PRINCE'S DRESSING CHAMBER, PALACE OF ARCHENFIELD

Prince Jared stood before his looking glass. Outside, he could hear the noise of the people massing in the palace grounds, and the stewards keeping them firmly but good-naturedly under control. This was the third trip to the palace for the citizens of Archenfield in little more than two weeks: first, to hear with their own ears the news of Prince Anders's assassination and to glimpse Anders's successor, and then to claim a front view of the funeral procession. Only members of the court would be permitted into the Palace Chapel for the afternoon coronation ceremony, to witness the moment when the Prince's Crown was placed on Jared's head. As important as that moment was, arguably it would be eclipsed by Prince Jared's subsequent arrival on the palace balcony as he greeted the citizens of Archenfield for the first time as their crowned Prince.

He stared dispassionately at his face in the mirror. Recently, each time he glanced at his reflection, his features seemed to have undergone a subtle but significant metamorphosis. He wanted to try to remember the way he looked that afternoon, if only to ask himself the *next* time he looked in the mirror if anything had truly changed. Would the coronation imbue him with a new sense of ... what? Authority? Gravitas? Royalty? Was it even possible to trace such qualities in one's own face, when one knew all too well the frailties lurking just beneath the skin?

'Someone to see you, Your Majesty.' Hal's head poked through the chamber door, then disappeared again as he made way for the Prince's visitor.

His brother strode into the room. Prince Edvin looked utterly transformed in his robes of state. His appearance gave Jared a deep jolt. Edvin and Anders had always looked remarkably similar; now, it was as though Jared's dead brother had risen from the dead, a hundred thousand flakes of ash reuniting until they alchemically became glorious flesh once more. As Edvin opened his long arms to fold him into an embrace, Jared closed his eyes, unable to shake the notion that his dead brother had returned from his own Valhalla to wish him well as his successor.

'What's the matter?' Edvin asked. 'There are tears in your eyes.'

'I was thinking of Anders,' Jared said, opening his eyes again. 'You remind me of him.'

Edvin smiled tenderly and shook his handsome head. 'Don't do that,' he said. 'Today is your day, Jared. Own it. Savour it.'

It was just the kind of thing Asta might have said.

'I really ought to wear ermine more often, don't you think?' Edvin said now, twirling around to give Jared the full effect of his cloak.

Jared laughed at the sight of his brother deliberately

playing the fool. 'Just a piece of advice,' he said. 'I would strongly suggest that you don't give in to your inclination towards pantomime when we're out on the balcony.'

Edvin grinned. 'It would almost be worth it, if only to see Mother's reaction.'

'No,' Jared said huskily. 'Let her have faith that at least one of her surviving sons might one day make her proud.'

Edvin was quick to respond to the bait. 'Yes, I heard things had grown a tad frosty between you two.'

'From her?' Jared enquired.

Edvin shook his head. 'I have other, ah, *sources* in the Queen's Chamber,' he said.

'Do you, indeed? Well, I don't think I want to know anything more about that.'

'And nor do I intend to tell you.' Edvin smiled again. 'All I'll say is that if you had only told our dear mother that she was not, in fact, going on her trip a little sooner, you would have spared a lot of frenzied packing and unpacking.'

Jared chuckled lightly. 'Yes, I'm aware of that.'

Edvin sighed and when he spoke next, his voice had acquired a new edge and urgency. 'So I'm just going to get straight to the point here … I want to come on this quest of yours.'

'It's *not* a quest,' Jared said, vehemently. 'It's a mission.' His voice grew more measured. 'I wondered if perhaps that's where this was leading.'

'You have to agree I'd be a tremendous asset,' Edvin forged on. 'First, I'm miles better with the crossbow than you are. I understand you have Kai along for the ride, and Hal of course, and that new bodyguard with the rather inappropriate name, but you can always use more muscle.' He paused to tense his biceps, before breezing on. 'Second, I am irrefutably more charming than you. I think we can agree I would cut quite a swathe through foreign courts, especially – but not exclusively – when there are females involved in the negotiations. And third, and perhaps most important, I can guarantee I would keep your morale boosted in a way no one you currently have on your list will.'

Jared waited to see if Edvin had any additional ways to bolster his case. It appeared not.

'Come on,' Edvin said, giving his most winning smile. 'You know it makes sense.'

Jared smiled back. 'I'm touched by this, really I am.'

'Don't be touched, brother. Just give me an official commission or whatever passes for protocol in these situations now—'

'I'm greatly touched,' Jared continued, stepping closer towards his brother. 'But I'm afraid I cannot take you with me.'

Edvin frowned. 'Please explain.'

'I should have come to see you myself,' Jared said. 'Because I want you to know that I *did* think about this, long and hard.' He could see the surprise in Edvin's face and was glad to have the chance to explain. 'You're right – you *would* boost my spirits on the journey. There's no question of that. And as far as the ladies go, well, yes, I probably could broker at least one alliance based on my offering you up for a royal marriage—'

'Steady on!' Edvin recoiled. 'I said I'd charm them, not marry them!'

'As for your talent with crossbows,' Jared continued, 'well, it's true you are gifted in that area. But, actually, Kai and I have been working daily on my own skill. We'll be fine. I need you to stay here, safe. If anything happens to me . . .'

He didn't have to finish his sentence: the look in his brother's eyes told him he understood that Jared needed him

42

to be alive and ready to play his part, should anything happen to the Prince.

Outside, they could hear the chiming of the Bodyguard's Bell. Before the nine chimes had finished, there was a knock at the door and, perfectly on cue, Hal appeared in the Prince's chamber. He waited patiently for the bell to subside before speaking. 'It's time,' he said.

Edvin straightened his ermine cloak. 'Come on, brother,' he said to Jared. 'Let's get out of here and make you official!'

Which, out of the many vivid details of his coronation, would he carry with him for ever? Jared wondered. The sweet smell of burning incense as he entered the Palace Chapel? The purity of the choral voices as he walked down the nave towards the altar? The face of his mother watching closely as, helped with his long robe by Edvin, Jared took his seat on the Prince's Chair? The ancient gold cloth woven centuries before, and still as lustrous as sunlight, which covered the chair? The face of Asta Peck? The lingering scent of shaving soap on Father Simeon's cheek as the Priest leaned in to ask if he was ready? The pervasive sense of ritual that connected him back to each of the priests and princes who had occupied their places there before?

But for Prince Jared, his coronation was to become distilled into one single moment: Axel, his chosen Edling, standing before him, in his hands the Prince's Crown. It was, at close range, a fearsome thing: shaped like a soldier's helmet in burnished blue steel, around the base of the crown was a leather band, riveted there with twelve gold bolts – each of them polished to a mirror-shine – signifying the Council of Twelve and the Prince's responsibility to the Twelve. Midway up the helmet was a broader band of leather, studded with four gold engravings of a dragon – the symbol of the Wynyard family. Between the engravings, stitched into the leather band itself, were the marks for north, east, south and west – demarcating the responsibilities of the Prince to the farthest reach of each of the borders. Welded to the top of the helmet was a golden rendering of a stag's head – paying tribute to the very beginnings of Archenfield and to Jared's most distant ancestors, who had been crowned with – *There but by the grace of God, go I* – the actual head of a slaughtered stag, antlers and all. Sitting on the Prince's Chair, his senses suffused by the wafting incense smoke and transported by the beautiful singing, Jared had looked up into the wide engraved eyes of the stag. He thought back to the stag hunt of only two weeks before, which had ended not only in ignominy but with the news that his brother was dead and that he would now ascend the throne. Jared felt as if everything was circling about one moment. He lifted his gaze from the eyes of the stag to those of his cousin, Axel, standing above him. Axel looked solemn, distant. Jared wondered if he was imagining that it was he and not Jared who sat in the Prince's Chair; that it was his own Edling who stood before him, ready to crown his head with the ancient blue-steel helmet.

Suddenly, there was a moment of utter silence and stillness. Father Simeon had addressed Jared and he had given his answer. Then Axel stepped forward, his eyes meeting Jared's at last. Axel raised the crown high above the Prince's head, so that all in the chapel could see the ancient artefact. Then, in one slow, steady movement, he brought it down to rest on Jared's head.

Nothing had prepared Jared for the weight of the crown. His first thought was that Axel was ramming it down on his head but then he saw Axel stepping away, the Edling's role in the ceremony complete. Father Simeon, too, stood back, smiling benignly at him as Jared felt the pressure of the crown bearing down upon his skull and neck.

Everything came into focus. This was the true meaning of being the Prince of All Archenfield – this burden that he and *only* he could bear. The message, passed down the line of his forebears through the medium of the crown, could not have been any clearer if the princes had risen in unity from the Burning Place at the edge of the fjord to come and whisper their secrets in his ears: '*You might have a Council of Twelve to advise and support you. You might have the gift of glorious lands encompassing fjords, mountains and forest. But, ultimately, being the ruler means bearing this weight alone.*'

Father Simeon was gesturing to him now. Jared knew that he wanted him to stand up. Summoning all his strength, gripping the arms of the Prince's Chair and pressing his hands down upon them, Prince Jared, new ruler of Archenfield, rose to his feet.

Jared began the slow walk back down the nave, towards the chapel doors. He was more aware than ever of the immense mass of the crown, pressing into his temples, and walked more carefully than he had ever walked before. The Prince's steps were accompanied by a fanfare of trumpets, which heralded fresh, jubilant singing from the choir. Jared was aware of all the courtiers' faces directed towards him, their eyes wide with expectation. Few princes could have been crowned at such a dark moment in Archenfield's history, but Prince Jared could see that somehow the ancient coronation ceremony had delivered them new hope. It was down to him and him alone to make good on that promise. His father and brother had devoted their lives to serving the people. Now it was his turn.

Feeling renewed strength, Prince Jared walked out to greet

his people from the palace balcony. As he left the sanctum of the Palace Chapel behind, the trumpet fanfare was drowned out by the cheers of the expectant crowd. He looked at the faces turned up to him and waved his hand to them. More cheers erupted and, just for a moment, Jared was able to forget the terrible deadline he'd set to save his kingdom.

In six short days, either these would still be his people, or ... Jared tried not to shudder.

The alternative was not worth thinking about.

SIX

THE CAPTAIN OF THE GUARD'S VILLA, VILLAGE OF THE TWELVE, ARCHENFIELD

Axel Blaxland gazed into his glass tumbler, filled almost to the brim with aquavit. Returning from the palace to his mansion in the Village, he had found the drawing room prepared for him – the fire drawing well, the lamps lit – just as it always was in the hours following dusk. Closing the door with a force surprising even to himself, he had swiftly extinguished each of the lamps, needing not only solitude but also the comforting embrace of darkness. But the servants had been remiss in one aspect of duty in failing to fully draw together the room's heavy curtains: a rogue shaft of moonlight cut across Axel's shoulder and bisected the polished table in front of him like a dagger.

There was a sudden clamour on the other side of the door. He heard footsteps on the flagstones, then the opening of the mansion's main door, and voices.

'He's not in here, the room is in darkness!' His father, Lord

Viggo, stood at the threshold, a dark silhouette against the light of the hallway.

'I am here,' he said, rising from his seat.

Axel's mother, Lady Stella, and his sister, Lady Koel, joined him and his father in the room.

'Well,' Axel said, with soft resignation, 'I see the whole family has come for an after-hours visit.'

'Light!' Lord Viggo's voice boomed. 'Let's have some light in here!'

Axel's head steward arrived at the threshold to the room but hovered there for a moment, evidently unsure which Blaxland he should be taking his orders from.

'Yes, fine,' Axel told him. 'You may light the lamps.' He turned to his female visitors. 'I know Father will be happy slugging back my aquavit, but can I have brought for you anything from the kitchens? Some tea or warm milk, perhaps?'

Lady Stella nodded. 'Some tea would be very nice, thank you, Axel.'

Axel gave a nod to his steward and the servant left the room. Then he turned back to his family. 'Please,' he said, 'make yourselves comfortable. I'm sorry I was not more welcoming. I was not expecting visitors.'

'Do you often sit here in the dark?' Koel asked.

Axel did not answer. Instead, he reached for his glass.

'Well,' his father said, taking a seat. 'Quite a day, eh? Quite a day! Archenfield crowns its new Prince.'

'If you have come to reflect, blow by blow, on the coronation ceremony, I'm not in the mood,' Axel told his father.

Lord Viggo chuckled. 'No, my son, I have no interest in that. I suppose the ladies might be keen to discuss the fashions and so forth ...' This comment, typical of Viggo Blaxland, was met by three pairs of disdainful eyes. 'No? Well, that isn't why we have come.' He took a sip of his drink,

48

then resumed in a more energetic tone. 'Things have reached an interesting pass, you must agree. I have come – *we* have come – to discuss what happens next.'

Axel's eyes felt heavy. He could feel the familiar overture to a pressure headache and pinched the bridge of his nose. 'Go on,' he said. He knew from experience that it was best to frog-march his father to the point.

Lord Viggo glanced towards the door, checking that there were no servants in earshot. 'This is the moment we have been waiting for. The Wynyards have never been so weak. Now is ripe for you to make your move and seize power.'

As Axel turned to address his father, he noticed that Koel was watching him with those intense, feline eyes of hers.

'As Captain of the Guard,' Axel said, 'it is my responsibility to defend the Princedom against this fresh attack from Paddenburg. It would be a dire enough situation even without the Prince throwing obstacles in my way.'

'You mean by refusing to declare open enmity with Paddenburg?' his mother said, her voice cool as the waters of the fjord.

Axel nodded. 'Yes. But his mind *is* changeable. Yesterday, when the ultimatum arrived, we talked immediately about the necessity of acting swiftly and in the most decisive terms – in other words, taking war to Paddenburg before they deliver it to us.' He sighed. 'But then, at the meeting of the Twelve, where we are supposed to ratify the decision to go to war, he tells us that no, he is intent upon forging alliances that he hopes will eliminate the hostilities even before they commence.'

'It is a noble aim,' Lady Stella pronounced. 'Though surely a misguided one.'

Koel nodded. 'How on earth does Prince Jared think he can forge the necessary alliances in less than one week?'

Axel shrugged. 'I agree with both of you. But Jared's been down blind alleys before.' He leaned towards them. 'I argued from the very beginning that Prince Anders was assassinated for political reasons. And so it proved. But Jared, urged on by his little friend ...'

'Asta,' Koel added. 'The Physician's apprentice.'

Axel nodded. 'The two of them somehow convinced themselves that no, in spite of all the evidence to the contrary, Anders's murder was a crime of passion. And so they embarked on a dangerous diversion that almost cost each of them their lives.'

'To be fair,' Koel broke in, 'it was true that Prince Anders *was* having a reckless affair.'

Axel slammed his glass down more forcefully than he had intended. 'So, a Prince cheats on his wife? It wasn't that reckless, Koel. Believe me, it was not without precedent in the palace of Archenfield. But the fact that this Asta seems to wield some influence on Jared – a greater influence than I or even Queen Elin – is troubling. Especially when the future of Archenfield rests on his actions ...'

'No!' Lord Viggo cried, rising to his feet. 'That's just the point! The future of Archenfield no longer depends on Jared Wynyard's actions.' He moved towards Axel. 'This nation's future depends on *you* and what *you* do next.' He shook his head. 'I don't understand why you fail to see that the power is there in front of you. You just have to learn to seize it!'

Axel had risen to his feet also. 'I told you before, Father – I am neither a fool nor a procrastinator, but the facts are simple. This is not the time for me to distract myself, or others, with a *coup d'état*. My first and foremost duty is to make safe the Princedom, whatever expedition my cousin has decided to embark on. Somehow I have to find a way to give him his head and let him ride across the borders with his chosen fellows, while I ready the troops for the hell-hounds the twin Princes of Paddenburg will let loose upon us six days from now!' He let out a strangulated cry of frustration. 'I could work alongside Prince Goran,' he continued. 'Even Prince Anders was fairly straightforward. I don't know what it is about this sixteen-year-old boy, but I find him impossible.'

His confession was met by silence. Then his father spoke.

'Neutralise him.'

'What?' Axel's eyes met his father's.

'If Prince Jared is such a thorn in your side, remove him.' Lord Viggo reached for Axel's shoulder. 'You need to change the way you see this situation.' He gave his son's shoulder a little shake. 'You think you and I are poles apart, my son, but we're not.'

'Perhaps not,' Axel conceded. 'But I can't contend with this external threat to our nation *and* launch a plot to overthrow the Prince.' He looked at his father with exasperation. 'You were just the same when I was dealing with the investigation into Anders's assassination, telling me then it was the time to strike. Father, I know how ambitious you are – for me and for our family. I'm ambitious too. But you have to let me handle these crises in my way.' He lowered his voice. 'And be assured that as soon as things are settled, I will deal with Prince Jared. In *my* way.'

'But you are thinking about this all wrong!' his father insisted. 'It's *just* these moments of crisis – when Jared is so wrong-footed – that are the very times to take action against him. You already missed one powerful opportunity, during the investigation, to embarrass him.' Lord Viggo's eyes narrowed. 'And you even rushed to his aid when Wilde plunged his dagger into him during the funeral procession ...'

51

'Yes,' Axel acknowledged with a shrug. 'And in doing so, gained his trust and that of those closest to him – those who might perhaps before have doubted my intent. Should I not have done that, Father?'

It was Lord Viggo's turn to shrug. 'You could have waited a moment or two longer, so that he bled out a bit more.'

Axel shook his head, smiling. 'How unusual ... you of all people to advocate waiting.'

Lord Viggo swept his hand through the air as if swatting away a horsefly. 'We're getting away from the point. You need to act right now, and take advantage of a weakened Jared, to assert your rival claim to the throne.' He stepped closer to Axel, his eyes surveying his son with confusion. 'What's holding you back? I'm starting to think you're actually scared of power.' His tone became crueller. 'I'm starting to think that all these years we've spent preparing you for glory have been a poor investment.' He shook Axel hard by the shoulder before releasing him. 'Our time would have been better spent looking to your sister.'

Axel was too angry to speak. Furious, he threw his glance towards his sister, and noticed that she was grimacing, as though she shared his ire. Axel turned back, slowly, towards his father's livid face. 'I did not invite you into my house tonight,' he said, his voice as cold as the fjord in winter. 'And you are not a welcome guest. I am going for a walk. When I return, I expect to find you gone.' Head down, Axel strode out of the room.

'Axel, wait!' Koel called after her brother. It was no joke trying to pursue him across the dense lawn of his garden, encumbered as she was by long skirts and dainty shoes.

He stopped and turned half towards her, his face bathed in moonlight.

'I know you are angry,' she said carefully. 'And you have every right to be. I see the way our father piles pressure upon you, and at the most ill-judged times.'

Axel shrugged. 'I can deal with Viggo. I'll make things happen in my own time and my own way.'

'I know that,' Koel said. 'I have never doubted your abilities.'

Axel observed her curiously. 'What exactly do you want, sister? Lately, you've taken to following me around like a dog. Wherever I turn I find you, hard on my heels.' He frowned. 'I don't need this. I'm beginning to feel suffocated.'

It was her turn to frown. 'Believe me, that is not my intention. I simply want to help you. I believe I can. But you always push me away. I'm not a child, Axel. I know how things work. Let me help.'

He sighed. 'I have told you before. I do not want – or need – *your* help. You have beautiful, wide eyes, sister. Open them and look around you.' The smile evaporated. 'I have people close at hand to help me. I have good friends and unfailing allies on the Twelve. I have my deputy, Elliot, and the rest of my teams. I have all the support I need. What I *don't* need is this constant interference from my family. I am keenly aware that the pressure is on me. It always has been. Our father wants me to claim power in order to satisfy his own frustrated appetite.'

Koel nodded, her agile mind more than keeping pace. 'You're right, of course.' She gazed up at him. 'You wouldn't resist power just to defy him, would you?'

Axel pursed his lips. 'You're no better than he is, Koel, whatever your protestations to the contrary. You have the same one-track mind; you pose the same needling questions. I don't need it from him and I won't take it from you! It's time you started living your own life and cease interfering in mine.

We're not allies. I hold an inordinate amount of power in this Princedom. You hold none.'

His words cut her deeper than she would let him see. Koel was used to being pushed away by her brother, but never had he used such direct or brutal words.

Axel hesitated for a moment. Feeling flushed and queasy, Koel wondered if he might be about to attempt to draw her into a patronising embrace. That was the last thing she wanted. She folded her arms tightly, drawing herself together, and let out a breath into the chill air. It was a relief when he turned and walked away. She watched her brother's silhouette blend into the shadows of the hedges and ivy-clad walls. Within moments, his form was lost.

She began her own walk back towards the lights of Axel's mansion. She was keenly aware that her parents would be waiting for her report. She must compose herself, but Axel's vicious words echoed in her head, repeating and layering themselves, like a peal of bells: *'I hold an inordinate amount of power . . . you hold none.'*

'No!' she cried, her outburst causing an owl to take startled flight from the hollow of a tree in which it had been resting. Koel watched its wings beat its path of retreat and suddenly felt a certain sense of satisfaction. Her brother might not believe that she wielded any power; her father – perhaps her mother, too – might suffer from the same delusions. But she would make them all see. If there was one thing she had learned from observing the workings of court, there were some to whom power was given – often for no discernible reason – and others who were driven to claim power for themselves. She knew which camp she belonged to.

SEVEN

THE PHYSICIAN'S HOUSE, VILLAGE
OF THE TWELVE, ARCHENFIELD

'It's your play, Asta,' Nova reminded her.

'I know,' Asta said, glancing up guiltily.

Nova smiled softly and lifted the cup of herb tea to her lips. A spiral of steam rose over the Falconer's strikingly beautiful features. She glanced back down at the serried faces of the tiles on the rack in front of her. Elias and Nova had also succeeded in collecting sets of similarly patterned tiles and laid them down in front of their own racks. Elias had two quartets – one of the Huntsman, the other of the Beekeeper, and a trio of – and this had pleased him greatly of course – the Physician. Nova had two trios – the Bodyguard and also the Huntsman – but had in addition achieved an 'honour quartet' with the four highly valuable Season tiles. Meanwhile, Asta herself had laid down only one trio so far – the Edling – and, judging by the eclectic assortment of tiles in her rack, would not be laying claim to further points anytime soon.

'I'm very grateful, Nova,' Elias said, 'that you were able to come and join us this evening. It's been an age since I dusted off my set of gaming tiles and, of course, you need a minimum of three to play.'

Nova smiled, setting down her cup. 'It's my pleasure, Elias. But I rather suspect that your true motive in asking me over was to see how my recovery was proceeding.'

Elias flushed slightly. 'No, of course ... well, all right. *Perhaps.*'

Asta smiled. Her uncle was saved any further embarrassment by a brisk knocking on the front door. Grateful for the diversion from her move, Asta jumped out of her seat and darted into the hallway. She opened the door to find Prince Jared standing on the threshold. As ever, Hal Harness stood a few steps behind him.

'Good evening, Asta,' Prince Jared said. 'May we come in?'

'Yes, of course!' She nodded.

Asta led the Prince and his Bodyguard through the hallway and into the parlour, where the others were still seated on either side of the gaming table.

Elias began scrambling up to his feet.

'No, no, Elias. There's no need to get up,' Prince Jared said. His eyes ranged across the array of tiles. 'Ah, the Game of the Gates,' he said, with twinkling eyes.

'Feel free to take over my hand,' Asta said. 'I don't think I have a knack for this at all.'

The Prince smiled. 'I'm sure that's not true.' His smile was only fleeting.

Asta knew Prince Jared's face well enough by now to see the blend of disquiet and purpose swimming below the surface of his handsome features. 'I'm sorry to call upon you late in the evening,' the Prince said, his voice a touch more formal, 'but there's a matter of court business too pressing to wait until morning.'

Elias nodded, pushing back his chair and drawing himself upright. 'Of course,' he said. 'Perhaps you would prefer to speak to Nova and I in private?'

Prince Jared looked suddenly sheepish. 'I'm sorry. I should have been clearer. It's actually Asta who I came to see.'

Elias and Nova turned to look at her; Asta was aware of her face reddening. Elias hovered awkwardly midway between standing and sitting. 'Nova and I can leave—'

Nova nodded, but Asta broke in. 'There's no need for you to abandon the game or your drinks.' She turned towards their visitor. 'That is, if Prince Jared is happy to step out into the Physic Garden with me? The full moon will light our way.'

The Prince gave a nod. 'Of course,' he said. 'Lead on!'

Stepping through the pair of doors into the garden, Asta felt the bracing chill of the night air on her face and regretted not fetching a warmer item of clothing on her way out.

'You're shivering,' Prince Jared said, close at her side, his jacket already in his hands.

Jared's woollen jacket warmed her, as did the thought that, only moments before, it had been pressed close to his own body. Asta glanced up into Jared's face and, finding this somehow too intimate a connection, quickly looked past him. She noted Hal, standing at a discreet remove from them close by the house. The Prince had crouched down to examine one of Elias's neatly ordered herb beds. Intrigued, Asta walked over to join him, dropping down at his side.

Jared surveyed the plot, then looked more closely at a plant over on his other side. It had lacy, blue-green leaves. She watched as the Prince carefully broke off a sprig from it, then lifted it to his nose. She smiled at the expression he pulled and the speed with which he snatched the herb away. 'That is ... pungent!' he gasped, offering it to her.

Asta accepted it with a laugh. 'Pungent is a polite way to

describe it. But as bad as it smells, this is one of the most powerful plants in my uncle's arsenal. It's rue. It's thought to be the antidote to all kinds of poisons.' Her words trailed off as she saw the colour rapidly drain from the Prince's face. Asta chided herself for her lack of sensitivity.

Jared rose to his feet. Asta drew herself up, half tempted to discard the foul-smelling rue but, on second thoughts, slipped it into her pocket.

'Time isn't on our side,' Jared said, 'and there is an important matter I must talk to you about.'

Her eyes locked on to his as he continued. 'Perhaps you know by now that I took your advice. Tomorrow, I embark on a mission to recruit allies from some of our neighbouring states. Much against the advice of my mother, Cousin Axel and a good many of the Council of Twelve, I might add.'

She nodded. 'I'm glad you came to this conclusion, though I shall miss you and worry about you until you return. But, Prince Jared, I didn't advise you to go any more than I did to stay. All I did was encourage you to see there were multiple possible actions you could take.'

He smiled at her, and for a moment she wondered if he felt she was trying to duck out of responsibility – which she certainly wasn't. 'How carefully you choose your words,' he said. 'That should come in handy.' His gaze intensified. 'Asta, I wish to appoint you as the new Poet.'

This was too much. She must have crossed from reality into a dream state. There could be no possible way that he was asking her to join the Twelve.

'I want you as Logan Wilde's replacement.'

Asta shook her head. 'The Poet is one of the most pivotal positions in court. I have no training.'

'That's of little concern to me,' Jared said defiantly. 'Logan Wilde had plenty of training, and look what a multitude of benefits we reaped from his appointment! What I want from my Poet is honesty, and a voice that resonates with the people.'

Asta nodded, understanding the Prince's point. Still, he had ducked her important question. 'Shouldn't this role go to someone with suitable position and talent?'

Prince Jared held her gaze. 'Position be damned,' he said. 'What matters to me is that the Poet is someone I can trust.' His voice softened. 'I do trust you, Asta, and I have absolute faith in your talents. I know we haven't known each other long, but there have been times in the past weeks when you have been the only person in court I could depend upon. We are venturing deeper into the unknown now, and the next days and weeks are likely to be even more challenging than what has come before. I fundamentally need people around me whom I can trust, Asta. I need you.'

She nodded, tears pricking her eyes. 'I want to help. I just don't want you to overestimate my capabilities.'

He reached for her hand. 'You will never disappointment me, Asta, if that's what's on your mind.'

She gulped. 'I'm really touched – staggered actually – by your belief in me. But how can you really be sure that I'm ready for this? I'm still new in court. There's so much I don't understand.'

'Remember what I said to you when we first met in the woods?' He paused, then resumed with a smile. 'I said we were both fish out of water. And so we were. We still are. But we are learning to swim together.'

She nodded. She liked what he was saying, but could she really fulfil his great expectations in her?

Once more, he seemed to intuit her question. 'Just speak your mind and do this job your way. Don't let anyone try to mould or influence you, or distract you from what needs to be done. Above all, Asta, just be your wonderful self.'

The scroll of Asta's life had already unfurled much further than she could ever have expected. Six months before, she had been living in the settlements; two weeks ago, she had been thrust into the heart of court proceedings on the tragic day of Prince Anders's assassination. Now here she was, sharing whispers with Jared, Prince of All Archenfield.

'All right,' she said. 'I'll do it.'

'You're sure?'

She nodded again. 'It would be my honour, Prince Jared, to serve you and the court.'

'Thank you,' he said, relief making him smile broadly.

Asta had a sudden fresh thought. 'What about Uncle Elias? Have you talked to him about this?'

Jared shook his head. She realised that it was further vindication of his respect for her that he hadn't first sought out her uncle. 'No, but I'm sure Elias will understand. He, more than anyone, knows how talented you are.'

Asta frowned. She wasn't so sure. Uncle Elias might indeed be assured of her talents, but he had brought her to court to help *him* in *his* work.

'You look worried,' Jared told her. 'Please don't be. Trust me, it will all fall into place.' He sighed. 'I wish we had more time, Asta, but I ought to head back to the palace now.'

She began to slide out of her borrowed jacket. 'You need some sleep before tomorrow. Don't forget about that. You're not superhuman.'

He affected a pout. 'I'm disappointed you think that.' His face brightened. 'Rest assured, I will sleep a lot more soundly knowing you have agreed to my request.'

She pressed the jacket back into his grasp. Their hands made contact; his flesh was surprisingly warm. 'Let me walk you back inside,' he offered.

She nodded, then changed her mind. 'Actually, I might stay

out here for a moment. My head is spinning ... in a good way. I think I just need a moment or two to come back down to earth.'

He nodded, gazing fondly at her. His face was close. Closer, she thought, than it had been before. With a shiver of anticipation, she wondered if he might be about to lean in and kiss her. He did not. Smiling at her, he slung his jacket casually over his shoulder, then turned and began making his way back towards the lights of the Physician's house.

Asta watched Hal extinguishing his latest cigarette under the sole of his boot, preparing to escort the Prince back to the palace.

'Wait,' she called after Jared.

Immediately, he stopped and turned around, as she strode to catch up with him. She dug her hand into her pocket and produced the sprig of rue she had squirrelled away there before. 'Please take this with you,' she said.

He wrinkled his nose. 'Do I have to? It smells *so* rank!'

She kept her hand stretched out towards him. 'I told you before,' she said, 'it's an antidote against all kinds of poisons. Some people believe it has the power to repel plague and evil spirits. That's probably overstating the case but, all the same, I'd feel better if you took it with you on your journey.'

He hesitated for a moment, then reached out and took it from her. 'I know I'd better do as you say and take it with me,' he agreed, tucking it carefully into his own pocket. 'Even if all it succeeds in repelling are my travelling companions!' He smiled. 'I'm grateful to you for thinking of me, Asta.'

Jared turned away from her and followed Hal back inside the house.

She was all alone in the Physic Garden. The wind was colder now that the Prince's jacket and his close company no longer warmed her. She brought her arms across her chest, mustering what heat she could, and turned her eyes up towards the night sky. Things were changing fast now. She was shedding another skin. It was at once terrifying yet completely exhilarating. As the stars faded and the night sky was pushed away by the new morning, it would become known that she, Asta Peck – the girl from the settlements – was to be one of the Twelve. She had already come so much further than anyone could ever have thought possible. But she also sensed, with the thrill of momentum, that her journey was only just beginning.

EIGHT

THE DINING CHAMBER, THE BLACK PALACE OF PADDENBURG

'Why is there so much food?' Prince Henning asked Lydia as yet another platter was set down on the already laden table.

Lydia smiled. 'I talked to the kitchens. I wanted you to have a taste of all your favourite dishes before you and Ven set off with the troops in the morning.'

Across the table, Nikolai – cousin to the two young Princes and poised to assume greater powers during their absence – smiled approvingly and lifted his black-glass goblet of wine. 'A noble intent!'

'Roast duck with preserved cherries,' announced the steward, raising the silvered dome from the latest platter and releasing a plume of steam and the sweet perfume of cherries into the air. Lydia was momentarily transported to a lazy afternoon in the heat of the summer, when Henning and she had enjoyed an impromptu picnic in the palace's glorious cherry orchard. She remembered him tenderly feeding her cherries, their flesh still warm from the kiss of the August sun.

'Oxtail stew, spatchcock quail, slow-cooked pork, roast duck,' Henning said, his eyes roaming across the many dishes deployed along the centre of the table, as he comically pushed out his stomach and gave it a pat. 'If I eat all of this, I fear no horse in our stables will be able to carry me to the border of Archenfield!'

Lydia turned her head and rested the tip of her chin gently on the shoulder of his stiff serge jacket. 'You don't have to eat *all* of it. Besides, if a horse can sustain you in your heavy armour, I'm sure a little extra body weight will prove neither here nor there.'

Prince Henning laughed. 'Well, when you put it like that . . . !'

Nikolai set down his glass. 'Will Prince Ven be joining us this evening?' he asked, glancing at the empty seat beside his own.

Lydia watched Henning's carefree smile disappear, unhappy that Nikolai had raised the question. She had made such a concerted effort to bolster Henning's mood; now she could see her good work was already being unpicked.

'Prince Ven seems to have little appetite these days,' she said. 'I hope some of these delicious dishes might tempt him to eat tonight. But I do not think we should wait any longer for him to join us.' Her eyes met the steward's, propelling him into action. 'We don't want the food to spoil.'

'Where exactly is Ven?' Nikolai asked, as the steward attended to the Prince's plate.

'Take a guess!' Henning snapped. 'Where is my brother ever to be found these days? He is in our father's bedchamber with the latest quack whom he has summoned from afar and to whom he throws ridiculous amounts of gold in exchange for increasingly ludicrous *cures*.' Henning's face flushed as he continued. 'Last week, it was leeches; then, two days ago, imagine my surprise and delight as I observed Ven assisting his latest miracle worker in placing dead cockerels on either side of Prince Leopold's head.'

Lydia watched the steward closely as he put a generous plate of food down before Prince Henning. Though the steward gave no indication he had taken in a word of Henning's outburst, she still couldn't shake the fear that he might report it verbatim to the other servants.

'Poor Ven,' Nikolai spoke softly as he set down his glass. 'He wants so very much to find a cure for Prince Leopold in spite of the terrible odds against him.'

Henning frowned darkly. 'My brother acts as if he is the only one who wishes my father to recover.'

Lydia placed her hand over Henning's, her long, graceful fingers stroking his wrist. 'We all know that is not the case. Your father's decline is equally painful for both of you. I hope this will not sound callous' – she saw Nikolai observing her carefully – 'but perhaps it is for the best that tomorrow Ven must ride out with you. It will take his mind away from sick Prince Leopold and towards matters central to the future of Paddenburg.'

Henning shrugged as he tore apart a quail with his fingers. 'I would be far better off taking you with me to the border and leaving my brother to mope around the palace.'

'No,' Lydia said with a shake of her head. 'It is important that you ride out together. This is, and always has been, about the two of you.'

Henning dropped the quail bones with a clatter on to his plate. 'As usual, dear Lydia, you are right.'

'Why don't I go up and talk to him?' Lydia suggested. 'Perhaps I can persuade him to leave Prince Leopold's bedside for a short time. It will be good for you two to have some time together – before you set out tomorrow.'

'No!' Henning trapped her hand under his own. She felt the oily residue of quail juice transfer from his fingers to hers. 'There is no reason for your dinner to spoil,' he continued. 'Let my brother wend his way here in his own time.'

Lydia discreetly wiped her hands clean and reached for her knife and fork.

'Ah, yes!' Henning continued, chomping through a portion of duck. 'This is the taste of home! I shall savour its sweetness and subtlety as I resign myself to lesser fare over the coming days and weeks.'

Lydia couldn't help but laugh. 'I have no doubt you will be well catered for in camp,' she said.

'Indeed,' Nikolai added, his dark eyes twinkling. 'Let it never be said that the army of Paddenburg does not march on its belly!'

As Henning turned to Lydia, guffawing at his cousin's small joke, a globule of thick cherry sauce slipped from the corner of his mouth.

The effect was chilling – the dark red stain too perfect a match for blood. It sent an icy chill from the nape of Lydia's neck to the base of her spine. She leaned across to apply her napkin to his mouth; it came away streaked with crimson.

'You seem a little on edge,' Henning observed.

Once again, Lydia was reminded of Henning's knack for seeming entirely caught up in his own thoughts and then surprising her with his lucid observations of her mood.

'You know I am always sad to be parted from you,' she told him. 'You have no idea how slowly time moves when you are away from the palace.'

'I know,' he reassured her. 'But, in this instance, it will be only a matter of days. You will, as discussed, ride out in two days' time with the second flank of troops and join us at the border camp.' His eyes were bright as he warmed to his theme. 'Your glorious body will be encased in the armour I had forged for you. And you, Ven and I will ride side by side across the border and on to the soil of Archenfield to take it for our own!'

Lydia nodded, feeling her heart beat faster. 'That is a heady thought.'

Henning nodded. 'And who shall be waiting for us on the other side, but Logan? I know how you ache to see him again.'

Lydia closed her eyes for a moment.

'And, as you know,' Henning continued, 'there is important work for you and Nikolai to conclude in my absence.' He reached to the chair on his other side and produced two parchment scrolls – one slightly larger than the other. Each had been neatly tied with a black silk ribbon. Henning handed the smaller scroll to Nikolai.

'Cousin, this is the decree signed by myself and Ven, which makes you Prince Regent in our absence.'

Nikolai took the decree. Lydia watched as his nimble fingers unpicked the tight knot. He carefully set the snake of ribbon down and unfurled the parchment. From across the table, her keen eyes traced the intricate copperplate detailing the substantial powers with which Nikolai was being invested. Her eyes dipped down to the signatures of Prince Henning and Prince Ven – Henning's wild and looping; Ven's small and scratchy, like a spider pressed into the fibres of the parchment.

Nikolai nodded, then carefully rolled up the decree and replaced the ribbon.

'Of course, the Prince Regent's decree has no value without us first obtaining a signature on this.' Henning offered Lydia the second scroll. 'I shall entrust this to you.'

She took it but did not untie the ribbon. She knew exactly

what was inside. Though it was only parchment, it suddenly seemed as heavy as a sceptre.

'Prince Leopold *must* sign this before our horses set their hooves on the soil of Archenfield,' Henning said. 'No one must be able to say that my brother and I are not the legitimate rulers of Paddenburg.'

Nikolai nodded. 'It is regrettable that Prince Leopold has not rallied before your departure to sign this decree. I am sure you would ride out with a lighter heart knowing that all was in order.'

Henning shrugged. 'Unlike my brother, I do not waste my time or energy merely wishing for things to change. If things are not to my liking, I make the necessary alterations.'

Lydia met his eye. She quickly set down the scroll. Footsteps rang across the room. Glancing up, she saw Prince Ven walking towards the table.

'You greedy pigs!' Ven exclaimed, pulling out the chair next to Nikolai. 'Look at all this food! It's enough for the entire army.'

'I hardly think so,' Henning said quietly.

'What's that, brother?' Ven asked, reaching for the platter of quail. 'Where is the steward? Must I serve myself?'

'I will serve you,' Lydia said, rising to her feet.

'No,' Henning said, seizing her wrist. 'You will not serve my brother. You are his equal now.'

Ven raised an eyebrow. 'You talk as if you are already married,' he said.

Lydia saw with relief that the steward had returned to the dining chamber and was striding towards the table.

'It matters little whether Lydia and I have been through the formalities of a ceremony,' Henning announced. 'She has already done enough for us and for the Princedom of Paddenburg to sit here as our equal.'

'You will not hear any argument from me,' Ven said, as the steward prepared his plate. 'A little more generous with the duck, if you please!' Ven's eyes met his brother's. 'Both Lydia and Logan have earned their place in our nation's history.' He picked up the wine decanter and poured a large measure into his goblet. 'A toast,' he announced. 'To Lydia and Logan Wilde!'

'To Lydia and Logan!' Nikolai and Henning echoed. Henning squeezed her wrist gently as he lifted his goblet.

'Now tell us,' Nikolai turned to Ven, 'what news of Prince Leopold? We hear tell of an unusual treatment involving dead cockerels.'

Ven swallowed his wine. 'Oh, I'm sure my brother has made great mockery at my expense.' Henning shook his head and was about to protest, but Ven lifted his hand. 'But the fact is that the latest treatment seems to be working.'

'It is?' Nikolai said. 'But that's wonderful news.'

Lydia saw his fingers come to rest lightly on the bound scroll in front of him. It seemed that, after all, Henning would have an answer before his departure.

'Has he returned to consciousness?' Henning asked. 'Is he able to talk?'

Ven smiled. 'What you want to know is – is he able to hold a pen? He has shown moments of lucidity and I have seen faint glimpses of the father we used to know. But he is still very weak and given to tiredness. He is sleeping again now.'

Henning shook his head. 'It doesn't sound quite the miraculous recovery we were promised. I fail to see why you remain so confident.'

'Because the physician tells me that he is responding to the latest treatment. And I put store in the physician's words.' Ven pushed back his chair and picked up his plate. 'I shall eat in my chamber,' he announced. 'I do not care for the company here.'

Nikolai turned to Henning. 'You need to bring him into line. This is not the way for the two of you to embark on the most important mission in Paddenburg's recent history.'

Henning chewed meditatively on his quail, spat the bones into his palm and dropped them on his plate.

'I will take care of my brother, Nikolai. You need have no concern about that. Your job is to resolve this situation with my father.' He turned to Lydia and traced the curve of her cheek with his finger. 'Let's retire,' he said. 'I have an early start in the morning. I'll not waste any more of this precious night.'

NINE

THE DUNGEONS,
PALACE OF ARCHENFIELD

Koel Blaxland moved through the dank underbelly of the palace. There were few places within the court that she had not explored at least once in her seventeen years but until now she had had no reason — nor any desire — to visit the Dungeons. The light was poor down here, but her quick eyes soon began to discern shapes in the darkness. She felt her heart rate accelerate at the prospect of entering this new, forbidden territory.

Thoughts of her earlier argument with her brother pulsed in her head, each of his lacerating comments wounding her anew: *What exactly do you want, sister? I don't want or need your help ... It's time you started living your own life ... I hold an inordinate amount of power ... You hold none ... What exactly do you want, sister?*

It was a good question and, she realised, not one she had thought to answer before. What *did* she want? What was the reason she had taken this diversion on her way home to

Blaxland Manor? She couldn't put it into words yet. All she knew was that the subterranean darkness had exerted a powerful pull upon her. Heightened as her senses had been, she had had a sudden vision of a hand reaching up from under the ground to grip her and drag her down through the layers of the palace. Down here, to the very darkest level.

Walking onwards, she experienced a sudden chill as she realised that it was not a question of *what* had brought her down here, but *who*. She had come to look into the eyes of the assassin. To bear witness to that ultimate kernel of darkness.

Logan Wilde was not a stranger to her. She had watched him manoeuvre his way expertly through courtly politics, dropping careful phrases into Prince Anders's – and then Prince Jared's – ear. She was intrigued by Wilde now, more than ever, for here was a man capable of single-handedly bringing a Princedom to its knees.

Her thoughts were momentarily halted as she found her path blocked by the solid bulk of Morgan Booth, the Executioner. Koel's eyes traced the complex artwork on his muscled forearms. There were detailed inkings of flowers and ships. She had not chanced to gaze upon them before; now they whispered to her of new worlds and journeys of discovery.

'Lady Koel,' he said, inclining his head. 'You are the last person I expected to welcome down into my domain.'

How sweet that he thought of this as *his* domain. Smiling, she brushed past him, noticing the thrilling rows of axes above his workbench.

'May I?' she enquired. When he didn't answer, she reached out and pressed her fingers against the cold blade of one of the weapons. She wondered when the blade had last been employed to cut through some undesirable's neck. She brought her fingers to her nose and inhaled the odour of metal. It was strange how similar the blade smelled to the blood it unleashed.

'Is there something I can do for you?' Booth asked.

'No,' she said. 'It's the prisoner I came to see.'

The Executioner raised an eyebrow, but before he could speak, another, more cultured voice than his emerged from the gloom.

'Well, well,' it said. 'I am honoured indeed. Greetings, my lady.'

Koel hadn't realised that she was standing right before the prisoner's cell. She turned around as the disgraced Poet's face emerged into the meagre light. He stood in the centre of his cell, sinewy arms folded – arms, she supposed, that had only ever wielded pens rather than swords. But no, Logan Wilde had used a dagger with great skill on poor Cousin Jared – and, frankly, that was the least of his crimes. He had pumped poison into Prince Anders, killing him little by little until his feet turned gangrenous, his head was filled with terrifying visions and his heart gave out. Next, Wilde had turned his attention to Lady Silva. The wicked Poet had battered her to death, then staged things to look as if she had drowned herself and her unborn child. Finally, he'd moved on to Nova Chastain, revealed as Prince Anders's true love. He had used those same sinewy arms to send her flying from the top of her tower.

'Did you just come here to gaze upon me?' he asked, his confident voice cutting through the silence. 'Did you take it upon yourself to come and look into the face of a murderer? Well, do take a look, Lady Koel. See what you can decipher.'

Her eyes met his. Yes, this was exactly what she had come for ... but now, with a flash of disappointment, she saw that he was just another man.

He grinned at her, perhaps guessing her thoughts, and took

73

a seat on the stone platform that served as his bed. 'Well, since you *are* here, my lady, what news from above ground? We sewer rats like nothing more than to feast on the tasty scraps of palace gossip.'

Koel hesitated. Surely it was not politic to share any matters of court with him? Yes, he was trapped down here and there was certainly no way he could escape but, according to the terms of the Paddenburg Ultimatum, he could not be harmed. And, in a week's time, he would be reunited with his comrades from Paddenburg. She knew that anything she told him would be passed on to them.

'Why so tongue-tied?' he asked. 'I've no doubt you have stories to tell, my lady.'

She frowned. 'You know nothing about me, Mr Wilde.'

He shook his head, smiling. 'I know more than you might think. You're a spectator, Lady Koel. You stalk the palace corridors, absorbing it all. Most people fail to notice you but don't let that lull you into thinking you are invisible to me.'

His words took her by surprise. 'You've made a study of me.'

'Yes, something like that.'

The prisoner was talking to her as though he were her equal. As much as it irked her, it also intrigued her. But they had to be careful. She glanced over her shoulder, seeing Morgan Booth busy at his workbench.

'We should be circumspect,' she whispered. 'We are not alone.'

Logan smiled. 'Regrettably not,' he concurred. 'But if it's the Executioner you are concerned about, fear not.'

What did he mean? Was Morgan an ally of Logan's? She was shocked to think of it. How many co-conspirators did Logan have in court? On the Twelve?

'In my days of freedom,' Logan resumed, 'Morgan and I

were friends – at least, it's fair to say he thought of us as such and I saw no need to disillusion him. Friends confide in one another and Morgan was no exception.' The prisoner paused, a smile etched across his lips once more. 'He confided plenty in me – from his teatime dalliances with your aunt, the Queen, to his worsening deafness.'

'Deafness?' she echoed.

Logan nodded. 'The fact of the matter is that the Executioner is pretty much as deaf as a post. You may think he's looking intently at you when you speak, drinking in your every word. I've no doubt that Queen Elin is under that impression. The truth of the matter is that he is somewhat desperately attempting to read your lips.' Logan winked. 'But if he can't see you, he certainly can't hear you.'

Glancing from Logan to Morgan, then back again, Lady Koel decided to take a chance.

'You asked for news from above,' she began.

'Yes.' He nodded. 'The deaf Executioner is not exactly a bundle of entertainment and my only other visitor, thus far, has been Father Simeon. It seems he's intent on saving my mortal soul.'

'But you're not?'

'I haven't decided yet.' His face suddenly lit up. 'Maybe I *shall* let him grapple with some of my innermost demons. It would give him some point, some purpose, don't you agree?'

Koel was intrigued. 'You don't think Father Simeon has a purpose?' she asked.

'I think he struggles sometimes. He doubts himself.'

'But you – someone like you – would never doubt yourself, I suppose?'

Koel expected a flippant answer, but she saw he was giving her question careful consideration.

'Of course I have experienced doubt. You cannot be a

75

rational being and not be subject to moments of doubt, can you? The difference between Simeon and me is that I don't let it get in the way of getting the job done, while he dithers and ties himself up in knots of one kind or another ... '

'You poison princes,' Koel said flatly.

'If that's what the occasion demands.'

'Or what your masters in Paddenburg demand.'

He smiled again. 'What makes you think *they* are *my* masters? It could just as easily be the other way around.'

'I ought to be going,' she said. 'It's late and I'm not sure I can match your energy or talent for verbal sparring.'

He shook his head, laughing. 'You're actually very clever, my lady. I know no one tells you that very often but I have observed you, both from afar and now up close, and I have no doubt that you are indeed very clever. Far cleverer, I suspect, than the rest of your kin.' Their eyes met briefly. 'Oh yes, I'm sure you'd love to know my take on Axel. But that's something for another time.'

'Another time?' It was her turn to laugh. 'That's exceedingly presumptuous of you. What makes you think I'll come back? It smells foul down here. And it's hardly appropriate for me to consort with you. If my father found out, he'd—'

'He won't find out,' Logan said. 'He's far too preoccupied with moving your brother into position.' He nodded. 'Oh, yes, Lord Viggo will be in no doubt that this is the golden moment your family has been waiting decades for.' Koel tried not to give anything away in her expression, though it hardly mattered. He clearly had a keen sense of the goings-on in the palace, even from down here in his cell. 'No,' he continued. 'Lord Viggo has a very skewed sense of his daughter and her talents. You know that as well as I do. Why, most of the time, he acts as if he has only one child.'

His ready smile belied the brutal truth of his words.

'Sorry,' he said. 'I didn't mean to wreck the beginnings of this beautiful friendship.'

'We are not friends,' she said defiantly. 'We cannot be friends.'

'Spoilsport.' He stood up and stepped closer, his hands reaching for the bars. 'You can handle the truth. You're one of the very few people in court who can. That's just one of the things we have in common.'

'I'm not sure that I care to examine what traits we may have in common.'

'Of course you do.' He was unrelenting. 'You can see the truth for what it is, and accept its consequences. You see what's going on – and you don't just see it – you absorb it, you process it. You have everything your brother does not ... except position in court. But, of course, that could soon change.'

It unnerved her the way he seemed to know her from the inside out. Almost better, she thought with a shiver, than she knew herself. It was as if he were drawing words, thoughts, desires, up from deep within her. But then, she reasoned, was it also possible that he had planted them there?

Koel attempted to compose herself. 'What makes you think I even want a position in court?'

'Don't play games with me,' he said. 'I know just what you want. I told you before – I understand you.' He lowered his voice. 'I know exactly how you tick. I think I unsettle you a little, but that isn't my intention. We're cut from the same dark cloth, you and I. We both want power. We both want as much power as is there for the taking – and then more besides.'

She shook her head as a strange rush – at once new and yet strangely natural – flowed through her body.

He smiled again. 'You've never even allowed yourself to

think it until now, have you? All those days and nights hearing your father go on and on about how Axel was the one to take power. But now I've found your desire, lying there like a pearl in an oyster at the bottom of the ocean. I have found it and I have named it. Now it is out there. And it is only going to grow stronger, believe me.'

She recognised the truth of his words. Strange sensations pulsed through her head and body as if energies long held dormant were now being unleashed. She had come here to look straight into the eyes of a killer, to know what darkness lay within him. And she had done so. But she had found in Logan Wilde a strange kind of mirror. She sensed she could confide in him, share with him the darkness deep within her that she had learned to keep hidden from the others. It was at once a terrifying and yet utterly exhilarating thought.

FIVE DAYS UNTIL
INVASION...

TEN

THE PALACE, ARCHENFIELD

It was still dark as Prince Jared and Hal made their way to the stable block; the only sound was the crunching of their boots on the gravel. The palace was shrouded in a rare blanket of peace. The next time I lay eyes on this place, Jared mused, will be either as its champion or as another kingdom's prisoner.

The thought chilled him.

As they neared the stable block, the Prince saw the glow of lanterns and caught the earthy aroma of coffee.

'Prince Jared, good morning to you!' Lucas Curzon said, as the Prince and his Bodyguard walked through the stable doors. 'You are earlier than expected.'

'I thought we should make as early a start as possible,' Jared said. 'I am keen to ride out before the palace wakes.'

Lucas nodded. 'I understand. And everything is just about ready, I think.' He turned back to watch the other grooms make the final preparations.

'Good morning, Prince Jared ... and Hal.' Kai Jagger emerged from the shadows.

Jared shook the Huntsman's hand. In spite of being the Prince of All Archenfield, Jared had struggled long and hard to regard himself as Kai's equal. But now at last he felt on the verge of being able to do so.

'I'm honoured to be coming with you on this important journey,' the Huntsman said.

From behind Kai appeared a lanky young man of a similar age to Jared. He had black eyes and dark, curly hair.

'I am not sure you have been formally introduced to Bram Gentle,' Hal whispered in Jared's ear.

Jared started a little. He had forgotten that Hal was so close, but quickly recovered himself. 'We have not properly met,' he said, offering his hand to Bram. 'But I hear great things about you.'

The boy met the Prince's gaze timidly and shook the Prince's hand quickly but with surprising firmness. He flushed red as beetroot in the glare of everyone's attention.

Jared smiled. It was a great relief to encounter someone more ill at ease than himself. 'Gentle is an interesting name for a bodyguard,' he said.

'It is my father's name, sir,' Bram answered. 'And his father's too.'

Kai laughed. 'You know, I think we might have guessed that. Bram, have you had a cup of coffee yet? No? Then come with me and we shall knock the last remains of sleep from you.'

As they moved out of earshot, Hal turned to face Prince Jared. 'Do not be fooled, Your Majesty. That boy is sharp as a dagger when it comes to offence and defence. Words are, however, not his forte.'

The grooms led the horses out into the yard, accompanied by their chosen riders. Jared was gratified to see that, although each of the horses had been loaded with panniers containing essential changes of clothes, spare weapons and provisions, the baggage had been kept to a minimum. If Queen Elin had had her way, the horses would have been weighed down with treasures from the palace vaults to help him barter and bribe his way to agreement in the foreign courts. Jared had insisted that he would not win alliances through bribery but only through straight talking and common goals. The look his mother had ended the conversation with was one he would remember for the rest of his days.

'All right then.' Lucas reappeared at his side. 'There you are, Prince Jared. Four of Archenfield's finest beasts of burden – and the horses are pretty impressive too.'

Lucas's joke helped break the undertow of tension, which spiralled through the early morning air like the exhalations from the horses' nostrils. Lucas now offered Prince Jared the reins to his own horse, Handrick, and stood back as he climbed into the saddle. There were few places that Jared felt more relaxed than in Handrick's saddle. Handrick had been the Prince's favourite horse for many years now. It had been love at first sight when Prince Jared had seen the new foal gambolling around the palace meadow. Undoubtedly the journey ahead was to be their greatest challenge to date, but he had no doubt that the tireless nine-year-old was more than up for the challenge. Glancing over his shoulder, Jared saw his three travelling companions poised and ready to depart. The Prince turned back towards Lucas.

'We'll see you in a few days' time,' Jared said. 'And don't worry.' He patted Handrick's glossy black flank. 'I promise to take good care of him.'

'Travel safe,' Lucas said. 'Here's wishing you good speed and fair weather.'

All at once, they were off, walking and then trotting away from the palace. Although the Prince's Bell had yet to sound,

Jared saw that one of the palace's upper chambers was lit and the curtains open. He glimpsed the silhouette of his mother. He raised his hand.

If Queen Elin saw him, if indeed she was watching, she did not reciprocate.

Before long, they were trotting along the side of the river – the same river which snaked through all of the territories Jared intended to visit. The river was perhaps the only common factor linking these territories but, he hoped, would prove a crucial point of connection. Just as Axel had suggested, he would put on the table to each of the foreign rulers an unprecedented alliance of the river territories. His only departure from Axel's vision was that this would be an alliance not of four territories but of five, because, against the Captain of the Guard's clear advice, the first port of call would be Woodlark.

The queendom of Woodlark was not merely important in practical terms: its size, its exemplary militia – under the helm of Princess Ines – and its proximity to both Archenfield and Paddenburg; no, Woodlark was also important in other ways: Jared had to make good his debt to Francesca by telling her the truth about Silva's death.

Even if he did not gain her alliance, he would regain his self-respect.

They were passing the charred remains of Prince Anders's bathing house, the place that his brother had come to betray his wife, Silva, with another woman. Close by, Silva's own life had ended. He remembered how Axel had told him about the fire and put forward his theory that Silva had set fire to the tainted hut before hurling herself to her death in the river. This had not proven to be the true shape of events. Both the burning of the hut and Silva's death had been executed with icy precision by the hand of Logan Wilde – the Prince's right-hand man – who had now been revealed as the architect of destruction and a true ally of Paddenburg and its two ambitious Princes.

The sky was growing lighter all the time. Now, at last, Jared heard the sonorous chime of the Prince's Bell. *The bell chimes once, for there can be only one true Prince.*

The traditional line snaked sinuously through his brain. With the Paddenburg Ultimatum hovering over the Princedom like the sword of Damocles, Jared was Archenfield's only hope.

Once again, Jared felt the awesome weight of that responsibility, just as he had when Axel had set the Prince's Crown on his head. Thankfully, the crown was stashed safely with his other things on the back of Hal's horse – it would be brought out only if absolutely necessary. He dug his heels into Handrick's sides and felt the pleasing sensation of gathering momentum as he and his three fellows hastened to the borders with Woodlark.

ELEVEN

THE CAPTAIN OF THE GUARD'S VILLA, THE VILLAGE OF THE TWELVE, ARCHENFIELD

Axel's eyes snapped open. He was sitting up in his bed, the sheets twisted around him. He caught sight of his face in the mirror on the wall directly opposite the bed. He looked pale and haggard.

He freed himself from the clutch of the bedclothes and leaped up. The room was bitterly cold. He wrapped a fur cloak around himself and nudged his feet, sockless, into a pair of boots.

He had no idea of the time but as he strode out of his chamber he was struck by the smell of brewing coffee. On the landing, his valet was lighting the lamps. It had to be just before the Prince's Bell.

'Lord Axel!' The valet paused in his duties. 'You have risen early this morning.'

'There is much to do,' Axel answered, without slowing his pace. 'I'll take my coffee in my office.' He continued on his way, not bothering to exchange pleasantries with the other servants making their way about the mansion. He plunged into the sanctuary of his office and slammed the door shut.

The room was still dark. Axel pushed back the curtains. The door opened again and his valet followed him inside. He set a tray with a coffee pot and a neat stack of buttered toast down on the desk, then glanced guiltily at the Captain of the Guard. 'I'm sorry that the room was not ready for you on entry.'

Axel met the valet's eager-to-please expression with a frown. 'You need to wake up,' he told him. 'Take notice of what's going on around you. The Prince is on his way across the borders and we are on the verge of a new war.'

'Yes, sir.'

'Just get the fire lit,' Axel snapped. 'We might as well be in Elias's Ice House.' He turned away and directed his attention to the rows of books before him. He soon found the one he was looking for and carried it back to the desk. It was, fittingly, a heavy book: two hand-spans long and another two wide, bound in maroon leather, its vellum pages edged in gold. On its front cover were the embossed words: *THE LAWS OF ARCHENFIELD*.

Axel set the tome down on his desk and began turning its pages, quickly drawing comfort from the familiar titles: 'The Priest', 'The Beekeeper', 'The Captain of the Guard'. The Book of Law was the touchstone that Axel turned to in times of uncertainty. Written long ago, it laid down the key responsibilities of each of the Twelve. Axel was unsure as to why it soothed him so to see their roles and duties laid out in ink on vellum; perhaps it was merely that in moments of stark uncertainty, it gave him some reassurance that there *was* definition and certainty, if one only took a breath and searched for it.

His hand rested on the first of the pages devoted to the duties of the Captain of the Guard. He had no need to concentrate on the all-too-familiar lines:

The Captain of the Guard shall advise the Prince on how best to make safe the borders in times of threat ... The Captain of the Guard shall muster the necessary forces to act to defend the Princedom ... The Captain of the Guard shall act as the Prince's deputy, as required, and in consultation with the Edling ...

Axel felt the calm he had sought. He was doing all that was asked of him; all that his predecessors had asked of him. He might be failing in his father's eyes, but according to this book, he was adhering to every last word of law.

His fingers brushed through the chapters devoted to 'The Groom', 'The Cook', 'The Executioner' ... He knew that there was no section dedicated to the responsibilities of the Prince – it was as if the ruler was never to be questioned or held to account like the rest of them were.

He heard a snap and glanced up to see the flames leaping in the hearth. The valet had done his duties and slipped away, unnoticed. He poured himself a cup of coffee. The liquid was scalding hot, just as he liked it. Axel continued to turn the pages until he reached the last section. This final chapter addressed the workings of the Twelve as a whole. He stilled his hand on the title: 'Extraordinary Measures to be Employed in Extraordinary Circumstances.'

His eyes skimmed the page, then – with a swift flick of his finger – the next. And there it was, staring at him in black and white. His answer.

*

THE PHYSICIAN'S HOUSE, VILLAGE OF
THE TWELVE, ARCHENFIELD

'What do you expect me to say?'

Asta stared disconsolately at her uncle across the breakfast table. 'I thought – I *hoped* – you might be pleased about this.'

Elias smiled thinly. 'Surely, Asta, as flattered as you may feel, even you must see what a ridiculous idea this is.'

Asta bristled. 'I want you to know, Uncle Elias,' she said, 'that I fully intend to continue as your apprentice in combination with my new duties.'

Elias shook his head. 'I'm afraid that is further evidence of your naïvety. Under normal circumstances, a position on the Twelve is all consuming.' His smile disappeared. 'With the threat of invasion hanging over us, things become still more intense.' He shook his head again. 'You really have to wonder – what *was* Prince Jared thinking?'

Asta brought her cup down angrily on the table, sending a knife clattering to the floor. Her uncle flinched, but he deserved that. Did he really have to be unkind? Did he really not have any sense that she already felt out of her depth? 'I *did* wonder how the Prince came to this decision,' she said, her voice wavering. 'In fact, I asked him why he would even consider me for one of the most pivotal positions in court, when I have no relevant training.'

'A fair question,' Elias said. 'And what did the young Prince answer?'

Asta glared at her uncle defiantly. 'He told me that he wanted someone he could trust.'

'I see,' Elias shot back. 'So you're being offered this position because the Prince trusts you?'

'Yes. He does.'

'And what exactly is that trust based upon? Certainly not your background or your training, relevant abilities, your knowledge of the way this court works—'

'No,' Asta interrupted. 'Upon none of those things. Prince Jared trusts me because during the past two weeks – during this cataclysmic time when his brother was assassinated and Axel bungled the murder investigation – I was there for him—'

'You were *there for him*?' Elias flushed puce. 'What does *that* mean, exactly?'

'I was someone he could talk to,' Asta said. 'In spite of my lack of knowledge and experience of the court – indeed, perhaps *because* of my lack of those qualities – he felt able to talk to me . . . as an equal.'

Elias's eyes widened. 'Just listen to yourself! You think you are talking *as an equal* to the ruler of Archenfield?' He shook his head. 'My, my, Asta, if your dear mother could hear you now.'

'She would be beside herself with pride,' Asta countered. 'Just as proud as she was the day I set off from home to make a new life here with you. All Mother and Father have ever wanted for me was to know a good life, to have opportunities that they did not.'

Elias's voice came sharp and low. 'Well, just look at you scrabbling your way up the greasy pole. It's quite a sight to behold.'

His words hung in the air like a noxious odour.

There was a knock at the door. For a moment, neither of them made a move to answer it. At last, Asta rose slowly to her feet. 'You are being grossly unfair,' she said.

There was a second knock, louder than the first.

'Answer the door, child,' he told her, his eyes lowered.

Hot tears welling in her eyes, Asta went to the door to find Nova waiting on the step. Her weight was propped on the cane she had taken to using during her recovery from her fall. It was made from a stag's antlers, its wildness perfectly suited to the Falconer.

'I'm sorry, I wasn't sure if you had ... ' Nova's expression changed. 'Asta, is everything all right? No, I can see that it isn't. You look quite upset.'

Asta just about managed to nod. 'Please come inside,' she said.

As Nova moved carefully over the threshold, she said, 'I came, as agreed, to accompany Elias to the meeting of the Twelve. But, first, you must tell me why there are tears in your eyes.'

Before Asta could speak, Elias bustled into the hallway. *Is he going to try to put a gloss over our spat in front of Nova?* Asta wondered darkly.

'Good morning, Elias,' Nova said.

The Physician glared at the Falconer. 'There's really nothing good about it, from my perspective,' he told her.

No gloss then.

Without further explanation, he brushed past them and made for the door to his surgery, Nova calling after him in surprise: 'Elias, I thought we had agreed to walk up to the palace together? It's a surprisingly clement morning—'

'Change of plan!' he called, already halfway through the surgery doorway. 'Walk with Asta if you wish!'

'But Asta doesn't attend ... ' Nova began, then broke off as the door to the surgery slammed shut.

'Asta, I think you had better tell me what's going on here. Clearly you and your uncle have had some kind of unpleasantness?'

Asta nodded, leading Nova through to the kitchen. 'Last

night,' she said, 'when Prince Jared came to visit, he asked me to be the new Poet.'

'Asta!' Nova exclaimed, light dancing in her eyes. 'What a bold and wonderful move on the Prince's part.'

'You really think so?' Asta asked, fresh tears welling in her eyes.

'Yes,' Nova assured her. 'But I'm not convinced that you do.'

'I was so happy about it. Surprised and anxious but happy beyond measure. To think that he would place such faith in me.'

'Faith you have swiftly earned,' Nova noted.

'I wish my uncle felt as happy for me as you do.'

'Oh, of course.' Nova's eyes met Asta's. 'So, that's why he's stamping around? I'm sure you know as well as I that your uncle does not adjust well to change. Give him some time.' Pressing her cane into the floor, she leaned forward confidentially. 'He's just being over-protective. You know how deeply he cares for you.'

'Perhaps you're right,' Asta conceded. They could both hear the Physician, shuffling about in the adjacent room. 'But, Nova, he has made it very clear to me that he thinks the Prince's confidence in me is misplaced. That I have no aptitude or experience to bring to this role.'

Nova reached out her hand to blot Asta's tears. 'Clearly, Prince Jared feels differently.'

Asta allowed her head to drop. 'Maybe Uncle Elias is right. Maybe the Prince's faith in me *is* misplaced. And if my own uncle thinks that, how do you think the rest of the Twelve are going to react?'

'With open minds, I hope,' Nova said. 'Some of the more traditionally minded – Vera, perhaps, or Jonas – may raise an eyebrow, but times are changing fast, Asta. If recent events have shown us nothing else, it is that we need to alter the way we do things around here.'

'You really think that?' Asta pressed her.

Nova nodded. 'I do. And I want you to think about this, as you take your place at the Prince's Table. The Prince himself is sixteen, the exact same age as you. But Morgan Booth, Emelie Sharp, Hal Harness and Lucas Curzon are all in their early twenties, Asta. There is almost no old guard left. That's a myth that people who oppose change like to cling to. The Council of Twelve has always welcomed new blood and fresh thinking. In many ways, it is what keeps us so strong.'

Asta felt a fresh shiver as the Groom's Bell began to chime.

'Come on, then,' Nova said, reaching out her hand. 'It wouldn't do to be late for your first meeting.'

Asta froze. 'I'm really scared. Just imagine – what if I really can't do this?'

Nova gave her hand a squeeze and looked deep into her eyes. 'Just imagine,' she said. 'What if you really *can*?'

TWELVE

THE FENCING COURT,
THE BLACK PALACE OF PADDENBURG

Lydia felt the blood pulsing through her veins as she readied herself for Nikolai's next attack. She watched carefully through the mesh of her mask as he extended his sabre towards the left side of her torso. Swift as a snake's tongue, he lunged towards her and, holding her nerve, she moved into his thrust to parry. But, as she did so, her opponent paused and withdrew, directing his attack to her right side. It was the classic disengagement and she knew she ought to have anticipated it. She twisted her own sabre in a circle just in time to catch the tip of Nikolai's weapon and deflect it away.

He drew back, nodding slightly in her direction. This was, she knew, as much praise as she was ever likely to elicit from him.

Nikolai had been in a merciless mood throughout their bout that morning and, true to form, he did not allow her any time to recover from his last attack before lunging towards her again. She met his energy with her own, using her sabre to push Nikolai's aside and gain access to the target area. She executed the move perfectly and was rewarded by the pleasing sight of her sabre pressed up against his chest.

This time, he did not launch another attack but instead lifted his hands in playful surrender. Their battle was over.

'Thank you,' she said, lifting her mask and shaking free her hair.

'Thank *you*.' He removed his own mask and bowed low before her. 'You certainly made me sweat today, Miss Wilde.'

'I'm glad to hear it,' she said, grinning. As he unbuttoned his fencing jacket, she caught sight of his chest, still widening and narrowing rapidly as his breath caught up with his exertions. His skin was slick with sweat. As she walked closer she caught his scent. Nikolai exuded a different kind of sweat to Henning; it was clean and pure, like the air in the mountains.

'You have proved a great help to me,' she said. 'These daily bouts with you have made me a better fighter than I ever thought I could be.'

He gave a small shake of his head. 'You came to Paddenburg as a fighter, Miss Wilde. I merely trained the sabre not to tremble with fear at being in your hand.' He held her gaze, then smiled. 'Well, I for one seem to have built up a sweat from our exertions. We should go and wash.'

She nodded and followed Nikolai out of the fencing court and into the corridor circling back to the Black Palace's main entrance but, as they moved further from the court, her exhilaration began to ebb away, and her head once again became crowded with the dark thoughts that had magically receded while she was stalking Nikolai through the mesh of her fencing mask. She thought of Prince Leopold slumbering above, behind the gauze curtains connecting each of his golden bedposts. She thought of Henning and Ven riding for the border in their golden armour. Each one of them had a job to do.

The hour of judgement was close now. Whatever games she might play with her mind to try to distract herself, there was no running away from that cold fact.

She had barely set foot on the grand stairway when she heard the woman's cry. 'Lord Nikolai, my lady! Thank heavens! I was looking all over . . . !'

It was Magda, one of the Black Palace's oldest servants, coming down the stairs from the upper gallery. The wrinkled skin of her face and neck was contorted, as if she was having trouble breathing.

'Whatever is the matter, Magda?'

'The Prince, my lady.' Lydia tensed, preparing herself for the worst. The old woman took a gulp of air before continuing, 'He is asking for his sons!'

Nikolai turned and glanced over his shoulder at Lydia. His eyes were dark, alive with purpose.

Lydia felt a fluttering in her chest and her heart rate accelerated again. She had a fresh vision of Henning and Ven riding towards the border. She remembered the particular way Henning had squeezed her hand during dinner. She knew with a cold certainty that she had to take control here.

'Thank you, Magda,' she said. 'Come, Nikolai. Let us go to greet the Prince.'

As Magda tottered down the stairs and across the marble floor of the hallway, Nikolai placed a steadying hand on Lydia's shoulder. She realised she was trembling.

'There is nothing to be frightened of, Lydia,' he said. 'There is no task that awaits you now that you are not capable of tackling. Remember this.'

'Yes,' she said, gathering herself. 'I know you are right. I will stop by my chamber to retrieve the decree.'

'Very good.' Nikolai nodded. 'And bring a pen and ink,' he added. 'Just in case the inkwell on old Leopold's desk has run dry. We may get only one chance at this.'

As Lydia walked towards the Prince's bed, each of its four posts mounted by a carved golden eagle, motes of dust danced before her eyes. The air in this room was always stifling and she was aware of a noxious odour – a mixture of various bodily smells and something else – perhaps one of the strange medicaments or dead animals delivered to Leopold by the latest of Ven's 'miracle workers'.

The gauze curtain on one side of the bed had been drawn back. Leopold was sitting up, propped on a pile of pillows. His eyes were fixed on the window, with its clear view of the palace gardens and his beloved maze. As Lydia drew closer, he gave a start. 'I thought you were an angel at first, dressed all in white, come to lead me away,' he said hoarsely. 'But no, I see it is fragrant Lydia.'

She curtsied before him, then took the limp, papery hand on which he still wore his obsidian ring – the sole visible remnant of his authority – and lifted it to her lips. 'Your Majesty, I am your humble servant.'

The crêpey skin around Leopold's eyes crinkled. 'A woman such as you is nobody's servant.'

She nodded gracefully, letting go of his hand and moving aside to allow Nikolai access.

'It is Nikolai, Prince Leopold,' he said, bowing low before him.

'Yes, yes,' Leopold answered. 'Do you think I cannot recognise my own nephew after all this time?'

Nikolai kissed his uncle's ring, then drew himself up to his full height. 'You have returned to us, after so many weeks in the wilderness, as sharp as my sabre.'

Leopold nodded, patting the side of the bed. 'Come, Lydia, take a seat here beside me.' The old Prince's eyes – a watered-down echo of Henning's – met hers.

Lydia settled herself on the edge of the bed. The Prince reached out his hand again and she held it gently.

He gave her hand a faint squeeze. The father's actions were a pale imitation of his son's. Lydia thought of Henning and tried to push the thought away.

As if sensing her discomfort, Nikolai piped up. 'Uncle, I gather from Magda you were asking for Henning and Ven.'

'Oh, yes. Where are they? I want to talk to them.'

'I'm afraid that's not possible,' Nikolai began. 'They rode out from the palace early this morning—'

'What kind of business has taken both my sons away from the palace?' Leopold asked. His voice was clearer now, more authoritative.

'Here, let me make you more comfortable,' Lydia said. Letting go of his hand, she reached forward to rearrange his pillows.

'What business?' Leopold repeated. 'How long are they gone for?'

'A day or two,' Lydia answered. It scarcely mattered that in two days' time – assuming he was still alive – he would discover this was a lie.

'Prince Leopold.' As Nikolai spoke, Lydia watched him walk towards the bed. 'Do you know how ill you have been? How close we feared you might be to ... the end?'

The Prince looked vacant for a moment, then shook his head.

'You have been very sick, dearest uncle,' Nikolai said. 'For several months, you have been confined to this chamber.'

Leopold's eyes clamped shut for a moment. Lydia glanced nervously toward Nikolai.

'In all these months, Prince Leopold, your sons have been running the Princedom most ably on your behalf,' Nikolai pressed on. 'When they return, they will be delighted to see you making these first steps towards recovery. But they will worry that any unwanted pressure, any stress, might—'

'What is it that you want, Nikolai?' Leopold asked.

'What I want, what we *all* want, is for you to make a full recovery and to live out the rest of your days in the bosom of your family and the heart of the Princedom. We want those days, which I hope will be numerous, to be light and unburdened with the business of running Paddenburg.'

Leopold gave a dry little laugh.

'And so,' Nikolai continued, 'if you would just sign your name on this document we have prepared, you will officially pass on the duty of rule – jointly – to your two sons. And, after all these years of care, you will be free to let go of the reins you have held for so long.' He set the decree down on the bedclothes, unfurled the parchment and slipped the pen into the Prince's hand.

Leopold's eyes turned towards his water glass, and Lydia brought it to his lips. He took a draught, then nodded and wiped away the excess with his liver-spotted hand. 'My days will be free, you say?' he resumed, clear as a bell.

Nikolai smiled. 'You can do just as you please, Uncle Leopold, safe in the knowledge that your heavy labour here is done and that your two sons, and those they command, will continue your glorious legacy.'

Anxiety coursed through Lydia's body, and she held her breath as Leopold nodded, then lifted his hand. 'Yes, yes, I see the shape of all this.'

The pen remained in his hand. He made no move to remove the cap. Instead, he looked past his visitors towards the window.

Nikolai reached across the bed. 'Well, then,' he said, removing the cap from the pen. 'Shall I find something to prop this document upon so that it's easier for you to sign your name?'

'No, Nikolai. It is my express wish that you go *now* . . . and leave me with Lydia.'

Nikolai frowned. Lydia held her nerve. Somehow, deep in her core, she had always known that she would be the one to take control of this.

'Please do as the Prince requests,' she said to Nikolai, surprised at how casual the words sounded.

Shrugging, Nikolai strode out of the room. Leopold waited until the door closed before addressing Lydia.

'I see what is happening here,' he said. He smiled, gazing intently upon her. 'I see how easily frustrated my nephew grows with me. I see how my sons have worked upon him to do their bidding.'

'No—'

'Please!' Leopold said. 'My sons have decided it is time to take the reins from me,' he said. 'I knew, of course, this time would come. They will have me sign over the right to rule to them, or, if I refuse, they will find another way to take power from me.' He gripped Lydia's hand. 'They will do whatever they feel is necessary.'

'No,' she said again.

'Yes,' he shot back. 'I know this because they are *my* sons. Their characters were forged in the fire of my own ambition. And this is exactly what I would do in their place.'

At last, he fell silent. Lydia knew how important her next words might prove.

'It sounds like you do indeed have a clear understanding of things,' she began, 'and, to a degree, an acceptance.' She paused, taking it step by gentle step. 'In which case, would it

100

not be better all around if you did sign the decree?' The words fell from her lips as gently as cherry blossoms stirred by the spring breeze.

Prince Leopold shook his head. 'No,' he said. 'No. I will not sign any decrees today.' He closed his eyes. 'All this talking has tired me,' Leopold announced. 'I think I shall have a sleep.'

She nodded and began to rise but, as she did so, he gripped her hand with the exact same pressure Henning had used. It sent a shock wave through her entire body.

'Before I submit to slumber, Lydia, I would like you to tell me a story.'

'Of course,' she said, smiling. 'What kind of a story would you like?'

'That's easy,' Prince Leopold said. 'I'd like to know the truth, Lydia Wilde.' His eyes snapped open. 'I'd like to know what your real motives are for being here in Paddenburg.'

THIRTEEN

PALACE OF ARCHENFIELD

'He's not here,' the servant told Asta, closing the door in her face.

The last person Asta had wanted to talk to – now or ever – was Axel, but the Captain of the Guard was in charge of the Twelve, and it had made sense to her to find out what he needed from her in her new position as Poet. Still, to be turned away from his office was more a relief than a disappointment. She set off once more along the palace corridor, feeling a weight lifting from her shoulders.

Asta passed through an unfamiliar set of doors opening on to a back stairwell. Looking around, she realised that she hadn't a clue where she was. She decided to go down. At least, that way, she'd be back on ground level and surely able to find her way from there.

But the stairs deposited her at the beginnings of another unfamiliar corridor. Then, with relief, she saw Jonas Drummond, the Woodsman, come out from a side turning in front of her and march on ahead, oblivious to her presence.

She was about to call out to him – he clearly knew where he was going and could point her towards an exit – but, just as she was about to call out, Jonas glanced cautiously over his shoulder, looking very much like someone who was checking to ensure that he wasn't being followed.

Asta remained hidden from him in the dimly lit stairwell. Judging by his brisk strides, wherever he *was* going, he was in quite a hurry ... Asta's curiosity got the better of her. Whatever was the Woodsman up to?

Still careful to keep distance between herself and Jonas, she followed him around a corner – this one darker than the previous, with a galleried area to one side. She saw Jonas reach the door at the end of the corridor and knock on it. Asta ducked into the shadows afforded by the gallery as the heavy door opened and Jonas slipped inside. Hearing voices echoing from within, Asta waited for the door to close. But although it swung back again, it did not close completely. Still, it seemed safe to approach, treading carefully so as not to make a sound, and keeping close to the covered gallery.

As Asta reached the end of the corridor, she saw a sliver of candlelight spilling from the unclosed gap in the door like a dagger and heard voices, including that of Axel Blaxland.

What she heard rooted Asta to the spot.

'Well, this is all very cloak and dagger,' Jonas observed, as he arrived at the table. 'Why are we meeting here and not in one of your *two* offices?'

'The doors are considerably thicker here,' Axel said. 'There's less chance of any unwanted interruptions.' He kicked a chair out from under the table. 'Take the weight off, Jonas. Morgan isn't drinking, but I'm sure you will.'

The Woodsman nodded. Jonas sat down and, noticing the hefty volume in the centre of the table, drew it towards him. 'The Book of Law. Have you actually read this?'

Axel nodded. 'From cover to cover. It's illuminating.' He smiled.

'So are we waiting for anyone else?' Jonas enquired, reaching for his glass.

'Nobody else.' Axel shook his head. 'Just the four of us.' His keen eyes moved around the table from Jonas to Morgan, and then to Elliot Nash. 'I extended this invitation to only my three most trusted allies.' He rested one hand on the ancient Book of Law, imagining himself drawing power from its pages. 'I summoned each of you here today to tell you that I have come to an important decision. I intend to put forward a vote of no confidence in Prince Jared.'

Morgan looked shocked but nodded. Elliot took another sip of his drink.

'When?' Jonas enquired.

'That is yet to be determined,' Axel replied. 'Though my feeling is the sooner the better.' He tapped the book. 'I just need' – he broke off and smiled – '*we* need to ensure that I will get a majority before I set the wheels in motion.'

Jonas nodded. 'So you don't have to table this vote – put it on some agenda to inform the Twelve that it's up for discussion?'

'No,' Axel said, smiling beatifically. 'That's the beauty of it. I can just bring it up whenever I care to and the vote happens right then and there.'

Morgan raised his hand to speak. Axel gave him a nod. 'We are currently missing two members of the Twelve,' Morgan said.

'Correct.' Axel nodded. 'And I would, on balance, prefer to await Kai and Hal's return.'

'Rather than depend on the votes of their deputies?' Jonas asked.

'Deputies do not have voting rights,' Axel told him. 'So either we delay the vote until Kai and Hal get back – with Prince Jared, of course – or we proceed ahead of that.' He sipped his drink. 'The reason I asked you to come here now is to assess the current loyalties and thereby likely voting of the Twelve. Put in its simplest terms, we need seven votes to pull the throne out from beneath Jared's sorry ... behind.'

'Well,' Jonas said, clearly amused, 'you are assured of one vote, at least. Your own.'

'I'm a little more optimistic than that,' Axel said. 'If I wasn't confident I had at least three votes in the bag, I would not have called you and Morgan here today.'

Jonas grinned. Morgan's expression was tougher to read.

'Elliot has made a list,' Axel said, turning to his deputy. 'Elliot rather enjoys making lists, don't you?'

Rolling his eyes, Elliot took up his ledger and addressed the members of the Twelve. 'The first thing you need to know is that Prince Jared has no voting rights, whether he is in court or not when the vote takes place.' He tapped his pen on the paper. 'And though Axel currently occupies two positions at the Prince's Table, he gets only one vote. That was established when he became Edling.'

'So, assuming we both vote for Axel,' Jonas said, nodding at Morgan, 'that's three votes in the bag.'

Axel smiled, reaching for his glass. 'So far, so good.'

'Presumably,' Jonas continued, 'if Hal and Kai are back from their journey with the Prince, those are your next two votes.'

Axel took a hit of aquavit. 'Well, Hal's a certainty,' he agreed.

'Are you sure?' Morgan said. 'The Bodyguard seems very

loyal to Prince Jared, just as he did to Prince Anders.'

Axel smiled, running a finger around the rim of his glass. 'Yes, he does *seem* that way, Morgan, doesn't he? As it turns out, Hal is rather a good actor. Could have had a career with a band of travelling players if he hadn't had such a liking for using his dagger in various interesting ways.'

Morgan grinned. Axel could see the mere mention of weaponry had cheered him up.

'Just between ourselves,' Axel continued, 'although it was Prince Jared who selected Hal to accompany him on his quest, I gave Hal a little briefing of my own before he departed.' That got their attention. 'I told him to keep the Prince safe, of course, but to keep him beyond the borders and out of my hair for as long as possible.' He smiled. 'Which should give us time to build our case. By my reckoning, the closer we come to the attack from Paddenburg, the more votes will land on our side of the table.'

'What about Kai?' Morgan asked. 'How do you anticipate he will vote?'

'Good question, Morgan,' Axel said, seizing the opportunity to flatter the Executioner. He wasn't entirely confident he had his vote yet. 'We can't take Kai's vote for granted. He's an independent thinker and I fear he's taken on a somewhat paternal role with Prince Jared. And the fact that Kai and Jared are out on the road together is, I fear, only going to make their bond stronger.'

'Unless,' Jonas interjected, 'Prince Jared does something to put the wind up him.'

'True,' Axel conceded. 'But it's hard to think what that would be. Kai's a hard one to ruffle.'

'I'm not so sure,' Jonas insisted.

'If you have something to say, spit it out.'

Jonas shook his head. 'Nothing conclusive. Just a feeling.'

'All right,' Axel said, growing bored. 'Elliot, put a question mark by Kai's name. Who's next on your list?'

'The Groom,' Elliot said.

Axel nodded. 'Lucas Curzon – the prettiest lad in all of Archenfield. Well, what do you think, Morgan? Which way will the ladies' favourite vote?'

Morgan frowned. 'That's a tough one to call. Lucas has an innate sense of loyalty and honour.'

Innate? Axel stilled his rising eyebrow with an effort. The Executioner's vocabulary grew more varied with every encounter – testament to the latest book he had devoured.

'I don't think the idea of betraying Prince Jared will sit comfortably with him,' Morgan finished.

'This isn't about betraying Prince Jared,' Jonas said. 'It's about making a choice about who is the strongest leader for Archenfield.' He glanced at Axel, who nodded with the grateful look he knew Jonas was expecting.

'I understand that,' Morgan said. 'I'm saying how Lucas might see this.'

'*Very* useful,' Axel said. 'Elliot, make a note that we may need to exert some gentle persuasion on Lucas.'

'Sounds like someone has some ammunition,' Jonas said with a grin.

'Let's just say that Lucas's halo isn't quite as bright as it might seem.'

Jonas raised an eyebrow, but Axel remained tight-lipped. He saw Jonas glance across to Morgan, clearly wondering if *he* knew to what Axel was alluding. To Axel's great pleasure, Morgan shook his head.

'I shall deal with Lucas,' Axel assured them. 'Let's move on.'

'The Priest,' announced Elliot.

'Father Simeon,' Axel said, rubbing his hands together.

'Jonas, you're the most frequent visitor to his chapel. Which way do *you* think Father Simeon will vote?'

Jonas considered for a moment. 'It's actually very simple with Father Simeon.'

'Good! We like simple.'

'Father Simeon feels fundamentally disconnected from power and purpose at the moment. He has for some time. The one to secure his vote will be the one who successfully restores his sense of purpose.'

'Excellent,' Axel said. 'We'll have a think about how best to reawaken Simeon's purpose so that we can claim his vote. Who's next?'

'The Cook,' Elliot answered, with a knowing grin.

Axel rolled his eyes. 'There's no way Vera would vote for me over Jared. She still hasn't forgiven me for the Michael Reeves business.'

Jonas smiled. 'That's unusually defeatist of you,' he said. 'I'm sure between us we could think of a way to bring Vera around.'

Axel shook his head. 'Actually, I'm not being a defeatist, I'm being a realist. Vera is as dangerous as her food. Frankly, if she even learned about this vote, there's no telling what she might do.' He turned to Elliot. 'We'll leave her alone, unless we're in absolute need of her vote. Hopefully, it won't come to that.'

Elliot nodded and began scribbling away. When he had finished, he tapped his sheet of parchment. 'The Beekeeper.'

Axel frowned. 'Emelie Sharp. Sharp by name, sharp by nature ... Well, she's anyone's guess, isn't she?'

'I'm sure you could use your powers of persuasion on Emelie, Axel,' Jonas said. 'You used to be quite cosy, didn't you? Remind me – my memory's a little hazy ... why did it end?'

Axel reached for his drink. 'Let's not go there,' he said. 'Another question mark for her, Elliot. Who's next?'

'The Falconer,' Elliot announced.

Axel groaned. 'We really left the fun ones to the end, didn't we?'

'What's your take on Nova?' Jonas enquired.

Axel shrugged. 'Well, she's clearly got a base loyalty to the Wynyards.'

'I think that's a bit of a leap,' Jonas said. 'Just because she was having an affair with Anders, I don't think you can interpret that as unswerving loyalty to the entire clan.'

'I'm sorry to bring this up,' Morgan interrupted, 'but when Prince Jared made Axel his Edling, didn't Nova say something about Prince Anders having good reasons *not* to offer Axel the position?'

'Yes,' Axel confirmed. 'Well remembered! And now she's running around with the Physician and his niece. You might as well put her down as a Jared vote, Elliot.'

'Put her down as a question mark,' Jonas countered. 'Nova and I are on pretty good terms. I might just have a little talk with her.'

'Might you just?' Axel wondered how this budding relationship between the Woodsman and the Falconer had slipped his notice.

'Anything for the good of the party,' Jonas said, helping himself to a fresh slug of aquavit.

'Just two names remain on the list,' Elliot said. 'The Physician and his niece – now the Poet.'

Axel nodded. 'Well, the girl's a definite vote for Jared. Those two are as thick as thieves. I'm only surprised that he didn't choose her for his travelling companion.'

Elliot made a note.

'But Elias,' Axel resumed. 'Now, he's another matter

entirely. For one thing, I sense he's concerned about his little prodigy being promoted to the Prince's Table. Added to which, he owes me a favour.'

'Owes you?' Morgan enquired.

'I've covered his back a few times – most recently during the investigation into Anders's assassination.'

'So he's a definite vote for you?' Elliot enquired, his pen hovering over his precious list.

Axel shook his head. 'Let's not get ahead of ourselves. He's surrounded by Jared fans. Put him down as a question mark and I'll visit him to see how the land lies.'

'That's everyone,' Elliot announced. 'Shall I tell you exactly how things stand?'

Axel nodded, though he was confident he already had it clear in his head.

'To remind you all,' Elliot said, 'Axel needs seven votes to topple Prince Jared and. . .'

'To take the throne,' Jonas said.

The Woodsman's words seemed to echo around the chamber. All eyes turned to him.

'Well,' Jonas said, aware of his fellows' scrutiny. 'That's what this is ultimately about, isn't it? Removing Prince Jared from power is only the first step.' His eyes met Axel's. 'He made you his Edling so power would naturally move to you.'

Axel said nothing but smiled softly.

Jonas shook his head. 'Prince Jared is certainly going to regret not making Prince Edvin his Edling.'

'What I was going to say,' Elliot resumed, shooting a dark look at Jonas, 'was that Axel needs seven votes *and*, by my reckoning, he currently has four definites – his own, you two and Hal—'

'Assuming Hal returns before the vote,' Axel cut in.

'Four votes is not enough,' Jonas said.

Elliot nodded. 'On a positive note, Axel, you have only two definite votes against you – Asta and Vera. The other six are all question marks.'

'Fine,' Jonas said. 'So we need just three of those, and the job is done.'

'All right then.' Axel slammed down his drink. 'It's time to go to work!'

Asta's head felt as if it might explode. The depths of their treachery!

As the door opened, she flung herself into the gallery that ran along the length of the corridor. She felt her body make contact not with the hard wall as she had expected but with something softer. Another body. Confused and fearful, she was about to cry out but a hand reached over her mouth and pressed hard against her lips, silencing her.

She remained frozen in the clutches of her captor as Jonas and Elliot passed by on their way back along the corridor. Then she heard the door close – all the way this time.

At last, the hand pressed to her mouth grew limp, then fell away. Asta was released and turned slowly – heart in her mouth – to see who was there with her. She was dumb-founded to see Lady Koel move out of the shadowy recess, holding a finger to her lips.

Lady Koel drew down her finger. 'You have no need to fear me,' she whispered.

Asta shook her head, unable to speak.

'You heard every word,' Lady Koel continued. 'As did I. We must talk about this, as friends.'

'Friends?' Asta managed to rasp.

Lady Koel nodded. 'Can you meet me in the morning near the Burning Place at the edge of the fjord?'

Dumbstruck, Asta nodded. But even so, her mind raced –

111

could she really trust Axel's sister, or was she throwing herself into the path of yet more danger?

Lady Koel smiled at her reassuringly. 'I'll see you there, at the tolling of the treacherous Woodsman's Bell. Now, off you go. I'll follow at a discreet distance. I think I'm a little better cut out for subterfuge than you are.'

FOURTEEN

THE PALACE AT THE FOUR WINDS, WOODLARK

Prince Jared stared queasily at the intricate geometric patterns of the tiles beneath his feet. The patterns were dazzling, both in symmetry and colour. And they could not have been more different from the simple black and white floor tiles in the palace of Archenfield – it seemed almost a crime to walk upon these in rough boots rather than soft slippers. A clock was ticking nearby. The alien sound was mesmerising to him, and he drew his eyes back to the clock face. It divided up time into the smallest of parcels, allowing the court of Woodlark to mark time's passing much more closely than did the bells of Archenfield.

Such signs hinted at Woodlark being a far more civilised land than Archenfield, but the rough treatment the Prince and his party had received on their route to the palace had revealed the stark truth of the matter.

Kai and Hal still looked as if they were in a state of shock. Kai stared across the vast hall, his face drained of colour, while Hal picked at a dark stain on his sleeve. As members of the Twelve, both were afforded an unquestioned level of respect by the other members of the court and those who dwelled in the settlements beyond. These were men unaccustomed to being jeered at or spat on in the street. Jared knew how difficult it had been for both men to remain stoic in the face of such blatant disrespect. It was testament to the value they all placed on Prince Jared's meeting with Queen Francesca that they had not lashed out.

His thoughts were cut off by the low groan of the hinges of the heavy wooden door at the end of the corridor, followed by the sound of precise, clicking footsteps. As Princess Ines, Woodlark's Captain of the Guard, strode towards him, Jared rose from his seat to greet her. Around him, his travelling companions did the same.

Jared was struck by the beauty of Queen Francesca's eldest daughter, despite her only fleeting smile at him as they exchanged their formal greetings. She was stunning – her features the shocking yet perfect meld of her parents'. She had the same lustrous caramel skin and deep olive eyes as Queen Francesca, combined with the sharp cheekbones and white-blonde hair of Prince Willem. Silva, of course, had sported the very same flaxen locks, but that was where the resemblance between the two sisters began and ended. Where Silva had always seemed fundamentally fragile, Ines was possessed of an innate vigour: her muscular yet lithe limbs spoke of days on horseback, hunting and combat training. As if to drive home the impression, Ines was not dressed in one of the pale, floating dresses that had so defined her sister but, instead, in high leather trousers that were bound at the waist with a metal belt cinched beneath an emerald buckle. A simple cambric shirt completed her ensemble.

'I must confess,' she said, now that the formalities were

over, 'you are the last person I expected to see in the Palace of the Four Winds.'

'I understand.' Jared nodded. 'But, as I would welcome the chance to explain to you and Queen Francesca, events have taken an unprecedented turn since we last met.'

Princess Ines nodded thoughtfully. 'I gather that the people of Woodlark failed to extend the welcome you were hoping for.'

Jared frowned to think of it. From the moment they had crossed the border, the riders had been met with hostile glares – as far as anyone in Woodlark was concerned, Archenfield had failed in its promise to protect Princess Silva as one of its own. News of the travellers' presence had spread like a forest fire and by the time they had ridden into the town that wrapped around the Palace of the Four Winds, a mob had been lining the streets. It took one lone voice to shout 'Go home' for the crowd to surge forward. Hal and Bram had instinctively positioned themselves either side of Jared so that he and his horse were protected. Kai stood close at hand. All three of his companions had an array of combat techniques to call upon, as required. Still, Jared had tasted the danger of the situation. His party was greatly outnumbered. It would not have taken much for the angry mob to surge forward and pull them from their horses. But, instead, they had merely shouted and spat and thrown scraps of rotten fruit and vegetables at their unwelcome visitors. It had been a far cry indeed from the cheers Jared had receivod from his own people as he was crowned Prince of All Archenfield.

He shuddered now to think how much worse things might have been had the people of Woodlark known the complete truth about Silva's death.

'To my surprise, my mother *has* agreed to see you,' Ines's voice interrupted his dark reverie. 'Please follow me.'

Jared started after her, aware of the others close on his

heels. The noise prompted Princess Ines to stop. 'I'm sorry if I was unclear. Queen Francesca and I will see *you*, Prince Jared, but this invitation does not extend to the remainder of your retinue.'

'Of course.' Prince Jared nodded.

Bram hesitated, looking to Hal for guidance. Kai shot Jared a warning look, which his reciprocal stare silenced. But Hal dared to address Ines directly: 'Your Highness, forgive my impertinence, but Prince Jared does not take a step without his Bodyguard at his side.'

His words, or perhaps merely his audaciousness, seemed to amuse her. She glanced over Jared's shoulder to meet Hal's steady gaze. 'Fair enough, Bodyguard. *You* may follow us inside. But only you.'

As they approached an intricately carved door, Jared's heart began racing. The last time he had met the Queen had been on the soil of Archenfield and, accordingly, he'd been flanked by Queen Elin and Cousin Axel, among many others. Now he was at the heart of her domain – which seemed so much more sophisticated than his own – and he was, in spite of Hal's footsteps close behind, essentially on his own. He could feel his heart beating wildly under his ribs as Ines pushed open the door and he caught a glimpse of Queen Francesca, sitting in wait for him.

As Jared briefly paused, attempting to calm himself, he became aware of the pervasive scent of cinnamon and orange blossom emanating from vast incense bowls placed at intervals around the large state room. The scent conjured up a warmth at odds with his reception.

'Your Serene Highness.' Prince Jared bowed low before Queen Francesca.

She nodded her veiled head but did not rise from her seat. This, of course, was her prerogative, but he knew that his

116

mother would have taken umbrage at the slight. Perhaps it was a good thing that she had not accompanied him.

'Please, sit down, Prince Jared.' Queen Francesca's voice was as bleak and formal as the mourning garb she wore. Her face – what Jared could make out of it beneath the veil – looked tired and pinched. 'What prompts you to invade our period of mourning?'

'I am deeply sorry to have done so,' Jared told her. 'It is the last thing I would have wanted, but events have forced my hand.'

The Queen smiled bitterly. 'Well, seeing as you are here, you had better come to the point then.'

Ignoring the sourness of her tone, Jared reached into his breast pocket and produced the furled missive from Paddenburg. 'This ultimatum was delivered to my court on the eve of my coronation,' he said.

'Of course,' Queen Francesca said. 'Since we last saw you, you have been formally crowned Prince of All Archenfield. I suppose we ought to offer you congratulations.' She motioned for him to approach more closely and took the note from him, lifting her veil to read it.

'The Princes of Paddenburg threaten to invade your lands in seven days,' Francesca said when she had finished reading, placing the parchment down, her veil dropping back into place.

'The note was received two days ago.' Jared paused. 'So the clock is now ticking fast.'

'What do you, or any of the court of Archenfield, know about clocks?' Francesca snapped. 'You still measure your days in archaic bells.'

Jared bit his lip.

'Why have you come to see us?' Ines interrupted, her voice smooth and kinder than her mother's.

She'd been standing in the shadows. Jared had the sense that she might be willing to support him. From what Axel had said, Ines was a pragmatic politician. Surely this pragmatism would inform her that an invasion of Archenfield by Paddenburg would not be good news for its closest neighbour and former ally? For the first time, he felt faint stirrings of hope.

'He has come to ask us to renew our alliance,' Francesca announced, as Ines took a seat beside her. 'The same alliance I burned down to my fingertips in the tarnished palace of Archenfield.' Jared swallowed, the memories of those moments – when Francesca had indeed burned the scroll of parchment the alliance had been written on in front of a shocked court in Archenfield – still etched on his mind.

He took a breath, then plunged in. 'I have come to ask you to consider a *new* alliance with us – with *me*, as the new ruler of Archenfield.'

Francesca did not respond, but Princess Ines nodded. 'I am grateful for your directness,' she said. 'It is a quality I appreciate in our allies and one that was not as evident as I might have wished in your brother's time.'

Jared was taken aback. Was she actually stating a preference for his way of doing things over his brother's? He could not resist pressing home this advantage. 'Although we have just five days in hand, you and I both know that the might of our united armies would conclusively see off the threat from Paddenburg. This would help Archenfield in the short term, but it would also serve to nip in the bud any aggression from Paddenburg towards Woodlark, which we might expect to follow.'

Ines considered his words. 'To your first point – yes, working together, our armies would almost certainly defeat Paddenburg. The intelligence from our spies in Paddenburg backs that up.' Her eyes turned colder. 'And if you are equally well briefed, why is it that this attack from Paddenburg has taken you and your court by surprise?'

Jared frowned. He knew they were coming to the more difficult matter now. It was time to deviate from any script.

'The Paddenburg Ultimatum does not mark the beginning of a new attack,' he told them. 'It was Paddenburg who sought and enacted the assassination of my brother. The ultimatum marks the escalation of their plot.'

Queen Francesca glanced up. 'We know all this. The renegade steward poisoned Prince Anders. Must we return to that sorry tale?'

Jared felt cold fear flush through him, but knew he had to tamp it down. 'I'm afraid we must revisit this,' he said. 'You see ... the steward was not, as we initially thought, the assassin. He was caught in a far more complex web and, while we drew false comfort that we had apprehended the culprit, the real assassin remained at large and was therefore able to strike again.'

He could see the effect this information had. He exchanged a discreet look with Hal, then pushed on. 'Queen Francesca, Princess Ines, one of the reasons I have come today is to correct a lie you were told when you came to Archenfield.'

The air seemed to suddenly chill. 'Go on,' Francesca said.

Jared felt the pricking of tears behind his eyes. 'Silva did not take her own life out of grief for Anders.' He swallowed. 'She was the next victim of the true assassin.' He watched their faces, waiting for the information to sink in. 'Silva was murdered on our soil, as part of the same plot from Paddenburg.'

The two women turned towards one another. Even before Francesca spoke, Jared had a terrible sense of foreboding.

'These facts have already been in our possession for several days,' Francesca said, the steel returning to her voice. 'I do not intend to tell you how, so spare me the impertinence of asking.' She raised her hands and swept back her veil. Now he saw the undiminished strength within her: the grey shadows he had taken for grief had vanished; her skin was almost as smooth as that of her daughter.

'I'll grant you this, Prince Jared – you alone of your clan have some strength of character to come and confess to this execrable lie.' Her hard eyes bored into his.

'I'm so sorry,' he said. 'I never wanted to lie to you.'

'I suspect that's the truth,' Francesca acknowledged. 'I'm sure your advisors left you little choice in the matter. That's what comes of bringing someone so young, inexperienced and vulnerable to the throne.

'You are a young man of some quality,' she added in a softer voice. 'It has taken great courage and humility to come here today.'

Princess Ines nodded, then smiled at Jared. This time he sensed genuine warmth emanating from her.

'You journeyed here to ask us a question.' Francesca rose to her feet. 'As you say, the combined might of our armies would conclusively see off the threat from the lunatics of Paddenburg.'

Jared's heart lifted. He was too anxious to breathe.

'Do you really think,' Francesca continued, 'that, after all of Archenfield's heinous crimes, there could ever again be an alliance between your nation and mine?'

Jared held his nerve.

'I hope you can see that Archenfield is being ruled in a new way now,' he said, talking quickly. 'Can you not find it in your heart to forgive our past crimes? Can you not find it in yourselves to trust that I will never disrespect you, your family or your nation again?'

'There is goodness in you, Prince Jared, I see this.' Francesca stood up, slowly. 'But it is not enough to make amends for all that has come before. And, lest you forget, you were complicit in that terrible lie. It happened while you were Prince. Though you may regret that, still you must take responsibility for it.'

There was finality in Queen Francesca's words. Princess Ines stood up, shoulder to shoulder with her mother. She too seemed to sense that this meeting had come to an end. But now Francesca lifted her hand. Turning her olive eyes to Jared, she spoke again.

'We have his name now,' the Queen said. 'We know that our daughter was murdered by a man called Logan Wilde.' Her eyes met Jared's. 'I would agree to a new alliance with you on one condition – that you bring Wilde here to the court of Woodlark.' She broke off. When she resumed, her voice was low and raw. 'I will tear him limb from limb with my own hands.'

Jared was careful to make sure that his voice betrayed no emotion. 'Forgive me, but you read the ultimatum,' he said. 'If we deliver Logan Wilde to you, all kinds of hell will rain down upon Archenfield. That is explicit in the Paddenburg Ultimatum.'

Queen Francesca nodded. 'The Princes of Paddenburg sound impressive, don't they? But, in uniting our two armies, that's a risk I'd be prepared to take. The more pressing question is – are you?'

Jared's heart was racing again. Of course, Prince Henning and Prince Ven would do anything to protect Logan Wilde, but against the combined armies of Archenfield and Woodlark—? Even 'anything' might be defeated.

It was worth a risk, wasn't it?

Jared extended his trembling hand to Francesca. 'On behalf

of my family and my Princedom, I extend my thanks and delight at a new alliance between our two lands.'

Queen Francesca gripped his hand firmly. 'We shall have the decree drawn up at once. I am sure you will be anxious to return to Archenfield with the good news.'

Jared retrieved the parchment from the table. It was strange, he thought, how the Paddenburg Ultimatum felt less powerful now. Merely a scrap of paper. 'Thank you,' he said. 'You will not regret this.'

Francesca nodded regally, then drew down her veil again. She folded her hands across her lap. Their interview was at an end.

As he turned to follow Ines, Hal moved out of the shadows to his side. His mouth was set in a thin line.

Francesca called after them. 'Just bring me Logan Wilde. That's all I ask.'

The Island of the Dead was as beautiful and tragic a sight as Jared had anticipated. It lay beyond a calm stretch of water, clouds breaking over its hilltops. Beneath those, Jared could just make out pillows of colour – the red banks of roses and drifts of snow-white lilies. Even now, a rowing boat made its way over to the island; a young woman sat in the back, flowers clutched to her chest, ready to pay homage to Silva.

Hal wandered over to join him. 'May I talk with you, Prince Jared?' he asked.

'Yes, of course,' Jared said, grateful for his company.

'Is it really your intention that we return to Archenfield today?' Hal enquired.

Jared nodded. 'Just as soon as Princess Ines delivers the decree.' He smiled. 'You have to admit, Hal, this alliance is a real coup – and with so many days in hand!'

'What if we *don't* have this alliance?' Hal asked.

Jared's eyes narrowed. 'What do you mean?'

'Are you sure that we *can* hand over Logan Wilde to Francesca and her court?'

Jared frowned. 'I am Prince of All Archenfield, Hal. If I decide that we hand him over, then we hand him over.'

Hal's brow furrowed. 'I don't mean to overstep my boundaries, but have you fully thought this through? How would the people of Archenfield react if they found out what Wilde had done and then saw that you'd failed to claim the Blood Price yourself from the assassin of their Prince?' Hal paused. 'Right now, the good people of our Princedom mistakenly believe that your brother was killed by Michael Reeves and that Silva took her own life. If you deliver Logan Wilde to Woodlark, the first risk is that you inflame the enemy. But, just as importantly, the common people would soon know that Prince Anders was not murdered by a renegade steward but by his closest advisor on the Twelve.'

'They need never find out,' Jared rasped.

Hal shook his head. 'I'm sorry to say this but that's a naïve thought. You can't expect to extradite a member of the Twelve without questions being asked.'

Jared felt a spiral of panic coiling through him. He knew there was truth in Hal's words. And how could he even know he *would* be in a position to hand over Wilde? Paddenburg had already successfully infiltrated the court of Archenfield – was it far-fetched to believe that they could spring Logan Wilde at any moment? How many other spies might they already have within the palace walls?

Jared turned to face Hal. 'I feel like you have a suggestion for me,' he said.

Hal nodded. 'Under the terms of the Paddenburg Ultimatum, we still have five days in hand. I suggest we ride on and explore the possibilities of further alliances with Rednow,

Baltiska and Larsson.' His voice was steady, his eyes open and clear. 'That was always the plan, wasn't it – an alliance of the five river territories?'

'Yes,' Jared confirmed, feeling steadied by Hal's words. 'That was the plan.'

'If Princess Ines allows us to ride through her lands, we can reach the border with Rednow as early as tomorrow morning,' Hal told him. 'From there, it's a fair ride to Prince Rohan's palace but, if we push the horses hard, we could get there by the end of the day.'

Jared nodded. 'You're right. We have our plan. I'll go now and inform Princess Ines that I intend to develop further strategic alliances, which will benefit Woodlark as well as Archenfield. There's no harm in her knowing the level of my ambition.'

'No harm indeed, Your Majesty.' Hal's eyes gleamed brightly at his master.

FOUR DAYS UNTIL
INVASION . . .

FIFTEEN

THE FJORD, ARCHENFIELD

Asta stood alone at the edge of the fjord, listening to the distant chimes of the Woodsman's Bell and, closer, the gentle lapping of the water. She had not slept well – thoughts of what she had overheard the day before and anticipation of her imminent meeting with Lady Koel turning over and over in her head. This time, she might really have gotten herself into deep water. What if Lady Koel was not coming to meet her at all, but had dispatched members of Axel's guard to 'deal' with Asta? She hadn't had any previous dealings with Lady Koel to know whether she could trust her or not. Of course, she had wanted to ask Uncle Elias for his thoughts and share with him the horror of what Axel Blaxland was planning, but that was the very worst of it – Elias seemed barely able to remain in the same room as her at the moment, let alone engage in such a necessarily difficult and loaded conversation. Asta fingered the small, sharpened kitchen knife she had stowed in her pocket – just in case – hoping with every fibre of her body she would not be called upon to use it.

'Good morning!'

Carefully letting go of the knife, Asta turned to find Lady Koel walking toward her. She was wearing elegant riding boots, silver-coloured jodhpurs and a matching silver cape, which billowed around her as she made her way over the stone-strewn path. So she *had* come, just as she had promised, and it appeared she was unaccompanied by guards or, indeed, any living creature besides her elegant grey horse, which she had tethered at the edge of the forest.

Lady Koel smiled at Asta as she drew closer.

Her companion, who, Asta reminded herself, was only a year older than herself, looked effortlessly beautiful. Another lady of court might have tamed her hair with hundreds of pins for the morning ride but, for the most part, Koel allowed her gorgeous chestnut locks to hang free, with just two simple plaits circling around the top of her head, like a pretty crown. And, as her long hair danced with the cool breeze of the fjord, Asta found herself envying Lady Koel her natural grace and her luxuriant dark locks.

'There's no more picturesque place to watch the coming of the new morning to Archenfield,' Lady Koel said, joining Asta at the edge of the fjord and settling her hands on her slender hips. 'The patterns of light on the water's surface are never the same from one moment to the next.' She turned confidingly to Asta. 'I've tried to paint it several times but I never do it justice.' A shrug. 'Perhaps I should just accept that, unlike my aunt, I have no talent for art.'

'It *is* a very special place.' Asta sighed. She remembered the time, not long ago, that she had met Prince Jared there. 'We need to talk,' she said. 'About what happened yesterday.'

Lady Koel nodded, her face composed. 'Yes,' she agreed. 'We do.' She turned her gaze upon Asta and reached out, squeezing Asta's hand. 'But before we go any further, I need to remind you what I told you yesterday.' Her dark eyes were wide. 'I am your friend, Asta. We are on the same side. Axel Blaxland may be my brother but Jared Wynyard is my Prince.' She sighed. 'I wish there was more I could say to make you believe me.'

Asta shook her head. 'I *do* believe you,' she said. 'Frankly, it is far easier to imagine that you would be appalled by your brother's ambitions than driven to support him by means of the loyalty instilled by your blood.'

Lady Koel nodded, gently releasing Asta's hand. 'That's eloquently put, Asta,' she said. 'I see my dear cousin's good judgement in making you his Poet.'

'Thank you,' Asta said, wanting to move off that subject quickly. 'So, Axel is preparing to launch a vote of no confidence in Prince Jared. What I am still not clear on is what that would mean in practice.'

Her companion grimaced. 'If my brother is successful, then Jared will be deposed as Prince and Axel – as Edling and therefore next in line – will claim the throne.'

'But isn't this treason on Axel's part?'

Lady Koel shook her head. 'I'm afraid there is precedent for this in the Book of Law. This kind of vote has not been incurred for centuries, but it remains perfectly legitimate. It's one of those articles of law that was put in place to protect Archenfield from dictatorial, incompetent or otherwise unfit rulers. It was designed to give the Council of Twelve genuine power to curb the whims of a tyrannous royal family.'

'But Prince Jared is neither dictatorial nor incompetent,' Asta protested. 'And the Wynyards are not tyrannous, are they?'

'Of course not,' Koel agreed. 'And this isn't a case of The Twelve applying a useful restraint to the royals. On the contrary, this is ruthless opportunism. My brother – and, in point of fact, my father too – views the current political crisis as a convenient opening to challenge Prince Jared and transfer power from the Wynyard line to the Blaxlands.'

'*Your* line,' Asta heard herself say. Immediately, she regretted it.

Lady Koel held up her hands. 'I cannot deny that I am a Blaxland. Though at times such as this, I would gladly erase myself from the family tree. What my brother and father are embarking upon here utterly appals me, Asta.'

Asta saw the pain in Lady Koel's eyes. 'We feel exactly the same,' she assured her companion. 'We could discuss his treachery all day and night. Let's focus on the tangibles. How soon do you think he will launch this vote?'

Lady Koel folded her arms. 'I cannot be sure when my brother will pounce but, rest assured, he'll do it as soon as he feels certain of achieving the majority vote.' She shivered. 'He needs time to work on the members of The Twelve. Though Prince Jared seems to have angered certain of your colleagues by crossing the borders to embark on this quest for allies, others remain steadfastly loyal to him.' She smiled. 'You, for instance. I'm fairly sure you would not cast a vote against Prince Jared, whether Axel called the vote today, or in a year's time.'

'I certainly would not,' Asta agreed. 'You're right. Jared, *Prince* Jared, has plenty of support in The Twelve.'

'I think you are right, Asta. I *hope* you are right. But we cannot take anything for granted. Those who do not willingly come over to Axel's side may be persuaded into doing so.'

'Persuaded?'

'My brother does not play by the rules. He has positioned his spies throughout the court. He knows things about all the key players – things that they would not wish widely known. He has been storing away such information for the right moment.' She removed a stray strand of hair from her eyes. 'Information is power, Asta. It gives Axel a very dangerous and powerful currency to deploy.' She shook her head. 'I feel bad you've been placed in this position. You have enough to concern yourself with adjusting to the responsibilities of your new role, without having to deal with my brother and his brazen ambition.'

Asta shook her head. 'I got myself into this. I was eaves-dropping.' She smiled. 'Just like you.'

Lady Koel acknowledged her smile. 'As a matter of interest, how did you happen to be there?'

Asta shrugged. 'It was quite by chance. I'm not well versed in navigating the palace corridors, and I was lost. I saw Jonas Drummond striding along the corridor and something compelled me to follow him.'

'It was fate, then,' Lady Koel decided. 'Fate and your good instincts.'

Asta couldn't help but smile. 'How about you? What brought you there?'

'Oh, I've pretty much made a career of spying on my brother,' Lady Koel said. 'I like to keep tabs on his schemes and secrets, though I have never discovered anything quite so incendiary before.'

Asta looked at her. 'You know, your brother is not the only one in court with powers of persuasion.'

'What on earth are you thinking?' Lady Koel asked.

'You and I are not the kind of people to sit back and let events buffet us this way and that, like driftwood.' Asta saw the faint stirrings of a smile on Lady Koel's lips. 'Well, we're not, are we?'

'No,' Lady Koel agreed. 'We are not those kinds of people.'

'If your brother is going to attempt to influence the members of The Twelve, then what is stopping us from doing exactly the same? We can fight Prince Jared's corner for him until he returns and is able to defend himself.'

Koel's dark brown eyes widened. 'Asta, I applaud your spirit!' But then her face fell. 'I want to help – I do – but I have to be supremely careful. I told you before that my brother and father have embarked on this campaign together, but even my mother is complicit. Nor am I entirely sure about Grand-mother Klara – my father and Queen Elin's mother. Each one sees the advantage of removing Prince Jared from the picture. If my family knew what I had already told you – if they had the merest idea that I was contemplating working against them ... well, you cannot imagine their fury.'

Asta nodded. She understood the difficult position Lady Koel found herself in.

'I envy you, you know.'

They were the very last words she had expected to hear slip from Lady Koel's noble lips.

'*You* envy *me*? How is that even possible?'

Lady Koel's face was sombre. 'Because you have everything I don't – a legitimate position on The Twelve, freedom to take action. You have *power*, Asta. I've been thinking a lot of late about what it means to have power; what it means to earn it and have it and not abuse it. Take Cousin Jared, for instance. He made no secret of the fact that he never wanted this level of power and responsibility, that it was thrust upon him by the most dire turn of events. But he has risen to his new role, just as you are now doing to yours. Yet here am I, with no power to wield – confined to the shadows and the galleries, pathetically spying upon my brother.'

'No,' Asta said, this time extending her own hand to take Lady Koel's. 'There is nothing pathetic about you. Even if your family position prevents you from taking further action, you have already taken an important stand. I have my own

132

friends on The Twelve. I can counter your brother's campaign myself, even if you must by necessity drop back into the shadows.'

Lady Koel took a moment to weigh Asta's words, then shook her head decisively. 'You know,' she said, her voice cracking with emotion. 'I am tired of spending my life in the shadows. Let's take up Prince Jared's cause. Let's give my back-stabbing brother exactly what's coming to him.' She grasped Asta's hand. 'Let's do this. Together!'

SIXTEEN

THE FALCONER'S MEWS, THE VILLAGE OF THE TWELVE, ARCHENFIELD

'A vote of no confidence,' Nova said, stroking the head of one of her beloved falcons ruminatively.

Asta stood beside the Falconer at the perch, which was home to her six remaining falcons – the seventh, her dearest bird Mistral, having been ravaged by the eagle courier from Paddenburg.

'At least we know what plan he is hatching,' Asta said. 'And we know *early*, so we can devise a counter-campaign.'

Nova frowned. 'Asta, this is a noble thought. But you have been a member of the Twelve for only a matter of days, and you're already talking about taking on the Captain of the Guard.' She shuddered. 'It's no secret I have little fondness for Axel Blaxland but we should stop and think for a moment before we rush into a "counter-campaign", as you call it. He has a ruthless ambition and he'll stop at nothing to get what he wants. Be in no doubt – he's a very dangerous man.'

Asta met Nova's eyes, her own blazing with determination. 'Yes,' she agreed. 'He is highly dangerous. And, evidently, only becoming more so. But we don't have a choice. We have to do what we can to protect Prince Jared from this conspiracy. We must be brave, Nova – and we are not alone in this. We already have another comrade.'

'Who?' Nova looked intrigued.

In answer, Asta walked to the main door of the mews. She opened the door to allow a hooded figure to enter, then closed it quickly behind her. The figure walked towards Nova and dropped down its hood.

'You?' Nova said, startled.

Asta could see the look of mutual suspicion pass between her two companions. She realised that she was going to have to work hard to build this alliance.

'Why should we trust you, Lady Koel?' Nova asked bluntly. 'This vote, if successful, would not only benefit Axel but also the rest of the Blaxlands – including you.'

Asta cut in. 'Lady Koel has placed herself in considerable personal danger by coming to meet us.'

'Not if she's a double agent for the Blaxlands,' Nova exclaimed pointedly.

'Look,' Lady Koel addressed Nova, calmly. 'I understand why I do not automatically merit your trust, but at least allow me to put my case before you. Firstly, I find the thought of what Axel is plotting utterly repellent. This is a time when the court should be rallying behind its new Prince, not turning against him. My allegiance is to Prince Jared, both because he is Archenfield's rightful ruler and because of my personal feelings towards my cousin. I have always found him to be honourable. I can scarcely say the same for my brother.'

Asta found Lady Koel's answer to be convincing. She

scrutinised Nova's face, hoping for some signs of a shift in thought there, however slight.

There were none.

'You expect me to believe that you are throwing family loyalty out of the window in order to take a stand?' Nova asked her now.

Lady Koel's usually composed face showed signs of stress for the first time. 'Do not think for one moment that this is easy for me, Nova. To separate from my brother and thereby my father and mother and the rest of the Blaxlands ... this is not a step I take lightly. But I have searched my mind and my heart and I find that I have no other choice.' She turned to Asta. 'Perhaps this was a mistake,' she said. 'Perhaps you two would be better carrying this forward without me.'

'No!' Asta said, desperate not to lose an important ally. 'We need you.'

Nova hesitated, then she extended her hand towards Lady Koel. 'I apologise,' she said. 'I have a deserved reputation for bluntness. But I am sure you understand why I had to put these questions to you.'

Lady Koel took her hand and shook it. 'I do understand, Nova. If I were in your shoes, I would do exactly the same.'

Asta smiled and nodded, but when she glanced at Nova, she saw that the Falconer's face was still clouded with worry.

'With the Paddenburg Ultimatum hanging over court like a deadly storm cloud, and Prince Jared venturing far from home ... ' Her eyes met Koel's once more. 'Your brother certainly has a gift for timing.'

Koel shrugged. 'In truth, this comes from my father even more than my brother. Lord Viggo has been pushing Axel to make his move since before Anders's body grew cold.' She met Nova's enquiring eyes. 'Axel may be the one embarking on this course of action, but our father has been propelling him in this direction for months, if not years.'

Nova nodded. 'It's hardly news that there is deep enmity between Lord Viggo and Queen Elin. Still, I had not thought it had come to this. It means that we are not only under attack from an external enemy, but from an insidious enemy within too.'

'The first thing we must do is consider the vote,' Asta said. 'Axel had a clear sense of who would support him without question, namely Jonas, Morgan and – and I have to admit this puzzles me – Hal. There is no point in us expending time and energy working on those members of the Twelve.'

'Quite,' Koel agreed. 'We risk Axel finding out if we do talk to the wrong person. The further we can progress without him knowing we are onto him, the better.'

'All the same,' Asta said. 'I am confused by his certainty of Hal's support. From everything I've seen with my own eyes, Hal seems to have gone out of his way to look after Prince Jared.'

Lady Koel shrugged again. 'Asta, I fear that, in court, sometimes appearances can be deceptive.' She paused thoughtfully. 'But, as the Bodyguard is currently with Prince Jared beyond the borders, for now let us focus our concerns on those remaining at court.'

Asta nodded. 'That makes good sense to me. So we need to determine who we can definitely count on for support, and tip them off. And we need to make a plan with regard to those we identify as floating voters.'

'Agreed,' Nova said.

'You should know, Nova,' Asta continued, 'that you are seen as a floating vote. Jonas plans to sway your opinion.'

Nova raised an eyebrow. 'Let him do his best!' She

walked away, as if their conversation were over.

Koel turned with a quizzical look to Asta. Asta shrugged. She at least had had the chance to grow used to the Falconer's often strangely detached behaviour.

'Don't just stand there,' Nova called. 'You're supposed to be my allies!' She had seated herself at a low table, and was busily removing small items from a casket.

As Asta drew closer, she smiled in recognition. 'The Game of the Gates,' she said. 'Genius!'

'I'm not sure that I follow,' Koel admitted.

'It's very simple,' Asta said, helping Nova to turn and sort the pieces until each member of the Twelve was represented by a single counter. 'Here's the Council of Twelve.' She took the counter bearing the Prince's insignia and brought it up to the top left of the table. Next she located the Captain of the Guard's token and placed it on the opposite side. 'Now we have to determine who is on Team Jared and who is with Team Axel.'

Koel smiled, taking her own seat at the table. 'Very good, ladies. Let's begin.'

'All right then,' Asta said, reaching a hand across the table. 'This is the state of play, as it stands. Prince Jared needs seven votes to ensure his majority. Right now, by our calculations, he has three – if he and his retinue return in time for the vote.' She reached forward and drew the Huntsman's tile down the table. 'But only two if they do not. Nova's and my own.'

'Meanwhile, we judge Axel already has three safe votes – which increases to four if Hal returns,' Koel noted.

Three pairs of eyes turned to the final column of gaming counters Nova had arranged on the table.

'There are six swing votes,' the Falconer announced.

Koel nodded. 'Those are the people we need to work on.' She pulled back and smiled at the other two. 'Ladies, I think we have a plan. And, best of all, my brother has no clue that we're onto his poisonous little scheme.'

Nova grimaced. 'Let's do everything we can to keep it that way.'

Asta nodded, her eyes bright. After the earlier difficulties, it felt like their team had come together and that they could be a force to contend with. 'It feels good to be one step ahead, doesn't it?' she said.

Koel nodded and smiled slowly. 'How about we increase the odds still further?'

Nova leaned back. 'And how, pray, would we accomplish that?'

Koel smiled enigmatically before giving her answer,

'So, it has come to this.' The Queen brushed past Asta and Nova – it had been agreed that, for reasons of her own safety, Lady Koel would not accompany them – and walked on towards the window of her office. She pulled back the brocade curtain, glancing outside. 'My mangy brother has finally summoned the nerve to make his bid for power after all these years.' Her tone remained level, whether from composure or from the fear of a servant overhearing her, Asta could not be sure. 'How entirely predictable that he should do so just when the Princedom is vulnerable to attack.'

Queen Elin turned and sat down in the window seat, her head and shoulders framed by the golden light of the afternoon, reminding Asta of one of the religious paintings in the Village chapel. 'Did anyone see you come to find me?'

'No one of note,' Nova answered. 'Perhaps one or two of the household guards.'

Queen Elin frowned. 'We have to be more circumspect

from now on. Who knows which of those guards might be feeding Axel and Viggo scraps of information about comings and goings?' She straightened her skirts with care. 'I wonder if he plans to make his move even before my son returns?' Before either of them could offer their opinions on this, the Queen tossed fresh questions at them. 'Who else does Axel think is already on his side?'

Asta and Nova exchanged a glance.

'Morgan Booth,' Nova said.

'Morgan?' For the first time in their interview, Queen Elin seemed perturbed.

'Yes, Your Majesty,' Nova confirmed. 'Morgan was there and, from what Asta and Lady Koel overheard, Axel can probably count upon the Executioner's support.'

It was as if a chill wind had penetrated the room. 'No,' Queen Elin said, her face glacial. 'Morgan will not support Axel. You may be very sure about that.'

'That is one of the reasons we came to see you,' Nova told her now. 'Asta and I have been assessing which of the Twelve is likely to vote for Prince Jared, which for Axel, and who the waverers are most likely to be. We feel our energies are best directed at the third category.'

Queen Elin nodded. 'I concur.'

'We would place Morgan, whatever he has said, into that category. So one of us ought to talk to him.' Nova paused. 'We felt that, on account of your special relationship—'

'I will talk to Morgan,' Queen Elin said briskly, rising from her seat.

'I don't mean to be impertinent . . . ' Nova began. Queen Elin folded her arms as the Falconer continued. 'But you will tread carefully with the Executioner, won't you, Your Majesty? If he is indeed in Axel's camp, we don't want them to know how much we know.'

The colour drained from Queen Elin's face. 'Please be assured that I appreciate the complexities of this situation,' she said. 'And, from what I have observed so far, I might venture to suggest that I am somewhat better suited to this game than you are.' Her eyes were as hard as ice, her hands fists. 'Leave the Executioner to me.'

Asta and Nova made to leave but the Queen's voice stilled them in their tracks. 'We must do our utmost to protect my niece in this. Lady Koel has taken a considerable risk in breaking from her venomous clan.' Queen Elin folded her arms tightly across her chest. 'I was, regrettably, born a Blaxland. No one knows better than I how ruthless they are – even with their own. *Especially* with their own.'

SEVENTEEN

THE ROYAL BEDCHAMBER, THE BLACK PALACE OF PADDENBURG

Lydia surveyed the pieces of her new golden armour, which has been laid out on the floor of her dressing room. It was vaguely disturbing to gaze down at the disconnected panels of metal: the greaves, which would encase the lower part of her legs; the poleyn, which would circle around each of her knees; the cuisse, which would soon compress her muscled thighs.

It was rather like looking at the broken remnants of a fallen goddess, she thought fancifully.

She crouched down to pick up the breastplate. It was a shock to view her reflection in its polished surface. The curve of the metal distorted her image horribly, elongating her head and neck, making her look deformed, monstrous. She knew it was simply a trick of the light on the convex surface but still, a sense of cold dread spiralled through her.

She realised her breathing had become unsteady again. Throughout the morning, it had seemed to her that her body was battling with the new current of energy building up within her. She set the breastplate back down among the rest of the armour and stumbled towards the open window, longing for a breath of cool air.

As she felt the cold winter breeze on her face, she reflected again on her agitated state of mind. Why, today of all days, should she feel this way? Today was, in so many ways, the day she had been waiting for – the day that would serve as a bridge from one truly extraordinary phase of her life to the even more glorious next. The bright morning sun would see her ride out from the palace at the head of the second movement of troops; by the time the sky glimmered once more with stars, she would not be in any doubt that her journey back to her beloved brother had begun.

Gazing out through the window, she could see far across the palace borders. She knew that with such fine weather, the riding would be good today. All things considered, her spirits should be soaring like the birds turning circles high above the courtyard. But how could her flagging spirits soar, when she knew that there was critical, unfinished business at the palace?

Behind her, she heard the door open and close. Assuming it to be her chambermaid coming to help her with the armour, she remained at the window. It was only as she smelled a musky cologne that she realised her visitor was Nikolai. Turning, she saw him surveying her armour.

'You should not be here,' she scolded. 'And you might at least have left the door ajar, to demonstrate propriety.'

'I needed to talk to you, away from prying ears and eyes,' he said.

'Why?' she asked. 'Is there bad news from the borders?'

'No,' he said. 'Everything is proceeding according to plan out there.'

'What then?' she asked.

'What are you going to tell Henning and Ven?' he enquired. 'About their father, I mean.'

'Yes,' she snapped. 'Of course about Prince Leopold.'

'We have failed in our mission,' Nikolai said. 'We were charged with making the two Princes' rule legitimate before the attack on Archenfield reaches the next stage.'

She nodded. 'In that case, we have not failed yet.'

Nikolai smiled. 'You are preparing to dress in your armour, are you not? The army is already gathering outside the barracks. In two hours hence, you will be poised to depart. How do you propose to achieve the desired result between now and your imminent departure?'

Lydia took a slow inhalation of breath. 'I will go and talk to Prince Leopold one more time before I depart.'

'I wish you luck,' Nikolai told her.

The door to her chamber opened. This time, it was her chambermaid.

'Oh, I'm sorry, Lady Lydia. I did not know you had company.'

'It's quite all right,' Lydia told the startled girl. 'Lord Nikolai was just admiring my new armour, but he has urgent business to attend to elsewhere.'

'Yes.' Nikolai nodded. 'So I do. But I shall come and bid you and the troops a formal farewell, of course.'

Lydia's maid stepped aside to allow him passage into the corridor. When he was gone, she turned to Lydia. 'Well then, madam, shall I help you with your armour?'

'Actually,' Lydia told her, 'I have to go and speak with Prince Leopold. I shall leave you to finish packing my things and meet you back here within the hour.'

'Very good, my lady.'

The girl's voice quickly faded from Lydia's mind as she bowed her head and made her way along the corridor, towards the Prince's chamber. Before she could knock on the door, however, another maid dashed out.

'I came to speak to Prince Leopold,' Lydia told her.

'He isn't here, Lady Lydia,' replied the girl agitatedly.

A jolt of unease throbbed through her. 'But where else can he be? He hasn't moved from his bed in months.' Her eyes met the servant's. 'Well? Out with it! Has the Prince simply evaporated?'

'No!' said the maid. 'Far from it, my lady. No, he has taken it upon himself to visit the maze.'

'The maze?' Lydia was incredulous. 'On his own?'

'He was quite insistent,' the maid told her. 'It always was one of his favourite places. He used to spend hours there, chasing—'

Lydia turned on her heel and strode back along the corridor, towards the main stairwell. She took the stairs two at a time and then strode across the marble hall towards the doors leading out into the garden. She said nothing to the guards who opened the doors for her, stepping out into the cool air and finding herself surprised by the warmth of the winter sun.

Before her stood the maze, in all its glory. She thought once more of Henning and Ven on the road to Archenfield; she thought of Logan waiting for her on the other side of the border: she knew that time was running out, along with her options. Taking a breath, she stepped into the maze, from the light world outside into an enclosure of deep, devouring green.

'Prince Leopold, where are you?' she called, her voice echoing on the winter wind.

Lydia made her way through the looping entrails of the maze. There was a tale of a visiting royal who'd once become lost in its embrace, found dead the next morning. Lydia had been following its green corridors for long moments now, with no one answering her calls but, as she turned a corner, she finally heard singing. She paused. It was a childlike voice singing a nursery rhyme of some sort. It *had* to be him. She just needed to work out which direction the sound was coming from and then track it down.

But identifying the location of the singer proved a good deal more straightforward than getting to him. The maze kept turning her around on herself and, just when she thought she was close, she realised she had been cunningly led away in another direction. Now she could no longer even hear the singing. As she started to fear that she might be trapped in the maze, Lydia found herself wondering darkly if this might have been Leopold's intention all along: the men of Paddenburg – how they enjoyed their games.

She thought of Nikolai. As the Prince Regent while Henning and Ven secured the annexation of Archenfield, he would have considerable power, if only for a short time. By rights, he ought to be the one feeling his way through the maze – if he failed to gain Leopold's signature on the decree devolving power to Henning and Ven then, in turn, the decree granting Nikolai the powers of Prince Regent was utterly worthless. Feeling anger pulse through her, Lydia turned a corner. And then, at last, she came upon old Leopold, sitting on a bench and waving her over to join him.

'*There* you are, Your Majesty!' she said.

'Here I am!' He nodded, wreathed in smiles. 'And here you are! Isn't this wonderful?'

'It's certainly good to see you up and about,' she said. 'But is this wise?' She took a breath herself before continuing, 'You are quite flushed. I hope you haven't over-exerted yourself. You haven't been outdoors for months now, have you? You have to be careful—'

'Careful! Pah! I'm sick to the core of being careful, of taking care. I need to feel alive again, Lydia. That's no life up there in my chamber, surrounded by all kinds of medication that is no use to me ... no damn use at all.'

Lydia frowned. 'You have to be patient,' she said. 'You do seem to be on the verge of recovery, so something must have helped—'

Leopold laughed. 'Really? You think that I've managed to make it out of bed thanks to my son's latest quack applying a dead cockerel to my ears?' He shook his head. 'Come now, Lydia. I think we are both a little too rational to follow that line of thought.'

Lydia smiled. There was a certain brutal honesty to Leopold which she could not help but admire. 'If it wasn't the cockerels, then to what do you ascribe this turnaround, I wonder?'

He considered the matter for a moment. 'Necessity. Willpower.'

She nodded. 'I suppose that could be enough. But now, while it is wonderful that you managed to make your way down here today, I think it's time we took you back inside to rest.'

But Leopold remained rooted to the seat. 'What's really going on here, Lydia? Where are my sons? And don't toss me some lie that they are on army exercises, because I don't believe that. I've seen the army massing through my own window. Something significant is about to happen, isn't it?'

Lydia took a breath. 'Let's talk about this in your chamber,' she said. Seeing him frown, she added, 'You are Prince of Paddenburg, and these are important matters. How do we know there is not someone listening to us on the other side of this hedge?'

He looked doubtful. 'I suppose—'

'Come on, take my arm!'

147

She watched as he creaked upright, on to his legs. For all his fighting talk, he was still obviously frail.

'I might need your help finding our way out of this maze,' she told him.

'That's not a problem,' he said. 'I know these pathways like the back of my hand.'

But these words proved to be a vain promise. Perhaps Leopold had once known the maze well but, today, he seemed at a loss. Lydia began to wonder if he had genuinely lost his bearings or if he was playing another game – if he knew that time was ticking by and he was doing everything he could to delay her.

Through a combination of exhausting all other possibilities and sheer determination on her part, they finally caught sight of the entrance. 'At last!' she exclaimed.

Leopold did not speak. His breathing was laboured and Lydia was shocked by his pallor. She realised that he had not been playing a game, but putting on a brave face.

'Come on,' she said, gently. 'We need to get you back up to your chamber.'

This time, he offered no protest.

There were no maids to be found near the Prince's bedchamber. Evidently, they were below stairs, discussing in excited tones Leopold's miraculous recovery. As Lydia settled the Prince back in bed, she heard the sound of many horses outside. She knew she was running late. How long would it take to put on her armour?

'What are those noises?' Leopold asked.

'It's the army,' she told him. She was past the point of lying.

'I knew it!' A brief flicker of his earlier fighting spirit returned.

'You were right,' Lydia said. 'Something significant is about to happen.' She leaned across him and rearranged his pillows.

'Tell me,' he said.

'I am telling you,' she said, stepping back with one of the pillows in her hand. 'Your sons are en route to Archenfield. They sent Prince Jared an ultimatum to surrender or prepare for invasion. Paddenburg is poised to take control of Archenfield.'

'No!' Leopold exclaimed, trying to sit up. 'They have no right to issue ultimatums! Nor to mount an invasion! I am ruler of Paddenburg, not they.'

Lydia shrugged. 'You know that and I know that. But no one outside beyond these walls knows that. They all think you signed over power to your sons months ago.'

Leopold made a fist. 'Well, they are going to find out the truth. Get me Nikolai! Tell him to gather my council! I will stop this invasion in its tracks.' His eyes were full of rage.

Lydia shook her head slowly. 'I'm afraid there isn't time. The wheels are in motion. It is time I was going.'

'Going? Where?'

'I'm leading out the second movement of troops to meet Henning and Ven at the borders,' she said. 'We will ride into Archenfield shoulder to shoulder, the standards of Paddenburg flying at our sides.' She saw the horror in Leopold's eyes.

'You too? *You* are part of all this?'

Lydia shook out her hair. 'Yes, I am very much part of this.'

Leopold tried to swing his feet out of bed. Lydia did not help him, and his movements grew more frantic with frustration.

'You're not going anywhere,' she said, determined to resolve this once and for all. They were so close to success; she wouldn't let this old man stop them now. She'd been patient for too long. 'You're not strong enough.' She leaned in closer. 'You're a man on the verge of death.'

'No,' he said, spitting the word at her.

She brought the pillow she had been holding down over his face until his cries were muffled. She watched his hands flail about but then grow weak. Strangely, this sign of weakness only seemed to nurture her own strength. She increased her pressure on the pillow and held it down over his face until all sound, all movement, ceased.

At last, silence.

She lifted the pillow and reached out to check the pulse in his neck. Nothing. There was no life left in him.

She closed his eyes. Rising to her feet, she lifted old Leopold's head and placed the pillow under his neck. Then she smoothed down his hair and turned away from the bed.

The door was ajar. A figure stood close by the chamber entrance.

'Nikolai!' she said, as he stepped out of the shadows.

'Lydia,' he said. 'You have played your part beyond all expectation. Now it is my turn to do mine.'

EIGHTEEN

THE PHYSICIAN'S SURGERY, THE VILLAGE OF THE TWELVE, ARCHENFIELD

'Remind me,' Axel said. 'How much is a pair of testes worth these days?'

The Physician smiled at his enquiry. 'That all depends, doesn't it?' Elias turned towards Axel. 'On whose testes they are, I mean.'

The two members of The Twelve were standing before a bank of glass jars of various sizes, in which different parts of the human body were suspended in alcohol. The preserving liquor had a purplish-blue tinge to it. Coupled with this, this part of Elias's surgery was lit by a strange, watery blue light. It seemed to Axel as if he were standing at the bottom of the fjord, watching this jumble of mortal flotsam and jetsam float before his eyes.

'As you may remember from your schooling,' Elias said, 'just as there are twelve members of the Prince's Council, so there are twelve parts of the body of equal rank – the two hands, the two eyes, the two ears, the upper lip and the lower lip, the two feet, the neck and the nose.' At the mention of each body part, Axel's eyes darted from jar to jar as if playing a macabre game; from the pair of hands that rested upon one another, as if in prayer, to the mouth which looked like no more than a lump of gristle. Axel had a memory of one of Vera's more unsavoury stews; it was only Elias's neatly written label which gave the game away.

'The value of each of these twelve separate parts is a cow and three copper ingots if the victim is a commoner, but the Blood Price soon rises if the victim is a member of the Twelve, and then again if he or she is a member of the royal family.'

'Six kine and ten silver ingots for the hand of a member of the Twelve,' Axel calculated. 'And a dozen kine and twenty gold ingots for the hand of a prince.' He paused. 'Though, of course, these are values attributable during times of peace and order. The traitor Logan Wilde took much more than the hand of Prince Anders but he has not paid the Blood Price – and perhaps he never will, if we hand him back intact to his comrades from Paddenburg.'

Elias nodded. 'To your earlier question about the testes ...' He paused to approach the relevant jar and inspect its meagre contents. 'The value of a pair is equivalent to that of a hand or any of the other parts of equal rank.'

'Another dozen kine and another twenty gold ingots,' Axel calculated.

'Indeed,' Elias said. 'I'm curious to find you so interested in the value of the human body today,' he said.

Axel shrugged. 'We are poised on the edge of another conflict, Elias ... no, not even poised. The conflict has already begun, but it will soon get much worse. We must anticipate the broken bodies piling up once more all across the Princedom. This is the price of war when it comes.'

Elias's eyes clouded. 'It is my fervent hope that we avoid war, that your defence of the borders proves watertight until Prince Jared succeeds in coming home with the necessary alliance.'

Axel nodded. 'Our hopes rest with Prince Jared and his team.' He tapped the jar of testes. 'He's certainly going to need those.' He turned back to Elias. 'You didn't seem overly enthused by the idea of Prince Jared embarking on this mission.'

'That's true,' Elias said. 'Prince Jared is young and new to his role, and all it demands of him. All things considered, I would have preferred Queen Elin, with her greater experience in cross-territory diplomacy, to have undertaken such an important journey.'

Axel folded his arms, observing the disjointed images of his reflection and the Physician's in the glass jars before them. 'You speak almost as if Cousin Jared's youth precludes him from doing a good job as Prince.' He paused. 'But he is the very same age as your niece, and look how capable she has turned out to be.' His tone softened further. 'She does you much credit in the way she has moved on so effortlessly from being your apprentice to taking up her new and unexpected position on the Twelve.'

Axel saw, exaggerated in the curve of a jar, the change in Elias's expression.

'You might praise her, Axel, but I see things somewhat differently. Where you see credit, I see another person of youth and inexperience who has arguably moved too far, too fast.'

Axel was surprised at the Physician's frankness, though not the import of his words. Elias had always been a stickler for tradition. His one departure from this stance had been his offer to give Asta a role in court; it seemed like this was a lapse he was now regretting.

'You sound disappointed in Asta,' Axel observed. 'I must confess I'm surprised,' he lied.

Elias shook his head. 'I'm not disappointed *in* her,' he said. 'I'm disappointed *for* her. But it was the Prince's decision to promote her.'

'I'm sure that Prince Jared was acting in good faith,' Axel said. 'Just as I am equally sure that it must be most ... inconvenient to you to have trained an apprentice for, what – six months – and now find her taken away from you.'

'Bah! I have no real need of an apprentice, Axel! I never did and I certainly don't now. Of course, it was useful for me to have someone to help with my notes and so forth, but Asta's position was never about *my* needs. It was about giving something to her – getting her out of the devastation of the settlement of Teragon and opening up a window on a different kind of life.'

'You sound almost sorry that you gave this chance to her.'

'I do not have children of my own,' Elias said. 'I have devoted my life to my calling and my duties to the court. I have no regrets. It was a sadness to me that my wife died so young but that is what fate determined. I understood that. I threw myself into my studies and my duties and I woke up, one day, twenty years later, all alone in my home. I thought of my brother's child and the chance I now had to make a difference to her.'

Axel had never heard Elias speak so openly before, in all the years he had known him – the Physician was almost trembling from the release of pent-up emotion when he finished speaking. But, after only a moment, he resumed in a far more controlled tone of voice.

'I do not mean to sound rude, but I am surprised that you have time to linger with me here, when there must be other, far more important conversations for you to be having with others.'

Axel shook his head. 'In my view, there are no more important conversations than this. I have given my team very clear instructions and they are activating my plans as we speak. If there is one thing I have learned from my experience as Captain of the Guard, it is to delegate what you can and ensure you always have time to check in with your allies.'

'Well, I'm certainly glad you think of me that way.'

'Of course I do,' Axel said silkily. 'Our friendship has always been founded on the utmost mutual respect, has it not? Throughout our lives, we have done many things for one another – from the stitches you threaded through my brow when I was just five years old' – he saw Elias nod at the memory and squint to seek out the now faint scar above his right eye – 'through to the discussion we had after Prince Anders's assassination about the presence of savin in the Physic Garden.' Elias squirmed at the mention of this – just as Axel had intended. 'My point, my good friend, is that we have always looked out for and helped one another whenever the need has arisen.'

'This is true,' Elias said. 'And I sense from your words now that you feel that this need has arisen once more. What I'm less sure of is *how* you would like me to help.'

Axel nodded, turning in the underwater light towards the Physician. 'I believe we share a common view,' he said. 'Which is that there is a regrettable void of experience on the throne at a time when experience is most necessary.' He waited for Elias's response, hoping he had not gone too far.

After a moment's pause, Elias nodded. 'We do share the same view. But what do you propose to do about this?'

'Regrettable though it is, I fear Prince Jared must be removed.'

Elias stared sightlessly for a few moments at the bank of jars in front of him – the strange mosaic of severed limbs and other, less substantial, body parts. 'You are right,' he said. 'It is regrettable. But we have to think, first and foremost, of the value of a stable Princedom, and of peace.'

'I couldn't have expressed that any better myself, good Elias.' Axel rested his hand lightly on the older man's shoulder. 'I knew I could count on you. Such loyalty is beyond value.'

'Nothing is beyond value,' Elias said, with a slight shake of the head. 'There is just one thing.'

'Go on.'

'I need your assurance that my niece will be protected. Whatever I have said to you here – in complete confidence, of course – I only wish the best for Asta.'

Axel nodded. 'Of course you do,' he said. He paused, allowing the Physician's tension to rise. 'And, of course, I readily give you my word. I will take good care of Asta. Have no fear about that.'

NINETEEN

REDNOW

Jared could barely comprehend how much the landscape had changed since they had crossed the border from Woodlark into Rednow earlier that morning. If he hadn't witnessed the gradual shifts in terrain with his own eyes, he'd have thought that he'd somehow been transported to another planet, rather than another Princedom.

Rednow could not be more different from the lush green topography he was used to. As they had journeyed north, the verdant landscape had steadily given way to first brown, then ochre, ground. Lost in his own thoughts – and sometimes with no thoughts at all, but simply the meditative rhythm of Handrick's hooves – he had suddenly become aware that there were no longer any trees. They had been replaced by ragged shrubs, clumps of dry, spiky grass and, as far as the eye could see, an expanse of orange scrubland, met at the horizon by a bright blue sky.

The tinkling of bells had made them aware of goats and goatherds quietly going about their business in this strange hinterland. The muffled music of the bells was the only thing to break the unearthly silence. It made Jared feel like they were less alone in this vast open space. Still, the goatherds seemed intent on keeping themselves to themselves, probably fearing that four strangers on horseback could mean only one thing – danger.

But, all the time, they had followed the river – the very same river which fed the swollen fjords of Archenfield and Woodlark, travelling down from the higher grounds to this alien land. Now, still riding along the riverbank, they had entered a deep gorge with majestic walls rising up high on either side, the rock surface shifting from orange to red to purple with the patterns of light and shadow. The canyon was so deep that he could no longer see out of it – only the sky above. Jared had never felt so small or insignificant.

'Spectacular, isn't it?' Kai said, bringing his horse up alongside Jared's.

'Yes,' Jared agreed. 'It's a landscape I could never have imagined. It's so different from Archenfield.' He nodded to himself, thinking of the vast canyon walls bearing witness to the four riders, making their trail of hoofprints in the dust. In the stiff, circling breeze, though, even that trail of prints would disappear before the setting of the sun.

There would be no evidence at all that they had travelled this way.

Jared turned towards Kai. 'It's strange, but I have the sense we are being watched.'

Kai nodded, seeming pleased. 'Your senses are alert, Prince Jared. Of course we are being watched.'

As Jared gazed at Kai in confusion, the Huntsman instructed him. 'Look up to the higher reaches.'

Jared saw the indentations of the rock and the patterns of small, shifting shadows, but only when he looked more carefully did he realise that he was not observing mere shadows on the cliff face. No, when he looked more closely, he saw there were structures carved out of the rock: rudimentary columns and walkways, windows and doors. And he could see, though barely, the movement of figures way up there.

Kai offered him his field glasses. 'Here, these may help you.'

Slowing his horse, Jared looked more closely at the upper reaches of the canyon. Intricate buildings had been constructed within the crevices of the cliff-face.

'It's amazing! I mean I've heard tell of this, but to see it with my own eyes? Imagine making such a sheer rock face inhabitable.'

Kai smiled. 'The people of Rednow are expert at making their homes in their native rock, as you will see when we arrive at the palace.' He paused. 'Which will not be too long now. Look up ahead!'

Jared saw a vast pair of wooden gates stretching from one side of the cliffs to the other, covering the river and both its banks: the gateway to Prince Rohan's palace. He felt possessed by new energy and purpose. Even the horses seemed to sense that the next staging post was in sight.

As they approached the gates, Jared felt his stomach clench. The next part of his challenge was coming sharply into focus.

'They won't let us through,' Hal announced, returning on foot from his meeting with the palace guards at the gate.

'What do you mean they won't let us through?' Kai retorted. 'Prince Rohan has no reason to deny Prince Jared an audience.'

'If you just let me finish, they *will* let Prince Jared through into the palace. So long as the rest of us remain here until the meeting of the Princes is concluded.'

Jared felt a cold dread. 'They'll let me through but only on my own?'

Hal nodded. 'I argued hard for at least me to accompany you – as your Bodyguard – but they are adamant.' He turned to include the rest of the group. 'I'm sorry to say this after such a long day's ride, but I think we have no choice but to abandon Rednow and journey on to our next—'

'No,' Jared found himself saying. 'If Prince Rohan will see me and me alone, then so be it.' Where had the words, the certainty come from? It was like hearing someone else speak through his mouth – his mother, perhaps, or Logan Wilde.

Jared jumped down from his horse and walked towards the gate. Behind him, he heard Kai and Hal arguing. He shut them out. He reached into the pocket of his surcoat and closed his fingers on the sprig of rue that Asta had given him. It was ridiculous, he knew, but somehow touching the now dried-out sprig renewed his confidence. He addressed the palace guards.

'Good evening. I am Prince Jared of Archenfield, and I have been riding all day, and much of the night, with the intention of speaking to Prince Rohan.'

The guards bowed formally to him and, without further delay, the gates opened, revealing another pair of gates. For a moment Jared was confused, then he realised the sense of it – the double layer of protection and control they afforded the palace.

With a crash that echoed down the canyon, the outer gates closed, cutting him off from his companions.

A pair of guards led him on towards the second gates. One of them gave a command to his comrades on the other side and these gates too began to open. Jared watched, with a growing sense of anticipation, as the palace of Rednow was revealed on the other side.

'Please come this way, Your Majesty,' said the first of the guards.

Jared saw that, just as the people dwelling at the top of the canyon had made their home by burrowing into the natural rock face, so it was down there at the base of the gorge. Ahead of him was the palace structure, but each room, each door, each window opening, had been carved from the red rock which had given the Princedom its name.

To one side of the palace was a dam, with small waterfalls tumbling down on either side of a series of stone stairways. The people of Rednow had been clever in appropriating what nature had given them – whether it was the rock in which they had created their homes, or the water that they had harnessed so expertly. He followed the guard up one of the stone stairwells to the top of the dam. As he reached the apex, he looked down into the vast reservoir of fresh water on the other side – it was more than enough to sustain the palace and all who resided here.

'This way, please, Your Majesty.' The guard urged him onwards and up, along another stone stairway. As Jared followed, his eyes darting back and forth, up and down, he became aware of the complexity of the palace building and the numbers of men and women going about their business.

Before he knew it, they had climbed high up into the rock. Looking back over his shoulder, Jared could now see over the twin gates. Beyond them, no bigger than ants now, were his companions.

Everything rested on his shoulders.

'The Prince is waiting for you in his apartment,' the guard told him, indicating an ornate doorway carved out of stone. So he knew I was coming, Jared thought. Those spies work fast.

The Prince of All Archenfield took a breath, and entered the palace.

161

TWENTY

THE PRINCE'S APARTMENT,
THE CANYON PALACE OF REDNOW

With every step Jared and his escort took, the palace seemed to – there was no other word for it – *evolve*. From out of the red rock walls emerged elaborate, painted carvings depicting, Jared surmised, three-dimensional scenes from Rednow's history, while intricate statues of the territory's former rulers seemed to rise up from the floor to meet him as he continued on his way.

His surroundings were dazzling, but Jared was struggling to take it all in. His heart was already starting to race at his imminent audience with Prince Rohan and the necessity of securing Archenfield's next strategic alliance.

Jared's escort led him across a series of wooden bridges over pools of turquoise water, illuminated by the numerous wall sconces – deep in the belly of the palace, there was no natural light, anywhere. The sound of the lapping water – like Jared's footsteps and the very rhythm of his breath – were all magnified by the vast, cathedral-like space.

The final bridge deposited them in the most elaborately decorated corridor yet, and they emerged at the top of a stairway so grand and smooth it might have been crafted from marble.

Down below, surrounded by fine tapestries and antiquities, sat Prince Rohan.

Knowing of Rednow's unparalleled reputation in trade, Jared had expected its ruler to be clad in fine silks, velvets and other rare materials, sourced from territories on its extensive trade routes. In reality, Prince Rohan was dressed in simple black robes, with a leather waistcoat and matching boots. The only nod towards his vast wealth and lofty status was the rings, in a rainbow array of metals and precious stones, which shimmered from each of the fingers on both his hands. Hands which now reached out to clasp Jared's own.

'Prince Jared of Archenfield,' Rohan declared warmly. 'Welcome to my humble home! Do take a seat. I'm sure you are tired from your long journey, and hungry too?' Rohan gestured towards a vast platter of fruit on the table before them and took a crescent of melon. 'Help yourself!' he told Jared. 'I'm a fiend for fresh fruit. My second wife got me started on this. She tells me she wants me to live a long and healthy life – in stark contrast to her predecessor, I might add!'

Jared smiled at Rohan's easy intimacy. Turning his eyes to the array of fruit, he found himself momentarily dazed by so much choice. The colours of the fruits, glistening in the candlelight, were as rich and lustrous as those of Prince Rohan's jewellery. By the time he had plumped for a quarter of fig, Rohan had already dismissed his escort.

'So,' Rohan said brightly. 'It's a good while since we had the pleasure of welcoming a Prince of Archenfield to the

Canyon Palace. Tell me the news from your court, my friend.'

As Jared began his sorry tale, Prince Rohan listened attentively. His bright eyes remained on Jared throughout, though the intensity of his gaze was not troubling to Jared – actually, his clear empathy was bolstering.

'So, the boys from Paddenburg have grown in ambition,' Rohan said with a nod, as Jared concluded his report.

Jared sighed. 'Ambitious is an understatement.'

Prince Rohan's hazel eyes twinkled. 'Well, let's get down to business, shall we? Beyond sharing your current woes with a sympathetic neighbour, what precisely brings you to Rednow today?'

In spite of Rohan's warm welcome, Jared felt the pressure of the moment. 'My reason for coming here today is very simple,' he said. 'I would like to invite you to enter into an alliance with us.'

'You require some help against the bully boys of Paddenburg?' Prince Rohan reached for the platter of fruit.

'Yes,' Jared agreed. 'But this is not only about Rednow coming to the aid of Archenfield to fend off the current foe.' He took a breath. 'I'm thinking of the future, and not only the future of my own Princedom. I am proposing an unprecedented alliance of the five river territories – Archenfield, Woodlark, Rednow, Larsson and Baltiska – to ensure that none of our domains falls victim to the whims of our less stable neighbours.'

Rohan leaned back in his seat, popping a grape in his mouth. 'An alliance of the river territories? An interesting thought. So where does this unprecedented alliance currently stand?'

'I have reached a new agreement with Queen Francesca of Woodlark,' Jared told him.

Prince Rohan arched an eyebrow. Jared guessed from this

that his companion knew something of the recent enmity between Archenfield and Woodlark.

'Francesca did withdraw the alliance for a brief time, due to a misunderstanding between our two courts,' Jared hastened to explain, 'but I met with her and Princess Ines in the court of Woodlark yesterday.' He paused. 'And I am happy to confirm that the alliance is back on the table.' *So long as you hand over Logan Wilde*, the demonic voice in his head taunted him. Pushing this aside, Jared focused on Rohan. 'So if Rednow were to join this alliance, you would benefit not only from Archenfield's army, but also Woodlark's own considerable military strength, and that of its existing ally, Malytor, to the east.'

Prince Rohan nodded. 'This is an appetising prospect, Prince Jared. Nevertheless, something puzzles me.' He leaned forward confidentially. 'Woodlark is a sizeable territory with a deliciously vicious army and, as you say, its own ongoing alliance with Malytor. Given your alliance with Woodlark, I'd imagine you and Francesca could take on Paddenburg together and be reasonably optimistic of victory.' He paused to twist one of his rings around his finger. 'Without wanting to disparage my own Princedom, I'm not sure what we – better known for our trade than our military capabilities – add to the mix. One could ask the same question with regard to Larsson and Baltiska. Our three territories are far smaller than yours and Francesca's.'

Jared nodded. It was a fair question, and one he had turned over in his head many times on the long ride there. Of course, one answer was that if Francesca pulled out of the alliance, then he would need the combined capabilities of the smaller three territories to even begin to make up for the shortfall ... but, he reminded himself, there were nobler, longer-term motives too.

'Rednow, Larsson and Baltiska are indeed smaller territories in terms of land mass, but you would each bring different assets to the alliance – your unparalleled reputation for trade, for instance.' Jared paused. 'You are right that if I was thinking only of the current conflict, the alliance with Woodlark would serve me well enough, but I'm thinking further into the future and not merely of Archenfield.' He heard new conviction in his own voice. 'I want to initiate an alliance that strengthens and protects each of the five river territories from aggression now or in the future from the west or south.'

'In other words, from Eronesia or Paddenburg,' Rohan said.

Jared nodded. 'Territories like yours and mine cannot go on being at the mercy of the shifting moods and mercurial ambitions of our neighbours. We need to find a way not only to avoid another war now, but also to broker a more lasting peace. So that, for instance, your own trade concerns may be allowed to prosper.'

Prince Rohan helped himself to a segment of orange. Jared wondered if he had said enough to persuade him. The voice in his head reminded him that there was one explosive matter he had not mentioned – Francesca's stipulation that Archenfield hand over Logan Wilde to the court of Woodlark. Until that was done, the alliance with Woodlark was effectively meaningless.

Jared felt bad about lying to Prince Rohan, but Rohan had not explicitly asked if there were any terms attached to his agreement with Francesca, so it wasn't exactly lying, was it? He didn't want anything to derail the agreement with Rednow. If he could secure an alliance here and ride on to conclude further agreements with Baltiska and Larsson, then he'd be in a far stronger position on returning to his own court to argue for the handover of Wilde in exchange for not one but *four* alliances.

We'll see, said the niggling voice.

Prince Rohan rose to his feet before his guest. 'You know what? You impress the hell out of me.' He rested his hand on Jared's shoulder. 'So you're what – seventeen, eighteen years of age?'

'Sixteen,' Jared said, irritated by the note of apology in his voice as he rose from his own chair.

'Sixteen!' Rohan exclaimed. 'The same age as my own middle son! Don't get me wrong, Prince Jared, I couldn't be more proud of my boy, but that's what he is – a boy. Whereas you – you are already a man, and a man of honour at that.'

Jared drew little satisfaction from his companion's praise: it only made him more keenly aware of his dishonesty. 'Circumstances have compelled me to grow up fast,' he said, anxious to remain outside the maelstrom of his own head.

'Circumstances challenge us,' Rohan told him. 'They question what we are made of. But it is you, my friend, who found the answer. When I think of everything you have faced these past few weeks. Other men – more experienced in rule – would have crumbled.'

Jared smiled. 'Perhaps my very inexperience is my secret weapon,' he said.

He realised it was one of the most honest sentiments he had shared.

Rohan returned his smile. 'You could be onto something there.'

Jared was conscious that he needed to bring things to a conclusion. 'So,' he said, his voice sounding far steadier than he felt. 'Will Rednow sign up to the alliance of the five river territories?'

Just say yes, he willed the man before him.

'There is just one thing I would like to clarify,' Rohan said.

Jared felt his stomach tense again. Was his lie about to be dragged out into the open?

'What specifically do you want from me at this point?' Rohan asked.

Jared had to resist grinning in relief. 'I want you to loan me your army,' he said, 'with you at its helm, primarily in order to make as strong as possible a show of force to deter Paddenburg.' He paused. 'That said, if there is a need to fight, I would expect your forces to stand shoulder to shoulder with mine on the battlefield.'

Prince Rohan's eyes were bright. 'I am not given to prevarication, Prince Jared.' He reached out his hand. 'It is my honour to agree to be your ally.'

'The honour is mine.' Jared shook his companion's hand. 'There is just one thing further I need to ask of you.'

Prince Rohan laughed lightly. 'There is always a footnote. Go on then – tell me what I can do for you. Have you taken a fancy to one of my four beautiful daughters, or are we talking about financial support in addition to military?'

Jared shook his head. 'Neither of those – thank you, though. All I ask is for you to work with me to bring Séverin of Larsson and Ciprian of Baltiska into our alliance.'

Rohan inhaled deeply. 'I see. Well, Séverin and I are on pretty good terms – thanks to some shared trade connections and a tactical marriage or three. I would not anticipate too much of a challenge in bringing him to the table.' He paused. 'Ciprian, I fear, is another matter altogether.'

Jared frowned. 'I'm aware, of course, of Prince Ciprian's reputation. That's why I'm asking for your help.'

Rohan clicked his tongue. 'I'm sorry,' he said. 'If I thought I held any kind of sway there, I'd petition on your behalf. But there was some unpleasantness recently.' He shrugged. 'To be honest, there is always some recent unpleasantness with Ciprian.'

Jared's mind was working overtime. An alliance between four of the five river territories was good – way better than good. And, in terms of land mass, Baltiska *was* the smallest of the territories. Maybe he could allow a slight revision of his ambitions? But there was no getting away from the fact that Baltiska occupied a crucial strategic position next to Schloss, the former ally of Eronesia. Jared shuddered as he remembered the struggle Archenfield had had in defending itself against Eronesia. As such, Baltiska was an important part of the jigsaw in stemming any future threat from the west. *But for now*, the voice in his head reminded him, *you need Baltiska in case Woodlark slips through your fingers.*

'I am sorry I cannot help,' Rohan said. 'Like I say – Séverin, yes, but Ciprian ...' Rohan reached over once more to the fruit platter, selected a peeled lychee and dropped it into his mouth. 'The thing that puzzles me, of course, is why you're asking for my help when you already have a perfect route into Ciprian's court.'

Jared's eyes narrowed in confusion.

Rohan chewed the lychee, then lifted his fingers to retrieve the purple stone from his curled tongue. 'Given that you are travelling in the company of Prince Ciprian's own cousin, why wouldn't you just send him into Baltiska to petition for you?'

Jared stared blankly at Rohan. Ciprian's cousin? What was he talking about?

Rohan shook his head in amusement. 'You don't know, do you? I mean, they're not on the best of terms, I grant you, but they are cousins, and that has to count for something.'

'I'm sorry,' Jared rejoined. '*Who* is Prince Ciprian's cousin?'

Rohan's eyes glinted in the candlelight. 'Three clues,' he

said. 'Silver beard, violet eyes and you certainly wouldn't want to run across him in a dark alley.'

'Kai Jagger!' Jared exclaimed, his head spinning with this new information.

'Kai Jagger,' Rohan repeated. 'If you want to unlock an alliance with Prince Ciprian of Baltiska, the Huntsman is your key.'

TWENTY-ONE

THE CANYON PALACE OF REDNOW

Jared was trying hard to keep calm. 'Why didn't *you* tell me? Why did I have to find this out from the ruler of another Princedom?'

He and Kai were in a large bedchamber deep in the palace, the other travel-weary Archenfielders stretched out asleep on the far side of the room. Jared stared angrily at Kai, sitting across from him on a stone bench.

Kai frowned. 'It was not a secret, Prince Jared. But it is ancient history. It has no bearing on my life now.'

'*No bearing?*' Jared felt his anger rising. 'Of course it has bearing! You are first cousin to the Prince of a territory with which we want to build an alliance. You are in the perfect position to exert influence.'

Kai shook his head. 'I have no influence in Baltiska any more. I left there under a storm cloud years before you were even born. Though it is true my blood directly connects me to

Prince Ciprian, my actions – and his – have severed that connection for all time.'

'What actions?'

Kai dropped his eyes. 'As I said before, it is ancient—'

'I'm sorry, Kai.' Jared shook his head. 'But I need to know this.' He realised that it was the first time he had openly challenged Kai in all the time they had known each other. A few weeks ago – a few days ago even – he would never have dared. But now the stakes had risen, and so too had his confidence.

Kai nodded. 'It's a simple, if rather pathetic story, but I'll share it with you if I must.' He sighed. 'Ciprian and I both fell in love with the same girl.'

'This is all about a girl?'

Kai smiled softly. 'Wars have been fought over less, Prince Jared.'

'Who was she?'

'Her name is Nina,' Kai said. 'The most beautiful girl I ever saw. I wasn't much older than you when I first got to know her. It wasn't love at first sight – no, that's not true ... I was spellbound. But I was ill at ease with young women and it took me some time to gain the confidence to even talk to her.'

Jared was amazed by how a few words could overturn the impression he had formed of Kai over many years – of someone who was frightened of nothing and no one.

'She was kind and patient,' Kai continued. 'And, in time, I found the courage to talk to her and, to my astonishment, she liked me too.' His voice grew husky. 'Later, she confided that she had known from the first time we saw each other that we were destined to be together.'

'Why didn't she make the first move then?' Jared asked.

Kai smiled. 'That was not her way. She saw no need to rush

things. We were young. We had the whole of our lives ahead of us.' His smile faded away. 'Or so we thought.'

'What happened?'

'It was three years to the day since we had met when I asked her to marry me. She said yes, but we agreed that we would keep our plans secret, for a time. We knew that the moment our families got word of our intentions, mayhem would break out.'

'Your families would have opposed the marriage?'

'No,' Kai shook his head. 'They would have been thrilled. Which means they would have taken control. We just wanted a brief period of time to be together and hug the secret close to us before everyone began to stake their claim in our lives.'

Jared nodded. He thought of his own family and the fanfare around Anders's betrothal to Silva. But then, he reminded himself, Anders and Silva's marriage had been incubated in the Council Chambers of Archenfield and Woodlark. By the time they had first met each other, their fate had already been decided by parents and councillors. Jared frowned to think of it. He would never submit to such manipulation. And it was strange to entertain the thought that, in this respect at least, he might be stronger than his brother. 'So,' he continued. 'You and Nina had agreed to marry, but you kept your plans secret. What happened to change that?'

'Not what,' Kai said, 'but *who*.' His face clouded. 'Ciprian. My cousin Ciprian.' Kai paused to collect his words. 'When I was twenty, he was thirty-one. Old enough to be married twice already.' He paused. 'I should clarify. He was not widowed, nor did he divorce. He had simply claimed a second wife in addition to the first. But it seemed two wives were not enough for him.'

'A harem?' Jared said, his nose wrinkling with distaste.

'Something like that,' Kai said. 'He kept them in separate palaces, with separate courts. And he moved from one to the other, how and when he pleased. Ciprian was Prince of Baltiska. Nobody dared to question him.' Jared began to have an ominous sense of where Kai's story was heading. 'As you know,' Kai continued, 'he and I were cousins but, for a time, we became as close as brothers. We had some similar interests – hunting, for instance. And, though it pains me to admit this now, I looked up to him.'

'You looked up to him? How is that even possible?'

'I was an only child and my own father was considerably older than me. I saw very little of him growing up, and then he died. In a short space of time, Ciprian became the perfect blend of father and brother to me.'

Jared was starting to get a sense of how complex Ciprian was.

'And then everything changed,' Kai said. 'Because Ciprian saw Nina, and the moment he saw her, he knew that he would take her as his third wife.'

'But she had agreed to marry you!'

'Yes,' Kai said. 'But, as I told you, that was a secret. Ciprian did not know – at least, at first he did not know. When I told him, he merely smiled and told me I was young and handsome and I would soon find another girl to love and marry.'

'What about Nina? She could have turned him down, surely. Why did she not?'

Kai sighed. 'I cannot speak for her. I have often asked myself the same question.'

'But did you ask her?'

'The Prince wanted her,' Kai said, sadly. 'Just as she could not refuse him, I could not defy him without losing my own life. I made the decision to leave the court. I left the day before Nina became Prince Ciprian's third wife. I saw the palace he was building for her, connected by bridges to the other two palaces. I left and I have never been back.

'So you see,' Kai said, 'I have no influence to exert on Prince Ciprian. In all honesty, I doubt he would even grant me an audience after all this time. What I did – effectively exiling myself from the Princedom – he would have taken as a great insult against him—'

'An insult against *him*, after what he did to you?'

Kai nodded. 'Ciprian is a very different kind of man from you or I, Prince Jared. I would not pretend to understand how he thinks.'

Jared frowned, still reluctant to give up on the possibility of an alliance with Baltiska. 'Kai,' he said, 'Prince Rohan has agreed to escort me to the court of Prince Séverin. He is confident we can make another alliance there. We leave tomorrow.'

Kai smiled. 'Well, that's good. There are still four full days until Paddenburg's promised invasion. You have already secured two alliances and, by the sounds of it, are very likely to land a third.'

'I'm worried,' Jared told him. 'If Hal is right and Francesca reneges on her promise—'

'Prince Jared,' Kai lowered his voice a little. 'I would not listen too closely to Hal. He is your Bodyguard but—'

Jared frowned again. 'Hal has as keen a sense as any of us of how things may fall. And he is right when he says that the alliance with Woodlark, which we all know has been deeply strained, is now contingent on us delivering Logan Wilde to Francesca and Ines before Axel signs his death warrant.'

'Axel wouldn't do that in your absence.'

'Why not?' Jared retorted. 'He brought forward the execution of Michael Reeves without my knowing.'

'That was different,' Kai said. 'Axel is a shrewd politician. He knows just how important Logan Wilde is in the greater scheme of things. Especially within the terms of the Paddenburg Ultimatum.'

'Maybe,' Jared said, 'but I can't be sure my cousin won't just get a rush of blood to his head. For all we know, Logan could already have been hanged, drawn and quartered. And even if he hasn't, I'm not convinced that we can prevent his allies in Paddenburg from "repatriating" him before we hand him over to Francesca.'

Kai let out a sigh. 'Then, at worst, the alliance with Woodlark fails. But we return to court with alliances agreed with Rednow and Larsson. Isn't that sufficient?'

'You can answer that question as well as I can. We know they are two of the smaller territories, and that Rednow's strength lies far more in trade than in war. I suppose the army of Larsson is a somewhat better proposition to deter Paddenburg ...' Jared paused, thinking. 'But if we don't have Woodlark, the one we really need is Baltiska.'

Kai's brows knitted together. 'What are you asking me, Prince Jared?'

'Tomorrow, when I head out to Larsson with Rohan, I'm going to take Hal with me,' Jared told him. 'So I'm asking you to take Bram and go to Baltiska and see if, even after all this time, you can talk to Prince Ciprian and persuade him. Put the offer of an alliance between the river territories before him. Surely his own self-interest will see how it strengthens his border position with Schloss?'

'I told you, Prince Jared, I doubt that he'll even agree to see me.'

'Then talk to Nina,' Jared said. 'Perhaps she can exert influence on her husband?'

Kai's eyes closed.

'I understand that this will be difficult for you,' Jared said. 'And if I could identify another way to get to Ciprian, I'd pursue it. But there is no other way.' He paused. 'I know what I'm asking, Kai. I need you to do everything you can to secure that alliance.'

Kai's features were veiled. 'Are you *asking* me to return to Baltiska to talk to Nina, or are you *ordering* me to do so?'

Jared met the Huntsman's gaze. 'I think you know the answer.'

TWENTY-TWO

THE PALACE GARDENS, ARCHENFIELD

Koel felt the Dungeons calling to her once more. What was their strange allure? Was it the thrill of the darkness and the utterly unembellished surroundings there exerting some kind of primitive hold over her? Or was it the darkness personified in Logan Wilde? How strange it was to think that, through these nocturnal meetings, she had found her own private counsellor ... in Archenfield's number-one enemy of state. She thought of him now, of the way he could intuit her thoughts and feelings, and was taken aback once more at the deep sense of connection she felt to him.

Koel knew she really ought to return home to Blaxland Manor. After all the events of the day, what she needed most was rest, not another close encounter with the provocative assassin. She hesitated. What should she do? If only fate would decide this for her.

Fate did indeed grant her wish but not in the way she had wanted or foreseen: Koel suddenly felt a pair of hands grab her roughly from behind and another wedge a ball of cloth in her mouth. She tried lifting her hands to remove it but realised, with cold fear, that her attackers already had her arms held tight behind her back. Now she was deprived of vision as a tight hood was drawn down over her head.

Panic pulsing through her, she struggled violently, trying to break free, but there were at least two men holding her and they were clearly stronger than she – already her wrist was burning at the pressure of one of her attackers' clutches. Only her legs were unsecured and, before the opportunity was lost to her, she launched a hard kick with her right leg. She was gratified both by the feel of solid contact with the fleshy part of another body and the accompanying pained cry. Bullseye!

But there was no time to savour this small victory. The ground was taken from underneath her and she found her legs too were held tight. She tried to kick out again but her attackers had somehow rallied. Perhaps there was a third or fourth of them, she thought, fearfully. The gag was wedged deeply into her mouth, and with the further pressure applied by the tight hood, she had no opportunity to ask their identity or plead the case for mercy.

Now she felt a pressure around one of her ankles and realised that a buckle was being fastened tightly around it. Her other ankle was clamped just as tightly shut. At last the hands were removed from her legs. She tried to move them, of course, but it was of no great surprise to her that she had little room for movement now. She knew what was coming next and, what was worse, she was powerless to do anything about it. Sure enough, each of her wrists was held down as a buckle was secured around them. Only then did her attackers let go of her.

Other than the cry when she had lashed out with her foot, none of them had said a single thing. They were being exceedingly careful, she realised, so that she would have no clue as to who they were.

Why had they fastened her like this? And what had they fastened her *to*? In the next few moments, she was granted some kind of answer as she heard the whinny of a horse and then felt a sickening lurch of movement. Clearly, whatever structure they had bound her to was also attached to a horse.

The horse gathered momentum and she was drawn along in its wake, bouncing up and down over the rough ground. Some instinct deep within told her that if she allowed her body to relax – no mean feat under these circumstances – it would be less painful for her. She did her best and tried to retain mental focus. She needed to ready herself to deal with her captors; indeed, to broker some kind of deal with them. Were they invaders from Paddenburg? Had they come early then? Had her 'counsellor' Logan Wilde summoned them through his network of spies? How had she allowed herself to fall prey to him? This rankled most of all. She was so much *smarter* than this!

After a time, in spite of her best efforts, it grew harder to focus on anything but the pain she was enduring and what paltry measures she might take to minimise it. How far were they going? Gradually, however, the ground grew softer but her momentary relief at this was undercut when she realised they must now be in the forest. Did they plan to take her all the way across the border like this? But she'd be saved by the border guards, wouldn't she? Unless the invasion was already under way ...

Her senses were restricted, her hearing muffled by the close-fitting hood. She strained to hear the sound of hooves, trying to assess how many horses were in this party. She knew that there had been at least two attackers, probably three.

Potentially more. Still, she was fairly sure she could hear only one set of hooves thumping on the forest floor.

She felt consciousness beginning to ebb away from her. No, she instructed herself. No, you have to keep awake and alert! This isn't an end in itself. Whoever has done this to you – and for whatever reason – you have to be ready to confront them and negotiate your way to freedom.

But it was getting harder and harder not to just slip away ... Was it her imagination or were they slowing down? No, they definitely were slowing! There was one final series of bounces over uneven ground, until at last there was no more movement and she lay there, summoning what strength she could muster for the next, undoubtedly decisive, part of her ordeal.

She heard the muted sound of someone jumping down and landing on the ground, then moving towards her. She knew that it was likely only a matter of moments before she would know the face of her attacker. Sure enough, she felt a presence beside her and, at last, the hood was lifted away from her head.

She opened her eyes and saw, at first, only darkness. The smell of pine trees, strangely pungent, told her that they were still in the heart of the forest. They seemed to be in a clearing. Then a face came into her range of vision. At first she thought she was hallucinating; then she realised that it made complete sense.

'Good evening, sister dearest,' Axel said. 'How did you enjoy your ride?'

Koel stared weakly up at him. She was flushed with a certain relief, but at the same time furious that her captor and torturer had turned out to be her own brother.

'Yes, it's me,' Axel said with a nod. 'I wonder, though – who did you think it might be?'

Koel glared at her brother, still unable to speak or scream due to the gag. She moved her eyes from him downwards, seeing that she was fastened to a basic frame of wooden struts and canvas, which in turn had been attached by chains to the saddle of Axel's horse. No wonder she had felt every nuance of the ground beneath her. She glanced down the length of her body, seeing the tight buckles at her wrists and ankles. Instinctively, she wriggled her legs and arms, knowing that it was hopeless but unable to allow herself to remain trapped like this any longer.

'Stay still,' Axel instructed her. He leaned over her, his face just above hers so that she had no choice but to inhale his breath. 'First of all, I'm going to take the gag away. Then, if you're quiet, I'll unfasten you from these straps. Nod if you understand.'

She had no choice but to nod. Upholding his side of the bargain, Axel removed the gag. She was grateful to sense feeling and movement return to her lips.

'Why did you do this?' she asked.

'Oh, I think you can probably guess,' he told her. 'But in any case, once I've released you, you and I are going to have a somewhat overdue brother–sister chat.' As he moved to unfasten the straps at her ankles, he raised a finger in a warning gesture. 'Don't lash out again with your legs. I've had to send Elliot home with a block of ice to nurse the wound you inflicted earlier upon his manhood.'

She lay there on the uncomfortable frame, gazing up at the star-filled sky with a certain satisfaction. No one could say that Koel Blaxland had gone down without a fight.

'What is this contraption, anyhow?' she asked as he moved up to free her wrists.

'Stretcher,' he said. 'For removing the war-wounded from the battlefield. I'd have thought that would be patently obvious but then, lest we forget, you have no experience of battle, do you?' He shrugged. 'It's good to know the equipment's in good working order. We'll have need of it soon enough.'

She propped herself up on her elbows, already aware of how much her body was going to ache the next morning. 'So you think war *is* coming again to Archenfield?'

'Almost certainly,' Axel said matter-of-factly. 'Which is why this is no time for playing childish games.' He glanced around, checking – it seemed – for prying ears and eyes. Evidently satisfied that they were alone, he sat down, cross-legged, on the ground beside her.

It was strange, Koel mused. She could not remember the last time they had sat like this.

'What games do you think I have been playing?' she asked.

'You know very well,' he said. 'You have been seen, sister. On your nocturnal trips to the Dungeons and your daylight flights to the Falconer's Mews.' He raised an eyebrow and paused, as if readying himself for her objections.

She decided, under the circumstances, that it was best to let him continue.

'Somehow you got wind that I'm planning on putting a certain vote before the Twelve. And you decided to throw in your lot with the enemy.' He paused again, his eyes scanning her face. 'You're unusually quiet,' he said. 'Aren't you going to protest that I've got this all wrong?'

She shook her head sharply. 'There's no point,' she said. 'You're right in all but one respect. I *was* angry at you the other night when you railed at me about how I had no power and how you had no need for my help. And I *did* overhear you conspiring with your cronies about this vote.' Her eyes widened. 'You left the door to the chamber open, Axel. You made it exceptionally easy for me and Asta to overhear every traitorous word you said.'

183

Axel was frowning. 'Asta heard us too?'

Koel nodded. 'She was standing in the corridor, and I was in the gallery. Honestly, what were you thinking?'

She could see he was vexed. 'I closed the door myself—'

'Well,' Koel cut in, 'somehow it opened up again. Or *someone* opened it. Surely you must have noticed, or were you too distracted by your own rhetoric?' She could judge how perturbed he was by the fact that he didn't rise to this barb.

'I was sitting with my back to the door ...' His eyes narrowed. 'That's why I didn't notice. But one of the others *must* have. Why didn't they say anything?'

Koel drew her arms around her knees. Ouch – it hurt! 'Either one of your comrades has issues about being shut in a confined space, or he wanted to allow for the possibility of you being overheard. I wonder which of them is working to undermine you?'

Axel bit his lip. 'No need for you to wonder,' he said. 'Be assured I will deal with this in my own way.'

'Fair enough.' She shrugged. 'But it shows you, does it not, that you really can't trust anyone around here any more ...'

Axel smiled darkly. 'If you start off from a position of trusting no one,' he observed, 'then you're less likely to be disappointed later.' He returned his full attention on her. 'Koel, I know you're frustrated at not having a position in court and I know you get angry because you don't think I have any time for you and your ideas. But when you threw in your lot with Asta Peck and Nova Chastain and started plotting against me, you crossed a line.'

It was her turn to smile. 'It might look that way, mightn't it?' She looked closely at her brother before she said her next words: 'Because that's *exactly* the way I wanted it to look. In reality, I didn't cross any line at all. I'm working *for* you, brother – I have been all along. What better way to bring down

184

the campaign against you then putting myself at the very heart of it?'

Axel's eyes narrowed once again. 'Let me get this straight. You're busy plotting with Asta, Nova and our deranged Aunt Elin to rally support for Jared, but in fact you're really working to strengthen support for me?'

Koel nodded. 'That's about the size of it. And actually it was surprisingly easy. You see it's not hard convincing people that I think you are a monster.' She smiled again. 'Oh, it's all right, brother. You can save the big "thank you" for when you win the vote and scoop the main prize.'

There was a short silence, then: 'You had better be telling the truth,' Axel said. 'Because, if you're not, next time I won't stop at a little ride around the grounds.'

She knew he was deadly serious. 'I'll prove my worth to you,' she said. 'Just give me a few more days.' Her eyes zeroed in on his. 'Trust me.'

He met her gaze, his eyes boring into hers. Then he shook his head. 'I told you before – I have no truck with trust.' He rose to his feet and brushed the earth from his trouser legs. 'And now I need to get the horse and stretcher back to the stables.'

She stood unsteadily. 'You could at least give me a ride back.'

He shook his head. 'That would be an obvious mistake. After what you've told me you're up to, it would not do for us to be seen out riding together.'

Once more, Koel realised her brother had out-manoeuvred her – even in something so petty as the journey home. As she watched him meander over to his waiting horse, scooping up the cloth gag on his way and tucking it into his pocket, Koel felt stabs of pain and aching spreading through her body as she began what she sensed would be a slow and painful walk back to Blaxland Manor.

THREE DAYS UNTIL
INVASION . . .

TWENTY-THREE

PALACE OF ARCHENFIELD

Lucas was accustomed to riding alone at this time of day. Although he was rarely lonely, it was an unexpected pleasure to have company. He and Nova barely exchanged a word as they cantered into the countryside, where their horses broke into a gallop.

It had been quite some time since the two friends had taken their horses out together, and Lucas was swiftly reminded what an expert horsewoman Nova was. As they galloped side by side over rain-sodden fields, their riding boots and clothes becoming spattered in mud, Nova seemed to have fully given herself over to the exhilaration of movement: her cheeks were flushed and her long, untamed hair flew out behind her like a dark pennant. Lucas smiled in admiration, recognition and also relief: to ride with such vigour, the Falconer must clearly be well on her way to making a complete recovery from her near-fatal fall. Glancing above them, Lucas glimpsed Pampero keeping pace a short distance above them. It always fascinated Lucas to witness the close connection between the

Falconer and her birds. On either side of the horses, two of the Prince's hounds kept pace with the riders.

As they reached a clearing, Nova turned her exuberant face towards him. Lucas eased up his horse's pace and Nova did the same with her own. The hounds, too, gratefully slowed as, above them, Pampero turned watchful circles in the crisp morning air.

'I really needed that,' Nova exclaimed.

'So did I,' Lucas agreed. 'This threat of invasion has rattled me more than I care to admit. I feel keenly these short winter days ebbing away, each one bringing us closer to the edge of the abyss.' He dismounted and went over to offer her assistance.

'The Paddenburg Ultimatum has deeply unsettled all of the Twelve,' Nova answered, waving away his hand. 'I don't mean to be rude,' she said as she jumped to the ground. 'I just need to prove to myself that I can do these things on my own again.'

'I understand,' Lucas assured her. 'It's wonderful to see you embracing life again.' He lowered his voice. 'Not only in the aftermath of your fall, but following the death of Prince Anders, to whom you were so close.' He noticed her face tighten at these words.

'We were *all* close to the Prince,' she said pointedly. Seeing him blush red, she softened her tone. 'I'm sorry, Lucas. I didn't mean to snap. I suppose I am still adjusting to the fact that the secret I kept buried so deep, and for so long, is now out in the open.'

'I'm sure this is uncomfortable for you,' he said. 'But at least now you can mourn your deep loss openly and not bear the burden alone.' He knew it would have been more politic to end it there, but he couldn't stop the words from pouring out. 'I know what it is like to carry the burden of a secret friendship.'

In response, the Falconer spoke just one word. 'Silva?'

Lucas nodded. It was a relief to feel his own weighty secret lift from his shoulders, but he was grateful for the distraction as they both heard a rustle of leaves in a nearby tree.

Nova turned, her sharp eyes focusing on one of the branches, where her falcon now perched, alert. 'I think Pampero has prey in her sights,' she said.

Lucas nodded, glad of the change of subject. 'Shall we send the hounds into the copse to flush it out for her?'

Nova strode over to the nearby copse with the hounds trotting beside her. As he watched, Lucas mused that Nova was as much of a huntress as her birds. Now that she had prey in her sights, she moved with new energy and purpose.

By the time he arrived at her side, the dogs had flushed a rabbit out from the undergrowth and were waiting and watching with Nova as Pampero went in for the kill. Lucas stared with dark fascination as the bird swooped down to claim the trapped rabbit. As the falcon's merciless claws and beak made contact, he saw the hounds straining to re-enter the fray.

'No,' Nova told them. 'You have played your part.'

The rabbit was not yet dead but the resignation in its eyes was pitifully plain to see. As the Falconer moved across to where the stunned animal lay, Pampero mercilessly began tearing through fur towards the still-beating heart. 'And now *you* must wait a moment,' Nova instructed her bird, reaching out with her gloved hand.

Lucas was surprised to see Pampero accept this interference, but he understood that this was all part of the rapport between the Falconer and her falcon. Nova took the stunned rabbit and in a quick, single movement twisted its neck. Its torture was ended. Only then did Nova allow Pampero to claim her prize.

The Falconer stepped back to join Lucas.

'There are parts of your job I think I'd struggle with,' he told her.

Nova shrugged. 'I tend to think that the brutality of nature serves as a useful reminder to us – our own impulses are not so far removed from those of the hounds or Pampero.' Her eyes met his. 'Really, is what we have just witnessed any more brutal than the threat from Paddenburg, or the conspiracy in our own court being launched against Prince Jared?'

Lucas felt a stab of fear and adrenaline. 'Conspiracy? What are you talking about?'

Nova's dark eyes met his. 'Lucas, I have a confession to make. I did not just ask to join you on your ride this morning on a whim. I wanted to get you away from the palace to talk to you in confidence about a scheme of Axel's.'

'Axel?' Lucas said. 'Are you telling me Axel is plotting against Prince Jared?'

Nova nodded. 'It is as true as it is abhorrent,' she said. As she folded her arms, he saw the scarlet smear of rabbit's blood on her gauntlet. 'But it is not too late to fight it.'

Lucas's eyes darted over to where Pampero was enthusiastically extracting the rabbit's vital organs. The Groom turned back to the Falconer. 'Tell me everything you know,' he said.

THE KITCHENS, PALACE OF ARCHENFIELD

Asta stared at the pig's head, then the bulbous mass of brains nestling beside it in the straw interior of the wide wooden crate.

'Mind yourself, Poet!' barked a voice. 'Another box of delights coming through!'

Asta stepped back as the kitchen boy deposited a fresh crate – groaning with what looked and smelled very much like a wet, sleeping dog – beside the one containing assorted pig parts.

'What's in *that* one?' Asta asked, covering her nose. 'It reeks!'

'Tripe!' Vera announced, sweeping into the kitchens grandly and, hands on hips, processing past the nine boxes of heads, entrails and organs, which had been laid out for her inspection along the full length of the kitchen table.

'What do you intend to make with all this?' Asta enquired.

Vera shrugged, reaching out to have a poke around the brains. 'I haven't decided yet. I'm experimenting with offal. If we're heading towards another war, I intend to make the most of everything in my larder. Waste not, want not!'

'Do you think for certain that war *will* come?' Asta asked, leaning back against the wooden bench.

Vera shrugged, her attention now firmly on the tripe. She had plunged her hands into one of the fragrant crates and was exploring its contents as if it were a favourite fur coat.

Asta was assailed by a fresh waft of damp dog. It made her think of Hedd, the Prince's beloved wolfhound. Though, to be fair, Hedd never smelled *that* bad, even after a long walk in the rain and mud.

'Axel seems to think the invasion is inevitable,' Vera said. 'But you know as much as I do. You were at the Council meeting yesterday yourself. And now you're here.' She pressed down on the surface of the brains again. 'You just keep popping up all over the place, don't you?'

Feeling queasy, Asta turned away from the boxes of offal. Watching her uncle dissect a human body was preferable to this – at least then she had known that it wasn't heading for her supper plate.

'Since you're here,' Vera said, a smile forming on her usually sullen features, 'why don't you make yourself useful?'

'I'm not very practised in cooking,' Asta said.

'No one's asking you to whip up a salmon soufflé!' Vera cried, returning with a lit taper, which she thrust into Asta's hands. 'You take this and get to work burning the hairs off that pig's snout.'

Asta stared at her in disbelief.

'Quickly now,' Vera barked. 'Queen Elin won't thank you if she finds bristly nostril hairs floating in her soup!'

Asta brought the lit end of the taper to the pig's gaping nostrils and tried to think of the crystal-clear waters of the fjord.

'That's more like it,' Vera observed, leaning in a little too close. 'I think we might just have found a job entirely appropriate to your talents!'

Asta didn't like the Cook's tone: clearly Vera was not thrilled that she had been given a position on the Twelve. Asta told herself that she could not afford to be derailed by Vera's slights – she hadn't come to the kitchens that morning to make a friend; she had come to win over a key ally to Prince Jared's side.

'How's that?' she asked Vera. Before she realised what she was doing, she found herself presenting the pig's head to the Cook to show off her work.

'What do you want? A medal, or a chest to pin it on?' Vera snorted, handing her another taper. 'Here you are – finish off his other porthole, if you please!'

Wrinkling her nose, Asta applied the taper to the pig's other nostril. 'Prince Jared seemed confident that he could forestall the invasion by securing those alliances,' she said.

'Good luck to him!' Vera said. Her tone was hard to read.

'It's very brave of him,' Asta said. 'Don't you think?' She

had completed her work on the second nostril and now stepped aside, as if to announce that she was not available for further kitchen tasks.

'He is the Prince,' Vera said, dropping the mass of tripe on to a large wooden board and beginning to slice through it. 'It's his job to secure alliances, just as it is mine to make lunch and yours to ... well, do whatever it is you're supposed to do, dear.'

Undeterred by Vera's latest barb, Asta stepped closer. 'So you support the fact that Prince Jared decided to go on this mission himself?'

Vera continued to chop. 'I don't feel strongly one way or the other,' she said. 'As long as someone brings in the alliances, I'll be happy.'

Asta nodded, thinking about what Nova had said to her and Koel the day before – that what mattered most to Vera was the security of the Princedom.

'I think Prince Jared has behaved with great maturity and dignity since the murder of his brother,' Asta said. 'Don't you agree?'

Vera glanced up from her labours, cleaver aloft. 'Are you president of the Prince's fan club, in addition to your other arduous responsibilities?' Setting down her knife, she waddled over towards a vast bank of cast-iron cooking pots.

'My new role is all about communications,' Asta told Vera, thinking quickly. 'So it is important for me to know how everyone on the Twelve feels the new Prince is doing.'

'He's doing as well as we might expect from a sixteen-year-old lad thrust into such a high position,' Vera declared. She looked hard at Asta, and her eyes grew steely. 'I know what you're doing, Asta Peck – I'm no fool. If you want me as your ally, you might do me the credit of speaking plainly to me.'

Asta blushed, watching as the Cook heaved a pot on to the

fire and emptied a thick slab of drippings into it. The fat melted, sizzling and spitting in the pan. Asta stood there, wondering what she could do in order to get things back on track.

Suddenly the door opened and Lady Koel appeared – an unexpected but welcome sight. Smiling, Koel strode confidently down the length of the kitchen, past the other busy members of Vera's team, towards them.

'Well, now,' Vera said, her voice brimming with warmth. 'You *are* a welcome visitor.'

'I thought you might welcome some help,' Koel said brightly, turning from Vera and winking at Asta.

Asta nodded and Koel gave a brief, graceful nod before turning her attention back to the Cook. 'I think I'd better be on my way,' Asta said, taking the hint.

'Such a shame,' Vera said, 'but if you must, you must!' She reached out for the board of chopped tripe.

'Here, let me help you with that!' Koel said.

'Oh, no, Lady Koel, you don't want to get tripe juice on that lovely blouse of yours! What colour is that by the way? Duck-egg blue? It's the perfect foil for your eyes.'

'It's no trouble at all,' Koel said, smiling serenely as she lifted the platter. 'It was lovely to see you, Asta,' she said.

'You too, Lady Koel,' Asta called as she made for the door. 'I didn't know you were friends with *her*,' she heard Vera hiss.

'Oh, yes,' Koel's reply floated over to her. 'But that's a story for another time, Vera. There's something else I really need to talk to you about.'

Asta pushed through the door, grateful for the blast of fresh air. She shook her head in admiration. Where Asta had failed, she had no doubt whatsoever that Koel would succeed. Now that they were working together, Axel wouldn't stand a chance.

*

THE CAPTAIN OF THE GUARD'S OFFICE, PALACE OF ARCHENFIELD

Axel's eyes fell on the glass that rested in his hand. He swirled it about, creating a miniature maelstrom in the honey-coloured liquid it contained. Then he steadied his hand and met the Beekeeper's steely gaze.

She was perched on his desk, a little too close for comfort. Her piercing eyes met his once more. 'I came to see you because I've heard about this daring vote, this unprecedented campaign of yours—'

Her words sent him reeling. 'You know—? *How* do you know?'

'Don't look so anxious,' Emelie said. 'I'm not planning to tell anyone else about it. Not for the time being. I just wanted to come to lend you my—' She cut herself short. 'To tell you how impressed I was.' She laid a hand on his chest. 'Don't take this the wrong way, darling, but I honestly didn't think you had it in you.'

Axel frowned. 'Emelie, I need you to tell me how you know about this. For reasons I'm sure you understand, the very few who do know are sworn to secrecy.'

Emelie nodded. She lifted her hand and stroked the front of his shirt, as if she was smoothing out a crease, brushing away a speck of dust. 'Now, don't get flustered—'

'I'm *not* flustered,' he said, reaching for her hand and lifting it away. 'I'd just like you to answer my question.'

Emelie made a cradle of her hands and glanced down at them. 'Jonas told me.'

'Of course, it *would* be bloody Jonas!'

'Now, don't be cross with him, Axel. He didn't mean to spill the beans. I think he thought he was doing you a favour.' She looked up at Axel again, eyes wide. 'By trying to recruit me to your team, you see?'

Axel sighed, shook his head and sat back down in his chair. Suddenly, the very air in his office felt suffocating.

Emelie seemed to be contemplating taking a seat beside him. Instead, she moved around and perched on the edge of the desk again, her leg stretching out the fabric of her tight skirt to brush against Axel's outer thigh.

'I feel bad,' she said.

'Give it a rest!' Axel said, immediately irritated at his own irritation.

She drew back. 'Leave it to me to completely ruin the mood, like rain at a summer picnic.' She leaned towards him again, one finger lightly tracing the scar on his brow. 'We never were very good for each other, were we?'

Axel shrugged. The last thing he cared to dwell upon at this juncture was how and why his budding relationship with the Beekeeper had taken a wrong turn.

'We're both solitary bees, you and I, Axel. We're not like the others. We might pretend to be part of the colony – to play the game – but we each know that, in truth, we can best accomplish what we must accomplish on our own. I suppose when you think of it, we are just too similar. Yes, I think that's why things didn't work out as they might have.' She smiled. 'You need a little playmate! It's only fair. Even Prince Jared has the jaunty Asta.'

He shook his head.

'But I didn't come here to gossip about the new Poet,' she said, her tone becoming more circumspect.

'All right,' he said, leaning back, knowing there was no way out of this. 'Tell me, what did you come here for?'

'Firstly to tell you that I am genuinely impressed that you have decided to make this move. As I said before—'

'You didn't think I had it in me.' Axel had decided he'd rather speak the words himself than hear them from her again.

'Sorry, that was wantonly brutal of me.'

'Sweetheart, I've grown accustomed to your sting.'

Emelie laughed. 'Touché, *sweetheart*. The second reason I came is to ask whether this manoeuvre is indeed your own idea, or if your father is operating your strings? This game has Lord Viggo written all over it.' She rose to her feet. 'I actually *do* care about you, Axel. And, you see, I care about Archenfield, too. So if you are asking for my vote – *when* you come asking for my vote – you need to bring me two answers. Firstly, that you are acting on your own instincts and driving ambition and not merely that of your slavering father; and, secondly, that you really feel that the Princedom will be better served by having your derrière on the throne than Jared Wynyard's.' She smiled. 'Not that young Jared *has* much of a derrière. Whereas yours, my sweet, is – as I fondly remember – as plump and firm as an August peach.'

TWENTY-FOUR

THE COUNCIL CHAMBER, PALACE OF ARCHENFIELD

'Word has come from the southern border.' Axel's resonant voice filled the Council Chamber. 'Paddenburg has already started to amass a worryingly large number of troops just shy of the border.' He paused, allowing this news to settle with his fellows. 'They are holding true to their threat of invasion.'

Glancing at the faces of her colleagues at the Prince's Table, Asta saw worry and bitterness etched upon each and every one. They had done nothing to incite this attack from Paddenburg. Up on the royal dais, Queen Elin and Prince Edvin looked equally sombre. Until now, the actions of the aggressor had been the subject of speculation; now no one there could deny that war *was* coming. She closed her eyes, just for a moment. There were many things in which Asta lacked experience; war, regrettably, was not one of them.

'Camps have already been set up at Inderwick and Grenofen,' Axel resumed, 'with reserve troops based at Dalhoen.

Armour and weaponry have been dispatched to Dalhoen and will be distributed to the two southern camps there.'

Although his tone was grave, Axel still sounded calm, confident and in charge. Asta was keenly aware that since the arrival of the Paddenburg Ultimatum, Axel had asserted that there was only one logical conclusion. Now he had been vindicated. And clearly he was on top of the preparations.

"Troops are being recalled from the northern fortress settlements of Teragon and Miryfyd, where they have been stationed since the war with Eronesia.' Asta felt a renewed chill as she heard Axel speak the name of her home settlement, Teragon, in the same breath as its nemesis, Eronesia. She fought to control the feelings of panic that were threatening to seize hold of her. She reminded herself of what Axel had said before – that Paddenburg was building up its forces in the *south*. In the coming conflict, Teragon was as far away from the line of fire as was conceivable. Still, she could not dispel her fear. Teragon had borne the brunt of the war with Eronesia; the settlement had been all but devastated in the conflict. It had been little more than a miracle that she and her parents had made it through alive. So many others had not been so fortunate. Now, even if Teragon did not face the same level of danger, those living in the many southern settlements would be bracing themselves for equal devastation. And Teragon and its close neighbour Miryfyd would not luxuriate in their northerly positions for long. If Paddenburg succeeded in taking the southern settlements, it was only a matter of time before the invaders began the journey north.

Axel's next words only confirmed Asta's darkest fears. 'Even with the redeployment of troops from the north to the south, we must face facts. The forces of Archenfield are small compared with the military might of Paddenburg.'

He paused to take a drink of water.

As he did so, Father Simeon took the opportunity to pose a question. 'Can you tell us,' he enquired, 'about the mood in the southern settlements?'

Axel nodded. 'I'm afraid it's an all too familiar picture. Fear and panic have taken hold.' He shrugged. 'There was no way of keeping either the fact of the Paddenburg Ultimatum or the massing of enemy troops a secret from the people. The fact is, they have nowhere to run. To the south is Paddenburg. Since the breaking of our alliance with Woodlark, they will no longer be granted sanctuary in the east—'

'Unless,' Emelie interjected, 'Prince Jared has been successful in rebuilding that alliance.'

Axel did not turn to meet Emelie's face, but kept his eyes on Father Simeon. His lack of response to the Beekeeper's interruption spoke volumes.

Asta felt a heated flush of anger. How did Axel know that Prince Jared had not concluded a fresh alliance with Queen Francesca? She wanted to add her voice to Emelie's, but Axel was already in full flow once more. 'In the north, we are bordered by our old enemies, Eronesia and Schloss. Tanaka, on our western border, would be a close refuge but remains a neutral territory. They would never open their borders up to refugees from Archenfield, out of fear of repercussions from Paddenburg.' He lifted his eyes from Father Simeon and addressed the whole of the gathering. 'Every man, woman and – dare I say it – child who dwells in one of the southern settlements has no choice but to fight.' Asta felt a fresh heat, compounded by nausea and a pounding in her head. Axel continued, mercilessly. 'Recruitment is being stepped up in each of the settlements—'

She could take no more of this. She had to say something. Pushing back her chair with a scrape, Asta rose to her feet.

'You look a little sickly,' Axel observed. 'Do you need to take some air?'

She shook her head. 'I have something to say.'

Axel smiled softly at her. 'I know you are fairly new to these proceedings, Asta. But if you wish to make a contribution, you have only to raise your hand.' Extending his own hand, he gave her the floor.

'I do feel sick,' she told him and the others. 'I think you all know that I come from Teragon. That, until six months ago, I lived there, though in truth there has not been much life to live there, since the war came.' She felt a strange wave of energy coursing through her and did her best to steady herself. 'I mean no disrespect to my fellows, but how many of you have been to Teragon since the conclusion of the war?' She cast her eyes around the chamber, watching as face upon face dropped to the surface of the Prince's Table. 'How many of you have visited Miryfyd?' she continued. Her voice was husky. She could feel tears welling but she did everything in her power to swallow them down. This was too important. 'Because if you had been to see those two northern settlements – seen what is left of them – you would see the legacy of death and destruction. You sent troops to the northern fortresses and yes, perhaps, they prevented the enemy from crossing the borders again—'

'There's no perhaps about it,' Axel countered her, displaying for the first time a flash of anger. 'Our troops have protected those settlements from further devastation.'

Now Asta felt hot tears coursing down her cheeks. 'There is nothing more to devastate,' she said. 'And now you are taking those troops away! Are you really serious when you say that children should be taught to bear arms?'

Before Axel could answer her, Vera spoke up. Her voice was not unkind. 'Asta, I'm sure I speak for all of us when I say how much we sympathise with what you and your family and your neighbours endured. You have spoken with great passion and eloquence about that. Your hurt is palpable, we see that. But I don't know what you are arguing for or against here. We are discussing the threat from the south now, not the north. Surely there is no question that we should move troops down towards the southern settlements, in the hope that we can prevent the terrible things which happened to you and your family happening to those who live in Vollerim and Grenofen and Inderwick and the rest?'

Asta nodded. 'You're right,' she said, drawing herself together. She turned towards Axel. 'I apologise for my outburst. It was ... inappropriate.' She sat back down. Nova reached across and squeezed her hand.

Axel shook his head. 'There is no need to apologise, Asta,' he said smoothly. 'We have always depended on our Poets to speak with eloquence. You have honoured that tradition. It is clear to me – to all of us, I am sure – that we have someone sitting at the Prince's Table who understands the settlements. This will be of great value to us.' He glanced from Asta across the table to Elias. 'Elias, I think we owe you a considerable debt in bringing your spirited niece into our ranks.'

Elias glanced up at Axel but did not respond.

'And now,' Axel continued, 'Elias, perhaps you could update us on your own preparations for engagement?'

Asta saw her uncle's face grow purposeful. 'The main field hospital will be stationed at Kirana,' he informed his fellows. 'This location served Archenfield well during the last war. Vital supplies have already been dispatched ... '

Uncle Elias continued, in his soft voice, to outline his plans. Asta tuned out his report. Her thoughts were far away – with her parents on the northern border. Her head was crowded with dark images of the previous conflict: the

sounds of her friends and neighbours fighting – and failing –
to cling on to life; limbs lying like broken toys on the ground;
newly orphaned children stumbling around as if they were in
some strange game of hide-and-seek. She thought of a particular child – a young boy whom her mother had found,
playing happily enough in the rubble. She had brought him to
their own barely standing home and shared what food they
had with him. Asta remembered watching as her mother had
cleaned the boy's mud-and-blood-streaked face and rocked
him gently to sleep. She remembered later that night waking
to his screams as he realised that this was neither a game nor
a bad dream. There could be no pleasant waking from the
horror of his young life. That was the reality of war in the settlements.

'Then we are resolved,' she heard Axel say. 'And this
meeting is concluded.' He sounded as sure and confident as
ever.

Asta watched as the others began rising to their feet. Nova
brushed her hand once more.

'I need to talk to my uncle,' Asta told her.

Nova went on her way. As she did so, Asta noticed Jonas
fall into step with the Falconer. So the Woodsman had
decided that now was as good a time as any to recruit Nova to
Axel's conspiracy? Asta drew comfort from the fact they had
been one step ahead of the rival faction. She watched as Nova
nodded pleasantly at Jonas, perhaps agreeing to a more
private rendezvous. She turned her attention away, scanning
the crowd for Uncle Elias. He was almost level with her, on
his way out of the chamber, embroiled in discussion with
Father Simeon.

'Uncle Elias,' she said, putting her hand on his arm.

He paused and turned towards her. There was something of
a resemblance between him and Asta's father, but Elias's face

was colder, hardened perhaps by the politics of court – politics she was only just beginning to grasp the extent of.

'You spoke very movingly, Asta. I think we all needed to hear that perspective.' It was Father Simeon who addressed her. 'You must be very proud of your niece, Elias.'

Asta shook her head. 'I don't think he is at all proud of me,' she said sadly. 'I suspect he rather regrets his decision to transport me here into the heart of court.'

Elias looked coldly at her, saying nothing, then turned towards the Priest. 'If you will excuse me, I have further preparations to expedite.' Without glancing back at Asta, he continued on his way out into the corridor.

Father Simeon gave her a sympathetic look. 'I have a good idea of what you are thinking, Asta. But, trust me, he cares about you more than you could ever know.'

TWENTY-FIVE

THE ROAD TO BALTISKA

Kai and Bram had spent the better part of the morning trav-elling north-west along an old trade route. The further they rode, the more dramatic the landscape became: columns of silver rock rose out of the ground, and deep crevices and ver-tiginous cliff-side trails opened up towards the snow-capped mountaintops to the far north.

As they rode through a wide, verdant valley that was flanked by rocky outcrops, Kai felt the butterflies fluttering beneath his taut abdomen. Not far now; not far until he made his ascent once more – not long until he gazed into her eyes.

They rode on into the low-lying settlements of Baltiska, where the landscape became more and more densely inhab-ited. The vast majority of the homes were of the most humble kind, built in the shadows cast by the vast cliffs, at the top of which stood the ornate, tripartite palace of Prince Ciprian and his three wives, with their interconnecting 'sky bridges' stretching out high over the valley floor.

'That is some citadel!' Bram exclaimed.

Kai nodded. Even from this far down, he could glimpse the

different coloured banners adorning each of the palaces. His eyes were drawn – how could they not be? – towards the scarlet banners tumbling down from the heights of Queen Nina's royal residence.

The two riders were forced to slow their pace as the road brought them to a bustling market square, crowded with stalls and people, and the tempting aromas floating from the food and drink merchants.

Kai watched Bram drink in the colour, noise and revelry of the bazaar. 'Think there's enough of interest here to keep you entertained for a few hours?' he enquired with a grin, as he dismounted from his horse.

'Oh, yes!' Bram confirmed, watching two attractive young women busily negotiating in front of a stall laden with bolts of richly coloured silks. He jumped down from his horse, his face suddenly solemn as he stood eye to eye with his companion. 'Good luck to you, up there. I hope you succeed in your mission.'

Kai strode off in the direction of the stone archway that marked the entrance to the cliff path. He reached in his pocket for coins to pay the gatekeeper. No one made it up to the palace or the sky bridges without the exchange of funds – such was Ciprian's way.

'Do you require an escort?' the gatekeeper enquired. 'For a small additional fee.' As he spoke, he kicked the boot of a young man who lay sprawled fast asleep next to a barrel. The boy shook himself awake and gazed around.

Kai shook his head. 'I know the way of old,' he said, surprised that the gatekeeper had not recognised him.

Of course, he had been a lot younger the last time he had planted his boots on these stone steps.

As he climbed up the stairway, he found he had to stop and catch his breath. 'What's this, Kai Jagger?' he asked himself.

'Getting old?' Glancing down, he saw the splatters of dried mud on his riding boots. Lifting his hand to his face, he realised that his skin was caked in dust from the morning's journey. And he must smell a treat too. He was in no fit state to greet Queen Nina – she would think him a ruffian. Well, there was always the option of a quick trip to the palace hammam. He continued on his way.

When he finally reached the summit of the stairway, feeling the exertion in every muscle of his legs, he paused to take in the vertiginous view back down the cliff. It was as if, with each step up to the summit, he had travelled back further and further into his past.

The impression was only enhanced as he emerged from the cliff stairs directly on to one of the palace's three sky bridges. Courtiers and visitors bustled in both directions across the bridge, too tangled up in gossip to stop and appreciate the rare view.

Kai stood for a moment, allowing them to pass hurriedly by. He was beginning to feel as if he had never been away.

And then he saw her. She was standing on the opposite side of the bridge. She had put up her hair. It accentuated the swan-like curve of her neck.

'Nina!' he called out to her, his voice husky with dust and his recent exertion.

She did not respond.

He lifted his hand to wave at her but, just as he did so, people surged past and cut off his view. His heart beat wildly. 'Nina!' he called again, but as the people dispersed, he saw nothing but an empty space. He circled on the spot. She had vanished into thin air.

'Kai Jagger.'

Just the sound of her voice speaking his name again after

all this time caused the hairs on the back of his neck to stand on end. He turned, and the sight of her instantly soothed him. She stood, framed in the open doorway of the palace chamber, majestic in a blue dress that emphasised not only the colour of her eyes but also how well she had kept her figure. A stray shaft of sunlight coming in at the casement played on her blonde hair. He was pleased that she still wore it long. He drank in the sight of her: her cool, commanding eyes, even more lovely than in his memory; her sharp cheekbones; her narrow lips closed but smiling in that particular way of hers, hinting at secret thoughts. The few fine lines etched in the corners of her eyes only enhanced her beauty.

'So it really is you.' She smiled. 'I thought it might be some kind of trick.'

He shook his head, feeling a weight of emotion surging through him. 'No, Nina. It is no trick.'

'How long has it been?' Still she did not move towards him.

'Too long. Much too long.'

He noticed for the first time that she had not entered the chamber alone but in the company of a maid. She turned to address her companion.

'You may leave us, Bathsheba,' she told her. 'But perhaps our guest would like some tea?' She caught Kai's eye – and he was seventeen again. 'Yes. Bring us some tea, if you would be so kind.'

The young woman made a discreet exit. Nina waited a moment, then walked towards him. As she did so, he saw that the bodice of her dress was studded with diamonds that shimmered as she made her approach. She lifted her hand and traced the side of his cheek, her thumb and forefinger brushing the soft hairs of his beard.

Her touch was electric. Kai felt as if he were coming to life again after a century of slumber.

210

'The years have been good to you,' Nina said.

He smiled, instantly at ease with her. 'I'm not so sure. When I see my reflection in the waters of the fjord, my first thought is that I'm looking into my father's face.'

Nina shook her head. 'No, Kai. You are as handsome as ever. A little beaten by the wind and the weather, but still every bit as handsome.'

'And you ...' he began. But words would not come. They were drowned out by the swell of emotion sweeping through him. He took a breath and was aware of her hand, reaching to take hold of his.

'We don't have much time,' she said. 'I'm sorry for that.'

He closed his eyes for a moment, luxuriating in her touch and the summer scent of her. 'Do you remember when it felt like we had all the time in the world?' he asked.

She did not answer, but took his hand and led him slowly towards a window seat.

Her touch was magnetic. Kai felt as if he had truly come home – more than that, as if he had never gone away. They sat side by side on the velvet cushions.

There was a knock on the door. At the sound, Nina withdrew her hand. 'Enter!'

The same young girl had returned with a tray of tea things. She placed the small pot, delicate tea-bowls and a plate of kumquats on a low table beside them. 'Will that be all?' she asked.

'Yes, thank you. You may go.' As the girl withdrew, Nina poured them each a bowl of sweetly perfumed tea.

'How is Prince Ciprian?' he found himself asking.

Nina considered the question. 'Manipulative. Angry. Easily bored.'

Kai frowned. 'I am sorry to hear that.'

'Ciprian is Ciprian,' she said. 'He has always been predictable in his changeability.' Her eyes met his. 'Kai, why are you here?'

He took a breath. 'I need an audience with the Prince.'

'What do you want from him?' Nina asked.

Kai set down the bowl of tea. 'Archenfield is under the threat of imminent invasion from Paddenburg. Prince Jared is intent upon securing alliances to strengthen not only Archenfield, but all five of the river territories.'

'You have come seeking an alliance,' Nina said, as if to herself, then her voice strengthened. 'But why did Prince Jared send you, rather than coming here himself?'

Kai nodded. 'Time is in short supply. Prince Jared and Prince Rohan of Rednow have concluded an agreement. Together, they are now en route to see Prince Séverin. I agreed to come to talk to Prince Ciprian.'

She leaned back on the seat. 'I am so sorry,' she said. 'But he won't see you, Kai. He believes that you turned your back on your Prince and your homeland all those years ago. He granted me the briefest of audiences with you, but he is adamant that he will not set eyes upon you himself. And you must leave the Princedom before the sun falls, or he will set his guards upon you.'

'Can you not exert your powers of persuasion upon him?'

Nina turned her face from his, gazing out through the window. 'In truth, my influence upon him diminishes each day. I am but one of three wives, remember.'

Kai shook his head. 'How could I ever forget?' A note of bitterness crept into his voice. 'You chose a third of the Prince over the whole of a life with me.'

'No,' Nina said, turning back towards him. 'I made no choice. The Prince chose me.' Her eyes were suddenly as sharp as flint. 'When the Prince chooses you, it is treason to say no.' She looked suddenly pensive and lowered her voice. 'The one thing I draw comfort from now is that his health is erratic. There was an incident a few months ago . . . It is just possible that he will not endure to wear his wedding robes once more.'

Ciprian's health was failing. He might not live to see another summer. This changed everything. Possibilities took flight like butterflies.

'You're smiling,' she observed.

'It is wrong, I know, but I cannot help my emotions, Nina.' He leaned forward and grasped her hands in his. 'You will be free. At last, you can leave Baltiska!'

She smiled, gazing down at their interlaced fingers. 'Is that how you imagine this ... fairy tale will unfold? That the brutal prince will die and I will suddenly be liberated after all these years in my ivory tower? That you and I will ride down to the river and on through the gates? To where? To Archenfield?'

Each thing she said was thrilling to him. 'Yes,' he said. 'Any of that. All of that.'

'None of that,' she said, drawing her fingers free. 'None of that can happen, Kai. If Ciprian dies – when he dies – my life grows more complicated, not less.'

'I don't understand.'

'There is my daughter to think of,' she explained. 'Nelufar is Ciprian's oldest surviving child and, in that respect, his first heir. But there is a boy, by the second of his wives – yes, the one everyone thought was barren. He is just sixteen – the same age, I believe, as your Prince Jared – and a year younger than my Nel. And he has his sights set most intently upon the throne – as do those who swarm around him.' She shook her head. 'So you see, I cannot leave. I must remain here to protect my precious Nel and her interests. I must stay to protect my daughter's life.'

As he heard the words, something clicked into place for Kai. 'The girl on the bridge,' he said.

'I'm sorry—?' Nina seemed confused by his words.

'I saw a beautiful girl on the bridge,' he said. 'With blonde

213

hair and blue eyes. I thought it was you. But it was your daughter – Nelufar. She is very lovely.'

'Yes,' Nina said with a smile. 'She is the most precious thing to me in all the world.' She reached out her hand and took his again. 'But know this, Kai Jagger – you are the only other one who matters to me. When the time comes, Nel will need all the allies she can muster. Though you left the Princedom many years ago, still you are cousin to the Prince and have valid claim to your father's lands.' She hesitated. 'You once asked me to go away with you. Would it be wrong of me now to ask you to stay? For the sake of me and my daughter.'

Kai held tight to her hand. Her words had opened up a door he had thought for ever closed to him. But, nonetheless, he was not free to make the choice. As much as he loved her – and he loved her with a vastness that called to mind the winter skies – his actions were circumscribed by his position. 'I'm sorry, Nina, my precious Nina,' he said. 'For now, my duties lie elsewhere.'

Nina nodded. 'Then you must go. Our time has come to an end. But I will not have you leaving here without knowing the weight of what you mean to me. In all these years, I have thought of you not only every single day, but every hour.'

Kai did not know how to respond. He had come seeking an alliance and he had utterly failed in his mission.

Yet he was leaving with something infinitely more precious.

Slipping her fingers from his, Nina rose to her feet. 'I am sorry that this has proved a wasted journey for you.'

He shook his head. 'I assure you, this was very far from a wasted journey.'

TWENTY-SIX

THE QUEEN'S LIBRARY,
PALACE OF ARCHENFIELD

'She sent for me,' Morgan told the portly guard, standing outside the door to the Queen's Library.

The guard nodded, a familiar glint in his eye. 'I'm sure she did ...'

Morgan was used to such looks, such remarks. He was tempted to reach out a muscular arm, take the guard by the throat and remind him where he stood within the hierarchy of Archenfield. Instead, he smiled a well-practised smile and waited a moment.

As the heavy oak door closed behind him, the Executioner found himself alone in the octagonal-shaped room with which he had become so familiar. The room had a very particular smell – the commingling of the thick, wooden bookcases and the multitude of leather-bound, parchment-rich volumes lining them.

Long ago, standing in that room as a mere boy, he had

wrinkled his small nose at it. Now, the very particular odour delighted him.

Was it best described as *dank*, he mused, or *fusty*? *Stale*, perhaps? No, on balance, he would have to say – *musty*. He smiled to himself. Had it not been for Elin and the care she had taken with him over the years, he would not have been able to conjure any of those words.

Still smiling, he crossed the room to what had become his favourite section of the Library. There, on a low shelf, was a collection of books gifted to Elin by a royal family from Litaria, one of the more distant territories. Morgan reached out and removed the first in the collection. The touch of its smooth leather binding was now as familiar to him as the skin on his own cheek.

Holding the book in his left hand, he reached into the gap it had left on the shelf and depressed a lever that lay hidden beyond. The entire panel of wall nudged gently open, creating another doorway for Morgan to step through. He could already smell the trademark scent of mimosa that awaited him beyond – in what he often thought of as his secret garden.

Replacing the leather-bound volume, Morgan walked through the narrow aperture into a hidden chamber. There, draped like a dryad on the velvet chaise – the fabric the perfect match for her lapis eyes – was Queen Elin.

Morgan closed the panel.

Beside the reclining queen, one of her favourite beeswax candles burned low in its glass, not only scenting her bower but sending the softest light across Elin's strikingly handsome features. Morgan could not help but stare, knowing that she would not scold him for doing so. His eyes hungrily reacquainted themselves with the noble line of her nose, the arch of her eyebrows and the strong cheekbones that imbued her face with such nobility. She gave the slightest twist of her elegant neck to meet his gaze but otherwise lay still as he moved over to her, bowing down so that he could kiss her tenderly on the lips.

She smiled. 'And after a hundred years of solitary slumber,' she said, 'the kiss from the handsome prince woke the maiden as gently as the touch of fresh mountain rain.'

He liked it when she quoted from stories they had read together. She moved her hand up towards his cheek. 'You grow more handsome every day,' she said.

He moved to a chair opposite as she sat up – sheaths of soft tulle floating like the soft wings of butterflies.

'My darling Morgan, there are things we need to discuss. Much is changing within the court at this time.'

Morgan felt a tightness in his chest. Was she about to utter the words that he so dreaded; that they could not continue with these afternoon meetings?

'You look tired,' she said. 'Come over here.'

He sat down beside her on the chaise. She patted her lap and, needing no further encouragement, he lay his head down in the folds of her skirt, extending his legs so that the backs of his boots rested on the wooden edge of the chaise and would not soil the blue velvet.

As he lay there, cosseted by the softness of her skirts – the surprising softness of *her* – he felt as if he were floating on water, or perhaps a cloud.

'With the threat of the Paddenburg Ultimatum hanging over us all, and Prince Jared away pursuing alliances, I fear that there are unscrupulous people within the court who might seek to take advantage.'

Elin paused in case Morgan had something to say, but all he did was gently exhale.

'I say unscrupulous,' Elin continued. 'But in truth, such people would better be described as reckless. This is not the moment to challenge the status quo – when we are facing the enormity of an attack, it *is* nothing less than reckless to contemplate another attack from within the very heart of court.' As their eyes met, she saw something akin to panic in his face. 'Don't you agree?'

He swallowed. 'Yes, my lady.'

She smiled warmly. 'I'm glad, Morgan. I felt sure you would.' She leaned back again and resumed stroking his hair. 'Your family and mine have been connected for such a long time now. Your grandfather, Atticus, fought on the same battlefield as my late husband, in Prince Goran's younger days. Then your father, Atticus Junior, took up the fight in his turn.'

She saw traces of tears in Morgan's eyes as she spoke of his forebears. Moved, she took his hand, and was surprised by the force with which he grasped hers. 'And you have continued that same loyalty. You fought alongside my husband at the battle which took his life, and you served my first son as now you serve my second.'

She watched, surprised, as the tears fell from Morgan's eyes. 'You have honoured your father and grandfather so well. I know you would have made your father proud. I remember when I first offered to help school you, he was grateful beyond measure.' She paused, smiling. 'What a rough scrap of a thing you were back then, Morgan. All long limbs and wide eyes, like some crazy insect – not at all the handsome creature you have transformed into now. But it was my pleasure to take that rough-hewn beast and teach him the power of words and speech and stories. It began as a kindness to your dutiful father, but in time it became something I wanted to do for you and you alone.'

She gazed fondly on him, seeing that though he had closed his eyes, still water was escaping from under his thick, dark lashes. 'Don't cry, Morgan. Times are difficult now, but the way through them is to stand up for what we believe is right. The Wynyards and the Booths have always looked out for each other. That's all we need to do now.' She smiled as his eyes opened once more. 'I know I can count on you.'

She leaned down to kiss him; his lips were salty from the trail of his tears.

As she drew back, she heard him speak, his voice husky.

'And after a hundred years of solitary slumber,' he said, 'the kiss from the beautiful maiden woke the youth as gently as the soft spring breeze.'

Queen Elin took her leave first, having kissed him again tenderly, her hands running up and down his arms as he gazed at her lips and she told him how pleased she was they had had the chance to talk about such important matters.

After she had gone on her way, he lay back down on the blue velvet chaise and cried again. This time, he did not try to control his upset but allowed his emotions to emerge in violent sobs, which sent tremors through the length of his body.

He knew his moans must have made a racket but to his own broken ears, they were as muffled and distant as the lapping waters of the fjord, as muffled and distant as the Queen's voice had been. Every day now, he seemed to be able to hear less and less distinctly – as if he were moving deeper, inescapably deeper, into his own cocoon. He knew that when the time came that he could not hear a single sound, it would be the tender music of her voice that he would mourn above all other things.

TWENTY-SEVEN

PALACE OF LARSSON

Prince Jared couldn't help but smile in awe and delight as he and his companions arrived on horseback at the open gates. On a normal day, the palace of Larsson would have been spectacle enough in itself on account of its fine architecture and its idyllic setting right on the water; today, with the fjord completely frozen – its surface glistening like spilled diamonds in the late afternoon light – it was a scene from a fairy tale.

Closer by was a riot of colour – some sort of celebration was taking place on the frozen water of the fjord, and its hubbub and delicious smells as people noisily meandered between scattered tents and food and drink stalls was en ticing. Jared watched as friends exchanged jokes and warm hugs, the air heady with festivity. It made him feel suddenly sad: this place was a world away from his home. He felt both the aching chasm of distance and a sense of envy that all could be so joyful and carefree in Larsson. As light and bright as everything felt here, it only made him more conscious of the dark storm clouds clustering over his own court.

He was pulled from his ruminations by the sudden arrival of a pretty young girl. She skated gracefully towards the new-comers, a glass of brimming liquid – amazingly stable – in each of her mitten-clad hands.

'Good afternoon!' She beamed, her teeth as pure white as the ice-crystals underfoot. 'May I offer you gentlemen some mulled cider?'

'You most certainly may,' Hal's voice rang out. Jared watched Hal nudge Prince Rohan's bodyguard. 'We may be further north, but it has to be said – you get a *much* warmer welcome here than in your neck of the woods.'

As the girl handed over the drinks ands skated off to fetch more, Jared turned to Rohan. 'What on earth's going on here?'

Rohan shrugged. 'Some kind of seasonal nonsense, no doubt. Welcome, my friend, to the court of crazy Prince Séverin!'

Now a young man on skates whizzed up to them at full pelt, performing an impressive turn before coming to a dead stop right in front of the two Princes.

'On behalf of Prince Séverin and Princess Anastasia, a hearty welcome to Larsson!' He beamed toothily. 'Wonderful to have you here for the annual Ice Fair! In a jiffy, we'll get you folks sorted with valet stabling. First, there's the tiny for-mality of checking your names off my list.' He lifted a vast scroll from a tube strapped to his back and unfurled it the-atrically. 'All righty ... so, who do we have here?'

'I am Prince Rohan of Rednow. And this fine fellow is Prince Jared of Archenfield.'

The young man's face looked fit to burst at the news that there were not one but *two* royal Princes in the party. 'As Princes, you will be on the VIP section of my list!' He began scrolling down at a rapid rate. 'Here we go! Prince Rohan ... hmm, I don't think we actually received an RSVP from you,

Your Majesty.' He glanced up, looking somewhat pained, to meet Rohan's imperious gaze. 'But obviously, that is *not* a problem!' His eyes dropped back to the scroll. 'And ... this is strange, but it would seem that we did not in fact issue an invitation to Prince Jared.' He glanced up sheepishly. 'No offence, Your Majesty. Traditionally, only our immediate neighbour royals are invited to this event.'

Prince Rohan cleared his throat loudly. 'Prince Jared is my guest. Now, put down your scroll and be so kind as to send urgent word to Prince Séverin that we wish to greet him in person, at his earliest convenience.'

The flustered lad began rolling up his scroll again but, in his flummoxed haste, it slipped out of his hands and bounced down on to the ice, unrolling itself as it went.

Jared felt for him.

Just then, quite possibly the loudest voice Jared had heard in his life boomed out from the melee: 'Prince Rohan of Rednow! Can it be true, or do my ancient eyes deceive me?' A tall, generously bearded man, dripping in furs and jewels in roughly equal measure, strode towards them. 'No, it really is you! Well, jump down from your horse and give a fellow a kiss!'

Jared watched in wonder as Rohan dismounted and submitted to Prince Séverin's embrace. A volley of kisses was exchanged, until the host Prince released his guest.

'What an utter joy to see you!' Séverin exclaimed. 'I was told you hadn't even responded to our invitation, so to have you here, and in time for the big race ... well, I'm flushed with euphoria and surprise in equal measure.'

'My dear fellow,' Rohan responded amiably, 'you know I can be somewhat lax with the niceties, but how could you think I would miss this wondrous event? And, look here, I have brought you a very special guest – Prince Jared of

Archenfield. He has travelled all the way from Archenfield just to see you.'

Jared now found himself subjected to the full beam of Prince Séverin's attention: Séverin's delighted face was as bright as the sunlight bouncing off the mirror-like surface of the fjord. Jared knew he should probably jump down to greet his host, but he felt rooted to the spot. Instead, he removed his glove and extended his bare hand.

Immediately, Séverin pounced – not shaking Jared's hand but kissing it. His host's beard tickled and Jared couldn't help but laugh. Fortunately, Séverin took it as mutual delight. Shaking his head, he stepped back, hands on hips. 'Young Prince Jared! What a gargantuan pleasure to make your acquaintance! Welcome to our humble home! What an honour to have you here for our little fete!'

'Thank you,' Jared said, dismounting from his horse. 'Your Majesty, I wonder if we could talk?'

'Yes, yes, we shall certainly talk! We shall talk and sing and drink and feast ... You will, of course, stay for the dance tonight, and meet my dear wife. And my oldest daughter, the incandescent Princess Celestia!'

'That sounds wonderful,' Jared said. He saw Rohan shoot him a warning look, but he had to go on – whatever the air of celebration around him, he wasn't here for the party, he had come to discuss a vital strategic alliance with Larsson. 'But Your Majesty, I would really appreciate some time alone—'

Jared found himself silenced as Séverin clapped his hands together excitedly. 'I have just had the most wonderful idea!' He stamped his feet for emphasis. 'Yes, though I say it myself, it's a complete humdinger – something to make this year's Ice Fair one for the history books.' He paused to draw breath. 'Fellow Princes, would you accord me the very great honour of each taking a sledge in the culminating race of the day?'

'I would love to,' Rohan shot back immediately, but reached for his leg. 'Sadly, this old knee injury prevents me.'

Séverin's lips turned down, but his eyes sought out Jared's. 'All our hopes now rest with you, Prince Jared,' he said. 'I am confident a young athlete such as yourself has no injuries to cite.'

Jared thought of the chest wound recently inflicted by Logan Wilde. It was, in truth, causing him some discomfort with all the riding of the past days, but he could see that now was not the time to mention it. 'I will gladly take part in your race,' he said.

'Hurrah!' cried Prince Séverin, punching the air with his fist.

Séverin stepped to one side, allowing Jared a clearer view of the frozen fjord. In the distance, dark shadows broke through the ice and Jared realised that these must be tiny islands. In the foreground, he saw that the near side of the fjord had been transformed into a vast racing arena.

Now, in a blur of jewel-like colours, a succession of horses and riders hurtled past. Jared heard the ominous sound of cracking ice and saw a spray of ice crystals spinning through the air.

'You look a little anxious,' Séverin said, placing his arm around Jared's shoulders. 'You have no need. There's plenty of solid ice below to support the runners and riders.' The ebullient Prince grinned. 'And, later on, the sledges!'

A mere hour later, Jared was being helped into the harness of his sledge – one of nine competing in the all-important final race of the day. The sun had dipped low over the distant mountains and, before him, the crisp expanse of the fjord was a tempting sight – for a leisurely skate, perhaps, but not necessarily for racing around in a potential death-trap ...

Jared knew he was tired and that this was compounded by the guilt he felt about wasting time taking part in a sledge race when his comrades and subjects back home were depending on him securing another vital alliance. But he reminded himself that his participation in the race was the price Séverin had exacted for talking to him later. His host had not said so in so many words, but the implications had been pretty clear.

Here goes nothing! Jared thought, as he shook up the reins to get his horse moving more quickly. He didn't want to have to use the long whip at his side unless he had to. They began moving at speed to join the others at the starting line. He was aware of the crowd all along the palace side of the fjord, shouting and cheering. Jared kept his eyes directly ahead. He knew he had no real chance of winning but if he could just bring the sledge back after the designated three laps of the fjord, without falling out, he'd at least acquit himself with some dignity.

Glancing up at the royal party in the stands, Jared lifted his hand to Séverin. He was rewarded with a whoop and a wave. Jared sensed that beneath his host's jocular and somewhat effete exterior lurked a ruthless and possibly dangerous leader.

The starter moved into position. Jared tapped the pocket where he had stowed Asta's sprig of rue for luck, then he turned his eyes to the front again, looking along the back of his horse to the vast expanse of white ahead. Jared felt his horse tense with the desire to break free. Any moment now ...

The starting signal was given: a vast flag of many colours was brought down. Suddenly, they were off.

To his surprise, once his horse got going, Jared felt entirely comfortable. In fact, as the race got properly underway, he felt exhilarated for the first time in a long time. The further they went, the more confident he felt as he noticed strategies being used by the other competitors, and he put those to good use – to the extent where he began taking in the positions of the other eight racers.

As they raced past the last stand of spectators, Jared was aware of the cheers falling away and only the sound of drumming hooves filled his ears. He kept his eyes trained to the front, marvelling as his horse thundered across the compacted ice of the fjord, flicking ice up into his face. To his amazement, he soon found himself in the middle of a central pack of four horses and riders.

There were rocks jutting up from the surface of the ice on the far side of the fjord, and the front riders broke formation so they could get through the widest gaps between them. Rounding one such obstacle, Jared realised he had gained a lead over one of the other horses – but he was still pretty much neck and neck with two of the other competitors. Ahead of them, the front-runners looked impossible to catch. But this was only the first lap, and Jared had a taste for it now. It would no longer satisfy him simply to finish: now, he was racing to win. As soon as the thought occurred to him, he realised that he was not the only competitor to have raised his game – he was joined by another rider, and penned in by sledges on either side.

They were rapidly approaching another rock-infested patch, made more difficult by a tight turn in it. Flags marked the course. It dawned on Jared that there would be space to fit only two sledges between the rocks, not three. He flicked the reins, urging his horse on faster.

His right-hand neighbour must have had the very same realisation: he was leaning forward, teeth bared.

All three were travelling at an equal pace, bearing down on the gap in the rocks before the turning but, suddenly, the rider to his left made a sudden lurch to the side. He had lost control of his sledge and had veered towards the wrong side of the rocks.

Jared saw the rider's horse rear up just before he shot safely through the gap in the rocks. The other sledge had made it through too, and they were now racing shoulder-to-shoulder along the far side of the fjord.

He dared to take the tight turn at the end of the fjord at a fast pace – a dare he took almost without contemplating the consequences of it going wrong. But, as he began racing back towards the start line to cross it for the second time, he knew he had gained a crucial advantage over his rival. It brought a smile to his ice-encrusted lips and, as he raced past the spectators' enclosures, it was as if their cheers were for him and him alone.

Approaching the end of the fjord for the second time, Jared noticed that the two sledges in front of him were moving closer and closer together. Then, as they began to turn, disaster befell one of the sledges: in order to avoid colliding, the rider had tried to change direction but just at the wrong moment. The horse had already chosen its turning circle and, confused perhaps by his rider's instructions, lost its footing. The horse fell down hard and, moments later, rider and sledge both spun away over the ice. Jared was momentarily transfixed by the sight, but he knew he had to tear his eyes away if he wasn't to suffer a similar fate.

Any concerns he might have had about the race being called off due to this accident were soon banished as he noticed the lead sledge thundering down the far length of the fjord. Even on this remote side of the ice, he could hear the muted cheers from the palace side. Clearly the spectators were getting ready for the grand climax.

The only horse and sledge he cared about was the one in front. And, as they raced on towards the end of the fjord and the final turn before home, he caught sight of the horse's number: number five.

There were white trails of spit around his horse's mouth and its mane was glistening with sweat. Still it showed no sign of tiring. If anything, his horse seemed even more determined than he was to shorten the distance between themselves and the leader.

As they approached the turn, his horse was equal with the other rider's saddle. Number five steered in close to them. Jared thought of the collision at the other end of the fjord and knew he had to avoid enduring the same fate. Looking across at the other rider, he realised he was close enough to see the angry expression on the rider's face, and close enough to hear the angry cry: 'Move over! This is *my* race!'

It was a young woman's voice.

Jared had absolutely no intention of moving over. He could hear number five cursing him, but he knew he'd gained the lead now. By holding his nerve and his line, he'd emerged from the final turn a little ahead. Against all his own expectations, he began the final half-lap of the course leading the field. But sledge number five had made a decent turn and was now hammering along, clearly intent on regaining the lead.

'Not going to happen,' Jared muttered determinedly. He could see the clear track ahead, could see the finish line was his for the taking. 'Come on, boy!' he cried.

Just when they needed it, his horse dug to his deepest levels and came up with more reserves of energy and speed. Though number five was working hard to catch them on his near side, Jared could feel they were edging ahead.

Then, out of nowhere, another horse and rider appeared on his other side. Risking a quick glance, Jared then refused to divert his attention by looking. Even so, he still saw number five nudging ahead of him. 'No!' he cried, cursing himself for allowing his attention to slip at that crucial moment. Like it or not, the rival sledge was edging ahead, with the finishing line coming ever closer.

'Come on!' he cried.

His horse needed no further urging. They were soon back level with number five; then, they were a nose ahead ...

As they thundered across the finishing line, Jared pumped his fists into the air. He'd done it! By some miracle, he'd won the sledge race! He pulled back on the reins and felt his horse slow down. They came to a standstill, some distance from the crowds.

For a moment, everything was quiet and Jared enjoyed the tranquillity of being alone in the centre of the frozen fjord. He leaned back in his sledge and laughed.

And then it hit him.

Nobody was cheering.

He heard the scrape of runners and turned to see another sledge pull up alongside him. It was no surprise to see the familiar pink and black silks of rider number five.

'I've got a bone to pick with you!' the young woman cried angrily, turning her reddened face towards him. 'This was *my* race! You cut me up on that last corner!'

Jared frowned. 'Actually, *you* tried to cut *me* up – just like you did to that other sledge over on the far side.'

'You don't know what you're talking about!' the woman snapped. 'You weren't even supposed to be in this race!'

'I know,' Jared said, at last able to smile with pride. 'Yet I won!'

'Ha!' she exclaimed, reaching up to remove her helmet. A shock of golden-blonde hair tumbled down over her shoulders. She would be rather beautiful, he thought, were she not quite so red with anger.

'Allow me to introduce myself,' she said. 'I'm the Princess

Celestia.' Her pout transformed into a smile. 'It's very rare that anyone beats me at anything. Who on earth are you?'

'I'm Jared, Prince of Archenfield,' he told her.

'Archenfield!' she exclaimed. 'You are a long way from home, Prince Jared.'

He nodded, smiling slowly. 'You're not wrong there.'

'Well,' said Princess Celestia, tensing her reins again. 'We should go and get cleaned up. The races may be over, but we have a long night of dancing ahead of us. And, after the way you treated me out here on the ice, I intend to punish you on the dance floor.'

'I'm really not much of a dancer,' Jared began, but he found himself addressing only the chill air. Princess Celestia had whizzed away on her sledge. It seemed she was every bit as unpredictable as her father. Only a hundred times cuter.

Jared smiled, shook his head and sped off in hot pursuit.

TWENTY-EIGHT

THE STABLES, PALACE OF ARCHENFIELD

Axel watched as Lucas tended to his horse. The Captain of the Guard stood in the shadows on the other side of the stable door, observing with scant interest as the Groom cleaned out each of the horse's hooves.

Lucas's movements were precise. First, he slid his hands down the foreleg, then squeezed the back of the leg between the hoof and the fetlock and said 'Up', which prompted the horse to raise the hoof under scrutiny. Next, Lucas employed a pick to pry out the grit and mud lodged in the sole of the horse's foot. After each excavation, he carefully placed the foot back down on the straw-covered floor and moved on to the next.

'I need to talk to you,' Axel said. 'This is important. Perhaps we could go somewhere else?'

Lucas shook his head, dropping the hoof pick into a wooden pail and retrieving a comb. 'Cleaning this beauty is important to me. We can talk here.'

Axel glanced over his shoulder.

231

'If you're concerned for our privacy,' Lucas resumed, 'you have no need. We're all alone. Why don't you step into the stall with me?'

'I'm quite comfortable standing here,' Axel assured him.

Lucas smiled softly. 'You always were a little nervous around horses, weren't you? One accidentally kicked you when you were a boy, didn't she?'

Axel stroked the faint scar above his eyebrow. He remembered how, when it had happened, there had been so much blood pouring down his face that he had feared he might drown in it. Even though the wound had soon healed – helped along by the stitches and ointments applied by Elias – he had suffered blood-soaked nightmares for months afterwards.

'To your credit, it never stopped you from riding,' Lucas observed, bringing the comb to the horse's shoulders. 'You're one of the best horsemen in court. Still, it's a shame you've never quite succeeded in overcoming your fear of horses.'

'I have no fear of horses,' Axel said crossly. 'I'm not frightened of any creature, whether two-legged or four. I wonder how many of my fellows in court – or on the Twelve, indeed – can give you the same assurance.'

Lucas knew he had jabbed at Axel's pride. 'Nonetheless, I'm sure there are places you would far rather be at this time of night ... others you would prefer to be with.' He paused. 'Well, spit it out. What is it that you want to talk to me about?'

Axel set his gloved hands on the stable door. 'I am instigating a vote of no confidence in Prince Jared. I assure you it is not something that gives me any pleasure, or that I have undertaken without a great deal of thought. The Princedom is in a heinous state and it is my duty to act. It is time for someone other than a Wynyard to take the throne.'

'Someone like you, perhaps?'

Axel did not flinch at the challenge. 'I *am* the chosen Edling.'

'Chosen by Prince Jared, who you are now preparing to betray, even as he risks his life trying to secure an alliance for us.'

Axel shook his head. 'He should never have set out on this mission, Lucas. We all agreed that it was to be Queen Elin's job. The Twelve expressed their feelings very clearly, as I remember. Neither the Prince nor the Captain of the Guard should depart the Princedom while the threat of invasion hovers over us.' He gripped the ledge in front of him. 'I took those feelings on board. Don't you think I'd have welcomed the opportunity to ride off heroically? It wasn't an option – I stayed to do my duty, but the same cannot be said of Prince Jared.' He paused, his voice becoming softer. 'There are those on the Twelve who feel Jared's actions to have been reckless.'

Lucas shrugged. 'There are those who might deem the Prince's actions noble.'

'Noble,' Axel echoed. 'It's a powerful word, isn't it? But one I personally struggle to apply to the Wynyard family these days.'

'Really?' Lucas glared at Axel. 'Explain yourself.'

'I'm thinking of Silva,' Axel said, noticing the change in Lucas's demeanour at the mention of her name. 'You were quite close to her, I believe?'

Lucas nodded. 'We were ... friends.'

Axel smiled pleasantly. 'I'm glad of that, Lucas. She needed friends in court.' His eyes met Lucas's. 'In my view, poor Silva was betrayed by the Wynyards – firstly in life and then a second time in death. Perhaps you agree?'

'What do you mean she was betrayed?'

'She was a sweet, intelligent young woman, who entered into a marriage with a foreign Prince. She committed herself wholeheartedly to that marriage, whilst he betrayed her by pursuing Nova like a dog chasing after a bitch in heat.' He watched Lucas recoil at the thought. 'Prince Anders did not just humiliate Silva – he took her pure heart and trampled on it in his hunting boots. He hadn't a care, so long as he possessed the alliance with Woodlark on the one hand, and the sultry embrace of the Falconer on the other.' At last, Axel drew breath, observing how pale Lucas had become.

'I don't disagree with anything you have said.' The Groom's increasingly firm ministrations on the horse provoked a whinny of protest from the beast and, with an effort, he gentled his strokes. 'But surely these are Prince Anders's crimes? They have nothing to do with young Prince Jared.'

'It was Anders who betrayed Silva in life, yes – but, after she died, both Jared and Elin treated her with the same disrespect. When Queen Francesca and Prince Willem came to retrieve Silva's broken body, did they tell them the truth – that their daughter had been murdered? Of course not – they were too intent upon preserving the alliance, whatever lies they had to conjure up to do that.'

Lucas looked queasy. 'No,' he said. 'I can't believe they'd do that.'

'You weren't there, Lucas,' Axel said gently. 'But I was. I heard the two of them tell those grieving parents that their precious daughter had taken her own life. Now, you tell me, Lucas – does that strike you as fair treatment?'

'No,' Lucas stammered. He moved the comb through the horse's mane. 'Of course not! But I understand that they needed to protect the alliance—'

'The alliance crumbled in any case,' Axel continued. 'Maybe that was fate's way of telling Jared and Elin Wynyard that they should have accorded those grieving parents the respect of telling them the truth.'

Lucas was trembling. If his feelings for Silva had ever been in doubt, they were no longer. He stumbled closer to Axel, standing just on the other side of the stable door.

Axel did not wait for the Groom to compose himself. 'This is just one instance of the way the Wynyards have abused their right to rule,' he resumed softly. 'I fear that they have held the throne in their grasp so long, they have consistently abused the trust and faith we have all placed in them. That's why I'm going to call this vote, Lucas. That's why I hope I can count on you.'

He reached a gloved hand across to Lucas's shoulder, but Lucas shrugged it away.

'Thank you for telling me about the vote,' he said. 'But I'll make up my own mind about Prince Jared.'

Axel could not excise the impatience from his voice. 'I'd have thought his deeds alone would have made up your mind by now.'

Lucas looked at Axel. 'Sometimes people think they can manipulate me, because I speak softly and I don't throw my weight around in the Council Chamber.'

'I would not make that mistake,' Axel said.

'You already did,' Lucas said, turning away and walking back towards his pail of equipment. 'I think you had better go now. We have nothing more to discuss.'

Axel smiled to himself. He had barely gotten started.

'I'll take my leave, shortly, Lucas, and leave you to finish your work. But before I do, let's talk about your *friendship* with Silva.'

Lucas shook his head. 'I don't care to discuss my relationship with Silva with you.'

'*Relationship?* Yes, it's interesting that you would choose that word. Because I fear, Lucas, that "friendship" is not quite adequate to describe the true closeness – the intimacy – of your dealings with the Prince's Consort.'

'Don't try to twist something good and innocent—'

Axel smirked. 'Again, an interesting choice of vocabulary, my friend. "Innocent", for instance – not exactly apropos in this case, I fear.'

Lucas seemed about to respond, his comb raised as Axel might lift a dagger.

Axel shook his head. 'I think our fellows on the Twelve would be *very* interested to know the full extent of your relationship with Silva.' He smiled again. 'The things you two got up to down here in the stables ... Or,' he proceeded relentlessly, 'as if that wasn't insulting enough to the Prince and his marriage, climbing up into her bedchamber – the chamber next to that of her sleeping husband.'

Lucas's eyes narrowed. 'These are lies! Vindictive, wicked li—'

'I have informants, you see,' Axel continued smoothly, fingering his scar. 'I have informants in the Prince's quarters and informants in these very stables. So I have a pretty good idea what *was* going on, and equally what was *not* going on.'

Lucas's eyes narrowed. 'What do you mean by that?'

'I'm glad you ask,' Axel said. 'Because that's the question it all boils down to. Since my spies in the Prince's quarters assure me that, before his assassination, Anders and his Consort hadn't ... *consorted* for some time ... it does lead to one particular question, doesn't it?' He paused before going in for the kill. 'Who was the father of Silva's baby?'

Lucas tried to protest but seemed to struggle to find the words.

'It's quite a thought, Lucas, isn't it? That if Silva hadn't been clubbed to death beside the river, she might have put the bastard child of the Chief Groom on the throne of Archenfield.' Axel grinned. 'Why, the little bastard might have inherited that rather particular dimple in your chin – the one that sends all the women of court into a tizzy. Imagine the chatter *that* might have provoked! No, when all is said and done, it was probably best all round that Logan Wilde took her out of the picture.'

'You *disgust* me!' Lucas spat.

'I'm sorry you feel that way, Lucas. Especially since I have always had the utmost respect for you.' Axel smiled. 'Setting those awkward emotions to one side, I'm sure I can count on your support. At least that way, we can keep this whole sordid business hidden, rather than sharing it with the rest of the court.' He tapped the stable door with his gloved hand. 'I fear I've taken up more of your time than I intended,' he said briskly. 'You have your work to do and, as you observed before, the company of others *is* far preferable to me than that of an adulterer and a hypocrite.'

TWENTY-NINE

THE BORDER CAMP, PADDENBURG

Lydia brought her horse to a standstill at the top of the hill, catching her breath as she gazed down at the glimmering lights in the crook of the valley. Exhaling, she could trace in the dark night air the pattern of her own breath, blending with the thicker spirals rising up from the nostrils of her mount. She brought a hand to the horse's mane and stroked it gratefully. She had ridden him hard, she knew, but he had not flinched; together they had led the second tranche of troops here to the border camp in excellent time.

Below was illuminated the temporary camp created by the two Princes of Paddenburg and the troops that had ridden out with them, ahead of her. The war machine, though vast, looked strangely peaceful from this distance, its array of tents glowing softly in the moonlight.

Within the hour, she would be reunited with the two Princes who were now – thanks to her and her *alone* – the legitimate rulers of Paddenburg. Lydia scanned the hundreds of tents, attempting to pinpoint the one where Henning was likely to be waiting for her. It was strange to think that they had been apart for only two nights. It really did seem an eternity since he and Ven had ridden out from the palace.

The first of those two long nights apart from him, she had lain awake in the sleigh bed, missing his body lying next to her. She had even missed his nocturnal grunts. Alone in the vast bed, having failed to persuade Prince Leopold to sign the decree, Lydia had fretted through the small hours, wondering how on earth she was going to change the old man's mind.

The second night had been spent in a far less salubrious setting – a roadside camp. But while those in her party had drifted easily to sleep after the long hours of riding, driven by her own cracking pace, she had sat alone by the open fire, deriving little comfort from the flames. Tasting the smoke on her tongue, it had seemed to her like the fires of hell as she gazed into it, through it, seeing only the thing she had done earlier that day.

In the dancing light, she had watched herself – over and over – leading Prince Leopold out of the maze and up the palace stairway to his bedchamber. She had seen her own fingers clasp the pillow, at first gently, then rigid with intent. She had seen the pillow press until it entirely masked the Prince's confused face, then watched as his frail hands had flailed about in a pathetic effort to claw back his life, even as it was slipping ever further from him.

She had killed the father of a man she now realised she truly loved.

Her brooding was interrupted by the voice of the captain of the First Regiment, at her side. 'Lady Wilde, do I give the command to ride on?'

She did not move her gaze from the tent city as she nodded. 'Ride on!' she cried. She jabbed her heels into the sides of her horse. Together, they flew down the hillside, the thronging second army of Paddenburg flowing in their wake like a dark and treacherous river.

There was a hubbub of noise and excitement as those already in the border camp welcomed their fellows. Lydia dismounted and passed her horse to a waiting groom, feeling the weight of her body encased in its golden armour.

As she moved through the camp the voices around her hushed, but she was scarcely aware of the movement of men and women on either side. Instead, it was as if she moved in a bubble of air, utterly separate. Unsure of whether to attribute this to her status or to the terrible thing she had done, Lydia felt she had been marked out to wander alone, not just through that camp but through the rest of her life.

She was, she suddenly realised, not just tired but exhausted. *So* exhausted, she felt she could simply fall down there on the wet soil. It wasn't merely the question of two long days of riding, cushioned by far too little sleep, nor even, in isolation, the events of the day or two preceding. No, she was exhausted from a journey that had begun long ago.

'Lydia,' Henning said, suddenly at her side. 'Darling Lydia. You cannot imagine how much I have missed you.' He could only achieve the semblance of an embrace as she was still clad in her armour, and his own body was wrapped in thick furs.

Lydia's heart beat with so many powerful emotions, she found it impossible to speak.

'I watched you lead the riders down the hill,' he told her in a voice full of pride and wonder. 'You looked so glorious in your armour – like a goddess from ancient times bringing fire to the world for the very first time.' He smiled again, lifting his hand towards the nearest tent. 'Come inside, my love. Let us unburden you from your golden shell.'

He led her into a several-roomed tent. Encountering a

maid, Prince Henning sent the servant off to fetch hot water for Lydia to wash. When the two of them were alone, the Prince himself began removing her armour piece by piece.

She must have flinched as he removed her gambeson, for now he stopped his labours and drew her into his arms. He had removed his outer coat when he began his labours and now their bodies fitted together again in a way that was reassuringly familiar.

'You're trembling,' he said. 'We will bathe you, and then you must eat before you rest.' The maid arrived with a cauldron of hot water. Prince Henning nodded. 'Thank you. You may leave us.'

The maid seemed surprised but knew better than to offer any protest. After she had gone, Henning began to lift the final layer of Lydia's clothing from her body.

She shook her head. 'No, wait. There is something I have to tell you.' She placed her red-raw palms on either side of his face. 'My darling Henning, I have sorrowful news. For you and your brother.'

His eyes met hers but he did not speak.

'Your father is dead,' she told him. 'Prince Leopold is dead.' She was surprised by the hot tears welling in her eyes.

Henning's remained dry, trained carefully on her face.

'He seemed to be on the verge of recovery,' she said, 'on the morning you and Ven departed. We thought – Nikolai and I – what a cruel trick of fate it was that he should recover just at the point when his beloved sons were riding away.' She sighed. 'We took him the decree. We told him how you had run the Princedom during all the months of his sickness and that it was best for him to sign.' She waited for Henning to speak. He remained silent. She felt him bidding her to continue. 'He would not sign,' she told him. 'Not that day.'

'Go on,' he said.

She could not bear the coldness in his voice. He had utterly withdrawn from her.

'The next morning – yesterday—' She broke off. Was it really only yesterday? It seemed so long ago now. And yet the vision of his face – the pillow, his arms ... all so fresh, so present.

'Yesterday—?' Henning urged her on.

'He took it upon himself to explore the maze. I found him there, exhilarated to be out in the air after such a long time. He was singing to himself!' she said, desperate for Henning to say something, anything, further.

'I must go and tell Ven,' he said finally – and she found this was the last thing she wanted to hear. The very last thing she wanted was to be left alone – and for this conversation to finish.

'Wait!' she pleaded. 'I need to tell you exactly what happened.'

'No.' He shook his head. 'No, Lydia, I do not think I could bear to know the details. You understand, I am sure. He was my father. To know that he had this moment of recovery and then—'

'I did what you asked of me,' she said.

He looked at her. 'That's a strange thing to say.'

His words sent a shaft of cold fear spearing through her body.

'All that you asked of me,' she added.

He moved away from her. 'I must see Ven. I must comfort him, and he me.' His voice turned even colder. 'Get back on your horse, Lydia, and ride west. You know what needs to be done.'

'*Now?*' Once more Lydia's sense of time seemed out of kilter. 'But we are only just reunited. I thought we would have this night together.'

He offered her the flicker of a smile. 'No, Lydia, there is no need for you to wait. It was always to have been this way.' He shrugged.

The gesture seemed so casual, as if he had succeeded in throwing off the dark, difficult emotions he had experienced just moments before. He gazed at her intently, the smile now faded from his lips. His eyes were like stars in the gloom of the tent.

'So, I have been dismissed,' she said, overwhelmed with fatigue. 'If this was the plan, I should have known. Henning, we should not keep any secrets from each other.'

He shook his head. 'I'm afraid I cannot agree, darling Lydia.' His voice was softer now and he stepped towards her again. 'There is beauty in secrets. For our relationship to continue to prosper, there must always be things we do not share with each other.'

As he finished speaking, his lips were so close to hers she could not voice any protest. He leaned forward and kissed her. Then, in one fluid movement, he turned and walked away. Gone to tell his brother the news that Prince Leopold was no more and they were, at last, the legitimate rulers of Paddenburg.

'You might thank me,' she said to his retreating back, an old strength finding its way into her voice.

'For what, precisely?' he asked, not bothering to turn back to her.

'For everything,' she said. 'For every last one of the secrets I'm keeping for you.'

To her surprise, as he lifted the tent flap, he did glance back over his shoulder. 'Thank you,' he said, before disappearing into the chill dark.

THIRTY

THE OFFICE OF PRINCE SÉVERIN, PALACE OF LARSSON

'An alliance of the five river territories is *indeed* an intriguing proposition.' The words came not from Prince Séverin but from Princess Celestia, who – Jared was left in no further doubt – appeared to be taking the lead in this discussion.

He had been surprised to find Celestia waiting for him, alongside her father, in the Prince's office. She was still dressed, as was Jared, in the clothes she had sported for the sledge race. Her cheeks were flushed a now more faded pink from her recent endeavours, yet there was no sign that the race had drained her of energy – quite the reverse. Her bright blue eyes sparked with life and purpose as she stood before Jared, one arm folded tightly over the other.

Jared and Séverin sat opposite one another in elaborate chairs. At first, Jared had thought they were hewn from the ice of the fjord but, though indeed cool to the touch, the sinuous chairs were in fact made of glass and draped with thick furs. Séverin was lounging upon his, one arm dangling over its back.

His keen eyes darted back and forth between his oldest daughter and Prince Jared, as though he were watching a tennis match. Celestia had swiftly vacated her chair to take the floor between them. 'May I be blunt, Prince Jared?' she asked now.

He nodded and smiled at her, wondering if it was within Celestia's powers *not* to be blunt. In this respect, among others, she reminded him of Asta Peck.

'We had expected you only to request an alliance between Archenfield and Larsson. This would not, I fear, be a compelling proposition. Your Princedom is under the threat of imminent invasion and may soon fall into new hands.' Her face betrayed no obvious emotion. 'But an alliance with the other territories – especially Woodlark – well, that is certainly much more interesting to us.'

Stung by the callous way Celestia had talked about the fate of Archenfield, Jared found himself giving in to a little reciprocal bluntness. 'I thought the prospect of an alliance with Woodlark would appeal to you,' he said. 'And it strikes me as curious, given the significant border you share, that there is not already an alliance in place between your two territories.'

As Celestia raised her head haughtily, her father responded to Jared's question.

'Your point is valid, Prince Jared,' he acknowledged. 'You have candidly laid your own cards on the table, so it seems fitting for us to reciprocate.' He paused. 'Queen Francesca, an impressive woman with many fine principles, has never seriously entertained the thought of a formal alliance between her domain and ours.' He lowered his voice confidentially. 'I suspect she feels we have rather little to bring to the exchange.'

Jared nodded. It would be no surprise at all for Francesca, buoyed by the size and might of Woodlark, to adopt such an arrogant position.

'I must say,' Celestia resumed, 'that I am surprised that

Queen Francesca has so readily agreed to rekindle the alliance between Woodlark and Archenfield.' Her eyes met Jared's challengingly. 'I mean, after it was so recently severed due to the death of Silva of Woodlark on your soil.'

'Your information is impressively current,' Jared acknowledged – wishing that it was somewhat less current. Clearly Larsson had as effective a spy network as its larger neighbours.

'Francesca must have a very strong motivation for agreeing to reinstate the alliance, only days after she withdrew it,' Celestia said, coming to stand at her father's side.

Séverin said nothing, but Jared was in no doubt he was subject to equal scrutiny by father and daughter.

He cleared his throat. 'A lot has changed in the past few days. The threat from Paddenburg has become a clear and present danger, thanks to the ultimatum dispatched to me by the two Princes. But you need only glance at a map to see the extent of the border between Woodlark and Paddenburg. With Paddenburg mustering its forces, this alone may have changed her thinking.'

Celestia considered his words. 'It's possible. But I suspect there's more to it than that.' She took her seat once more, crossing her legs. 'Prince Jared, we should be very interested to see the decree from Francesca, detailing the specifics of the new alliance. I assume you have it on you, or else easily accessible?'

Jared froze. He had the decree in his breast pocket.

He could prevaricate, but that would only prolong this sense of deadlock – the one thing Jared knew he did not have was the luxury of time.

Reaching into his pocket, he withdrew the folded decree and passed it over into Celestia's outstretched hand. He knew it would not be long before she found her answer.

It took her moments to scan the text. Then she nodded and

passed it to her father, who fumbled in a pocket before retrieving a lorgnette.

As her father lifted the glasses to his eyes, Celestia rose to her feet once more. 'Well, now we are a good deal clearer on Francesca's change of heart. It's evident from the wording of this decree that your alliance with Woodlark is valid only if and when you hand over her daughter's killer – Logan Wilde.'

Séverin folded his lorgnette away again. 'Correct me if I'm wrong, Prince Jared, but wasn't this Wilde – until recent days – a member of your esteemed Council of Twelve?'

Jared was forced to nod in conformation to both their questions.

Celestia's eyes bored into his. 'It's shocking to think that a member of your own Council would be responsible for the deaths of Silva and Prince Anders.'

Ignoring the stab of her implied criticism, Jared nodded again. 'His actions have shocked us all to the core. Wilde infiltrated Archenfield at the highest level, as part of what we now know to have been a long-term plot hatched in the Black Palace of Paddenburg.'

'Indeed.' Séverin nodded, his face showing sympathy at Archenfield's plight.

Celestia's expression was more severe. 'It's not ideal having a critically important alliance with such a major string attached to it.'

Jared nodded. 'You're right, of course – especially when there's a strong strategic argument to be made for *not* handing over Wilde to Woodlark. But handing him over ceases to be a problem once the alliance of the five river territories is activated. Right now, we're all acting out of fear, prompted by this odious ultimatum, that Paddenburg will attack more viciously and sooner if their terms are breached. But if and when

Henning and Ven discover that the five river territories – Archenfield, Woodlark, Rednow, Baltiska and *Larsson* – are standing together in alliance, then the Princes of Paddenburg will be forced to rethink.'

Celestia pursed her lips, then turned and walked towards one of the room's large windows. The curtains had not yet been drawn and, through the glass, Jared could see thick flakes of snow falling heavily. For a moment, Celestia stood before the glass, as if lost in delight at the festive scene of the snow falling on the frozen fjord below. He had no doubt that she was simply biding her time, the cogs in her head spinning fast as she weighed up her decision. She held all the power in her tiny hands, which, even now, were pressed lightly against the window pane.

'We will offer you an alliance.' He heard her voice, but it took him a moment to process her words. She turned and walked back towards him.

'That's wonderful!' His words emerged as a weak rasp.

'Wait,' she said. 'I'm afraid that just as there are conditions attached to the Woodlark alliance, so there will be one with ours – to be drawn up by our scribe.' Jared noticed Séverin was listening as carefully to Celestia as he was. 'Our support is contingent on the full activation of the alliance between you and Woodlark.'

Jared could not fault her logic. Had he been in her shoes, he might have suggested the very same thing. Celestia had made no secret of the fact that the prize she sought for Larsson was an alliance with Woodlark.

Jared felt conflicted: he had gained a third alliance and that should have been cause for celebration, but, like the first of his alliances, it hinged upon handing Logan Wilde over to Woodlark. He knew that he'd have a tough job persuading Axel and the others to follow through with that ... Though surely, he reasoned once again – his mind going back to his thoughts after the alliance with Rohan had been agreed – he could make a very strong case for it, as it delivered three vital alliances? Four, if Kai had been successful in Baltiska.

Four alliances. Jared felt a momentary sense of elation. Against the odds, he had achieved what, days ago, had seemed impossible.

All he had to do was persuade his Council on the matter of the renegade Poet.

'Well,' Séverin said. 'A drink, I think, to seal the deal, and then we shall send at once for a scribe!' He rose to his feet. After he had taken a few steps towards a row of assorted shaped bottles standing on a cabinet, he stopped in his tracks and glanced back at Jared, curiously. 'But tell me, my friend, how did Prince Rohan respond when he heard about Francesca's terms?'

Jared froze again, saying nothing. For all his veneer of softness and joviality, Séverin could indeed be as merciless as his daughter. 'I mean, about the necessity of you handing over the assassin?'

Celestia's voice chimed in again. 'I don't think Prince Rohan asked you about that, did he? And I don't think you saw fit to volunteer the information.'

Jared felt sick to the pit of his stomach. He just didn't have the heart to tell another lie. Remaining silent, he felt the walls of the room closing in upon him.

Prince Séverin shook his head sadly. 'Typical Rohan. Acts with his heart, not his head.' His eyes met Jared's. 'In spite of appearances to the contrary, that is not how we do things here in Larsson.'

Jared rose to his feet, feeling suitably chastised. Now he was gripped by a fresh fear, which he had to voice. 'Do you intend to tell him?'

Prince Séverin's lips rose up in a half-smile, then his eyes narrowed. 'I hardly think it is my place to tell him. Surely that task falls to you, young Prince?'

'Yes,' Jared said, flushed with momentary relief. He sensed he could trust Séverin on this matter. However, while he wanted to tell Rohan the full truth – had wanted to all along – what if it cost him a vital alliance? Only moments ago, he had been congratulating himself on the alliances he had secured; now, he could feel the fragile house of cards collapsing. Nonetheless, his mind was made up. 'I *will* tell him,' he said. 'Be assured of this.'

'Very good.' Prince Séverin issued a nod. 'And now, a glass of grappa to warm your bones!'

Jared raised his hand, palm up. 'Thank you, but I should keep a clear head,' he said. 'I intend to ride out tonight – just as soon as I am in possession of your decree.'

'That's ill-advised,' Celestia told him. 'The snow is falling thickly again and the icy roads will be treacherous in the dark – not to mention the added danger of bandits, once you leave the palace borders.' She smiled at Jared. 'All things considered, I'd recommend that you stay the night and ride out at first light.'

Séverin nodded. 'You shall join us at the ball tonight. It marks the end of the Ice Fair.'

'Thank you so much, but I don't have anything to—'

'We shall have fresh clothes sent to your room,' Celestia told him. 'If you dance anything like you ride a sledge, Prince Jared, we should all be in for quite a treat.'

Jared realised he had been roundly outmanoeuvred. As tough a negotiator as Queen Francesca of Woodlark was, he could see young Princess Celestia might soon prove her equal. He sensed he was in for a punishing time on the dance floor.

Jared turned to Séverin. 'On second thoughts,' he said, 'I should be very grateful for that drink.'

TWO DAYS UNTIL
INVASION . . .

THIRTY-ONE

THE CHAPEL, VILLAGE
OF THE TWELVE, ARCHENFIELD

Asta closed the lychgate carefully behind her, checking to ensure that no one had seen her enter the churchyard. Satisfied that she had arrived undetected, she turned towards the chapel door just as it opened and Father Simeon stepped out into the morning air. He was wearing a coat over his vestments to protect himself against the winter chill. Asta lifted a hand in greeting but he did not seem to notice her.

The Priest seemed agitated. He clasped a small book in his hand – it looked like a book of prayer or perhaps a hymnal. She watched as he turned it over in his hands a few times, before lifting out a furl of paper from between its pages, scanning whatever was written on the note, then slipping it back again. His face set with determination, the Priest bowed his head against the wind and began walking purposefully around the side of the chapel. Asta followed at a discreet distance.

An icy wind was blowing up from the fjord. Asta had forgotten how cold it got here, at the northernmost point of the

Village. Her hood was blown down and she drew it back up again quickly before the wind had the chance to nip her ears. When she looked back along the path, the Priest had disappeared.

Asta had the strong feeling that Father Simeon had ventured out here to meet somebody. Proceeding with caution, she scanned the smaller pathways emerging to the left and right. There were myriad directions in which the Priest might have disappeared.

The sound of a bird breaking free from the branches of a tree made her turn. As she did, she saw a flash of brown cloth – the tail of Father Simeon's frock coat. Asta set off to follow him. As she turned the next corner, she saw him approach one of the larger tombs. On pedestals to either side of its entrance stood a pair of statues, each with a hand covering its face in mourning: the left-hand statue's eyes were just visible as the figure's forefinger lay along the bridge of its nose; the face of the right-hand statue was entirely covered by a stone-rendering of a kerchief. Between these two figures were ironwork doors, into which were wrought the outline of two trees.

Father Simeon opened the door, and disappeared inside. Asta glanced up and read the words inscribed on the top of the tomb. *Family Drummond*. Now she had a pretty good idea who the Priest had ventured there to meet.

As the iron gates clanked shut behind the Priest, Asta continued on, making her way along the side of the tomb. She could hear voices, indistinctly. She had to get closer if she was to learn anything.

At the back of the Drummond tomb, a cross-shaped hole had been made in the stone. The aperture was only slight but it was enough for Asta to see and hear through. First, she saw Father Simeon's face. The other occupant of the small room –

its only interior decoration a string of cobwebs – had his back turned towards her. But once she heard him speak, she was in no doubt as to who it was: Jonas Drummond.

'I come here often to visit my family,' she heard Jonas say.

'I know you do,' answered Father Simeon. 'You have proved an honourable child to those who came before you.'

'They laid down their lives on the battlefield for me,' Jonas continued.

Asta risked leaning forward, watching her footing carefully as she did to ensure she made no sound.

'The Drummond family is one of the most honoured in all the court,' Father Simeon said.

'Thank you, Father. I want to live my own life with the same kind of honour. If I die in war – well, so be it. But I know I have to take a stand. It is my duty, my purpose, you might say.'

'Your purpose?' Father Simeon echoed.

Asta saw Jonas nod. 'We are short of time now that the Paddenburg invasion has begun. It is up to each and every one of us to take a stand and determine the kind of future we want for Archenfield.' He paused. 'The kind of ruler we want for Archenfield.'

'We have a ruler, Jonas,' Father Simeon said.

'The sands of time are running out for Prince Jared. His folly across the border is, I fear, another sign of his inexperience and naïvety. At this point, he needs nothing short of a miracle ...'

Father Simeon smiled softly. 'It may not surprise you to hear that I believe in miracles—'

'I wish I could say the same, Father. But when I see my family tomb and read the names of those who died on the battlefield, I find myself grasping for something more solid on which to build my own belief.'

If Asta had not known better, she would have believed the Woodsman's sorrowful tone herself.

'Something or someone?' Father Simeon enquired.

'*Someone*,' Jonas confirmed. 'Father, I believe that if Axel Blaxland were to replace Jared as Prince, we would have a much stronger chance of addressing this threat. Axel is experienced at wielding the sword. Prince Jared is still training with haunches of meat from Vera's larders. Axel has played a key part at diplomatic meetings. Jared has not. Who do you think is better qualified to defend our borders and − I pray that it does not come to this − negotiate the terms of surrender? I don't want to sound disloyal ... '

'It is not disloyal,' Father Simeon said.

Asta's blood ran cold as the Priest continued.

'You can only do as your heart and mind instruct you, Jonas. That is the way to honour your family, both living and dead. That is the way to honour the Princedom.'

'Thank you, Father,' Jonas said. 'You cannot imagine what a great relief it is to hear those words from you. I feel a burden lifting from my shoulders.'

'I am glad,' Father Simeon said. 'I am glad you called upon me to help and that I was able.' A pause. 'Perhaps I should go now and leave you alone here with your thoughts and your ancestors?'

'Yes, thank you, Father.' Jonas's traitorous voice was husky now. It was taking all of Asta's powers of self-control not to race around the family tomb and charge through the iron doors to openly challenge the Woodsman about his duplicity.

'Father,' she heard Jonas speak again.

'Yes, Jonas.'

'How will you determine your own path through this chaos?'

'I will do as you have done,' Simeon said. 'I will search my soul and challenge myself with the most difficult questions. I will decide what is best for the Princedom. My duty, like yours, is first and foremost to Archenfield.'

'I hope, Father, this will not prove a tortuous process for you.'

'We must all wander through the darkest woods at certain moments in our lives,' the Priest said. 'Such moments are those which define us not only as men, but as God's creatures. You are right – it will not be a comfortable journey. But I shall embrace it nonetheless.' He paused. 'And having talked to you, I have already begun the process.'

Asta heard the scrape of footsteps and realised that Father Simeon was turning to leave. There was the sound of the iron gates clanking shut as he went on his way. She watched as Jonas Drummond rose to his feet. He turned and she briefly caught sight of his face. There were, as she had anticipated, tears on his face. But he was nonetheless smiling.

Of course he was.

Before he could notice her, she darted around the side of the tomb, only to find Father Simeon standing on the path, staring at her.

She stumbled towards him. 'Father, I can explain.'

'I'm not sure that I would care for your explanation,' he said. 'Skulking around tombs hardly seems fitting behaviour for the court Poet.' He shook his head. 'These are testing times for us all,' Father Simeon resumed, more gently. 'But, all the same, we must act with the dignity expected of members of the Twelve.'

'But surely you see what's going on here?' she protested. 'Surely you know what Jonas came here to accomplish, on Axel Blaxland's behalf?'

Father Simeon frowned.

'He came here to recruit you!'

'Recruit me?'

'He may not have said it in so many words, but Axel is poised to launch a vote of no confidence in Prince Jared. We will each have to pick a side.'

'Indeed,' Father Simeon said. 'Well, your actions here today may have helped me make my own decision.' Head down, he continued on his way.

'Please. Please!' she implored him.

'Leave me,' Father Simeon said, turning back briefly towards her. 'I am not given easily to anger, but your actions today have inspired it in me.'

She let him go. Furious not only with Jonas but herself, Asta stood impotently on the path. She was not looking forward to explaining what had happened to Nova and Koel.

As she watched Father Simeon disappear around a corner, she heard footsteps behind her. She glanced over her shoulder to find Jonas Drummond striding towards her.

'Asta, have you come here to pray?' His face was close now, gazing down at her. 'You should pray. You should devote every last breath to prayer, Asta Peck. Because you're going to need it.'

THE PHYSICIAN'S SURGERY, VILLAGE OF THE TWELVE, ARCHENFIELD

Asta found her uncle in the middle of his surgery, surrounded by a circle of evenly spaced wooden crates. In his hands was a long scroll of paper, which appeared to be covered – in his distinctive hand and green ink – with a detailed list. Asta watched as her uncle took up his pen and scratched rather viciously through one of the items on the list. Then he glanced up.

'Oh, it's you.' He made no pretence of being pleased to see her. 'I'm preparing these boxes of medical supplies for the troop divisions,' he told her, placing a sealed earthenware container into the box nearest to him. The table behind him was loaded with an array of similar looking containers – each with his typically immaculate labels – standing to attention beside vast wraps of bandages and, even more ominously, sharp-looking saws. She didn't like to think how such implements might be utilised, though she had a reasonably good idea.

'I assumed,' her uncle's voice cut across her thoughts, 'that you were busy helping Axel in your capacity as the new Poet. But when I spoke to him, he said that I was mistaken about this – that he has scarcely seen hide nor hair of you outside the meetings of the Twelve.' Elias's eyes met hers. 'Where are you spending your time, Asta? What are you up to now?'

'I've been with Nova and Lady Koel,' she told him. 'Uncle Elias, has Axel talked to you about his vote of no confidence in Prince Jared?'

She saw Elias flinch at her words. 'If he has, then that would constitute a private matter between two members of the Twelve,' he said.

Asta shook her head. 'This vote affects all of us on the Twelve. Not to mention Prince Jared, and the court, the Princedom as a whole—'

'Thank you very much for the informative lesson,' Elias said. 'Truly, anyone would think that *you* were the insider at court and *I* was the one lately sprung from the dust and dirt of the settlements.' He raised a finger at her. 'Just because you have the new Prince's ear, that does not give you the right—'

Asta could no longer contain her anger. 'What? The right to care whether Prince Jared has a throne to return to? The right to think about who is best placed to rule Archenfield? The right to defend the Prince and encourage others to do so?' She could feel tears gathering in her eyes – tears of sadness, anger and deep frustration. 'Uncle Elias, I don't understand why you would be angry with me about this.'

'No,' he said. 'I think that is true. You understand very little about me, it transpires. And, I confess, the feeling is mutual. From where I am standing, this gulf between us is only likely to grow wider.'

'It doesn't have to,' she said. 'We could find a way back to how things used to be.'

'I think that would be impossible now.' Elias sighed. When he resumed speaking, his voice was steadier. 'I think it might better suit us both if you were to move out of my house. The Poet's Villa has been vacant since Logan Wilde's incarceration. Seeing as you have taken over his position, I assume the villa belongs to you too.'

Asta was dumbstruck. 'You want me to move out?'

He nodded. 'It would enable me to get on, uninterrupted, with my duties. And you to do the same.'

'When?' she gasped.

Elias shrugged, and turned his back on her.

THIRTY-TWO

PALACE OF ARCHENFIELD

'Well, Vera, you have trumped even your own extraordinary standards tonight,' Axel told the Cook as he brushed past her chair on his way out of the dining chamber.

'Thank you, Axel,' she said smugly.

'It was not a compliment,' he hissed, before striding away.

Lamb testicle stew? *Really?* Hard on the heels of that vile tripe dish the night before. She was clearly taking his point about the need for frugality to new heights.

He was tired and now, on top of that, nauseous, but he needed to get back to his office by the striking of the Edling's Bell. Only two days remained until Paddenburg's threat of invasion became a reality. If the latest reports from his spies were correct, the enemy army outnumbered his own by four to one. Grim as this estimate was, the latest troop deployments needed to be finalised.

Military camps had been set up between key settlements and the southern border with Paddenburg. The most recent report from the south confirmed his worst fears. The people of Inderwick and Grenofen – the two settlements closest to the Paddenburg border and thereby most vulnerable to attack – were fleeing north with whatever possessions and livestock they could carry.

Just as Asta Peck had predicted, the southerners had no further appetite for war. The southerners had a reputation for being fiercely patriotic and they had been quick to enlist at the outset of war with Eronesia. In doing so, however, they had seen severe casualties in battle. With over half their population dead or bleeding in the north, those that had remained had struggled to harvest the crops; those who had not offered up their lives on the battlefield nearly starved to death at home. It came as little surprise that, one way or another, war had eroded what was left of their patriotism.

Others might have seen this flight of refugees from the south as the final nail in Archenfield's coffin, but what separated Axel from other, lesser, mortals was his ability to hold his nerve – even in what seemed to be the Princedom's darkest hours. Surrender to Paddenburg was no more an option than surrender to Eronesia had been. He would begin the fightback on two fronts – firstly, by halting the flight of the southerners and persuading them to return to defend their home turf; secondly, by convincing the settlements to the west of the necessity to bear arms.

THE BORDERLANDS

Lydia swung her sword. The power she had mustered was sufficient to unseat her target in his saddle. She leaned forward to deliver the killer blow with her blade but, as she did, the target's horse twisted round, unwittingly protecting its rider by taking him just beyond Lydia's reach. Adrenalised for the kill, Lydia plunged the length of her sword into horseflesh instead – one creature's blood was as good as another. She swiftly retracted her weapon, dripping crimson.

The horse, initially frozen in pain, began to convulse and its rider was thrown off on to the battleground, showered with the blood of his dying horse as it reared up into the air one last time. Lydia directed her own steed over the fallen rider's body, hearing the satisfying crack of bones underfoot.

Her next target came into focus before her. Like those she had already felled, she was not in armour but only the winter garb of a border guard. It left her woefully vulnerable as Lydia swung her sword and sliced through her rival's arm, watching the geyser of blood gush up in the air. Some of it sprayed on to her own golden armour, but Lydia had little care that her pristine armour was sullied: blood was a badge of honour. She continued on, inhaling the scent of death and new beginnings that permeated the thick air. She didn't have time to think about where her deputy and the rest of the troops were. Her sole focus was directed on clearing her way through the obstructions that lay between her and the stretch of land ahead: land she was taking in the name of Paddenburg. In her mind, she was the hero of a folk tale – such as those Logan had told her in her younger, more impressionable days – slashing her way through a vast forest of thorn-encrusted vines. Like the hero charged with gathering twelve roses to wake the sleeping king, she must do whatever it took to achieve her destiny.

She heard the clang of steel on steel as her next opponent's sword clashed against her own, and she could feel through the contact of their weapons the strength of this newest enemy. Digging her heels into her horse's flank, she surged forward. The two swords smashed together again. He was attempting to unseat her, trying to use the weight of her armour against her. As he came yet closer, Lydia judged the distance, then propelled herself forward, smashing her helmet into his exposed forehead. She was ready for more of a fight but as she drew back, she saw with a certain sadness that she had already rendered him senseless. Shoving him firmly from his horse to the ground, she moved on.

These people had not known what hit them. They were ill-prepared and outnumbered. On she went, slashing her way through the forest in her head. On and on and on again, until at last there were no more vines to slash, no more blood-red roses to gather. She found herself alone at last.

It was perfectly still and quiet: no more echoes of clashing steel; no more drumming hooves; the pitiful cries of the dying muffled by the circling wind. Ahead of her was land, as far as the eye could see, a beautiful expanse of empty green fields.

'We're in!' she cried in heady excitement. 'The border is ours!'

Glancing back, she saw her comrades manoeuvring their horses carefully over the moving, squirming sea of bodies beneath them. Earthworms. That was all they were – a field of slowly wriggling earthworms. Turning her eyes once more in the other direction, she inhaled deeply the sweet greenness of it all, feeling it flood her senses. Already, her mind was emptied of all thoughts of what had come before. This was her gift – a rare one indeed.

Her eyes were drawn to a falcon wheeling gracefully over-head. She felt almost overcome by the perfect peace and silence of the scene.

THE CAPTAIN OF THE GUARD'S OFFICE, PALACE OF ARCHENFIELD

Sitting alone in silence, Axel had barely had a chance to skim the lists when there was an urgent rapping at the door.

'Enter!' he called out.

His deputy, the ever-dependable Elliot Nash, pushed open the door. He looked flushed. 'I have news,' he announced. 'And you're not going to like it.'

'Well? Spit it out, man.'

'Paddenburg,' Elliot rasped.

Axel frowned. Even the name of that bloody Princedom now had the capacity to turn his stomach. 'I'm going to need more than just one word,' he told Elliot.

His deputy nodded. 'Word has just reached us from the western border. Neutral Tanaka has been invaded! They have surrendered, and now Paddenburg troops are racing towards the border between Tanaka and Archenfield.'

Axel rose to his feet. Tanaka shared a considerable border with Archenfield to the west, just as Paddenburg did to the south. If Henning and Ven had taken the time and trouble to annex Tanaka, then this was going to be a hell of a lot worse than he had predicted. The bastards of Paddenburg had shown their deadly hand: they were planning to simultaneously attack Archenfield on two fronts. Now the people of the western settlements would not be valiantly coming to the aid of the beleaguered south, but fighting to save their own land, homes and families.

'We have to face facts.' Elliot's voice was drained of emotion. 'It is now only a matter of time before Archenfield falls.'

Axel frowned but spoke calmly and quietly. 'I don't need

you to tell me when to face facts. Be assured that I am always one step ahead. That's why I'm in the position I am in.'

Elliot looked more flushed than ever. 'I'm sorry, Axel, but you know as well as I that our fighting numbers were slashed in the conflict with Eronesia. Paddenburg, in contrast, has a swollen army, which we now have no hope of defeating.'

Axel raised his hand to silence Elliot's increasingly grating voice. 'Our fighting numbers *are* diminished. You know that and I know that but, crucially, the twin demons of Paddenburg do not necessarily know this. If we can still mobilise energetic troops to both fronts, we can make Henning and Ven think that we have a greater force at our disposal than we do. We can still win this—'

'By smoke and mirrors?' Elliot was clearly unconvinced.

'Wars are won as much with the head as with the sword,' Axel told him. 'You, for example, seem already to be unfurling the flag of surrender, simply in response to news of enemy troops clustering in the vicinity of our borders. At times like this, it is vital to hold one's nerve.'

To his surprise, Elliot did not back down. 'There's a difference,' he said, 'between holding one's nerve and steadfastly refusing to accept the facts.'

Was his deputy accusing him of such a refusal? Where was this uncharacteristic impudence coming from? 'You have gone beyond your brief, Elliot,' Axel snapped. 'And yet, I sense you have more to say to me?'

Elliot nodded. 'Just as we are being briefed by our spies across the border, how can we be sure that Paddenburg's spies within Archenfield have not given their leadership the clearest of indicators as to the size of our fighting force?'

'What spies?' Axel moved towards Elliot.

His deputy shrugged. 'I'm just saying that in principle—'

'Elliot, it is *your* job to ensure there are *no* spies in

Archenfield – none who still draw breath, at any rate. Have I not always made my feelings on this subject plain?'

'Yes,' Elliot acknowledged. 'But, nonetheless, I think by this stage in the proceedings, we have to assume that one or two have probably ... *possibly* slipped through the net.'

Axel smiled nastily, then shook his head. 'This was *your* job,' he repeated. 'If a spy has slipped through your net, then it is *you* who has allowed him – or her – so to do.' He paused, considering. 'So, we have reached a crucial point in this conflict. It is time to take decisive action.' Yes, that had got his attention, cut him down to size. 'Here's what you will do. Take anyone you suspect of being a spy and make an example of them.'

'How much of an example?' Elliot asked.

Axel sighed. 'Should I draw you a picture?'

'No, sir.' Elliot's gaze lowered. He shook his head.

'There's no better way to sharpen Morgan Booth's blade than with the blood of a traitor,' Axel noted, his spirits already perking up at the thought.

It was always good to take control.

'What if I'm not certain?' Elliot pressed him.

'Then you keep that to yourself. Put the fear of God into any spies who may be contemplating remaining here – render them useless – and, as importantly, reassure everyone else that we are completely in control.'

Elliot was frowning. 'What about Prince Jared? He should be back in court any day now. He was none too pleased when you brought forward the execution of Michael Reeves. The Prince does not like any deviation from protocol—'

Axel put his hand over Elliot's mouth. 'Remember this – Cousin Jared is not returning to court as ruler.' His eyes bored into Elliot's. 'It's time to move into the endgame here. Tomorrow, I'll put forward my vote of no confidence to the Twelve.' Slowly removing his hand, he smiled at his deputy. 'So you need have no worries on that score.'

Elliot looked bemused. 'Surely now is the time to bring all this cloak and dagger stuff to a close and focus solely on the external threat?'

Axel sighed. There were those who cracked under pressure, and those who allowed it to transform them, like diamonds. Elliot had revealed himself as belonging to the former camp, but Axel was made of superior mettle.

'Can you even be sure that you have enough votes to carry this motion?' Elliot pressed him.

Axel clenched his fists. 'Those misguided fools loyal to my cousin are about to have the rug pulled out from under them. Jared Wynyard is an ill-prepared *boy*. He does not have what it takes to negotiate with the barbarians of Paddenburg. I, on the other hand—'

'You mean to surrender?'

'Surrender?' Axel spat the word out. 'I said *negotiate*. I might be a pragmatist, but I'm not a pushover. Paddenburg will not be allowed to simply ride in and gather its chosen spoils. Archenfield will fight.' Turning from Elliot, he walked to the bureau and reached for the decanter. 'Given our diminished army and the complete absence of any strategic alliances – for which I hold Prince Jared entirely responsible – it is looking increasingly clear to me that negotiation will ultimately be our only real hope of survival. And I am the best one to secure the optimum terms for our people. I really can't see anyone arguing against that. Can you?'

Elliot shook his head slowly.

Axel lifted the glass of aquavit to his mouth and let the liquid tumble down his throat, carrying fire to his insides.

'You sent for me?' Asta Peck looked anxious. As well she might. Axel gazed across at her, from behind his desk, saying nothing for a moment. Let her think he was onto her. He *was* onto her: her and her petulant scheme to bolster support for his incompetent cousin.

'I have a job for you,' he said at last. 'Do come in and take a seat.'

He watched as she settled herself uneasily in the chair across from him. He realised that he still thought of her as the Physician's apprentice, rather than the Poet – his putative equal on the Council of Twelve. How could she, with her youth and inexperience, ever be considered his equal?

'How can I help?' she enquired.

'Cometh the hour, cometh the Poet,' he said, a smile playing on his lips. 'I believe I have found the perfect opportunity for you to deploy your unique talents and experience.'

Her eyes met his. 'What is it, exactly, that you would like me to do?'

He leaned back in his chair, making a steeple of his fingers. 'You're going to write me a speech,' he said. 'To a very specific brief.'

He was gratified to see that she reached for a pen and paper, holding them poised to take down further instructions. At least now it was abundantly clear who was calling the shots. 'You have eloquently expressed the feelings of those in the settlements,' he continued. 'Your speech will connect with these people. Your first objective is to stem their panic.' He waited for her to finish her note. 'Second, you will rally them to bear arms – with a greater fervour than ever before.'

She glanced up from her notes. 'Which settlement specifically is this speech for?'

'Galvaire,' he told her. He had to give her credit for asking the right questions. 'As you know, they are one of the westernmost settlements. Their closest neighbours, Vollerim and Lindas, are about to bear the brunt of an attack from Paddenburg—'

'From the west?' Asta gasped. 'I thought the attack was coming from the south.'

'We all did,' Axel replied. 'But we now know that they are preparing to invade on both fronts. Your job is to convince the good people of Galvaire to put up the strongest possible fight against the invader. They *must* not flee. An empty settlement only opens up more routes into Archenfield for Paddenburg's advance.'

Asta made another note, then raised her pen again. 'Do you have anything in particular you think I should say to motivate them?'

He smiled. 'You're the Poet, Asta,' he said. 'Far be it from me to put words in *your* mouth.' He paused. 'That said, I think you might want to tell them that if they can hold off the invaders for a couple of days, their ranks will soon be swelled by one of the alliances Prince Jared has secured.' He saw the sudden shift in her features at the mention of her precious Jared – her face was suddenly transformed, like the sun breaking through storm clouds. Pathetic, really.

'Prince Jared has concluded an alliance? No, you said *alliances*. So he has secured alliances, just as he set out to do?'

Axel nodded, smiling. 'Yes, that's the kind of thing you should put in your speech.' He gestured with his hand. 'But, you know, work it up a bit more. It's certainly the aspect you should stress.'

At last the penny dropped. The sun disappeared again and the storm clouds returned. 'This is a deception, isn't it? There are no alliances – you plan to send the people of Galvaire into battle with a lie.' She shook her head with unmasked disgust.

'Do you think you can rein in your righteous indignation for just a moment, Asta, and consider what the alternative is here?'

She set down her pen. 'That we tell them the truth?'

'Interesting. By all means, give that a go. Tell them that Paddenburg is attacking on two fronts. That, by a conservative estimate, the enemy army is four times the size of our own fighting force. That Prince Jared, to the best of my knowledge, has not managed to secure a single workable alliance . . . Yes, by all means, put all that in your speech and see how motivational it proves.'

'Don't you think these people deserve to go to their deaths knowing the truth?' she said.

'How tediously predictable you are,' Axel said icily. 'The irony is that you think you're doing them a favour by being open and transparent with them when, in fact, you are the one taking away their hope. In contrast, *I* am proposing to instil in them fresh hope.' His eyes bored into hers. 'When people feel hope pulsing through their veins, they are capable of transcendent acts. You seem to be convinced they will be hurtling towards certain death. That is not a view I share.'

Asta was frowning, but she had picked up her pen again and made a fresh note.

'I bow to your greater experience,' she told him. 'I'll write just what you say.' She let out a sigh. 'At least I'm only writing the speech,' she said. 'Whereas you are the one who is going to have to sell them this lie.'

He shook his head. 'I'm sorry, Asta. Evidently, I was not clear before. I do not intend to give this speech myself. I cannot leave court at this crucial time. No, it will fall to you to deliver the speech, as well as to write it. I am dispatching you to Galvaire with immediate effect. You'll find a horse saddled in the stables and a party of escorts ready to journey out with you.' He rose to his feet – it was time to bring this meeting to a close. 'You will be gone for a day and a night at the very least. But, assuming you are successful – and I have every confidence in you – I may have cause for you to address other of the settlements.'

Her face registered raw fear now. 'I could be gone for days,' she said.

'Very possibly.' He smiled. 'This is all well within the remit of the Poet. And, as I said before, this is an ideal way to capitalise on your talents and insight.'

And to ensure that there is one less vote in Jared's favour tomorrow morning, he thought, but elected not to add.

Axel could tell that she wasn't far from the same realisation – he had to give her her due. She had played the game, but she had been outclassed.

Just wait until she discovered which side her new friend Koel was really playing for.

ONE DAY UNTIL
INVASION . . .

THIRTY-THREE

THE MARKET SQUARE, GALVAIRE, ARCHENFIELD

Asta stood on a small stone platform, in front of the settlement church, rubbing her hands together. Although she wore several layers of clothes, topped off with her riding cloak, she still felt cold. She suspected her internal chill might stem as much from tiredness and fear at what lay ahead as from the westerly wind, which whipped around the square.

She and her escorts had arrived in Galvaire at dawn. Already many of the settlement dwellers had been up and about – spurred out of their beds not only by the pressure of their daily duties but by the gnawing question of what was happening in the south. And as the new morning light had lifted from the low hills, the view had given them an ominous answer: plumes of black smoke were visible in the distance. They might as well have been funeral pyres for Galvaire's southern neighbours.

News that a visitor from court – *a member of the Twelve, no less* – had come to talk to them had spread swiftly from door to door: clothes had been thrown on with little care; children had been swiftly dressed; animals had been fed at record speed. All that mattered was getting to the market square by the time the Cook's Bell chimed, to hear how the people of Galvaire were going to be spared the terrible fate of their neighbours to the south.

Now Asta gazed out at the crowd, keenly aware of the depth of expectation in their eyes. There was no delaying the moment any longer. Even now, the priest of the settlement – a younger, more vigorous man than Father Simeon – had jumped up on to the platform beside her and was silencing his flock with a practised hand.

'They are ready for you now,' he told her, unsmiling, as he stepped aside to allow her to be the full focus of their attention.

'Good morning,' she said. The words came out as a croak and she cleared her throat to try again. 'Good morning! My name is Asta Peck, the Poet. I have come from the court to talk to you today—'

'But you are just a child!' came a cry from the crowd.

'I am sixteen years old,' Asta said, finding the face of the man who had called out.

'Like I said, a *child*!' he rejoined.

His words had a clear impact on the rest of the crowd. Some of them sniggered. Others began to mutter.

'I am sixteen years old,' she repeated, raising her voice to cut through the hubbub. 'I am the very same age as Prince Jared, ruler of Archenfield,' she said.

'Hah!' It was a fresh voice this time – a woman's. 'Now she's comparing herself to the Prince! Cheeky—'

'No,' Asta retorted. 'That's not what I meant.'

'What exactly *do* you mean?' the first of her challengers resumed.

Asta could feel a sense of unease spreading through her body. Her legs felt like jelly – she wondered if they could see how much she was shaking under her long cloak. She had travelled here all through the night and her body, unused to extended bouts of riding, ached from head to toe.

She had spent the entire ride trying to find the right words with which to address the people of Galvaire, but now it seemed they were not even going to give her the chance to make her speech. She might as well summon the escorts and hasten back to the palace for all the good she could accomplish there. Asta felt water pricking her eyes but refused to cry in front of this crowd. She thought of Elias saying that she was too young and too inexperienced to take on the role of Poet. She *had* to prove him wrong and vindicate Prince Jared's faith in her.

'I have been dispatched to talk to you in my position as Poet on the Council of Twelve,' she said, her voice gathering volume. 'Yes, I am young – there is nothing I can do about that. Nor can I claim to have much experience of life in court. In truth, I have been there only six months.' She looked around at the quieting crowd. 'I did not grow up in court. My home is Teragon.' She took a moment to allow her words to sink in. 'I am a girl from the settlements. As such, as far as I know, I am the *first* girl from the settlements to have a seat at the Prince's Table.'

'Bully for—' a voice began, but was silenced by a neighbour's elbow in their side.

'I'm not looking for congratulations,' Asta continued. 'My point is that I understand what life is like for you – in peacetime and during conflict. My family and neighbours were on the front line during the war with Eronesia. Our homes were destroyed. Many loved ones were lost. My community has done what it can to rebuild itself but none of us who lived through that time will ever be fully able to remove the imprint of war.' She allowed herself to take a breath. 'I see it as my job to represent you and your views at court. This is what I have done in my short time on the Council of Twelve and what I will continue to do as long as I hold the Poet's Chair.'

'Forgive me.' A new, kindlier voice piped up from the crowd. 'I know that you are only laying out your credentials and that you have been delayed in doing so by frequent interruptions.' Asta found the speaker's face. He was an older man and, judging by the expressions on his fellows in the crowd, a figure of respect within the community. 'But what we need to know right now is what military help is being dispatched from court. We have all seen and smelled the black smoke rising from our neighbour settlements in the south. Archenfield has been invaded. We need to know the plan.'

Asta nodded. 'Yes, of course you do,' she said, doing her best to think on her feet as her mind and body recoiled at the news that Paddenburg had reneged on the terms of its own ultimatum. 'The first thing to say is that you should not consider flight. You need to stay here in Galvaire and prepare to defend yourselves against the invaders.'

She saw heads shaking, including that of the man who had just addressed her. 'If you run,' Asta resumed, 'the enemy will surely follow. How far are you prepared to run? Into the arms of the Eronese?'

'Are these our only options?' the man asked her, his voice still kindly but now cut through with undisguised gloom. 'To wait here for the slayers of Paddenburg, or flee north towards our former foe?'

Before Asta could answer him, other voices threw yet more questions at her.

'Where are the soldiers of Archenfield?'

'*Where* are the forces of our ally Woodlark?'

She opened her mouth, framing a response, but was drowned out.

'The soldiers of Archenfield are deployed on the southern borders! What is left of our Princedom's army is fighting to protect Grenofen and Inderwick. We're on our own, just as the people of Vollerim and Lindas were!'

Asta wanted to argue that this was not the case but she could not. She knew that news travelled slowly to the settlements and that they did not know that the alliance with Woodlark was broken – unless, by some miracle, Prince Jared had managed to resuscitate it – but in their assessment of the deployment of the army of Archenfield, they were right on track.

'They're not sending any help,' someone else cried now. 'They're leaving us to the hands of the invader.'

'We don't have a chance!' came a fresh cry.

'Yes, we do,' Asta rejoined. 'Even now, Prince Jared is across the border building alliances with others of the Thousand Territories.' This at least was the truth, but in seeking to reassure them, she only succeeded in unlocking a new concern.

'You meant that Prince Jared is not even here, on the soil of Archenfield, while we face the threat of invasion?'

'No,' Asta swiftly responded. 'He is not because he made the courageous decision to go to seek fresh alliances, whilst leaving his Edling and Captain of the Guard, Axel Blaxland, to manage the military campaign.'

'Great job he's doing of that! Couldn't he have predicted the attack via Tanaka?'

'Perhaps he could,' Asta answered, her voice growing hoarse from straining above the mutterings of the crowd. 'But he did not. I will not lie to you. The simultaneous attack took us all by surprise. But he and his teams are working night and day to ensure the best possible deployment of the troops we have.' She paused, gathering her breath, knowing that she did not have much more fight within her. 'Your neighbours in Vollerim and Lindas were taken by surprise. They had no time to prepare for attack. Here in Galvaire, you have some time – not much, I grant you, but enough. You are a fighting community. We believe that you can see off the invaders. I am here today to ask you to defend your settlement and in doing so, silence this threat from the west.'

She had no more words for them. Had it been enough?

After a few moments, Asta heard the crowd begin to chant. At first their words were unclear to her. Were they mocking her?

'Death to the Paddenburgians!'

No, it seemed that – against all odds – her talk had sown the necessary seeds of fight in the settlement dwellers.

'Death to the Paddenburgians! Death to the Paddenburgians!'

What had begun as a lone cry was now taken up in unison and volume. The chant rang in her ears, and the arms of the crowd began punching the air above them to punctuate their cries.

Through her relief, Asta suddenly noticed an urgent movement at the back of the square. A rider had arrived. He seemed to be shouting at the people to the rear of the crowd, trying to make himself heard against the wall of noise. To Asta's surprise, the crowd parted to create a corridor through the centre of their ranks to allow the rider through.

The rider brought his horse to a standstill at Asta's feet. She saw that he was not riding alone but with a young boy, presumably his son.

'I come from Lindas,' he told her. 'Others from my settlement will follow here soon – those who have survived.'

His words gradually brought the crowd to silence once more. The man turned from Asta and addressed the people of Galvaire directly. 'Lindas has been razed,' he announced. 'They are destroying our houses, burning our grain stores and slaughtering the livestock in our fields.' He paused to suck in a breath, no doubt weakened by the dual exertion of riding and the inhalation of smoke. 'You need to take swift action. You need to flee. This enemy will slaughter every living thing in its path. Do not waste time.'

His words were like a touch-paper, reigniting the crowd, only now with panic and horror. Their previous inclination to fight was nowhere to be seen.

'Please!' Asta attempted to calm them. 'Please, listen to me! You have to stand firm. You have to fight. I told you. Help *is* on its way.'

'Help is not on its way.' In spite of his obvious exhaustion, the rider from Lindas matched the strength of her voice with his own. 'There is no time for help to reach you. The advance of the enemy is like brushfire. They will be here in Galvaire before you know it. Vollerim is razed, now Lindas too. How can you question that Galvaire will be next? Save yourselves. Save your children. Flee!'

Looking out over the panicking crowd, Asta realised she had no hope of bringing the people of Galvaire back to calm again. She stepped closer to the rider.

'How far away *is* the enemy, in your opinion?'

'They will be here before the day is out, probably sooner,' he told her, stroking his son's hair soothingly as he delivered the fateful news.

'It's good you were able to save yourself and your family,' she said.

The man dropped his head, continuing to stroke the boy's russet locks. 'I was not able to save us all.'

Asta closed her eyes, unable to ask the obvious next question. When she opened her eyes, she saw that the boy was looking up at her. Almost certainly, that morning, he had had a mother. Perhaps brothers and sisters, too.

'Where will you go?' she asked, as steadily as possible, her eyes remaining on the child, though her question was for the father.

'Somewhere. Anywhere.' His voice was resigned. 'How do you outrun a brushfire? Can you tell me that?' As he spoke, he dug his heels into the side of his horse and turned from her to continue on his journey.

'Wait!' she called. The man glanced over his shoulder. She saw the complete absence of hope in his eyes, having lost so much in so short a time. She guessed that his young son was the only thing keeping him going now.

'Ride on to Mellerad,' she told him. 'The fortified city walls will offer you greater protection than the fir forests to the north.'

The man nodded to her. It was the smallest of gestures, but she hoped that she had given him an injection of hope, however fleeting.

There was a new voice at Asta's side now. 'We need to get out of here.' Turning, she saw one of the palace escorts there. His words were urgent, his voice tinged, to her surprise, with panic.

'Where do we go from here?' she asked him.

'Back to the palace,' he said. 'Our horses are waiting on the other side of the church.'

Asta absorbed the words, then turned back towards the crowd. It was thinning fast now. Spurred on by the bleak messenger from Lindas, the people of Galvaire had gone to swiftly prepare for flight.

Standing there, Asta knew that she had failed in her

mission that morning, but she would *not* fail in her bigger duties to these people, and the people in each and every one of the settlements of Archenfield.

She turned back to the guard. 'We cannot ride back to the palace,' she told him.

He opened his mouth to protest, but she spoke over his protest. 'We'll ride to Mellerad.'

The escort shook his head. 'Our orders were to take you back to the palace.'

'Everything has changed,' Asta told him. 'Flee to the palace if you want, but I am riding on to Mellerad. I may be of some help to the people there. At least I can warn them to prepare for this flight of refugees from the west.'

The guard hung his head. 'If you're riding to Mellerad, we'll come with you. We've been charged by the Captain of the Guard to escort and protect you at all times.'

Asta sighed with relief. It was some irony that in riding to Mellerad, she was fulfilling Axel's wishes – not only to use what talents she had to help the settlements but, of course, to stay away from the palace while he launched his iniquitous vote against Prince Jared. But there was nothing she could do to challenge the vote now. She could only hope that the work she and her allies – Nova, Lady Koel and Queen Elin – had already undertaken would be enough to protect Prince Jared at this crucial time. She nodded to the guard and followed him around the church to where their horses stood waiting.

THIRTY-FOUR

THE COUNCIL CHAMBER, PALACE OF ARCHENFIELD

'I trust that you will all believe me when I tell you that it gives me no pleasure to do what I am compelled to do next – no pleasure at all.' Axel looked grave. 'I take my duties as Captain of the Guard and as Edling most seriously. I am this Council's and this Princedom's humble servant. But Archenfield is facing yet another threat from invasion. In order to combat this threat and make the Princedom safe not only for ourselves but for the generations to come, we must take decisive action.'

Axel could see the uncertainty in each pair of eyes watching him. It was nothing he had not anticipated.

'We have heard nothing of what Prince Jared has accomplished during these days of absence from the court and the Princedom. And, again, it gives me no pleasure to state that I expect his achievements to fall woefully short of the mark. Securing alliances that are strong enough to repel the threat from Paddenburg was always going to be a long shot. If we are to truly find a way through the current crisis, then I believe critical action is required. And that is why I am invoking a vote of no confidence in Prince Jared.'

'Have you no shame?' Queen Elin cried from the royal dais.

Axel glanced across to where Queen Elin and Prince Edvin sat side by side. Edvin looked as outraged as his mother. Then Axel noticed that his aunt and cousin were not alone on the dais.

On Elin's other side, watching the proceedings with great interest, was his sister, Lady Koel.

Koel was not supposed to be present at meetings of the Twelve, any more than his parents were. She turned her face a fraction and her eyes met his across the room. She nodded and smiled discreetly.

'I recommend that you still your tongue, *dear* aunt,' Axel replied. 'It is as a courtesy that you are allowed to view these proceedings. Do not take that position for granted. It could very easily be revoked.'

The tension in the room was palpable. It had been building up all the while Jared had been away – all the manoeuvrings on both sides had been leading to this one moment. Now it was here, the moment of decision. The moment, Axel supposed, that his entire life had been building towards.

'Remind us.' Emelie was, refreshingly, all business. 'How does this work? Are there ballot papers?'

Axel shook his head. 'No papers, Emelie. No secret ballot.' He smiled briefly. 'No black balls or feathers. We simply go around the table and each of you in turn will state whether you vote for or against Prince Jared.'

Axel could see the Beekeeper's mind working overtime, trying to calculate who had the majority.

However long the vote took to go around the table, Axel was confident that he would be the Prince by the end of the procedure. All the same, gallingly, he felt the pressure of the moment getting to him – his left hand had started shaking, and he was aware of sweat pooling between his shoulder blades. If he forged on, perhaps the others would not notice.

'The absent Prince has no vote,' Axel announced. 'Neither does any member of the Twelve not here today at this table – namely the Bodyguard, the Huntsman and the Poet.' He took a breath, congratulating himself at having dispatched Asta to Galvaire. 'As Edling *and* Captain of the Guard, I have only one vote. But before I cast it, I want to say one thing.' His eyes looked down the length of the table. 'If Prince Jared had returned, I would be the first to commend him on all the considerable efforts he has made since Prince Anders's untimely death.' He risked a glance at Queen Elin, but her eyes refused to meet his. 'I know that Prince Jared was not prepared for succession, that this was not something he sought. Nonetheless, I feel he has acquitted himself to the best of his abilities, and actually beyond, in this time.'

'These words, I am sure, will be a great comfort to him when he returns to find you have displaced him as ruler,' Elin cut in, her words like ice.

Now Prince Edvin – his voice rarely heard within this chamber – added, 'If you think so well of my brother, why are you challenging him?'

Axel met Edvin's stare. 'For the future of Archenfield,' he said. 'The safety of the Princedom is bigger than all of us.' He returned his attention to those gathered at the Prince's Table – those with voting rights. 'And so, with great regret, I must cast the first vote against Prince Jared.' He turned to Emelie, who was seated next to him. 'The vote is with you now.'

Emelie nodded. She did not rise to her feet. 'I vote with Axel,' she said.

Two votes against Jared.

Hearing Nova gasp, Axel suppressed a smile. Koel had assured Axel that Emelie was with him, despite having also convinced Nova and Asta that they had secured Emelie's vote. All eyes now moved to Jonas, who sat next to the Bee-keeper.

'I vote against Prince Jared,' he said.

Axel had known from the beginning that the Woodsman was one of his chief allies, but there was still a way to go. Jared had no votes but Axel had only three. And Nova was next. They all knew how this would go.

'My vote is *for* Prince Jared,' Nova confirmed.

Though the Falconer's vote came as no surprise to Axel, still he found it rankled.

'I, too, vote *for* Prince Jared,' Lucas said.

Axel gazed coldly at Lucas. Over on the dais, Axel saw Elin smiling at the Groom. He wondered who had talked Lucas around, even after he had attempted one of his nastiest pieces of manipulation. It was now two votes to Jared and three to Axel.

On Lucas's other side sat Morgan. Axel glanced once again at Elin, knowing the role she had played in trying to secure the Executioner's vote.

'I vote against Prince Jared,' Morgan said.

Queen Elin looked thunderstruck, no doubt wondering how Axel had coerced the Executioner into coming over to his side. Axel was now two votes ahead: things were where they were supposed to be, but there were three votes to go.

'Father Simeon,' Axel said. 'We have come to you.'

'I am aware of that,' Simeon said, shaking his head. 'I'm sorry, I find this to be an iniquitous business.'

'And I'm sorry you feel that way,' Axel said smoothly. 'But as you know, it is not without precedent in the Book of Law.'

Simeon glared at Axel. 'It's the Book of Law,' he said. 'Not the Sacred Scrolls.'

'You have your rulebook and I have mine,' Axel said with a smile. 'Are you abstaining?'

'I don't think any of us feel entirely comfortable about this,' Emelie interjected. 'But we have all nailed *our* colours to the mast. Forgive me, Father – no pun intended – but why should you be any different?'

'I do not intend to abstain,' Simeon said angrily. 'But, as long as I am one of the Twelve, I am certainly permitted to make my feelings known in this chamber.'

Axel had known that whoever restored to Father Simeon his sense of purpose would have secured his vote. Had Jonas done enough?

'My vote is with Prince Jared,' Father Simeon said, nodding directly at Queen Elin.

Elin acknowledged the Priest with a grateful nod of her own.

Axel glared at the Woodsman. If his failure had cost Axel this vote, there would be hell to pay.

The next vote lay with Elias.

'My vote ...' he began huskily, then stopped to clear his throat. 'My vote is also with Prince Jared.'

No! Father Simeon's foolish allegiance to Jared was one thing, but Elias's vote was pure betrayal.

'I, perhaps more than anyone else in this room,' Elias explained, 'have felt that Prince Jared was too young and ill-equipped to rule Archenfield. But I have come to see that I was wrong. I was quick to underestimate what someone of Jared's age is capable of. Sometimes youth has to take control of the Princedom for it to begin anew.' Axel rolled his eyes, but it seemed the Physician had not yet finished. 'I fear that a change of ruler now would be a signal to the Princes of

Paddenburg that Archenfield is growing ever more chaotic and vulnerable.'

Axel flushed with panic. 'But we *are* vulnerable, you ancient fool!' he cried. If he lost this vote, he would make sure that Elias Peck's decision would be his undoing.

Vera Webb cleared her throat.

Even in his upset state, Axel noticed Nova and Elin exchange a look. He was under no illusions: the Cook would be voting in Jared's favour. He clenched his fists under the table and cursed himself for all the times he had openly bad-mouthed the woman's cooking.

'. . . Prince Jared,' Vera was saying.

Axel realised that it was over. He would never be the ruler of Archenfield. In fact, it was only a matter of time before he would be officially removed from the Council. Axel had given everything to the twelve, to the court and to the Princedom. And this was how they repaid him?

'Well,' Emelie said, her tone level, though she was smiling. 'By my reckoning, Axel, that is five votes in your favour. It seems you are now our Prince.'

Axel blinked at the Beekeeper. Then he realised his error. Vera had just said she was voting *against* Prince Jared. Flooded with relief, he nodded at Emelie, an overwhelming sense of gratitude threatening to overcome his swiftly regained composure. 'I thank those of you who voted for me for your confidence. I will not let you down.' He paused. 'And to those four of you who cast your vote with Jared, please do not be fearful of any repercussions. Let me assure you that what happens in this chamber, stays here.'

'Except it doesn't, does it?' Queen Elin rose angrily from her seat. 'Because you and your clan have finally got what you wanted. You have taken advantage of the dire external events to wrest the throne from my son and claim it for your own.'

THIRTY-FIVE

THE COUNCIL CHAMBER,
PALACE OF ARCHENFIELD

'There are,' Axel said, 'just a couple more matters of court business that we must attend to. Starting with my replacement as Captain of the Guard.' He paused to ensure he had everyone's full attention. 'I am pleased to announce that my successor will be my long-time comrade and deputy, Elliot Nash.'

There were murmurs of assent around the table. There was nothing controversial about this choice. Nash was a respected and popular man.

Axel smiled, buoyed up by the support of the Twelve. 'Now seems as good a moment as any to welcome Elliot to the Prince's Table.' He turned to the guards at the chamber door and nodded. 'If you would.'

The guards opened the doors to reveal Elliot Nash. It was like a perfectly executed game of chess, thought Nova. Axel had had all his people in the correct positions.

As Elliot walked into the Council Chamber, Axel began to clap. This was taken up by some, but not all, of the Twelve.

Though she had no personal argument with Nash, Nova's own hands remained carefully placed on the table.

'Welcome to the Twelve!' Axel cried warmly, drawing Elliot into a bear hug. 'And now, you must take your place at the Prince's Table.'

Elliot moved towards the empty seat. He seemed genuinely thrilled as he took his chair, and ran his fingers contemplatively across the table, where the words 'The Captain of the Guard' shimmered in the light.

Nova took some comfort from the fact that each member of the Twelve still possessed genuine power, even with the over throw of Prince Jared. This power would help keep a check on Axel's ambitions. As the vote had demonstrated, he currently possessed the support of the majority, but only just, and allegiances could shift fast. Especially with a little help. Nova felt the stirrings of a fresh campaign. It was not as if she were alone in her contempt for Axel. Far from it.

She became aware that she was being watched. She looked up and met the eyes of Lady Koel, sitting on the dais beside Queen Elin. Perhaps Lady Koel was thinking the very same thoughts, as she too absorbed the body shock of these extraordinary events – not least the Cook's betrayal. Lady Koel had been utterly confident that they had Vera's vote, just as Queen Elin had been that they had Morgan's.

Nova's eyes moved on to Queen Elin: Elin, who today had lost the tight hold she had maintained on the throne after so many years. It was strange how she already seemed to have lost some of the lustre of power. It made Nova wonder if that lustre came from within, or was purely something imbued on those in authority by others.

'And now, to my choice of Edling.' Axel's voice brought Nova's focus back to the room. Of course! She should have foreseen that, just as Axel had had his Captain of the Guard waiting in the wings, so too he would have positioned his chosen heir.

The new Prince was smiling and glancing around the table. And it was then that Nova realised that Axel's Edling was not standing out in the corridor; he – or she – was already within the Council Chamber. Axel was going to award the honour to one of his supporters on the Twelve; indeed, perhaps this had been agreed as the price of support. Her heart racing, Nova glanced across the faces of those who had supported Axel in the vote of no confidence. The Beekeeper, the Woodsman, the Executioner, the Cook. Which of them was it going to be? Nova found their expressions impossible to read, but she could no longer doubt that the Prince's Table was home to many skilled actors.

'My choice of Edling is . . .' Axel began, then hesitated just a moment longer. The tension in the room was palpable. Nova let out a sigh.

'My sister,' Axel announced. 'Lady Koel.'

Axel's arm was extended towards his sister. Nova's gaze moved, with horror, to the dais, where Lady Koel had risen to her feet and was smiling graciously. Whereas Queen Elin now seemed stripped of power, Lady Koel seemed equally transformed: her eyes, her hair, her clothes, all seemed brighter – as if she had darted out, without them noticing, and returned transformed to the dais in readiness for the announcement.

Nova sought out Lady Koel's eyes, wondering if she might find guilt there at her complete betrayal. But when, at last, Lady Koel deigned to look upon her, there was no trace of guilt. She simply nodded, with utter poise and grace. No one, Nova now realised, had been more ready to claim power than Axel's clever, ambitious, duplicitous younger sister. It was simply how the Wheel of Fortune worked: taking one person down as it raised another aloft.

Suddenly, the doors to the chamber opened again and members of Axel's guard strode inside, accompanied by Adam Marangon, Nova's own deputy.

'Prince Axel!' How easily the words tripped off the guard's tongue, Nova thought. 'We apologise for the interruption to your meeting, but we have grim news to share.'

Nova looked towards Axel. To his credit, he did not seem fazed by the words of the messenger. 'Go on.'

The guard nodded. 'Our borders have been broached in three locations by advancing troops from Paddenburg.'

'No!' Elias exclaimed, looking as if he had taken a body blow.

'How bad is it?' Axel enquired of the messenger.

The man cleared his throat. 'The invaders have taken over several of the settlements and are advancing fast on the other two southern fronts.'

'All hope is lost,' Vera cried.

'Pull yourself together, woman!' Jonas snapped. 'We aren't defeated yet.'

'Which settlements?' Axel asked.

'Inderwick has fallen, and our troops to the south of Grenofen have been surrounded.' The messenger replied. 'There has been significant loss of life. Paddenburg's army has also breached our border with Tanaka in the west. Lindas and Vollerim have been razed. The barbarians are systematically moving from one settlement to the next and destroying everything in their wake.'

'Asta!' Nova cried. 'What news from Galvaire?'

The messenger shook his head decisively. 'Galvaire has also fallen into enemy hands.'

Nova felt giddy. She glanced across the table towards Elias but he had his head in his hands. She bit down on her lip, sending a prayer for Asta's safety.

'Has the enemy reached Mellerad?' Axel demanded.

'No,' the messenger replied. 'They have spread northward to Galvaire and south of Vollerim, creating a wide front line in the west. I expect that they won't waste time before advancing eastward.'

'We must move fast!' Axel announced. 'I will lead troops to Mellerad. It's a former fort and our only western stronghold. The ancient stone walls and battlements will slow the advancing army but it cannot survive for long without reinforcements. Mellerad *cannot* be allowed to fall. If it does, there's little hope of stopping our enemy from swarming across the central plains to the gates of this very palace.'

There was surprise around the table at his words, and it was Vera who summoned the words that were surely waiting on others' lips too: 'Have you forgotten how we rule this Princedom?' she asked. 'In times of crisis, especially, it is the Twelve who make decisions together.' She rose to her feet, standing before Axel and folding her arms.

But Axel seemed unflustered. 'Be assured, Vera, I know better than anyone the inner workings of Archenfield. Key decisions cannot always be picked over and ratified by this group – there is a time to sit around a table and debate one course of action over another, but this is not such a time. We need to defend our people and our Princedom. *Now*.'

Vera remained standing, as solid and unyielding as the tree from which the Prince's Table had once been hewn. 'I'm sure that I speak for all of the Twelve when I say that we want the same thing, Axel. I just want to be part of those discussions.'

'As you wish,' Axel said. 'If I make a tactical decision that you disagree with, speak up. I guarantee you that your objection will be noted.'

Vera sat down, her arms still folded tightly across her chest.

'What do you want me to do?' Elliot asked.

'You, Emelie and Lucas will ride to Grenofen,' Axel replied. 'There are troops stationed at Dalhoen. Should Grenofen fall, then your priority is to defend the valley settlement of Pencador. It is the only route that Paddenburg's army can take north from Grenofen. With Inderwick in enemy hands, it is most likely that Tonsberg will be the next settlement in their sights. It's across the fjord from Woodlark and, if it falls, Paddenburg's army will have a clear run north. Jonas and Morgan, you will ride south to defend Tonsberg and the east. Elias will ride with you as far south as Kirana, where the central field hospital is stationed.'

'Koel,' Axel said, turning now to his sister. 'You will stay at the palace. As Edling, you are to make decisions in my stead. If our greatest fears are realised, and Mellerad, Tonsberg and Pencador are defeated, then you must decide if and when surrender becomes our only remaining option.'

Koel nodded, seeming at ease with such responsibility.

'Simeon and Vera,' Axel said. 'You will also stay at the palace.'

'What good can I do here?' Father Simeon cried. 'Our people are dying, Axel. They need a bearer of faith beside them before their final breath escapes them.'

'If our circumstances are as dire as you suggest, Father – and I pray that they are not – then your services are best utilised elsewhere.' Axel said. 'I need you both here to support Koel. We cannot dispatch the entire leadership of Archenfield to the battle lines.'

'And what about me?' Nova enquired. 'Do I even still have a role to play here?'

Axel turned towards her. 'I mean no disrespect, Nova, but you have not recovered enough to join the fight. You too must stay. As soon as you are able, send a falcon to the east. If my cousin has had any success there, we'll need as many troops as he is able to muster.'

'I understand,' she answered, unable to fault the logic behind Axel's decision. Every one of them had a job to do now. Innocent people to the south and west were being slaughtered by a seemingly unstoppable enemy. She shuddered to think that Asta might have met such a fate. Nova glanced through the mullioned window towards the mountains of Woodlark. She prayed that Prince Jared had succeeded in his mission, and that he be granted a swift return. Archenfield was at war. And without help from the other river territories, the lives they had built here would be torn to shreds by the merciless talons of the invaders from Paddenburg.

THIRTY-SIX

THE CANYON PALACE, REDNOW

Kai and Bram were nervously pacing about Prince Rohan's council chamber when Prince Rohan strode down the stairs, followed closely by Jared and Hal. Immediately, Kai and Bram turned to greet their comrades.

Jared swiftly embraced Bram's gangling form, then turned to Kai. 'It's *so* good to see you,' he exclaimed. He felt the reassuring solidity of Jagger's body against his own as they hugged. Stepping backwards, he grinned sheepishly at both his fellows. 'I'm sorry! We have ridden solidly from Larsson. I must reek to the heavens!'

Kai looked sombre, but shook his head. 'No, Your Majesty.'

'I shall have hot oil baths drawn for us all,' Prince Rohan announced. 'And massages to swiftly soothe our aching limbs.'

'So,' Jared enquired brightly, 'what news from Baltiska? How did you fare with Nina?'

Kai's expression gave Jared his answer, even before he spoke. 'I'm sorry,' Kai told him. 'I did warn you that there was little possibility of even gaining an audience with my cousin, let alone of concluding an alliance with him.' He bowed his head. 'It gives me no satisfaction to confirm that this was indeed the case.'

Feeling the weariness of defeat, still Jared placed his hand on the Huntsman's shoulder. 'I'm very grateful for your efforts.'

'Do not be too downcast,' Rohan said, coming to Jared's side. 'You have succeeded in putting together an unprecedented alliance of four river territories – Archenfield, Woodlark, Rednow and Larsson. Trust me, Ciprian would only ever have proved a thorn in our sides.'

Jared nodded but found it hard, in his weary state, to put on a brave face. The unshakable truth of the matter was that Woodlark's alliance was contingent upon his delivering Logan Wilde to Queen Francesca. The alliance with Larsson also waited upon this action. What if those in Archenfield would not allow this? Only the alliance Jared had concluded with Rohan had no such strings attached, but even this felt shaky. What if Rohan learned the truth and felt he had been lied to? Jared bitterly regretted not having been straight with Rohan from the start. He found himself looking into the bright eyes of a man who thought he had secured three strategic alliances when, in fact, he might not even have succeeded in concluding one of them.

Kai placed his hand on Jared's shoulder in a way that told him bad news was about to follow. 'I do not know if you have already been told, but there is more grim news from across the borders.' Kai's voice was doleful.

'We have just ridden through the palace gates,' Rohan told him. 'What news do you have?'

'Word from the Falconer was received this very day,' Kai said. 'Firstly, Paddenburg invaded Tanaka yesterday.'

'Tanaka?' Rohan said, his voice light. '*Not* Archenfield, Prince Jared. There is still time to—' His smile froze as Kai indicated he had more to say. 'My second piece of news is that Paddenburg's army has now directly attacked Archenfield.'

Jared felt each of Kai's brief bulletins stab him deep in his gut. It hardly mattered now whether he had secured the alliances or not. Events were moving at a dizzying speed. Paddenburg had not, after all, allowed them the full seven days of the ultimatum. Any sense of control he might have felt riding back towards Rednow all but ebbed away as Kai continued.

'They stormed our border in three places – in the south at Grenofen and Inderwick, as we correctly predicted they would, and in the west at Lindas. It was a highly coordinated attack.' Kai's violet eyes met Jared's. 'The Princes of Paddenburg made good on their dark promise – only they attacked us a day ahead of the time specified within their ultimatum.'

Jared's mind flashed back to the Council of Twelve's meeting the day they had received the Paddenburg Ultimatum. Emelie Sharp had been quick to predict this very outcome. Even though Axel had been determined to send troops to protect the border, Jared, in his naïvety, had hoped that the Princes of Paddenburg might play by the rulebook. But this wasn't a game or a sport; it was war, and his lands were now host to an invading army.

Jared turned to Kai. 'How far have they advanced?'

Kai's eyes narrowed. 'By the time the message was sent, the enemy had progressed northwards along our western border as far as Galvaire. The settlement of Grenofen is surrounded and Inderwick has now been lost. Our troops held their own for several hours but were forced to draw back by the sheer number of Paddenburg's force.'

'Things could have grown much worse since the message was written,' Hal pointed out.

'What loss of life has there been?' Jared asked.

'It is too early to say,' Kai answered. 'The note from Nova simply indicated that the protocols of war had been employed.'

'Then we must act swiftly,' Jared told his comrades. 'The Twelve will be moving to reinforce the front lines, which means that the palace and northern settlements will be left vulnerable in the event that Paddenburg's army breaks through our defences.'

Jared turned towards Rohan. He fully expected his voice to be tremulous when he spoke but, to his surprise, his words emerged surprisingly clear and resonant. 'It seems that I must call upon you to make good on your promise of help.'

Rohan nodded. 'You will have all the help you need,' he told Jared. 'The bandits of Paddenburg will not steal your lands from under you.'

'You promised two thousand men and women,' Jared said, feeling that the only way to navigate through this crisis and the attendant maelstrom of emotions was to deal in hard facts. 'How soon can you have them ready?'

Rohan's hand squeezed Jared's shoulder. 'I will go and talk to my officers. I know that time is of the essence.'

Kai looked at Jared. 'Two thousand troops *is* a significant offering,' he said. 'But how did you fare in Larsson? What additional support can Prince Séverin bring to bear?'

Jared hesitated, waiting for Rohan to exit the room.

'Prince Séverin agreed to an alliance,' Jared answered at last. This time – damn it – he heard the lack of conviction in his voice.

'What kind of numbers are we talking?'

'In the decree, Séverin has pledged the support of three thousand troops, but,' Jared paused again, 'there are terms attached to Séverin's decree.'

'*What* terms?'

It was a fair question but Jared found himself hating Kai for asking it.

'What terms?' He heard Kai's voice enquire once more.

'Séverin's offer of an alliance is contingent upon us having a full accord with Woodlark,' Jared informed the others.

'And the Woodlark alliance,' Hal stepped in, 'is dependent upon us handing over Logan Wilde to them.'

'Which,' said Kai, looking meaningfully at Jared, 'we simply may not be able to do. Especially now that the Paddenburg army is over the border and hacking its way to the palace.' He shook his head. 'Surely one of the first things they will do is spring Wilde from the Dungeons.' He shook his head glumly. 'I failed to bring you the alliance with Baltiska. Now it appears the rest of this house of cards is coming tumbling down.'

Jared felt a severe chill at Kai's ominous words. 'I have secured *three* alliances,' he maintained.

'Yes,' Kai said, his tone gentle, even if his words were not. 'But only one of them holds any real value.' He paused. 'And surely it is only a matter of time before Prince Rohan learns the true state of affairs.'

'Prince Rohan cannot find out about this,' Jared snapped. 'He cannot know about Woodlark, or that Prince Séverin has added an impossible clause.'

'How do you propose to keep that from him?' Hal's voice was tinged with uncharacteristic panic. 'He's going to find out sooner or later. And when he does, we risk losing his two thousand troops.'

'I shall tell him,' Jared said. For days, he had known this was what he would have to do. 'Rohan is a good man. I'll lay all my cards on the table. Then there will be no more to fear.'

Saying it somehow helped him to steady himself, and Jared

could see that he had once more asserted some level of control and authority within the company.

But it was to prove only fleeting.

Kai spoke up again: 'Prince Jared, I am afraid there is one last piece of news that I must share with you, though I hate to even give voice to these words.' He broke off, dropping his head.

'What is it?' Jared asked him. 'Spit it out! After everything else you have told me, with our enemies ranked against us, what else can hurt us now?'

Kai lifted his head once more. His eyes were tinged with tears. 'Axel called for a vote of no confidence in your absence,' he said, his voice soft but neutral. 'The remaining members of the Twelve voted in his favour. I'm so sorry, Prince Jared, but your cousin is now officially Prince of All Archenfield. He has deposed you.'

Jared felt the bitter import of Kai's words. Days earlier, possibly even hours earlier, they might have had the power to fell him. Now, after so many body blows, he felt numb. His cousin's betrayal was hardly a surprise – its timing almost made him want to laugh at Axel's cheek. But he was no more able to laugh than he was to cry or scream. He stood there, feeling as if he were not made of mortal flesh but of stone, like the statues of dead princes they had passed on their way to Rohan's council chamber.

He was aware of Kai reaching a hand towards his shoulder and he felt the Huntsman's hand come to rest there. Then, suddenly, the absence of sensation was replaced by a sudden surge of energy from deep within him. Jared shook off the Huntsman's hand and turned to face Kai, Hal and Bram.

They were all watching him, each face etched with the same expression of sorrow and pity.

'What do you expect me to do now?' he asked them. 'To

slump down at your feet or throw myself from the battlements of the Canyon Palace?' His eyes flamed with passion. 'After all that I have come through – after all that we have come through together – is that how little you think of me?' None of them spoke. 'Answer me, damn it! Is that what you think of me?'

'No, Prince Jared,' Bram was the first of his fellows to find words.

'Thank you, Bram,' Jared said.

'There are limits, however,' Kai began, 'to what one man can endure. You have endured much over these past few weeks—'

'Yes,' Prince Jared's voice cut over Kai's. 'Yes, I have. Any one of the challenges we have faced might have broken me – I'll be the first to admit that. But, to my surprise, I am *not* broken. There is still much to be done. We need to ride back to court. My own position is of little care to me now – what matters is saving Archenfield, keeping its people safe.'

'Yes, sir,' Bram said.

'Yes, Your Majesty,' Hal answered.

Jared was about to correct Hal's terminology when he heard footsteps on the stairway above. Glancing up, he saw Prince Rohan making his return.

'It is done,' Rohan called out as he strode over to join them. 'Two thousand troops will be ready to ride within the hour. We will make camp within the border of Archenfield as a show of force. We will advance further when you call. I have also arranged fresh horses for you. And,' he paused at last to take a breath, 'I have sent a courier to Séverin and told him to dispatch as big an army as he can offer.'

The mere mention of Séverin caused Jared to blanch.

'Prince Rohan, there is something I need to tell you,' Jared said. 'Something I should have told you days ago.'

Rohan's eyes narrowed. His characteristic energy fell away and he became still, his eyes trained curiously on Jared.

'When I told you we had an alliance with Woodlark,' Jared resumed, 'I should have been clearer. Francesca has agreed to an alliance only on the condition that we hand over Logan Wilde to her to impart her own choice of justice upon her daughter's murderer.'

'I see,' Rohan answered, his voice neutral.

'I did not share this information with you when we were discussing the alliance between Archenfield and Rednow – firstly, because I was confident that I could follow through with Francesca's terms and secondly because, I confess, I wanted nothing to stand in the way of Rednow joining the alliance.' He took a breath. 'I see now that I was wrong. I should have been plainer with you from the outset.'

Rohan nodded. Jared found the gesture hard to interpret. Was Rohan agreeing with him, or simply registering his understanding?

'When I met with Séverin and Celestia to discuss Larsson joining the alliance, they asked to see Francesca's decree. So they know of her stipulation,' he continued, 'and they included a stipulation in their own decree. That Larsson would activate its own alliance only once Woodlark had done so.'

This time, Rohan did not nod, but merely blinked.

'It was never my intention to deceive you,' Jared said. 'But I did deceive you, Prince Rohan, and I'm so very sorry about that. I will understand, of course, if you wish to withdraw your own alliance only and your offers of military support.'

There, he had said it. And, strangely, though they had been difficult words to say, he felt somehow lighter for giving voice to them. Now the ball was firmly in Rohan's court.

He watched as Rohan, eyes down, contemplatively twisted one of the rings on his fingers. Jared had noticed him do this before – same ring, same finger.

Rohan looked back up at him. 'I said when we first met that I found you to be an honourable man,' Rohan began.

Jared's face dropped. 'I remember,' he said. 'I'm just sorry that I failed to live up to your expectations.'

'Please,' Rohan said, more forcefully, 'let me finish. I said that you were an honourable man. It was a mistake on your part not being frank with me about Francesca's stipulation. But, just so we are clear, I would not have acted like her or Séverin and insisted on a condition of my own. You would have had a full, working alliance with Rednow.'

Would have. The words dug into Jared's consciousness. If he'd told the truth, he would have still come away with Rohan's alliance. Now, due to his deceit, he was about to lose it.

'You still have the alliance,' Rohan told him. 'It took guts to tell me the truth today. But this comes as no surprise to me – courage is a quality you possess in abundance. I still think you are an honourable man, Prince Jared, but, like the rest of us, you are a work in progress.'

Jared could not believe his ears, but there was no mistaking Rohan's smile or the hands that stretched out to take his own. And, once their hands were clasped, there was no mistaking the strength of Rohan's grip as he squeezed Jared's fingers reassuringly.

'You have already slain more dragons than most men twice your age,' Rohan told him. 'Now, let's waste no more time in getting back in the saddle. Your Princedom has never needed you or your wise rule more than today.'

Jared smiled at him, but bitterly shook his head. 'That's something else you need to know, friend. In my absence, it

305

seems my cousin – my own Edling – has taken it upon himself to oust me from power and take my place.'

Rohan shook his head in disbelief. 'I am very sorry to hear this.' He frowned. 'Does this change our plans?'

Jared considered his ally's words, then shook his head decisively. 'No, it changes nothing. We ride on. Archenfield needs me.' He shook his head, his eyes taking in all four of his companions – Kai, Hal, Bram and Rohan. 'What I mean to say is, Archenfield needs *us*.'

THIRTY-SEVEN

BORDER COUNTRY

The landscape fell away at Jared's left side and, in the distance, beyond the point where the forest grew dense once again, a wide expanse of blue peeked through the treetops. This fjord marked the border between Larsson and Woodlark and was joined to the great fjord of Archenfield by a fast-flowing river. This Jared thought, with mixed emotions, was the river that might have joined five territories in alliance.

Perhaps, against all odds, it still might.

Rohan of Rednow rode beside him. He had proved steadfast in all his dealings with Jared since knowing the truth of the alliance. They were two Princes leading an army into battle. As they approached the fork in the river that cut northward into the heartlands of Baltiska, Jared turned in his saddle and glanced at the great column of men and women on horseback, keeping a steady pace behind them. There were so many that Jared was unable to see where their numbers ended. His cousin and his Council may have lost faith in him, he may have lost his title of Prince of All Archenfield, yet nobody could take this away from him. He alone had forged the alliance with Rednow and indeed with Woodlark and Larsson. It was he who would lead these soldiers into his Princedom.

Jared was resolute that, whatever events had occurred in his absence, Archenfield was rightfully his. First, he would take on the Paddenburg army; then he would turn his full attention on Axel and attempt to undo the tangled threads of his cousin's duplicity.

There were tears in Jared's eyes as he rode towards the dark stone arch that marked the brief border between Rednow and Archenfield, and he felt his heart soar with the relief of coming home. He had not been away many days, but so much had happened. Now he wanted to drive the bandits of Paddenburg, as Rohan had called them, off his land once and for all.

As Jared dismounted, a border guard ran over and bowed before him. When the guard rose up, Jared saw dark circles beneath his grey eyes.

'You are a welcome sight indeed, Your Majesty,' the guard said. 'Especially with that throng riding behind you. Almost all of the border guards have been called up to fight. I wish I were down there helping them.'

'On the border or the battlefield, know that your service to the Princedom is equally valued,' Jared told him. 'We must ride on now. Stay safe.'

He led Rohan's troops west until he saw the familiar silhouette of the palace of Archenfield looming across the meadows. He had seen other palaces now – some, like Woodlark, might be grander; some, like Rednow, might be miraculous feats of architecture; some, like Larsson, might be located within the landscape of a fairy tale. But none could ever compete in his own heart with the palace of Archenfield, where he had lived all his days.

'Your troops should rest a while here,' Jared told Rohan. 'We will continue on to the palace, tell them of our alliances and determine where our numbers are most needed.'

Rohan nodded. 'On you go, Prince Jared. I will stay here with my people. They are about to go into battle. It is important for their leader to be with them.'

'I understand,' Jared said with a nod and a smile to his friend and ally.

On he rode – alongside him Kai, Bram and Hal – the final distance towards the palace. He had half expected to return there to find the palace razed to the ground. But, on riding up beneath the main balcony, he saw that the palace was strangely unchanged – and disconcertingly quiet.

Jumping down from the saddle, he felt the solidity of the ancient stone beneath his feet. Climbing the familiar steps up to the balcony, his thoughts turned to the two state occasions when he had taken his position there before his people. Twice they had pledged their allegiance to him; twice he had made his own oath to serve them. Today there were no crowds, but as he walked across the flagstones of the balcony, he knew that he was willing to die fighting, if that was what it took to honour his side of the bargain.

'Prince Jared!'

His mother ran out towards him. He felt hot tears pricking his eyes and then his whole body began to tremble with relief as she swept him into her arms.

'You are home safe,' she said, holding tightly on to her oldest surviving son. She had never held him in this way before. Somehow, this one embrace made up for all those he had been deprived of growing up.

'There is so much to tell you,' she said, when at last

309

she released him. 'Not much will be pleasing to your ears, I fear.'

'I know all about the vote of no confidence,' Jared told her. 'All I care about at this moment is stopping the advancing army of Paddenburg. We rode home with two thousand Rednow troops. They are ready to fight where they are needed most.'

'That is wonderful news,' his mother told him, stepping back but holding on to both his hands.

'Cousin Jared!' He turned to see Lady Koel, dressed warmly against the chill weather, striding out from the palace to join them.

'Though your brother has deposed my son,' Elin said, turning to her, 'the correct form of address is still Prince Jared, I think you will find.'

Lady Koel smiled as she came nearer. 'Jared was always my cousin first and a prince second,' she said. 'Now may I hug my dear cousin in welcome?'

'Yes, of course,' Jared told her. Awkwardly, he slipped free from his mother's tight grip in order to embrace Koel.

'I'm so glad to have you home safe,' she whispered in his ear. And though he knew she must somehow have been part of her brother's conspiracy, still Jared felt convinced by the warmth with which she spoke. He had always felt there to be a strong bond between himself and his cousin. Perhaps it was something he could use to his advantage in order to challenge the new set-up.

'You know, of course, that Lady Koel is the new Prince's Edling?' Elin told him now, her voice full of undisguised venom.

Jared nodded. 'Congratulations,' he told Lady Koel. What else could he say?

He saw his mother shake her head in horror and disbelief.

He knew how devastated she must feel at Axel's having seized the throne. In many ways, he suspected this was more of a blow to her than it was even to him. But he would deal with Axel – in his own time and his own way. There were other, more important battles to fight first.

'Lady Koel, I have news from my travels,' he told her. 'I have returned with alliances.'

'Yes,' she said. 'I heard you mention two thousand troops from Rednow—?'

'That is only part of it.'

'Let us go inside, into the warmth,' Koel suggested. 'Your face is pinched from the cold.'

Jared shook his head. 'If you don't mind, I'd prefer to talk out here. I intend to ride out again soon with the troops, and I fear if I go into the warmth, I might find myself reluctant to leave, when leave I must.'

Lady Koel smiled serenely. 'You are as noble as ever, Prince Jared,' she told him. 'All right then, we shall talk out here. Tell me about these alliances.'

Jared took a breath. 'I set out to achieve an alliance of the five river territories – Archenfield, Woodlark, Rednow, Baltiska and Larsson.'

'An ambitious plan in the number of days you were granted by the Paddenburg Ultimatum,' Lady Koel observed.

'Yes,' Jared agreed. 'You know already that I have returned with a fully operational alliance with Rednow – Prince Rohan is waiting in position to lead his troops into battle.' Koel nodded, urging him on. 'But, you see, this is only the beginning. Queen Francesca is ready to send us the troops of Woodlark, and back-up from Malytor if required.' Registering the surprise on the faces of his cousin and mother, Jared continued. 'All we need to do to unlock such an army is to hand over Logan Wilde to Francesca.'

Queen Elin nodded at this but Lady Koel frowned.

'You know as well as I, cousin, that as much as we may desire the renewal of our alliance with Woodlark, we cannot deliver Logan Wilde to Francesca or anyone else.' Her voice had wavered for a moment but now grew more resolute. 'Remember the terms of the Paddenburg Ultimatum.'

'What does the ultimatum matter when their troops are hacking their way, settlement by settlement, towards the palace walls? Paddenburg's threat was that they would invade *early* if we harmed Logan. But they invaded early in any case. Everything has changed. They're not playing by any rulebook, so why should we?'

He could see conflicting emotions on his cousin's face, and sought to bolster his case. 'If we give Wilde to Francesca, we not only gain the alliance with Woodlark but open up a third alliance – with Séverin of Larsson!' He paused. 'You hear what I'm telling you? I can offer you alliances with three of the four territories I petitioned. All we have to do is hand over my brother's assassin.'

Over Lady Koel's shoulder, Queen Elin had never looked more proud of her son.

Lady Koel cleared her throat. 'I am, of course, greatly impressed by what you have managed to achieve in so short a span of time. But the fact remains, we cannot simply *hand over* Logan Wilde.'

Jared shook his head in disbelief. 'Why ever not? Haven't we agreed the Paddenburg Ultimatum is meaningless now?'

'Forget about the ultimatum!' She cut him off. 'As you say, Wilde was Prince Anders's assassin. Our people would never condone us releasing Archenfield's number-one enemy of state.'

'That's the point,' Jared cut in. 'Wilde is *not* an enemy of state. I fear your inexperience is showing. What you fail to

312

appreciate is that the people do not know that Logan Wilde was Anders's and Silva's murderer – and for very good reason. Wilde's imprisonment is a well-kept secret. As far as the people know, Michael Reeves was the assassin and the Blood Price has been paid.'

'But it hasn't,' Lady Koel rejoined.

'I am keenly aware of that fact and of the importance of the Blood Price,' Jared resumed passionately. 'But need I remind you that the Blood Price is not owed to the people? It is owed to Anders's family – *my family*. And I'd far rather it not be fulfilled and the alliance with Woodlark be saved.'

Lady Koel eyed him with undisguised disdain, then shook her head. 'I fear things have moved on considerably in your absence. Even if we did as you wish, there is no time for your allies to ride to our rescue now. The fight is already too far entrenched.'

Jared could not believe his ears. 'It sounds as if you are about ready to surrender.' His voice exposed raw frustration. 'Or negotiate,' he added darkly.

'We will do what we need to do to preserve this Princedom,' she told him. 'My instructions from my brother, before he rode out from the palace, were plain.'

'But you said it yourself,' – Jared could not resist one final attempt – 'everything is changing so fast. *You* are Edling now. *You* can make your own decisions. You have that power!'

She nodded. 'I know the powers at my disposal,' she told him.

Behind her, Queen Elin's face was a picture of disgust.

Kai Jagger, who had been standing quietly by, now stepped forward. 'What is to stop us going down to the Dungeons ourselves and carrying Logan Wilde away from there?'

His words were full of fury but Lady Koel's voice was calm personified as she gave him her answer. 'Guards,' she said. 'Guards who report to Prince Axel, and to me. Logan Wilde is not going anywhere. We will not discuss him any further.'

Jared could see that Kai was not ready to back down, but he was growing weary of this line of argument. It was clear that Koel was not going to release Logan and that he would be unable to call upon either Francesca or Séverin for support. Still, he had Rohan and his two thousand troops waiting for him.

Jared's eyes met Lady Koel's. 'I told you before, cousin, that I am ready to ride out with such forces as I can muster.' His voice was neutral, business-like. 'I think you had better tell me where, in your view, we can best impact the fight.'

Lady Koel nodded. 'Prince Axel is leading the fight at Mellerad. The battle in the west has been most intense, but our position holds. In the south, our troops have fallen back and are defending the settlements of Tonsberg and Pencador. Although we fear that our hold at Tonsberg is fragile at best.'

'If Tonsberg falls, our enemy will move on towards Kirana,' Kai observed. 'If they reach Grasmyre, you'll be able to hear the death cries from this very balcony.'

'Then we ride on to Tonsberg,' Jared declared.

'No,' Lady Koel countered, equally firmly. 'Jonas sent a messenger this morning. The township had no natural defences and it was impossible to protect for long. The Woodsman intends to fall back from Tonsberg to the forests north of the settlement. He hopes to hold off the enemy from there.' Jared couldn't help but be impressed at his cousin's mastery of the situation – it seemed she had adapted to leadership far more swiftly and naturally than he had. 'The fighting may be intensified at the settlements,' she continued, 'but scouts have identified enemy troops flanking the battle zones and heading northward along the valleys. The land between Dalhoen and

Kirana is vulnerable and that is where your troops are most sorely needed. You will find additional supplies at Dalhoen. A military camp was set up there but the northern recruits have since joined the fight on the front lines.'

'All right then,' Jared said, nodding. 'We'll go there.' *We have our orders*, he almost added. 'Please send word to Prince Axel and the other members of the Twelve where we will be, in case they need us.'

She nodded again, her face softer now. 'I will, of course.'

Before departing, Kai leaned in towards Lady Koel. 'It never ceases to surprise me how people behave when they have the backdrop of war as their excuse,' he said huskily. 'If I survive this conflict, I assure you that your betrayal will not be forgotten.' With that, he turned and strode across the flag-stones to where Bram and Hal were already waiting on their horses.

Lady Koel stood for a moment, as still as a statue but for the wind buffeting the long, dark strands of her hair. Then she turned slowly to Jared. 'None of this was personal, you know.'

He did not answer her. What answer could he find? His strikingly beautiful, fiercely intelligent cousin had always been an enigma. That was never more true than now. He turned and walked away from her, down towards the stone steps. He heard footsteps following him. Turning, he came face to face with his mother once more.

'I cannot – I will not – lose another son,' Elin told him.

'Then let us pray you do not have to,' Jared replied, sub-mitting once more to his mother's embrace. 'Please tell Asta to stay safe,' he said, as she released him. 'Knowing that she is out of harm's way will allow me to stay strong.'

His mother opened her mouth as if to say something, but then she simply nodded. Jared hurried on to join his fellows.

THIRTY-EIGHT

ARCHENFIELD

Father Simeon felt the cool wind against his face as he rode out towards the settlement of Dalhoen. As his horse gained momentum, he settled into a more comfortable rhythm in the saddle and wondered why on earth he did not take the opportunity to ride more often. He had an entirely new appreciation of the beauty of the Princedom: the blue-green forest to the right, leading down to the silver fjord; up to the left, the stark beauty of the glen and, beyond, the purple-hazed mountains. If he had needed a reminder as to why he was doing what he was about to do, these views would have given it to him. But he needed no reminder.

As the white army tents came into sight, he saw a pair of soldiers riding out to meet him and, with some reluctance, slowed his horse. He felt the exhilaration of speed drain away as he drew level with the first of the soldiers. More than anything, he didn't want to be led into the army camp – the risk was too great. Either Prince Jared, Kai Jagger or Hal Harness could be somewhere within those barricades. They would attempt to deter him from his course.

'Halt!' The young woman – also on horseback – raised her hand towards him.

Simeon took in the girl's battle-weary face, the dried blood on her shirtsleeves. She was far too young to be witness to such bloodshed.

Holding tight to her reins, she leaned forward in her saddle. 'Where are you off to at such a pace?'

He had anticipated this question. 'I need to ride out to meet and talk to the advancing Paddenburg party.'

The girl's eyes narrowed. 'You do? Under whose orders do you undertake this act of madness?'

'Do you not recognise me, child? I am Father Simeon. The Priest.' He submitted to the girl's scrutiny.

'I'm sorry to ask this, Father, but has Lady Koel dispatched you?'

'That is correct,' he replied.

'Do you have any form of written decree? Something to verify that what you say is true?'

Father Simeon glanced down at his breastplate. He was not accustomed to wearing armour. It was marked with a cross, readily identifying him as a man of God. He reached beneath his breastplate and pulled free the roll of parchment he had secreted there. The message was written in his own hand, of course, but how qualified was this child to recognise a forgery from an official palace decree?

'Are there others in your party?' She glanced over his shoulder, searching for signs of riders he might have outpaced.

Father Simeon shook his head, smiling. 'No,' he said. 'I am riding alone.' The words brought a bittersweet smile to his lips. For the longest time, he had had the sense that he was riding alone through this vale.

The young soldier frowned, returning the parchment. 'I'm afraid, Father, I must ask you to turn back. It just isn't safe for a lone rider. Frankly, even for a group—'

Father Simeon met the young woman's eyes. 'You must let me on my way. My authority outstrips yours. And I travel under a greater authority than either of ours.'

She shook her head. There was water in her eyes – it might have been from the stinging wind. 'Please, Father, do as I ask. Turn around!'

'I cannot turn back from this path.' He heard the certainty in his own voice and smiled again, as if running into a once cherished but sadly long absent friend.

She shook her head slowly. 'I wish with all my heart you would not do this, Father. But if you must, then, I beg you, be vigilant. The enemy has advanced beyond Mellerad. There will likely be Paddenburg scouts looking to pick off anyone in their path.' She cleared her throat and called to her soldiers. 'Make way for Father Simeon.' When they turned to her, questions on each of their faces, she adopted her previous, more forceful tone. 'Just do it.'

Lydia rode at Henning's side as they led the phalanx of troops. Though she had argued against this – asserting the unnecessary risk arising from two of Paddenburg's commanders-in-chief travelling together – she had known that this was an argument she would lose. They had each left a sizeable contingent of troops to break the dwindling defences at Mellerad and Pencador – their role was to lead Paddenburg's troops into battle, not to undertake a dirty and prolonged street combat. The foot soldiers of Paddenburg would finish the job Lydia and Henning had begun.

It was of paramount importance to Henning and Ven to advance towards the palace of Archenfield together: if all was going to plan in the east, Ven would join them south of Grasmyre. Archenfield would be the second of the Thousand Territories beyond Paddenburg they would lay claim to, but it was a far more glorious prize than Tanaka. When the story was laid down in the history books, it must tell of the two brothers riding side by side.

On hearing Henning describing it thus, Lydia had wondered how history would record her own contribution to the seismic shifts within the kingdoms. She had a sudden vision of the maze.

'I'm walking Lydia! See, how I'm walking!'

'Yes, I see. And it's wonderful. But you must not over-exert yourself.'

The vision of the maze was pushed aside by one of the pillow, claiming the last of Leopold's breath.

'Lydia, darling, you're miles away!'

'What's that?' She turned to find Henning gazing upon her.

He looked sad. 'Sometimes you seem to disappear from me and I just can't bear it. I want to follow you everywhere you go.'

She sighed. 'Trust me, it is much better for both our sakes that you cannot.'

The tiny village of Malyx was quite deserted. It was distressing to see the remnants of the people's lives strewn through the streets: articles as commonplace as shirts, sewing baskets and copper pots had been left behind as they fell from carts and horses, or perhaps simply from a pair of overloaded arms.

It was the pervasive silence that Simeon found most unsettling – the utter absence of life.

The Paddenburg scouts had been following him for some time now. He had become aware of their movement in the shadowy fringes of the forest that marked the northern outskirts of the village, and they had quickly emerged into the light, charging towards him with alarming speed in their black armour. In that moment, he had understood that his mission would soon reach its end.

He was no match for these invaders. He was not a man of war. Still, he must stick to the path he had chosen.

Once he had cleared the military camp at Dalhoen, Simeon had dismounted and removed a tunic and riding blanket from his cloth satchel. Both articles bore the Wynyard crest and the vivid blue, gold and green of the Princedom. In these rich colours he would never be mistaken for an ordinary soldier or a fugitive villager. It would be obvious, even to the lay soldiers of Paddenburg, that this was a rider of some importance, perhaps even nobility.

When the black-clad soldiers had first come bolting out of the forest, he had thought that he had failed – that a scout's indiscriminate sword would soon sever his spine. But then the riders had slowed and, with weapons extended, taken Simeon into their custody. Just as he had invited them to do.

Lydia heard it first: the drumming of hooves, soft initially but growing louder all the time. 'What's that?' she asked, her head cocked.

'It could be our scouts,' Henning replied, drawing his horse to a stop. 'Or a small posse of enemy riders.'

Lydia shrugged. What did it matter? What threat did a few horsemen pose when they had several hundred following in their wake?

They sent back the command to halt. As the phalanx grew still, they were enveloped for a time by a curious silence, broken only by the sound of the approaching horses.

Lydia glanced around at the countryside, thinking how accurately Logan had described it in his secret letters.

At last, the riders came into view. Two were dressed in the black armour of Paddenburg, but between them was a rider in the blue, gold and green colours of Archenfield.

Lydia knew their soldiers were ordered to kill on the spot. This man must be of some perceived value to have been taken alive.

If their prisoner was disconcerted by the sight of the army, he gave no sign of it. He drew to a standstill before them.

'Prince Henning,' he said.

'The one and only,' Henning answered. 'And who might you be?'

The man smiled. 'My name is Father Simeon, the Priest. I am one of the Twelve who assist our Prince in the rule of this Princedom. I have come to welcome you to the soil of Archenfield.'

Lydia smiled. 'Of course.' She nodded. 'If in doubt, send out the Priest.'

'You have come to welcome us?' Henning scoffed. 'You do understand that we are invading your little Princedom? Soon, these flags you see behind me will fly from the roof of your palace, signalling that Archenfield is now a dominion of Paddenburg.'

Father Simeon nodded. 'I am under no illusions as to why you have come. But still, you are strangers in my land, and I humbly bid you welcome.'

Henning nodded slowly. 'That's very *decent* of you, I suppose.'

Father Simeon shrugged. 'Perhaps it would surprise you to know that I do not set much store by decency.'

'Really?' Henning answered. 'You said you are a priest!'

'Oh, I am a priest,' Father Simeon replied. 'And there are many things which concern me. But decency is quite a long way down the list.' He looked at Lydia for the first time and he smiled serenely in greeting. 'Decency speaks to me of conforming to a certain standard of outward morality or respectability. It is, to my mind, a rather superficial quality.' His eyes blazed with conviction. 'What interests me far more is genuine goodness.'

'If it's goodness you are looking for,' Lydia told him, 'I fear we're probably not your kind of people.'

Simeon shook his head. 'I don't think that's true.' He turned back to Prince Henning. 'Your Majesty, they say that your brother moved worlds to find a cure for your father and bring him succour. The way sons treat their fathers tells us much about a nation.'

Lydia leaned close to Henning. 'This could be a trap,' she said quietly. 'They could simply have sent him out to buy them time.'

'It's Miss Wilde, isn't it?' Father Simeon resumed. 'Yes, of course, I see the considerable resemblance to your brother.'

'How is Logan?' She could not help but ask him.

'He is ... troubled,' Father Simeon said. 'He has lost his way, I fear. But there is goodness in him too. I know it. I have seen it on many occasions.' His kind eyes met Lydia's and she believed he meant every word he said.

'Father Simeon.' Henning's voice had its familiar mastery restored. 'It is so very kind of you to ride out to engage with us on such matters, but I am afraid time is pressing. We must ask you to stand aside so that we may proceed.'

'Yes, of course.' Father Simeon nodded.

'Then you will stand aside?'

Father Simeon appeared lost in thought for a moment. 'No.'

Henning frowned. 'But you said—'

'I meant that of course you would want to be on your way, to continue on your journey towards the palace. But you must understand, I cannot let you proceed any further. The palace and all those within it mean too much to me. This Princedom ... this "little" Princedom, as you called it before, is too precious to me to allow you to claim it as some kind of trophy.'

'I understand your position,' Henning told him. 'And your words might, under other circumstances, prove stirring. But the fact remains – we are going to claim this Princedom and there is nothing you can do about it.'

'You are, of course, welcome to your opinion,' Father Simeon said.

'I *told* you,' Lydia hissed. 'This is some kind of trick. We don't have time for this! Every moment we lose here, they have more time to prepare God knows what for our arrival.'

Simeon shook his head. 'You are mistaken, Miss Wilde,' he said. 'There is no trick. I am not here to stall you or distract you. Quite the opposite.'

'What is it you want from us?' Henning asked, his patience at an end.

'I thought that I had been more than clear, Prince Henning. I am here to ask you to reconsider your actions. I'm here to implore you to turn around and retreat.'

'And why would we do that?' Henning asked.

'Because, Prince Henning, this is not your land, and you have no genuine claim upon it. You are under the illusion, perhaps, that the more land you gather under your name, the greater a man you will become. This kind of thinking is a trap I have observed many men – and women – fall into. You may devote the rest of your time on earth to taking each of the Thousand Territories under your command but, believe me, you will never find peace or fill the void inside you.'

Letting go of his reins, the Priest began to dismount. He had a deep need to feel the soil of Archenfield directly beneath his feet. But then he found that simply standing was not enough either. He creaked down on to his knees on the ground in front of Prince Henning's horse. 'I plead with you, Prince Henning – in the name of the thousands who will be slaughtered, displaced, orphaned, that you turn around and go back to Paddenburg.' His voice cracked. He paused, then resumed, as resonant as a bell. 'I kneel before you to beg you to go home.'

'Father Simeon, *good* Father Simeon,' Henning said softly, as he dismounted from his own horse. 'You can talk to us from now until the turning of the year, but you will have no luck in changing our minds or deterring us from our course.'

'I am very sorry to hear that,' Father Simeon said.

'What's that?' Lydia asked suddenly, her head on one side. 'Do you hear it?'

Henning glanced at her, puzzled. 'No. What?'

'Listen!' Lydia shouted. 'Horses' hooves. There *are* others in his wake! I told you this was a ruse—'

'I swear to you,' Father Simeon implored them. 'I came to you on my own.'

'Then how do explain the sound of horses?' Lydia asked. 'You do hear it?'

Father Simeon seemed genuinely confused, but Henning had clearly had enough.

Lydia saw him reach for the hilt of his sword. 'Henning, no!'

She watched impotently as Henning drew his sword from its sheath and swung the blade towards the Priest's neck. Father Simeon's eyes were strangely tranquil as the sharp metal edge made contact. His expression remained calm as his head was sliced cleanly from his body and tumbled down on to the muddy ground beside his body. He was still kneeling before his killer.

'Was that absolutely necessary?' Lydia rasped, as Henning wiped clean his sword blade.

'He left me no choice,' Henning said, returning his weapon to its sheath. 'We have come too far – you and I and Ven and Logan. Nothing and no one must stand in the way of our victory.'

THIRTY-NINE

THE FORT, MELLERAD

From the heights of the fort's bell tower, Axel had a vertiginous view down to the settlement and across to all sides. He had come up here to gain a clearer perspective on the fighting. From there, the combatants seemed little more than ants or flies. A dark swarm clustered beneath him and it was all but impossible to distinguish the soldiers belonging to the invading army from Archenfield's own forces. The latter's ranks had been swelled not only by the settlement dwellers from Mellerad, but also by the influx of fugitives from the western settlements which had been toppled, one by one, in grim succession.

Axel strained his eyes in a vain attempt to distinguish the abhorrent black armour and purple silks of the warriors from Paddenburg, but the fact that the dark mass below was clustering closer and closer to the edges of the fort left him in no doubt that the enemy had the upper hand.

The forces of Paddenburg were closing in. If the fort fell, then the settlement of Mellerad was lost. And if Mellerad fell, there would be no other option but to order his own forces to retreat and wave the flag of surrender: there were no further viable defences beyond this fort to halt Paddenburg's advance to the palace of Archenfield. Was he destined to be consigned to the history books as the Prince who ruled for barely a day?

Axel opened his mouth and allowed all his pent-up rage and disappointment to stream out. What emerged was a base, animal roar.

It caught the attention of the soldiers on the battlements a level below him. Questioning eyes met his from below. 'Keep firing!' he barked angrily. Glancing down again, it seemed to him that the swarm was drawing ever closer.

'What if we hit our own forces?' one of the archers cried up to him.

'Doesn't matter,' he snarled back. 'Keep firing!'

The archer and his fellows did not delay in sending more of their deadly rain down upon the heaving mass below. Let the aggressors be in no doubt: they broached the fort at their own peril.

But now Axel watched with fresh terror as tall, thin ladders were moved into position. Where the hell had they come from? The ants below hoisted the ladders up to the higher levels of the fort. Within moments, the insects began climbing.

'Increase your fire!' he screamed at the archers below.

But all was not yet lost: he watched as the first of the ladders began to tremble, as if caught in a sudden breeze. His own forces were pushing the ladder away with long poles. It peeled away from the wall and those at the top had the choice to either cling on or jump. He had a fleeting sense of satisfaction at their screams. But, within moments, a second ladder was hoisted and, seemingly undeterred by their comrades' fate, yet more dark shapes began scurrying up the sides of the fort. Spurred on by its success, two more ladders then began to rise. There was no way they could push back such a sustained, coordinated attack.

Now Axel heard a low thud. Throwing himself to the other side of his lookout, he saw that another group of soldiers was running at the main doors of the fort with a battering ram. *Wham.* He heard the sound echo up from below. The fort doors were fashioned from the thickest slabs of oak Archenfield could muster; the selfsame oak that had been crafted into the Prince's Table. Only in this case, it was reinforced with iron. The doors had been designed to hold off invaders like these. *Boom.* The battering ram made fresh contact. This time, Axel felt – or maybe only imagined – the reverberations through his body. The doors *would* hold – for all their sakes, the doors had to hold. *Wham.* The battering ram came again. Axel was powerless to do anything to prevent it. *Crack.* He felt sick to the pit of his stomach. How much longer could the fort hold out?

THE FOREST, NORTH OF TONSBERG

With one hand holding tight to his horse's reins, Morgan steadied his other hand on the shoulder of the dying soldier. He had buried his sword deep in the man's gut and the victim's body issued a distinctive squelch as he pulled it back out again. He saw the familiar expression in his victim's eyes: as the man slipped from his saddle, he was already well on his journey from this world to the next. Without lowering his eyes, Morgan wiped away a thick splash of blood from his face. On the other side of the now riderless horse, he could already see his next combatant.

It would be easy to lose count of the number of enemy riders he had dispatched to their deaths from the dissembling green of the forest, but it was important for Morgan to keep count. Twenty-three so far. Their battle might be located in the pine-perfumed forest just north of Tonsberg, but it was nonetheless brutal for its picturesque surroundings. Morgan and his comrades were holding their own: he had a sudden sight of Jonas up ahead, wielding his sword. Then the rider-less horse moved off, trampling its fallen rider underfoot, and Morgan bought his full attention to the next soldier lying in wait.

Like all the others, the rider was clad in the purple silk and dull black armour of Paddenburg. They looked, he thought, like giant flies. This one, a woman, was far more skilled at swordplay than the last. She met each of his attacks with a counter-move of her own and, as their sweating horses turned about one another, she gained the upper hand.

Morgan felt an undeniable excitement as he parried her attack. A good duel like this was rare and, he knew, would only strengthen his own fighting skills still further. He was almost sad when she unwittingly allowed him an opening to insert his sword deep into her flank. She opened her mouth to scream but no sound came out – only blood.

Past the dying woman's head, Morgan saw a fresh volley of enemy arrows flying through the air. One bounced off a breastplate; another hit the flanks of a horse; others fell impotently to the forest floor. Morgan watched as the last of the arrows found the exposed flesh between a rider's helmet and his back armour, the arrow burying itself deep into the rider's neck.

The rider turned. It was only then that Morgan realised, with a feeling of deep dread, that the victim was Jonas.

As the Woodsman slumped in his saddle, Morgan jumped

down from the back of his own horse – he *had* to reach his friend and do what he could for him. He raced over the fallen bodies slumped on the carpet of pine needles that was thickly spattered with the blood of Jonas Drummond and so many others. Was it already too late?

'Jonas!' He could not prevent the sob in his voice as he saw the undisguised agony in the Woodsman's eyes. Jonas's boots had become tangled in his horse's stirrups as he had fallen. Morgan sliced through the thin strips of leather in order to free him.

Alert to the ever-present danger from enemy swords and arrows, Morgan employed one hand to drag Jonas into a nearby copse; his other hand gripped tightly to his out-stretched sword, ready to see off any soldier in purple and black who stood in their way.

He succeeded in ferrying Jonas out of the fray and into the clearing. The battle continued to be fought only yards away from them – on the other side of the majestic pines.

'This must be one of the most beautiful spots in all of Archenfield,' Jonas rasped, as he glanced past Morgan to the perfect patch of winter-blue sky above them. 'Not such a bad place to die.'

The sides of the Woodsman's bloodied lips rose into a half-smile. Morgan reached, instinctively for the fatal arrow, but his hands froze. He knew the worst thing he could do was to remove it. He felt utterly impotent.

'Take it out,' Jonas instructed him.

'It will hurt like hell,' Morgan told him, tears filling his eyes. 'And it won't do any good. We both know that.'

'Please take it out,' Jonas begged. 'Don't let me die with an enemy arrow embedded in my flesh.'

Morgan reached for the arrow and drew it firmly towards him. Tears coursed down his face as he witnessed Jonas's intense pain. Blood sprayed out from the Woodsman's neck, covering Morgan's own face, neck and clothes. Then, free from the arrow, the Woodsman's body began to convulse.

Morgan gripped tightly on to his friend's hand. He could feel the life swiftly ebbing away. Morgan had been around dying bodies since he was a boy, but he had never once felt so sad.

With his free hand, he pressed down against the open wound but the blood soon escaped between his fingers and dripped on to the forest floor. His other hand clasped Jonas's all the more tightly. He knew if he loosened his hold, Jonas's hand would simply slip away from him.

Already Jonas's face was white, almost transparent. It made Morgan think of the fjord in winter, when it was thick with ice.

'Where are we?' Jonas asked, his voice fainter than before.

'We are in the heart of the forest,' Morgan told his dying friend. 'In the beautiful forest of Archenfield – the place you know better than any man. The place you love above all others.'

He glanced from Jonas's face up to the patch of sky. It was, he thought, the purest blue he had ever seen. It was only the briefest glance but, when he returned his eyes to Jonas's face, he knew that the Woodsman had gone.

NORTH OF PENCADOR

'*You* said to come north, Elliot!' Emelie Sharp harangued the newest member of the Twelve as she stood beside Nash and Lucas Curzon on the craggy hillside just north of the settlement of Pencador.

'Be fair, Emelie,' Lucas intervened. He had become well practised in the role of peacekeeper between his two hot-headed companions. 'We had little option but to flee in this direction.'

'Thank you, Lucas!' Elliot swept his arm around him. 'We got our troops safely out of the line of fire, did we not? You might give me some credit for that.'

Emelie drew down her field glasses and thrust them towards Elliot. 'You might not be quite so cocksure if you care to take a look down there!'

Frowning, Elliot took the glasses. As he lifted them to his eyes, Emelie continued at full pelt. 'It appears that we're riding into a fresh battle currently underway in the foothills between Dalhoen and Kirana.'

Elliot's expression was resolute as he removed the field glasses from his eyes and passed them to Lucas. Lifting them to his own eyes, Lucas heard Emelie's voice ringing in his ears.

'Well? We appear to be caught between the proverbial rock and hard place. You're the new Captain of the Guard. You got us into this situation. What do you advise now?'

As she spoke, Lucas felt a chill running through his insides. It was true: they were very far from a place of safety. Through the glasses, he could see the scope of the battle underway in the foothills – it looked like a rout.

He shook his head. Their troops had barely had the chance to draw breath after their last battle. Soon, though, they would be in the heart of the melee once more.

'We cannot go back,' Elliot declared decisively. 'We must continue north, on towards the palace.'

Emelie frowned. 'In other words, you intend to lead us into the heart of this conflict below. Are you a complete fool, or simply dead set upon leading us into enemy territory?'

Ignoring Emelie, Elliot turned towards Lucas. 'Our chances are significantly higher in taking on the smaller enemy force down there in the foothills, than the considerably larger one pushing north behind us.' He glanced back at Emelie. 'Success in circumstances like this is determined by taking calculated risks.'

'Pah!' Emelie spat. 'Which military manual did you grab that maxim from?'

'No manual,' Elliot rejoined with a thin smile. 'I learned everything I know from Axel Blaxland – of course, I *should* now say *Prince* Axel.'

FIELD HOSPITAL, KIRANA

Elias turned from the flayed leg to the nurse at his side. 'I'll have to amputate just below the knee,' he confirmed. 'Fetch me the' – he paused to lower his voice – '*equipment*, and do what you can to prepare the poor soul.'

Moments later, he had the saw in his hand, feeling the regrettably familiar sensation of its sharpened teeth slicing easily through flesh and tissue, but then making its first contact with the bone beneath. He was dimly aware of the soldier's screams, but only dimly. There was nothing wrong with Elias's hearing – he had simply acquired the necessary skill of tuning out any distracting noise in order to remain focused on the job at hand.

There had been a two-year hiatus between his last amputation and the first of this new conflict, but his touch was as precise and certain as if he had performed such an operation only yesterday. In truth, it seemed barely yesterday that he had been stationed, for months on end, in a field hospital identical to this – filled with the stench of death and the moans of the dying. He had convinced himself in the interim two years that life in court was the norm and his wartime experience the anomaly. Now he realised he had been mistaken: these tortuous sounds and horrific smells *were* the norm of life in Archenfield – a Princedom more practised in war than peace. Though this latest conflict might prove more definitive than those that had come before, he reflected briefly. The home army was now so weakened, the advancing enemy as vast – as it was predictably ruthless – that the struggle might simply be the very last of Archenfield's wars. Soon, very soon, Archenfield might cease to exist in its own right, swallowed whole by the insatiable hunger of its warmongering neighbour.

The Princedom Elias had loved and served so long had as much chance of returning to its former glory as this poor soldier had of growing a new lower leg.

Elias felt the curious weight of the limb as it became detached from the body. Remembering Axel in his surgery, discussing the value of the different parts of a body, Elias placed the damaged leg carefully on the ground. He could no longer remember the standard remuneration for a leg: it was if his mind could no longer maintain any pretence towards order.

His assistant – who seemed, thank heaven, able to focus squarely on the task at hand – passed him the earthenware pot containing the ointment to dress the wound. Its scent was pungent and familiar, going deep into Elias's nostrils. It momentarily overpowered the stench of decay – though, in truth, the two smells had come to indicate the selfsame thing to him.

As he applied the dressing to the exposed tissue, he became more alert to the patient's cries. He was unsure if they were cries of fresh pain, or grief for the loss of the limb.

'Give him more brandy!' Elias instructed his assistant.

The Physician took a spool of bandage and began to cover the inflamed flesh. How many more operations such as this would he be tasked to perform? However many broken soldiers and brave-hearted civilians he managed to fix, there would be far more who met their end either in the battle itself – where death at least might be mercifully swift – or here, at a slower, crueller pace. What, in truth, was the point in saving one more of them? Maybe he should make this patient his last. He was not quite a single man poised against the war machine, but the odds were not far removed from that.

War would win in the end. It always did. Why pretend otherwise?

Elias finished the bandaging. 'There,' he said with a sigh. 'All done.'

As the unfortunate soldier was stretchered away, Elias gazed at the familiar staining on the palms of his hands. He allowed his eyes to close briefly. It was one of the only ways he knew to cut himself off from the horrors around him.

As he did so, his mind became unusually empty and clear. A face appeared. It was Asta. He realised its import. The Princedom could descend into hell – it was well on its way in that direction already. All he truly cared about was the safety of his niece.

MELLERAD

Asta gratefully took the fresh pile of sheets from the woman whose house had been transformed into a makeshift surgery, at the heart of the settlement.

'You're sure about this, Zayna?' Asta enquired.

The woman nodded, even managing a faint smile. 'I

335

couldn't sleep on these sheets again if I thought we hadn't done everything to do our bit to help.'

Zayna sat down beside Asta and they began tearing through the sheets as neatly as possible to create strips that might be used as bandages. As she busied herself with her work, Asta thought of Elias and the caskets of medical supplies she had seen him organising for each of the settlements. The supplies had proved woefully inadequate here in Mellerad, where they were dealing with the war-wounded not only from the home settlement, but those who had fled from Galvaire, Lindas and Vollerim.

Across the room, another young woman was busy stitching a head wound with a needle usually employed for needle-point. It appeared to be working just fine. Asta felt a sense of pride that they had accomplished so much in such a short space of time there.

'You're quite something, you know.'

At first, Asta didn't realise that the words were directed at her, but then she felt Zayna's hand on her shoulder. 'We couldn't have organised ourselves as well as this without your help.'

Asta blushed, uneasy with the praise. 'I only did what anyone would have done.'

'No,' the woman said more forcefully. 'You did more than that. You came to warn us of the flight of refugees from the west. You somehow managed to rally the settlement dwellers whilst maintaining calm throughout, and set up this surgery for those of us cut off from medical help.'

Asta heard the words and they touched her, but it was as if Zayna were talking about someone else other than her. She had acted on pure instinct; indeed, she could barely remember any of her actions. She had simply kept focusing on what had needed to be done next.

'What now?' her companion asked.

As she tore through the last of the sheets, adding the strip to the basket in front of her, Asta glanced up at the kindly woman.

'You look exhausted,' Asta told her. 'You should go and rest for a while.'

'I can't—' Zayna began.

'You must,' Asta insisted. 'There are others here who can continue your work. You need to go upstairs, if only for a short while.'

'And what about you?' Zayna asked. 'You're a force of nature, Asta Peck, but even forces of nature cannot keep going without any rest.'

OPEN GROUND BETWEEN MELLERAD AND DALHOEN

Lydia and Henning rode at the front of their forces. They were not side by side, but close enough. So far, everything was going to plan – in certain ways, better than expected. Each of Archenfield's western settlements had fallen and by surrounding the fort at Mellerad, they were close to claiming their most significant prize so far.

Glancing back over her shoulder, Lydia saw a river – no, it was more of an *ocean* – of purple and black following in their leaders' wake. They were an unstoppable force and she had no doubt that she had played a significant part in making them so.

When she had first encountered the Princes of Paddenburg, she had found two young men full of ambition but lacking in any clear strategy. She had made them wake up to what was ripe for the picking beyond their borders. She had focused their energies and organised them into a force to be reckoned with. Her own success had already been proven by the swift taking of Tanaka: Archenfield was putting up more of a fight. All the same, it was almost certain now that the colours of Paddenburg would be flying from the palace flag-pole by nightfall. Where next? They had made plans, of course. But success brought the opportunity to create newer, bigger plans.

Turning back again, she saw that Henning had brought his horse to a standstill. The order to pause was passed through the ranks. What was wrong? She pointed her own horse towards his. The ranks soon opened up to allow her through.

'Why did you order the stop?' she asked, lifting the visor of her helmet.

Henning did the same. 'Look ahead, Lydia,' he told her.

She did as he asked. She could see the forces ranked on the open ground before them.

'What of it?' she asked dismissively. 'The last of the meagre army of Archenfield, buoyed by more ill-prepared civilians—'

'Look more closely,' Henning instructed her. 'Do you not see the colours of Rednow?'

She saw that he was right.

'So little Prince Jared managed to raise an alliance after all,' she said.

Henning nodded.

Lydia did not understand why he was hesitating. 'Rednow is only a small territory, my darling – far more adept at matters of trade than war. They might look like a force to be a reckoned with, but they pose no threat to the army of Paddenburg.'

Still, Henning seemed unsure. Was his nerve failing him at this late stage? It could not – not when they almost had the palace of Archenfield in their sights.

'We can still win this, with ease,' she told him. 'All you need to do is sound the charge.'

For a moment, he said nothing, his eyes focused on the army now advancing towards them.

'You must sound the charge,' Lydia told him. 'No one must sense your hesitation, your uncertainty.'

'You're right,' Henning said, lowering his visor. 'You're always right.' He raised his hand and gave the signal.

Flushed with relief, Lydia loosened the reins of her horse, dug her spurs in its sides and propelled herself towards her next golden victory.

FORTY

SOUTH OF KIRANA

The Paddenburg army had charged at them across an open stretch of land to the south of Kirana. The ground beneath them, sodden from the winter rain, had been ripped open by the thundering of a thousand hooves. Mud had splattered up the legs of their horses and mixed with the blood that had been spilled on both sides.

As Jared fought off his latest attacker, he caught sight of one of his own soldiers cut through by an enemy sword.

To the west, a flash of light caught his attention: it was as if the sun were casting off from the southern reaches of the great fjord. Then it dawned on him that it was the glint of sunlight on gleaming metal. Reinforcements were racing to join them – their swords raised above their heads. Leading the charge was Morgan Booth, his face contorted by his battle cry. The Executioner was a welcome sight, but his presence caused Jared to wonder – had Morgan and Jonas claimed victory over Paddenburg's army in the south, or had they been forced to retreat? Jared scanned the soldiers in

Morgan's vicinity but could not see the Woodsman amongst them.

Jared felt a unmistakable tension rise in the enemy around him. They were aware that they had been flanked by an Archenfield force from the west and were now outnumbered. Yet it did not stop them. With a sinking heart, Jared realised that these men and women had not been trained to consider the option of retreat or surrender; if anything, their weakened position had renewed their will to fight and, if necessary, die for their cause. Their dedication to their leaders was unwavering, even in the face of defeat. It was senseless and the senselessness of their deaths sickened Jared. Yet he had no choice but to meet each swing of their swords with his own and one by one they fell, dying in the battle-churned mud.

As Jared claimed victory, his eyes met Morgan's for the first time. The smile of reunion quickly faded.

'What is it?' Jared asked. He felt a sinking sensation in his stomach even before the Executioner answered.

'We lost the battle in the south. I made the decision for our troops to retreat.'

'I know you will have made the right decision,' Jared told him. 'Where is Jonas?' He saw the effect the mere mention of Jonas's name had on his comrade. 'He's dead?'

Morgan closed his eyes briefly. 'He's at peace, Prince Jared, in the forest at Tonsberg. He died a noble death, fighting to protect the Princedom he loved.'

'As these poor souls fought to wrench it from us,' Jared said, gesturing at the broken bodies spread across the battle-ground. 'I wonder what victory will mean to either side when this is the price we must pay.' Then he looked at Morgan. 'I am sorry for Jonas,' he said softly.

They stood, horses alongside the battlefield. Neither spoke

for a while. Then Morgan raised his hand up to shield his eyes from the low winter sun. 'Look,' he said, pointing towards the southern reaches of the plain.

Jared saw with utter shock what he was showing him.

A fresh wave of Paddenburg troops had advanced from the south. As far as he could see, there were ranks of soldiers, clad in purple and black.

MELLERAD

'I can't leave my *home*.' Zayna hesitated on the doorstep as a torrent of settlement dwellers ran past them.

'You have to!' Asta shouted over the noise of the crowd and their panicked cries. She grabbed Zayna's hand. 'We have to get out of here. Now.'

She tugged the woman away from the door and they became part of the fear-fuelled torrent. Men, women and children were pelting along the streets, unsure exactly where they were going, knowing only that the fort had fallen to the enemy. Asta knew that it was a sign of the people's fear and desperation that they had not even bothered to gather up treasured possessions from their vacated homes.

The narrow street soon became jammed by the sheer quantity of people moving down it, and Asta felt the crowd crushing dangerously in on itself. Now she was possessed by a new fear – that through their very desperation to escape, the settlement dwellers might crush one another to death on the streets. Children were screaming; babes in arms were held aloft to better protect them from the crush. What sounded like hundreds of voices were crying to go this way or that way or to stop pushing. As the crush became even tighter and the fear similarly intensified, the voices merged into a horrible caco-phony.

Asta could barely think, hardly breathe, any more.

With all the screaming and shoving going on, people were now moving but Asta realised she had become separated from Zayna. She turned, eyes ranging desperately to find her, but it was hopeless. The force of the crowd pushed her forwards, towards fresh horror.

At the end of the street, the thoroughfare widened and forked. This was cause for relief, as it enabled the crowd to begin to thin. Both roads led north and that was as good a direction as any in which to go. At least, it seemed that way.

As Asta reached the fork in the road and, for the briefest moment, weighed up which path to take, she saw that up ahead – on both stretches of road – were soldiers, bearing the colours of both Archenfield and Paddenburg.

With a ghastly clarity, she realised that the battle had pooled out from the fort itself – now, the very streets of Mellerad had become an urban battlefield. She turned and tried to stem the tide of panic-blind people. It was useless. They were running into the heart of the combat. Asta found herself being pushed again, and turned to face forward to be able to see where she was going. As she did so, her foot sud-denly came down on something that was not the road itself. Glancing down, she realised she had stepped on a dead body. Not a soldier but one of the settlement dwellers, stabbed and left to perish on the dust of the road.

Then she was pushed forward again, over the body, further into the melee. A breath away from her, a soldier of Archen-field ran her sword through an opponent. She found her mark and blood sprayed from her victim's throat. Asta felt the sudden heat and wetness on her face and realised that her face was now covered in the blood of the dying enemy soldier. She did not have time to wipe herself clean, even though she could taste the dead man's blood on her tongue. This was beyond anything she had witnessed before, even when Eronesia had taken Teragon. It was beyond even her worst nightmares.

Jostled forwards again, she saw that the road ahead only lay claim to worse horrors. It was littered with bodies of the dead – mostly soldiers, of both colours, but now the settlement dwellers too. It seemed that the army of Paddenburg had an unstoppable bloodlust. Taking the fort, then the settlement, was not enough for them: they would not be satisfied until every last man, woman and child had been massacred.

She recognised the boy's eyes at once. He was standing at the side of the road, staring vacantly towards her and the others. She managed to break free from the crowd to go over to him. Yes, there was no doubt in her mind. He was the boy from the market square in Galvaire – the one who had ridden there from Lindas with his father. Glancing at the ground at the boy's feet, Asta knew what she would find even before her eyes reached the ground: the slumped, lifeless body of his father.

Glancing back up at the young boy – no more than four or five, she guessed – she saw his stunned, expressionless eyes. In less than a day, this child had seen his entire family slaughtered.

Asta knew she could not leave him there. She wished she knew his name, but there was not even time to ask. She reached for his hand. As she did so, the vacancy in his eyes suddenly changed to show fresh fear. Turning, Asta saw why. One of the Paddenburg soldiers was charging at them, his sword held aloft. Instinctively, Asta wrapped her arms around the boy. She had to protect him.

*

THE FOOTHILLS NORTH OF PENCADOR

Kai Jagger stood on a craggy summit, a distance away from the men and women under his command. He had been looking down the same hillside for what seemed like hours now, aware that the foot soldiers gathered behind him at the top of the hill were restless and anxious for the situation to break.

Kai was not one to hesitate without very good reason and now, as his eyes glanced down the hillside, they met two very good reasons not to rush things . . .

About a third of the way down the hill, rough rocks broke through the grassland and formed a natural defensive ring. Just beneath this ring, the enemy force was biding its time. The soldiers of Paddenburg had been waiting there for many hours. Kai did not bother lifting his field glasses to his eyes in order to interrogate the faces of his enemy – it was enough to observe the back and forth movements of the dark silhouettes clustered below. By now, he was surprised that the enemy had not launched a charge on his own forces, and it made him wonder if they were waiting for reinforcements. This, in turn, increased his anxiety levels. The two opposing armies had been in this stalemate for too long now. He felt compelled to break the deadlock, but to do so meant making a near-impossible decision.

If he sent his forces racing down the open ground of the hill to tackle the enemy, they would be immediately exposed and vulnerable to the arrows of Paddenburg's archers. But at least he had a good idea of enemy numbers now, and he knew that he could muster an equivalent force, skilled and hungry for attack. If he stood firm and continued to do nothing, was he running the risk of a greater enemy force arriving, against which his regiments would have less chance of success or, indeed, survival?

Now, as he gazed down the hillside, something entered his peripheral vision: a new swathe of soldiers on horses was approaching the foot of the hill. Kai felt a rare sickness in the pit of his stomach. He knew that he had delayed too long. Just as he had feared, the enemy force was about to reinforce itself. After that, they would surely not hang back beyond their defences any longer, but begin to scale the upper stretch of the hill, caring little that Archenfield might send its own arrows down to decimate – at best – their numbers.

Kai was unsure what compelled him to lift his field glasses but, as he did so, he suddenly felt pure relief flood through his body. The horse-mounted troops were not clad in the purple and black of the enemy, but in uniforms of blue, green and gold. The new influx of riders were soldiers of Archenfield! This put his situation in an entirely different light. Rather than Paddenburg mustering double their force to overwhelm Archenfield soldiers gathered at the top of the hill it was, in fact, the soldiers of Paddenburg who were now in the most vulnerable position – with soldiers from Archenfield closing in on them from both above and below.

Kai saw no further reason to delay. Judging from the stirrings below him, the enemy was making its own difficult but necessary decisions. He raced over to address his troops. It did not take long to capture their full attention, and even less time to give the command for attack.

Kai was, as usual, at the fore of his troops as they raced down from the summit over the low scrub towards the ring of rock, from which they would propel themselves down into the midst of the enemy. Just as he had predicted, however, the moment they broke cover, arrows began flying through the air towards them. He was aware of several of his soldiers taking a fall on either side of him, but they were travelling fast down the hill, and only a small proportion of his force was lost. The vast majority made it to the rocks. So far, then, the gamble was paying off.

The wave of arrows thinned as the soldiers of Paddenburg set down their crossbows and took up their swords. Kai and his comrades swept over the rocks and jumped down among their enemy, beginning to tackle them in hand-to-hand combat. He could feel the energy pulsing through his soldiers as they finally got to channel their earlier tension into the fight. Head down, he made swift and brutal progress through the soldiers who dared to challenge him. Kai was the Huntsman and, when it came down to it, killing beasts or soldiers was pretty much the same thing. No one was more talented at the kill than Kai Jagger.

He was aware of the Archenfield soldiers fighting from the other direction, and the band of Paddenburgians between the two Archenfield regiments kept diminishing until there was simply no more enemy left for him to kill. Standing firm, he took in a deep gulp of air. His exposed flesh was covered in dirt and blood but he had sustained only the most minor of wounds – certainly nothing compared to the numerous death-blows he had inflicted.

Up ahead, he saw a familiar figure, still on horseback. It was Emelie Sharp, the Beekeeper. She raised her hand to him and he ran over to her. As he did so, he noticed Lucas Curzon and Elliot Nash, also on horseback, a short distance away. He was grateful that his allies had made it here safe.

'Emelie,' Kai said. 'I think we can congratulate ourselves on a battle well won here.'

She nodded, but did not return his smile. 'Yes,' she said. 'This was a decisive victory for Archenfield, but I do not know if it counts for very much in the wider scheme of things.'

'What do you mean?' he asked, disturbed by her tone as well as her words.

'We rode from the south not in victory but in retreat,' Emelie told him. 'Pencador has fallen and the enemy is mustering its forces to advance northwards. You and your foot soldiers succeeded in cutting a swathe through a moderate-sized force here' – she shook her head and he saw her face was drained of all colour – 'but let me tell you, Kai, a tidal wave of enemy forces is about to rise up against us.'

He felt his earlier feeling of sickness return. 'How can this be happening to us?' he said.

She nodded. 'I have asked myself the same question many times. And I believe I now have the answer. This attack is no sudden thing – these monstrous plans must have been incubating in the Black Palace of Paddenburg for months, if not years. I suspect that the ink was barely dry on the alliance with Woodlark when Henning and Ven began setting their foul plot in motion.'

'We should have been more prepared.'

'Yes,' she agreed. 'We have sleepwalked into this nightmare. And now, we will pay for our folly in blood.'

MELLERAD

Axel saw Asta pressed against the wall, holding a little boy tight in her arms. The bastard soldier, clad in black and purple, lunged towards the defenceless pair. Holding tightly to his horse's reins with his left hand, Axel leaned over as far and as quickly as he could to plunge his sword into the soldier's neck. He lost control of his weapon as the soldier slumped to the ground, barely more than inch from Asta's feet.

Axel jumped down from his horse, intent upon retrieving his sword and the girl but, as he stepped forward, he suddenly felt a searing pain in the flesh between his ribs. Turning, he saw that another of the Paddenburg soldiers had broken through the crowd and had jabbed a dagger between links in his chainmail. The weapon was still gripped tightly in the soldier's hands, poised to push fatally deeper. He saw the dark intent in his enemy's eyes.

Suddenly Axel's horse reared up above them, blocking for a moment the light of the winter sun. Axel felt the blade of the dagger move – any deeper and it would surely pierce his heart. But the dagger did not plunge in, but slipped out again. Why had the soldier left the job undone?

Looking up, Axel had his answer. Asta Peck had retrieved his sword from the body of the soldier he had slain before and used it to merciless effect on Axel's own attacker, plunging it with impressive efficiency into the gap between the man's breastplate and back armour. The dying man had fallen to the ground, his dagger tumbling before him, its tip shiny with Axel's blood.

Axel watched, amazed, as Asta calmly slid the sword out from the soldier's side and offered it to him. Taking back the sword, Axel gazed at Asta. Her face was drained of all colour.

'You saved my life,' he told her.

'You saved mine,' she answered matter-of-factly.

Axel realised in that moment that he had underestimated the young Poet. The thought also occurred to him that this might not be the first time she had killed somebody – she seemed dazed, but not entirely traumatised.

'We need to get out of here,' he told her, deftly resheathing his sword and climbing back into the saddle. 'And fast, before we're subject to another attack.'

Asta nodded, but instead of taking his hand to climb up

alongside him, she turned and lifted the boy she had been hugging so close to her.

Axel frowned and shook his head. 'We can't take him.'

Asta bristled with defiance. 'I won't leave him.'

He knew there would be no arguing with her, just as surely as he knew he couldn't leave her there to certain death. He found himself taking the stunned child in his arms and settling him in front. 'Hold tight to these reins and don't let go,' he instructed the boy.

His hands looked pathetically small in contrast to Axel's own.

Now Asta climbed up behind him. Axel turned his horse and, seizing his chance, used the horse's strength to push through the melee.

With the battle pushing deeper and deeper into the heart of Mellerad, they soon made open ground.

'Where are we going?' Asta cried in his ear.

'We have to fall back,' he called back to her. 'If Pencador and Tonsberg have suffered the same fate as Mellerad, all hope is lost.'

'What about the people of Mellerad?' Asta cried. 'Can't we do anything for them?'

He dug his heels deeper into the sides of the horse. 'No,' he cried. 'Let's just be grateful we escaped from that hellhole with our own lives.'

He felt a twinge in his side. Thanks to Asta, the enemy dagger had not gone in too deep but it had gone in deep enough to send shockwaves through his body – he had just been too flooded with adrenaline to notice it before. Now he began to wonder if he could actually complete the next part of the journey without medical help. No need to share that with the girl.

'Are you going to surrender to Paddenburg?' Her voice again – jabbing him deeper than the dagger had.

'No,' he told her. 'Not until I know what's happening on the central plains. There is still some cause for hope.'

'You need to surrender,' she cried, louder than before. 'Before more lives are lost.'

'*I*'ll decide when and if it is time to surrender,' he retorted, the pain of his wound flooding him with anger. 'You might have saved my life back there, but I am Prince of all Archenfield now. It is *my* decision and mine alone what happens next.'

Thankfully, the force of his words was sufficient to shut her up. He hoped he had sounded strong and certain. In truth, he had never felt more unsure – it would be nothing less than a miracle if Pencador and Tonsberg were not subject to the same atrocities as Mellerad. And at this rate, it would be a minor miracle if he even got them to the central plains. Still, Axel knew he had no choice but to ride on through his dying Princedom.

NORTH OF TONSBERG

Prince Ven felt the blessing of the winter sun as he emerged from the forest at the head of his regiment. He imagined how he must look, riding in his golden armour on his mighty steed at the head of his unstoppable force: like a hero from the old folk tales ... But no, not *like* a hero – he *was* the living embodiment of such a hero: he and Henning, and Lydia too.

He had thought it unnecessary for Henning to commission a suit of armour for Lydia, but his brother was smitten. He smiled to himself, thinking of the fourth suit of golden armour, of which only he was currently aware – the one he had had made for Logan with their intertwined initials engraved beneath the breastplate. Of course, it would not be necessary for Logan to don his armour for the current campaign, but this was only the beginning of Paddenburg's expansion through the Thousand Territories. Ven wanted to honour Logan's integral part in the journey so far. His heart soared like a mighty eagle at the thought of seeing him again – the ruffians of Archenfield had better not have inflicted so much as a graze upon Logan's perfect face, or there would be hell to pay. Though actually, a graze would only enhance Logan Wilde's handsome features, he thought with a smile.

Riding on, he reflected upon his achievements of the past days. The first of the settlements he had taken had been Inderwick. Next, he had pushed back the rag-tag army of Archenfield from Tonsberg, and fought them in the green shade of the forest. He had watched what was left of Archenfield's force scurry back north with its tail between its legs. Now, he had his next target in his sights: all he needed to do was push through the open grassland and Kirana would soon fall – with the ease of a leaf in autumn. After taking Kirana, he would rejoin Henning and Lydia at Grasmyre – the northernmost settlement before the palace of Archenfield. From there, it would be a short but glorious ride to the palace itself, where they would officially claim victory and grant Archenfield its new status as a domain of Paddenburg.

All three of them had played their part. Henning had taken Grenofen in the south, then moved on to Pencador. Lydia had been tasked with the smaller western settlements – Vollerim, Lindas and Galvaire. And then led her regiment to the fort at Mellerad. They had each triumphed, just as they had planned and promised. The relative ease of their success in no way diminished their achievements – it was testament to their intricate planning, tenacity and the superior skills of their army, honed for many months in the diverse terrain sur-rounding the Black Palace. But their inevitable victory – for yes, it was inevitable – spoke of something more, something larger, of far greater import.

Looking ahead, he saw the country opening up before him. It was as if the land itself was welcoming him, begging him and his brother to take it into their arms. *Don't worry, Archenfield, he thought. We are here. Henning and I will take good care of you. You were only ever a second-rate Princedom with impostors for Princes. But now, you will become part of Paddenburg, where we know what it means to be a Prince. At last, your forests and mountains and fjords will be blessed with a light so much greater than that of the sun – the light which emanates only from truly great rulers.*

He spurred his horse onwards, the sun making a halo around his golden helmet.

SOUTH OF DALHOEN

Axel rode out at the head of his regiment, but in many ways he felt he was utterly alone as he embarked on this new journey. He knew with grim certainty the task that lay ahead of him, as he and his force rode out to where Prince Rohan's soldiers – the one tangible result of Jared's quest for alliances – were fighting the regiments of Paddenburg under the leadership of Prince Henning. And, according to the latest intelligence, Logan Wilde's equally demented sister.

He had left Asta and the boy from Mellerad at the army camp at Dalhoen, taking the opportunity to have his wound dressed and bandaged as he had been given the latest, grim reports from the last remaining battle sites. Reassuring though it had been to hear that the enemy dagger had not punctured too deeply, it still hurt like hell.

'Your wound will soon heal,' Asta had told him. She was talking about his flesh, of course: the deeper wounds that the Princedom had sustained and was continuing to sustain were another matter altogether.

They had reached the summit of the hill. Now, below him, he saw the scope of the battle. A column of Paddenburg's forces, in the black armour that was now so horribly familiar, had divided into two the borrowed army of Rednow. He could see from this vantage point that Rohan's men and women were having a hard time of it, and could sense the relief as his own force came into view. They must have seemed like welcome reinforcements, arriving in the nick of time.

He continued down the hill, feeling the sting of the bitter wind, until he was just above the level of the battle. He scanned the ranks of the black-clad forces for the telltale golden armour. Were Henning and Lydia Wilde in the fray or, as he suspected, were they hanging back to let their foot soldiers do their dirty work for them?

He could not see them and he could not delay any longer. He brought his horse to a standstill and, hands trembling with the enormity of what he was about to do, began to remove the single object he had carried with him from Dalhoen. The ropes came away easily and he held it in his hands. It was only a light piece of wood but, in his hands, it felt like the weightiest slab of Archenfield oak.

He could hear the cries of the dying carried on the breeze. No more. It was time to end this. He unfurled the white flag of surrender and lifted it high above his head, for everyone to see.

*

SOUTH OF KIRANA

The two opposing armies smashed hard into each other, and the fight was on once more. As he took up his sword anew, Jared felt the enormity of the task still ahead of him and his allies. They were obviously outnumbered now – it was like fighting a supernatural enemy that had the ability to keep replicating itself. But he knew that there was nothing magical about Paddenburg's army. They had always had the advantage of numbers, and the more they diminished Archenfield's forces, so more starkly was the difference in scale revealed.

Jared thought how different things might have been if he had succeeded in bringing the troops of Woodlark and Larsson – and even Baltiska – into play. But, though he might wish this situation to be very different, now was not the time to focus on where he had failed. He had to concentrate on the job at hand – one fight at a time.

Still, moving from one duel to the next, he felt a new weariness setting in. He realised that though he had acquitted himself well enough in the fight so far, his stamina was beginning to fail him. He just could not shake the sense that the battle was already lost. Any more death – on either side – felt utterly pointless. The fundamental outcome would not be any different, after all. And where were these thoughts coming from? They were a trick. The battle was not over yet. He was still in the thick of it. It was simply fatigue and fear talking. He could not allow them to take hold. Fear and its paralysing effects, allied with physical and mental tiredness, would only make him more vulnerable.

Up ahead, in the heart of the melee, he saw a flash of gold. As he moved, he saw the legendary suit of golden armour. He had heard tell of this, but not seen it until now. He knew that beneath that suit of armour was either Prince Henning or Prince Ven or Logan Wilde's sister, Lydia – unless it was a trick and they had employed a decoy. With the princes of Paddenburg, anything was possible.

Jared felt drawn towards the golden armour, intrigued to learn which of his enemies might lie within its protective shell. He knew, deep down, that he didn't have much fight left within him, but the thought of taking down just one of the architects of the invasion and conflict was fuelling him with new energy. Just to do this one, last act for his Princedom would give him solace before his fight gave out and the vast opposing forces consumed him. He felt fresh adrenaline flooding his veins as he dug in his heels and directed his horse towards his target.

He had to unseat several other combatants to clear his path, but nothing was going to stop him now. He felt possessed of a strange new power as he wielded his sword with exquisite prowess. He realised this strength was fed by a well of anger deep within his core: anger at the wanton killing of his brother and sister-in-law; the near-fatal attack on Nova; the motiveless invasion of Archenfield; the cruel plot to take the Princedom back into a time of conflict, when his people were only just becoming familiar with peace. Anger too about having the throne stolen from under him, when he had been doing all he could to make his land and his people safe.

As he made his way ever closer to the rider in the golden armour, Jared felt as if he were confronting a dragon, responsible for all the hurts he and his people had suffered during the past few weeks. Suddenly, slaying that dragon was the one and only thing that mattered. And suddenly, there was no longer anyone separating them.

'Who are you?' he interrogated the armour. 'Which of my enemies?'

There was a pause, then a strangely disconnected voice, perhaps distorted by the curves of the helmet, emerged. 'I am Prince Ven of Paddenburg.' A pause. 'And you? Who are you?'

Jared felt his heart pounding. 'I am Prince Jared of Archenfield,' he cried.

There was a hollow laugh, which echoed from within the helmet. 'So it *is* true. This land *is* being governed by a child.'

Jared saw no reason to inform his adversary that he was no longer the legitimate ruler of Archenfield.

'We'll fight,' he said. 'One to one, you and I. Then we shall see if I am just a child.'

Prince Ven did not reply at once, and Jared felt his anger increasing. Was his opponent's arrogance so vast that he was going to refuse to even fight him?

'All right,' the reply came at last. 'Though it hardly seems fair.'

'You have never cared for fairness,' Jared spat. 'Why start now?'

He had no desire to trade further verbal blows with his enemy. Not when his sword would do a far more satisfying job.

Their battle was swift and furious. Jared could feel the greater weight of his opponent every time Prince Ven's sword made contact with his own. But that weight worked both for and against Ven – it added power to his strikes, although Jared's lighter armour enabled him to move more swiftly on his horse and to switch position with greater agility.

As they traded blow after blow, Jared knew that this duel was more important than any of those he had fought until now – an importance both real and symbolic.

Countering the latest of Ven's attacks, Jared saw that his opponent had become unseated in his saddle. Seizing his opportunity, he barged into him and attacked with his sword, forcing Ven out of his saddle entirely. The golden-clad Prince tumbled to the ground in a clatter of metal, down into the sea of mud below.

Jared did not waste any time. He jumped down from his own saddle and stood astride Ven, holding down one of the armoured arms with his boot as he threatened the other with his sword.

Ven's helmet had come loose in the fall. At last able to see his enemy, Jared felt a sense of shock. Stripped of his golden helmet, Prince Ven was slight, and clearly only a few years older than himself. His eyes were as wide as the night sky.

Ven stared up at him, his face contorted with hatred. 'What next?'

Jared considered his answer. He brought the tip of his sword to Ven's exposed Adam's apple. It was satisfying and terrifying at the same time to know that he now had the power to decide whether Prince Ven of Paddenburg would live or die.

'Do it then,' Ven spat out the words. 'If you have it in you. Run your sword through me. It won't make any difference. My brother will still claim this Princedom from you. But I will die the death of a hero, my Paddenburg blood bringing much-needed nutrients to the arid soil of Archenfield.'

'You're no hero,' Jared told him, pushing the sword deeper into Ven's flesh. He was keenly aware of all the reasons to take this man's life; all the atrocities that Ven had been responsible for. He had never been possessed of such pulsing anger before. But although Jared was no stranger to killing, something held him back.

'No, I didn't think you had it in you,' Ven sneered up at him. 'You don't even have a proper suit of armour! You shouldn't even be out on the battlefield, but back in the palace nursery, where children like you belong.'

That pushed Jared over the edge. He lifted his sword. It would be so easy. Sword held aloft, he became aware of a hand on his shoulder, Hal's voice at his side.

'Don't kill him, Prince Jared.'

He did not remove his eyes from Prince Ven's hateful, taunting face. 'Give me one good reason not to,' he rasped.

'Prince Axel has surrendered.'

Jared laughed bitterly. 'He has? Then what difference would one more death on the battlefield make?'

Now, for the first time, he saw genuine fear in Prince Ven's face. He couldn't deny that felt good.

Hal spoke again. 'It would make all the difference in the world to the future of Archenfield,' the Bodyguard told him. 'Prince Axel was very specific. We have surrendered – there must be no more bloodshed.'

'Yes,' Jared said. 'So you tell me. But surely you under-stand – I have little care these days for what Axel Blaxland desires.'

Hal's voice remained strong. 'You have always been guided by what is best for Archenfield. How many of your people will be slaughtered in retaliation for this act? Would you sac-rifice the life of even one of them for this kill? For that reason alone, you must let the bastard live.'

TWO DAYS AFTER
INVASION . . .

FORTY-ONE

ARCHENFIELD

Nova could hear the drumming of a thousand hooves advancing on the palace grounds. 'Here they come,' she announced, with grim resignation.

Queen Elin did not respond. Her slender fingers remained pressed against the cold, leaded window of the Queen's Chamber. It was as if she were incapable of separating herself from the palace that she had fought so long and tirelessly for.

Nova watched the serpent-like trail of the Paddenburg advance party pass beneath the avenue of trees on the road leading up to the palace. She recalled the weight of her armour and the blood of battle drying in her wild hair – then, it had been mid-summer and a rich canopy of emerald leaves had shaded them from the sun. Her beloved Anders had ridden beside her. He had come home a hero. Nova wondered if Elin was also lost in the memory of her eldest son's victorious return from war. This day, however, brought with it no such cheer. These riders – in their purple uniforms and hideous black armour – were an advancing enemy, and winter was now upon them all. The avenue had lost its leaves. In fact, Nova reflected, as she took in the bare, skeletal branches, the trees looked as if they were dead.

The first riders turned on to the final approach to the palace. The column of cavalry moved steadily behind them: merciless as a machine, unstoppable as the river. Nova sought out the faces of the two Princes of Paddenburg. That must be Henning and Ven, there at the front, armour audaciously hewn from gold. There was a third rider in golden armour too. Presumably this was Lydia Wilde, the Poet's sister. Nova's attention swiftly moved to another horse and rider, just ahead of the Princes.

Nova heard Elin gasp beside her.

The horse was moving erratically, pushing ahead of the press behind it. It was dressed in the colours of Archenfield, yet it was the distinctive cross on the breastplate of the rider's armour that revealed more clearly his identity.

The rider was Father Simeon. His hands gripped the reins just as tightly as his thighs pressed close against either side of the saddle.

But it was only when Nova looked more closely, in shock, that she discovered the true horror of it.

Father Simeon was riding back to the palace without his head. Where it should have been was a dark stump.

Nova could barely control the bile rising like lava in her throat. She thought of the old folk tale of how the day the Headless Horseman rode up to the palace gates would mark the end of order and the coming of chaos. She had always thought that story was a parable – had certainly never expected to see such a brutal scene played out before her eyes. And yet, as horrible as it was to watch, she could not draw her eyes away from the grotesque sight of Father Simeon leading the forces of Paddenburg along the road.

Nova felt desperately sad for the Priest, thinking of his kind heart and all his good intentions; understanding now his final act of unspeakable bravery – riding out to the enemy to make his claim for the court. His answer had been a brutal one, spoken with a sword rather than a tongue.

Axel, Prince of All Archenfield, stood on the palace's balcony, his fingers coiled tightly around the thick twists of ivy that had taken root there over the span of many years and countless changes of ruler. He was flanked by his newly appointed Captain of the Guard, his Bodyguard and the Poet.

The four of them watched as the lead members of the Paddenburg contingent made their final approach to the palace.

Could this unfolding of events, Axel wondered, prove any more surreal? Moments before, a gelding had cantered past the balcony, carrying the decapitated body of Father Simeon off into the nearby woodland. Now, the rulers of Paddenburg – who were clearly responsible for this atrocity, and many others besides – were trotting up the approach road themselves, in as relaxed and insouciant a fashion as if they had arrived a little early for a masquerade ball or weekend house party.

'How ought I to address the Princes of Paddenburg?' Asta asked.

'I gather they have a preference for "Your Infinite Majesty",' Elliot told her.

Axel frowned. 'I certainly shan't be employing those terms, not after they have decapitated my Priest.' He turned to Asta. 'And I don't think you need address them at all. Just watch and listen.'

Asta nodded. She seemed relieved, he thought. Axel was impressed with how steadfastly she had absorbed the news –

and, even more so, the sight – of Father Simeon's headless body. Of course, she had been deeply shocked, but where others might have screamed or fainted, Asta had only blanched and made tight balls of her fists. Perhaps such fortitude came from being cast – admittedly by his own doing – into a battle zone. He had saved her life and she, in turn, had saved his.

Axel had been planning to swiftly replace Asta as the Poet, on account of both her inexperience and her unquestionable loyalty to Jared; maybe, he thought now, he shouldn't be quite so hasty about it. Her surprising strength and her unquestionable straightforwardness might be useful assets. Although, he realised, the matter might well be out of his hands now.

The clip-clop of hooves below had slowed. Axel glanced down to observe Prince Ven and Prince Henning dismount from their horses. Henning then moved over to his striking female companion, offering her his hand. So this was Lydia Wilde, sister to Archenfield's renegade Poet, Axel thought. Yes, he could see there was a striking resemblance between the two: the same-shaped eyes, the same high cheekbones. Axel realised he might have thought her quite attractive had she not been his avowed enemy.

The three foreigners climbed the steps up to the balcony. Each of the three was flanked by an armed bodyguard. Henning and Ven strode purposely ahead, keen no doubt to proceed swiftly with matters; Lydia walked at a less hurried pace, her eyes ranging across the palace and the lands around it. Axel felt somehow grateful for this – at least she seemed to be taking some genuine interest in the territory she had come here to claim.

'Did the Prince not see fit to welcome us himself?' Prince Ven enquired, forgoing any formal manner of greeting.

'*I* am the Prince of All Archenfield now,' Axel snapped.

'You are—? Since when?'

'I'd have thought your spies would have been swift to bring you this news,' Axel said. 'Or were you too busy being humiliated on the battlefield by my cousin?'

With Prince Ven temporarily silenced, his brother seamlessly stepped in. 'And here we were worrying that Prince Jared might run into trouble on the open road, while all the while, his greatest threat was working against him at home. Do tell us, how did *Prince* Jared react to the news of your betrayal?'

'You need not concern yourself with his well-being. You need not concern yourself with him at all. The Wynyard family and their sympathisers have been placed under house arrest. I am ruler of Archenfield now and so your dealings will be with me.'

Prince Ven stepped in closer. 'You seem to have convinced yourself that you're in a position to negotiate. One word from me and you could lose that arrogant head of yours.'

'You underestimate me,' Axel said. 'I know that you come from an archaic Princedom, but even you can work out that I have no allegiance to the former rulers of Archenfield. In fact, I have very different views as to the future of Archenfield than my cousin's. You see, I was never in favour of our alliance with Woodlark and, by association, their southern neighbour, Malytor. Those Princedoms joined forces to ensure peace and stability – that is not what Archenfield needs. I want Archenfield to be a part of something bigger, something stronger, something altogether more aggressive.' He took a breath. 'Why not hear me out? What have you got to lose?'

Henning and Ven turned towards one another, as if weighing the matter.

Axel was now aware of Lydia staring intently at him. Getting the measure of me as well as my lands, he thought. 'I don't believe I've had the pleasure,' he said, stepping forward and extending his hand. As he did so, Lydia's guard moved swiftly into the space between them. Axel glared at him. 'I'm merely offering my hand in welcome,' he said. 'Perhaps such courtesies are alien to you.'

'Stand down!' Lydia instructed her guard. She took a step closer to Axel and placed her gloved hand in his. '*Prince* Axel, Your Serene Highness, I'm Lydia Wilde.' To his surprise, she had actually curtsied. As she drew herself erect again, she added, 'I believe you know my brother quite well.'

'Indeed,' Axel said. 'The resemblance between you both is remarkable. Are you twins?'

Lydia smiled. 'I trust my darling Logan is well. I should very much like to see him at the earliest opportunity.'

Axel savoured the moment. 'I'm sure he'll be glad of a visit. You'll find him in the Dungeons. Would you like me to have someone show you the way?'

If Lydia was disconcerted by his remarks, she gave no sign of it. Instead, her lively eyes simply moved to the man on Axel's right. 'Perhaps Elliot could walk me there?'

How did she know his deputy's name? Axel was himself now thrown. Had he introduced them before, then forgotten? No. Axel saw that not only did Lydia know Elliot's name, this was clearly not the first time they had met. He watched as Elliot gave Lydia the Paddenburgian salute. Elliot! Axel felt the red-hot stab of betrayal lance his guts.

Elliot Nash, his own trusted second-in-command – the man who knew him better than just about anyone else on earth; in whom he had confided just about all his secrets – was a court spy and traitor. How on earth had this been allowed to happen? How had he himself failed to notice? First Logan

Wilde, now Elliot Nash. How effectively the Princes of Paddenburg had manoeuvred their allies deep into the heart of Archenfield's court.

If he hadn't hated them with every fibre of his being, he'd be swooning with admiration.

'I'm afraid, Miss Wilde, that Elliot must stay with *me*,' Axel said, drawing some pleasure from Nash's evident discomfort. 'You see, he is my Captain of the Guard now.'

Lydia's eyes widened. 'My my, how the carousel spins,' she observed. 'Hey-ho, just point me in the right direction then, and I'll go find my brother myself.'

'Good idea,' said Prince Henning, nodding, as his gaze moved from Lydia to Axel. 'And then ... my own brother and I *would* very much enjoy a meeting with *you*.'

'No guards or lackeys,' Prince Ven added, his nose wrinkling as his eyes ranged over Elliot, Hal and Asta. 'Just the three of us Princes!'

'Not possible,' Hal spoke out.

Axel glanced towards the Bodyguard. He knew Hal was as reluctant to abandon him as he was to be abandoned. It would be madness to willingly enter a closed room with the two unhinged Princes. He supposed he could persuade them to leave their weapons at the door, but even if he did, they could surely still overpower him and put him to death with their bare hands if they chose to. Not that Axel was a laggard in the fighting department ...

'What's the problem?' Prince Henning asked. 'Have you changed your mind? Don't you want to meet with us any more?'

'We've come such a long way,' Prince Ven added. 'Don't we deserve a cosy chat? And a cup of tea wouldn't go amiss. Lady Grey by preference.'

Axel noticed a small smile play on Lydia Wilde's lips at

Ven's remark. It was strange the things that people found amusing. He turned back to his rival Princes.

'Well?' Prince Ven was clearly growing impatient, as well as thirsty.

'Hal, you and Asta wait here for me – with the Princes' guards. But Elliot, I'd like you to join us.' As he spoke, he looked not to Elliot but to the two Princes. 'It is clear that Elliot is up to speed with your plans. Whether he is my Captain of the Guard or – in reality – yours, I feel it appropriate that he should join our discussion.'

The Princes were clearly surprised but, after a moment's consultation, did not object. Elliot had already sauntered over to stand beside them. Axel could have killed him then and there if there hadn't been so much else upon which to focus his energies.

He saw Hal's expression of horror and could guess what he was thinking. Elliot was the traitor, which meant that Axel was about to walk into a private chamber with not two sworn enemies, but three. Axel rested his hand on Hal's shoulder. 'I'll almost certainly be fine,' he said. 'And, if I'm not ... well, I thank you for your friendship and wish you well.' He moved on to Asta, strangely reassured by the steadfastness of her gaze. 'Stay here with Hal. I'm likely to have need of your services, one way or another, when I emerge.' At last, he addressed Henning and Ven, with some irony. 'Gentlemen, please come this way.'

As the Princes, followed close behind by Elliot, took their first steps inside the palace, Axel turned to Hal once more. 'Perhaps *you* can point Ms Wilde in the direction of her brother?' Once again, he was aware of Lydia's intense scrutiny – she seemed greatly interested in him, and he looked across to her to meet her stare.

In spite of her allure, she was no better than her two

companions, Axel realised – this was all nothing more than a joke to them. Decapitating a priest. Invading a country. Laying waste to centuries of history. It really seemed as if it were all nothing more than sport to the demented trio from Paddenburg.

As Axel turned away from her, he realised he was shaking. He felt a renewed determination to fight them. However the odds were stacked against him, whatever he had to do – they would not take from him this Princedom that he had worked so long and so hard to claim as his own.

FORTY-TWO

THE DUNGEONS,
PALACE OF ARCHENFIELD

As Morgan's hearing had declined, so his other four senses seemed to have sharpened. Even within the gloom of the Dungeons, he found his eyes well equipped for reading even the finest print with the aid of only a single candle. His senses of touch and taste had also both grown more subtle, enriching his afternoon visits to the Queen's Library. But, in particular, he had found that his sense of smell had become more acute. So it was that, whilst he was sharpening a small dagger, he first became aware of the two visitors to his subterranean domain not by the sound of their footsteps, but by the scent of them.

He paused in his work, not yet turning. He knew at once that one of his visitors was familiar. The particular combination of clean sweat, shaving soap and tobacco was just the topnote that told him that it was Hal Harness. The first scent he caught from the second visitor was an unusual earthy cologne. As he inhaled more deeply, he had the sense of something utterly familiar about this person. Intrigued by the mixed messages his brain was sending him, he turned to face them. Even before Hal spoke, he had put the pieces of the puzzle together. She was the mirror image of her brother.

'This is Lydia Wilde,' Hal informed him, unnecessarily. 'She has lately arrived at the palace in the company of Prince Ven and Prince Henning of Paddenburg.'

Morgan inhaled again, deeply. The cologne had misled him. Beneath it, Lydia emitted the same animal scent as her brother. It was far from obvious and he doubted that others would have picked up on it, but he would have been in no doubt of the deep, tribal connection between the two even if a blindfold had been placed over his eyes.

The stranger silently scrutinised Morgan for a moment. He was aware of her eyes tracing the patterns of ink on his exposed arms, but her interest proved only fleeting.

As she stretched out her arm towards him, he at first had done the same in greeting, thinking to shake her hand. But as she turned her palm upwards, he saw his mistake.

'The keys, if you please,' she said, not unpleasantly.

When he did not immediately respond, she began to wiggle her fingers. 'The keys to my brother's cell,' she specified. 'Quickly now.' Her voice was resonant with authority. It reminded him of Queen Elin's.

Thoughts raced through Morgan's head. Was he supposed to take all this at face value and, following Hal's lead, be pleasant and cordial with Lydia Wilde and accede to her wishes? Or, bearing in mind that she was on the enemy side and had come here, it seemed, with no protection of her own, should he take the dagger which lay in easy reach and plunge it deep into her nearest available artery?

He met Hal's eyes, searching for some cue there.

As if sensing Morgan's question, Hal smiled at his fellow

gently. 'Miss Wilde is a guest of Prince Axel,' he said. 'Please give her the keys so she may be reunited with her brother.'

Morgan nodded slowly, then turned and walked towards his workbench. He was inclined to take Hal's words at face value. Nothing in Hal's tone of voice, or the expression in his eyes, told Morgan to act any differently. He shrugged to himself. Morgan had learned that sometimes Axel worked in mysterious ways. He was confident that Archenfield's new ruler would have a plan.

He retrieved the key and, turning, placed it carefully in Lydia Wilde's waiting palm. It was as small and fine as a piece of porcelain. Her delicate fingers swiftly closed over the key with the efficiency of one of Jonas's traps. It made him sad to think of Jonas. He still couldn't believe that the Woodsman was gone. He found himself back in the glade where he had reluctantly left his fallen comrade's body. He had been pained then, as now, not only by the abrupt departure of his friend, but by his own failure to bring Jonas's body back to the Drummond family mausoleum for its eternal rest.

After Jonas's death, everything had had the quality of a dream to Morgan. A surreal dream, which had sent Morgan deeper and deeper into himself. Now, as he watched Logan Wilde's sister slide the key into the lock, he thought that it was just another part of the dream.

She turned and glanced over her shoulder, rather haughtily. 'Some privacy, if you don't mind.' She addressed Morgan and Hal as one.

Nodding amiably, Hal turned to wander back to the other end of the Dungeon. Morgan strode after him.

'What the hell's going on here?' the Executioner asked the Bodyguard, when they were, he judged, safely out of the others' hearing.

Hal shrugged. 'Your guess is as good as mine,' he said.

'But Axel has some kind of plan, I assume?' Morgan hissed.

Hal nodded, reaching out a hand to rest lightly on Morgan's shoulder. 'Prince Axel always has some kind of plan, wouldn't you say?'

Lydia stood at the threshold of the cell, the door now open, her heart beating savagely as her brother began walking towards her through the gloom. His movements were, understandably, a little shaky at first, and he stumbled as he emerged from the cell, but then he reached out his long arms and drew her into a clumsy embrace. It felt so good to hold him in her arms – and to be held by him. So different from the way Henning held her. Lydia and Logan rocked together for a moment, as each regained their sense of equilibrium.

Logan's arms now fell to circle his sister's narrow waist. He seemed reluctant to let go of her, and she felt exactly the same. She reached up a hand to gently cup her brother's cheek. 'I'm not used to seeing you with a beard,' she said. 'How rugged you look! What will Ven say, I wonder?'

Logan shrugged. 'Is he here?' he asked.

She nodded. 'Yes, my darling. Ven and Henning are both here and in conference with the new Prince ...' She paused to correct herself. 'The temporary Prince.'

Logan smiled at her careful terminology. He had always enjoyed the precision of words. 'So everything is going to plan?'

She nodded, but not with the vigour he had anticipated. He could see the budding tears in her eyes. She lifted her hand to blot them dry.

'Here, let me,' he said, reaching into the pocket of his hessian trousers for a handkerchief. He half expected it to be a grimy scrap of cloth but it emerged as a perfect square of folded white linen. He realised he had had no call for it, throughout his captivity, until now. This pleased him disproportionately as he unfolded it and gently absorbed the moisture from his sister's troubled eyes with the soft cloth. He felt somehow that he was also drawing out some of her pain.

'Thank you,' she said. 'You don't know how hard it has proved being away from you for so long.'

He folded up the damp linen square without taking his eyes from hers. 'But of course I do,' he told her. 'I know exactly how hard it has been for you, because it has been just the same for me.'

She smiled now. 'We are two jagged pieces of the same mirror, aren't we?'

He returned her smile. 'Always have been. Always will be.' His lips pursed. 'You look tired,' he told her.

'I am tired, Logan. More tired than I can remember. These past few days have been gruelling beyond measure.'

He gave her a reassuring squeeze. 'It's over now.'

She shook her head. 'That's just it,' she said. 'It's not over, is it? It will never be over.'

'You're allowed to be weary,' he told her. 'But you know how you get, sister. When you are at a low ebb, you are inclined to forget how far you have come, how far *we* have come. You risk losing perspective on everything that lies before us.'

She nodded, her eyes showing fresh strain. 'You're right. I'm sorry. I'm just so tired of us playing these parts – the puppets of Henning and Ven.'

'I know,' he said. 'As am I. But it's only for a little longer now. Soon, very soon, we shall show everyone just who are the puppets and who are their masters.'

'You always know just what to say,' she told him.

He drew her back into his arms. 'And you – you always

know just what to do. That's why, Lydia darling, we are the perfect team.'

She settled her face in the crook of his neck and shoulder and felt her body relax for the first time in months. 'Two jagged pieces of the same mirror,' she repeated, her voice softer now.

'Exactly,' he said, planting a tender kiss on the crown of her head.

FORTY-THREE

THE COUNCIL CHAMBER, PALACE OF ARCHENFIELD

'Let me tell you how I see things,' Axel began, when they were all seated in the Council Chamber.

Henning smiled. 'Be our guest.'

Guest, Axel thought. A pointed choice of words. 'You need me. Now more than ever.'

Ven raised an eyebrow. 'That's an interesting idea. From where I'm sitting, there would seem to be an abundance of princes.' He turned to his brother. 'What *is* the collective noun for princes?' Faced with Henning's confused expression, Ven continued. 'You know how for nature, there exist these curious group nouns for certain animals ... "a murder of crows", "a parliament of owls" and so forth. What, I wonder, is the collective noun for princes?'

'A crown of princes?' Henning suggested with a shrug.

'An ambition of princes?' Elliot offered. 'No, wait – a *conspiracy* of princes!'

'Very good, Elliot,' Henning observed, with a nod and a wry smile.

Ven shook his head. 'No, they're not right.' His eyes turned to Axel. 'Do *you* know the correct terminology?'

Axel returned his gaze blankly.

'Well.' Ven looked perplexed. 'I'm sure I don't know the answer. But my point remains ... we really don't need another prince in the mix.'

'You *do* need me,' Axel asserted, pushing on before they were waylaid by another of Ven's meandering thoughts. 'I know how this Princedom works. I have the support of the Council of Twelve –'

'Not all of them,' Henning interjected. 'As I understand it, almost half of them voted to retain Prince Jared as ruler of Archenfield.'

Axel frowned. Had Elliot filled him in on these matters on their journey to this room? It was hard to think how else they could have been briefed so swiftly.

'Well, what we can be sure of is that if you ask any of the Twelve to choose between me or you, they will all choose me ... ' He broke off, realising his mistake.

Both of the Paddenburg Princes were glancing towards Elliot.

'We have the newest member of the Twelve here,' Henning observed. 'Let's ask him. Elliot, would you rather see Axel remain as Prince of Archenfield or would you be in favour of a suitable alternative from our ranks?'

Axel shook his head. 'I was overlooking the fact that Elliot has been on your payroll for some time. He doesn't count.'

'Charming!' Elliot sighed.

'That's where you're wrong,' Henning said. 'Elliot's opinion certainly counts to me. Tell us what you think, Elliot.'

Elliot nodded. 'Speaking for myself, I'd be very happy

to see an alternative candidate put forward for Prince,' he said.

'There's a surprise—' Axel began.

'Please, Axel, let him finish,' Henning said. 'Elliot?'

'I can only speak for myself,' Elliot said. 'My loyalties are with Paddenburg.' Axel marvelled at how easily those words slipped from the traitor's tongue. 'But I don't think that is true for the other members of the Twelve. I have every reason to think that Axel is right when he says that they would choose him over any candidates you might put forward.'

'Thank you, Elliot.' Henning looked across at Axel. 'You see, it was worth your while to let him finish. He seems to have endorsed your first point. I believe you have more to say?'

Axel nodded, somewhat surprised that Elliot had supported his argument. 'So, firstly, I have the Council of Twelve's support. Secondly, I have control of the army—'

'Ah!' This time it was Elliot who interrupted Axel. The way he shrugged his shoulders and smiled made Axel want nothing more than to strangle him quite slowly. 'The thing is, as we all know, I am now Captain of the Guard and, for some while now, I have served as Axel's deputy. So it would not be a major issue for the army to transfer its allegiance from Axel to me.'

'It *would* be more of a major issue,' Axel retorted, 'as soon as they discover that you have been working for Paddenburg and against Archenfield all this time.'

'Touché.' Elliot shrugged and folded his arms.

'I take your point, Axel,' Henning said. 'So what else do you have to offer us?'

Axel took a breath. 'You are clearly ambitious men, both of you.' He saw no reason to include Elliot in this and noted that the Paddenburg Princes did not, on this occasion, leap to his defence. 'You set out to take control of Archenfield with ruthless, single-minded ambition. You mobilised Logan Wilde to bring down the court from within and you achieved some success—'

Ven grinned. 'Flattery won't get you everything you want,' he said.

'My point,' Axel continued, 'is that it's clear to me that acquiring Archenfield cannot be the endgame for you, but merely the staging post in your ambitions. My intelligence leads me to believe that you have others of the Thousand Territories in your sights. With those kinds of grand plans, do you really want to be bogged down with the day-to-day running of one of the smaller Princedoms?'

'My, my, Axel.' Henning shook his head. 'I never thought to hear you speak of Archenfield, precious Archenfield, in such derogatory terms.'

Axel shook his head but when he spoke next, his tone was even. 'I am not talking Archenfield down. I would never do that. This Princedom may be small but it is a wondrous place and it has been home to my family for many centuries.'

'Fetch me a handkerchief.' Ven nudged Henning.

'All I'm saying,' Axel continued, 'is that what you need now is for Archenfield to settle into the rule of Paddenburg with the minimum of fuss. So that you two may proceed with the next stage in your plans to . . . expand.'

Axel had managed to get the words out, even if he felt positively nauseous at having done so.

He sat back in his seat, waiting for their response. The two Princes were silent for a moment, then Henning spoke.

'This is actually quite interesting. If I understand you correctly, what you are proposing is that you continue to rule Archenfield on a day-to-day basis, so that we don't have to. Is that right?'

Axel nodded. 'Absolutely. We can draw up a power-sharing

agreement. Your troops will withdraw from the borders and you will return to the Black Palace of Paddenburg, or go on to the next of your targets.'

Ven leaned forward. 'And the people of Archenfield will think that, once again, the plucky little Princedom has seen off a big bad enemy. Like the war with Eronesia all over again.'

'And who delivered such a victory?' Henning stepped in. 'But Prince Axel! Masterful Prince Axel. What a convincing way to announce your reign. Yes, I see.' He nodded, then fell silent.

'So,' Axel said, 'do we have a deal? Perhaps you'd like me and Elliot to leave the room so you can discuss this on your own?'

Henning shook his head. 'That will not be necessary,' he said, glancing at his brother. 'I'm sure I can speak for both of us. This deal is not possible.'

'Correct.' Ven nodded his agreement.

Axel's heart missed a beat.

'I'm very interested in your handling administrative matters within Archenfield,' Henning told Axel. 'Particularly with regard to the hefty tax we'll be placing on you – war costs, you know. Yes, this all has undeniable appeal and, as you say, frees us to focus on the bigger picture—'

'What exactly *is* the bigger picture?' Axel enquired.

Prince Ven set down his teacup. 'Now is not the time to go into detail, but what you said before was quite right.' He smiled. 'This was just the beginning.'

His brother nodded, his eyes remaining on Axel. 'I'm not opposed to cutting you a deal, with respect to our growing empire. You talk as if you'd be happy to live out the rest of your days in charge of Archenfield ... but I think not. I recognise us as beings of the same tribe. The walls of this

Princedom are too close to contain your own ambitions – just as they are ours.'

Still, Axel could not allow himself to breathe. What he could be offered was so much more than he had thought he could achieve. It seemed they weren't just going to allow him to keep hold of the reins of Archenfield, but be a partner in the expansion of their empire. This was as tantalising as it was unexpected.

'I sense I am talking your language,' Henning said. 'And yes, we can, as you said before, talk terms and draw up a decree. But before we do so, there is one thing you need to understand. No one within Archenfield will be under any misapprehension that this Princedom is anything but a spoil of Paddenburg. There will, I'm afraid, be no glorious tales of Prince Axel's first victory written in the history books.'

Ven nodded, glancing around the room. 'There will be some significant changes to the palace. This mural, for instance, has to go. It won't do any good reminding people of the way things were. It's time to look forwards, not backwards.' He tapped the Prince's Table. 'I don't think we have any need of this either,' he said. 'On the whole, I'm not convinced by the idea of the Council of Twelve. It's a little too democratic for my tastes.' He ran his fingers along the surface of the centuries-old table. 'But this is good oak. It won't go to waste. Winter is upon us and we shall have need of firewood.' He smiled at Axel's shocked expression.

'The flag of Paddenburg will fly from the palace flagpole before darkness falls tonight,' Henning told Axel. 'And these are just the first of the changes we must make, with your help. But here's where your proposal is so persuasive to me ... many of these changes may jar with the feelings and loyalties of the common man and woman. But you are right. They know you, they know your family. If you tell them that this is the way of things, they will heed your word. So yes, Axel, you may rule Archenfield for us.'

'You may even continue to call yourself Prince,' Ven assured him, 'if it pleases you to do so.'

'Why wouldn't I call myself Prince?' Axel asked. 'I would be ruling the Princedom, even if I was sharing in the greater empire of Paddenburg.'

'Yes,' Ven acknowledged. 'That is true. It's just that, assuming we do proceed with this intriguing proposition, there is one further matter we need you to be made aware of.'

Henning nodded. 'Yes, that's right.'

Axel didn't like the sound of this. At all.

'You see, when we embarked on this ambitious mission of ours, a promise was made. And it is very important to my brother and me to uphold our promises.'

Axel nodded. 'What kind of promise? To whom was it made?'

'Oh, it's very simple, really,' Ven explained. 'In exchange for successfully executing his mission, we told Logan Wilde that Archenfield would be his to do with what he wished.' He smiled. 'And I think we can all agree that Logan was extremely successful in executing that mission.'

Axel could not believe what he was hearing. 'So you told Logan that *he* would be Prince of Archenfield?'

'I don't think he's likely to be as hung up on terminology as you seem to be,' Henning observed. 'But he will be running the Princedom. By all means, talk to Logan – work out an arrangement. We don't need to get involved in that level of detail. If you want to be called Prince of All Archenfield, I doubt he'll object. Just so long as we're all clear that he'll have the final say on, well, everything.'

Axel was, at last, speechless. He couldn't even look upon the faces of the Princes of Paddenburg any longer. All his dreams lay in tatters, ground to dust. He turned instead to Elliot, who merely smiled and shrugged. *Damn* him and his traitor's heart! Damn them all! Elliot and Logan and his sister, and the two demon Princes of Paddenburg. They would pay – they would all pay. The Wheel of Fortune might have turned against his favour for the moment, but that wheel had a habit of spinning fast, and he would find a way to give it a hefty nudge in the right direction.

'All right,' he said. 'I'll talk to Logan.'

Ven smiled brightly. 'Speaking of Logan, I'm very keen to see him. I think our business here is concluded. I should now like to take possession of our rooms and catch up with Logan and Lydia.'

'Your rooms?' Axel enquired, caught off guard. 'Would you like me to have one of the guest suites prepared for you?'

Henning smiled gratefully. 'You're very kind, Axel, but no, that wouldn't be fitting under the circumstances. We'll be taking up residence, for the time being, in the Prince's Quarters.'

So, he was even to be denied the Prince's Chamber. Only for now, he told himself. Whatever indignity they impose upon you, it's only for now. Even so, the very thought of it made him retch. The minute he found a way to send them on their way, he'd have the entire palace fumigated.

'Let's all reconvene for dinner – around nine?' Ven suggested. 'I'll leave you to talk to the Cook. I know that it's customary to eat supper in Archenfield as soon as the sun sets, but our tastes are a little more sophisticated. I'm sure you will soon adapt.'

'I'm sure they will,' Henning said. The Princes of Paddenburg rose to their feet. Elliot rose too and lifted his hand in the Paddenburgian salute. The Princes returned it, then continued on their way.

Axel and Elliot were left alone in the Council Chamber. Axel waited until he heard the door slam shut behind them, then turned to his deputy.

But Elliot got in first: 'You see?' he said with a smile. 'They're not so bad once you get to know them. Oh, I'll grant you they have a few strange ways, Prince Ven in particular, but—'

'Shut up, Elliot!' Axel snapped, walking the length of the Prince's Table.

'Don't tell me to shut up,' Elliot said. 'Don't *dare* to address me in those tones. You are clinging to power here by a thread, and you really shouldn't be under any illusions.'

Axel nodded. 'I suppose, Elliot, that neither of us should be under any illusions.'

As Elliot nodded in return, Axel stepped closer and buried the small dagger he had been secreting in his hand deep into Elliot's heart.

Elliot's eyes widened with both shock and pain. 'How are you going to explain that ... to ... to the two Princes?'

Axel smiled, pushing the knife deeper into Elliot's flesh. 'If you wish to worry about such matters in the few final minutes remaining to you on this earth, be my guest. Rest assured, you traitorous little bastard, I won't be giving you another thought. Good night, sweet Elliot. May you rot in all eternity.'

Satisfied to see the weakness already overtaking Nash's traitorous body, Axel pushed his bleeding deputy to the floor. 'We don't want your traitor's blood staining the Prince's Table, now, do we?' he asked.

Looking down, he saw Elliot's lips part slowly. Axel brought down his boot and pressed it against the hilt of the dagger. 'No need to answer. It was a rhetorical question.'

FORTY-FOUR

THE QUEEN'S QUARTERS, PALACE OF ARCHENFIELD

'We make our own destiny, Jared,' Elin said, looking out through her casement at movements in the grounds. 'However dire events may seem, it is how we respond to them that matters.'

'Fighting talk, Mother!' Edvin said, from his position on the edge of her bed.

Jared was considering how best to respond but was distracted by a knock on the door to the chamber. He looked to his mother. This was her room.

'Enter,' she called wearily.

A guard stepped across the threshold of the chamber. 'Prince Jared,' he began, then broke off, as if embarrassed.

Elin stepped closer to the centre of the room. 'You are right to call him Prince Jared. Whether he is currently ruler of Archenfield or not, Jared is still a Prince and always will be.'

The guard nodded. 'Yes, Your Majesty.' His eyes returned to Jared's as he resumed, with more confidence. 'Prince Jared, Prince Axel wishes to meet with you in the Council Chamber at your earliest convenience.'

Jared nodded. 'I'll be there presently.'

'We'll come with you,' Elin declared.

'Actually,' the guard said, directing his words to Jared. 'Prince Axel asked only to see you, Your Highness.'

Elin now claimed the space between her son and the envoy. 'You have delivered your message,' she said. 'You may go now.'

'Yes, Your Majesty.' The guard gratefully disappeared into the corridor.

'Perhaps it would be better if I met Axel on my own,' Jared said tentatively.

'Nonsense,' Elin said, shaking her head firmly. 'In a time of crisis, the Wynyard family moves as one. Edvin and I will accompany you.'

'Yes, of course,' Edvin said, rising to his feet.

'What does Axel want from me now?', Jared wondered aloud. 'What more is there left to take?' As he walked along the corridor, his mother and brother at his side, he saw that the palace was now swarming with guards in the uniforms of Paddenburg. Two of them pushed briskly past the trio of Wynyards.

'Don't they know who we are?' Elin bristled.

'I suspect they *do* know who we are,' Jared answered. 'And this is exactly why they treat us with such disdain.'

Elin snorted. 'In that case, I wonder if your cousin Axel truly holds any sway here, after all.'

'Well,' said Edvin, 'I suppose we shall soon find out.'

They had reached the palace's main stairway. There were more guards there. They were taking down the family portraits from the wall.

'What are you doing?' Elin called, indignantly.

'Just following orders,' grunted one from the top of a ladder, as he passed down a canvas to his companion.

Elin seemed about to respond when her attention was diverted. Jared saw that Lord Viggo, Lady Stella and his grandmother, Klara, were at the foot of the stairs, waiting to ascend.

Lady Stella had the decency to look awkward; Lord Viggo, in contrast, could not disguise his smile. Klara turned to her son. 'What are they doing with the paintings?'

Before Viggo could answer, Elin swept down the staircase. 'Yes, brother. What *are* they doing with the paintings? And what hell have you and your kin unleashed upon the court and the Princedom?'

'This is not of my making,' Viggo told her. 'If you and your kin had not irretrievably weakened the Princedom, we would not be facing the challenging circumstances in which we now find ourselves.'

'You had a choice to make,' Elin told her brother. 'And you have made it. You could have shown support for my son when he most needed it, but instead, you chose to manoeuvre your own son in a desperate grab at power.'

Viggo smiled again. 'I did nothing you would not have done, sister. I think we can all agree on that.'

Elin reached out her hand and slapped Viggo viciously across the face. The weight of her blow sent him reeling. He laughed as he stumbled, his hand reaching the struck cheek, already rising with welts. Jared – he and Edvin stood midway up the stairs – watched as Lady Stella stepped forward. At first, it seemed she had done so to assist her stricken husband, but this proved not to be the case.

Instead, she extended her own hand and gave Elin as hard a slap as she had dealt.

Elin did not waver but stood stunned.

'You have held sway here for too long,' Lady Stella said icily. 'And you have come to confuse opportunism with divine right.'

As Elin lifted her hand to her cheek, Lady Stella reached out to help Klara on to the stairway. 'Come,' she said.

Elin was trembling as Jared and Edvin came to stand on either side of her. As they did so, Lord Viggo got to his feet. 'The time of the Wynyards is over!' he announced. 'The time of the Blaxlands is come!'

Elin shook her head. 'Are you quite blind to the flags of Paddenburg now flying from the palace roof? Congratulations, brother, you have managed to seize power at last – and to hold on to it for approximately two heartbeats. I do believe this may be your crowning achievement.'

Anxious to avoid any further discord, Jared nodded to Edvin and they led their mother down the last remaining stairs and past Lord Viggo. As they continued along the corridor towards the Council Chamber, there were yet more Paddenburg officers, traipsing along in both directions. One was walking towards the Council Chamber with an axe in his hand; others moved in the opposite direction, carrying something away from the chamber.

'The mural!' Elin said, shock reducing her voice to a whisper.

Jared saw that she was right. The guards were carrying away the painted panels of the precious mural that told the history of Archenfield.

'Stop!' Elin ordered them. Some residual authority in her voice caused them to pause. 'Where are you taking those panels?'

'We're making a bonfire on the palace lawn,' one of them told her, in discordantly amiable tones.

Elin shuddered. 'You most certainly are not. I command you to set them down.'

The guard looked at her vacantly. 'Sorry,' he said, dispensing with any formal address. 'We're just following orders.'

'Whose orders?' Elin enquired.

'The new ruler of Archenfield,' the guard told her.

'Come on!' Elin said, her voice high with manic determination as she strode ahead.

Jared exchanged a glance with Edvin, wondering what horrors might lie in wait in the Council Chamber itself. As they turned the corner, his question was answered. The mural had been dismantled, all save one final panel – the one which told of the Princedom's beginnings, steeped in mist and fire, myth and legend. Even now, another of the guards was busily engaged with tearing the panel roughly from the wall.

'No!' Elin cried out.

Jared realised that she was no longer concerned with the panel – she was spectator to an even more disturbing sight. The guard they had noticed before, carrying the axe, was now swinging the weapon at the Prince's Table. Jared watched, flinching, as the blade buried itself with a heavy thud into the table's thick surface. Were they about to bear witness to the destruction of the Prince's Table?

The blade seemed to be stuck. He could see the extreme effort in the guard's face as he tried to extract it. Under any other circumstances, it might have been comical. But Jared saw his mother's skin turn grey at the sight.

'No,' she said, more softly than before. She swayed uncertainly on her feet and he thought she might be about to faint. Jared reached out to take her by the hand as Edvin moved closer to her other side.

'You must be strong,' he told her. 'It is only a table.'

She gripped his hand as if her life depended upon it, then turned her face towards him. 'It is not only a table,' she said. 'It is everything. They might as well take the blade of that axe to my neck. Or to yours.'

Jared bit down on his lip. He was far from certain what the invaders had planned for him and his family. He stepped into the Council Chamber, anxious now to talk to Axel and find out how he could have countenanced the destruction of all that was sacred to the Princedom.

'Cousin Jared,' Axel said, sitting in the Prince's Chair at the far end of the table. He looked strangely calm as, around him, all hell broke loose.

'You sent for me,' Jared said.

Axel nodded. 'Yes, we have to talk. But I will talk with you alone.'

'The Wynyards move as one—' Elin began, but found herself cut off.

'You act as if you still hold some sway here, Aunt Elin,' Axel said, rising to his feet. Then he brought his hands together and clapped loudly. All motion within the Council Chamber ceased as all faces turned to the new Prince.

'I want everyone to leave the chamber. Now! I will see my cousin alone.'

Jared could see the reluctance and uncertainty in the faces of his mother and brother. 'Do as Axel commands,' he told them.

Edvin nodded, but his mother's feet stayed rooted to the floor. The guards brushed past them. Glancing around, Jared's eyes travelled from the broken mural, the last piece of which now hung by a final nail from the wall, over to the Prince's Table, where the guard's axe was still embedded in its surface. Suddenly, he understood his mother's point of view. The scene was as devastating to him as if he had stepped on to a battlefield.

Behind him, he heard the chamber doors close. He turned and saw that it was Axel who had closed them.

'At last, it's just you and me,' Axel said, walking towards him. 'Take a seat, Cousin Jared. Any seat you care for. What I have to tell you will not take long, I promise.'

FORTY-FIVE

THE BALCONY,
PALACE OF ARCHENFIELD

'Asta!'

Crossing the balcony, Asta felt her heart sink. The very last person she wanted to see or talk to was Lady Koel. Her eyes briefly met those of her erstwhile ally, but she quickly glanced away and kept walking.

'Wait! Please wait, we need to talk.'

Asta stopped dead in her tracks, unable to stop the anger from rising within her. 'What could we possibly have to talk about?'

Koel did not acknowledge Asta's fury but continued in her silky tones. 'We have much to talk about, Asta. But not here, let's go somewhere—'

'Somewhere more private? Somewhere we are less likely to be overheard?' Asta folded her arms. 'No, you and I have spent too long skulking in corridors and shadows,' she said. 'If we are going to talk, let's do it here – out in the open.' She made her way to the edge of the palace balcony, resting her hands on the stone and gazing out at the deceptively tranquil landscape beyond.

'It's cold,' Koel said, coming to stand behind her. 'It's starting to snow.'

'You'll live,' Asta said, hugging her own coat closer. 'Besides, this talk will not take very long. We both have things to get on with. You are the Edling now.'

Koel's eyes were bright. 'Yes, aren't you going to congratulate me?' Seeing the sour expression on Asta's face, Koel shrugged and leaned back nonchalantly against the balcony. 'I can see that you are angry with me, Asta. I know you think I betrayed you and your trust.'

'Yes, I do think that,' Asta confirmed. 'What else could I think? You said we were allies but in fact you were plotting against me – on behalf of your brother – from the beginning. It was all a big charade.'

Koel reached out her hand to Asta's shoulder, as if to squeeze it, but seemed to have second thoughts and merely brushed away a flake of snow that had settled there. 'You have to believe me when I say that this was never personal. I had a job to accomplish. And though you are angry with me now – and I do understand why – I have always very much enjoyed spending time with you.' She paused. 'I thought perhaps you felt the same.'

'No,' Asta said, shaking her head. 'You are mistaken.'

Koel hung her head. 'I know that I have broken the trust between us and I am sorry for that. You probably don't believe me, but it's the truth.'

Asta's eyes blazed with barely restrained fury. 'I'm not sure that you are the best judge of what is truth and what is fiction,' she said.

Koel shrugged again. 'I'll let you have that one. I deserve that.' She turned around and put her gloved hands down on the balcony, beside Asta's. 'I think there's still a lot I could teach you about the workings of life in court, you know. And I would do that with the utmost pleasure. You and I have two of the sharpest minds around here.' She smiled. 'Together, we could be powerful allies.'

Asta shook her head. 'The problem is that I'd never know if we actually *were* together,' she said. 'What you say and what you do are two very different things. I suspect that the only side you are really on, that you were ever on, is your own, Lady Koel.'

For the first time, Koel looked piqued. 'I am on the side of my family. I am on the side of Archenfield. I want what is best for this Princedom.'

'Prince Jared is—'

'Prince Jared was only ever a footnote in the history books, Asta. I know you have a great fondness for him, but you are smart enough to realise I am right. Under the current set of circumstances, we needed Prince Anders to be swiftly succeeded by Prince Axel, with his far greater experience and—'

'So he might hand over power to the Princes of Paddenburg?'

Koel frowned. 'He hasn't handed over power,' she said. 'He has negotiated with them. And, in my view, very successfully. My brother is playing a long game, Asta. When the dust settles, and we have a clearer sense of the new shape of things, there will be wonderful opportunities for people like you and me.'

'I don't want any part in the new shape of things,' Asta declared. 'What I want is Prince Jared back on the throne, where he belongs, and not under house arrest!'

Koel leaned in closer. 'Word of advice, Asta. I'd keep your voice down and treasonous thoughts like that to yourself. They won't help Cousin Jared, and they certainly won't help you.'

'Thank you, but you'll understand if I'm unwilling to take any more advice from you.' Asta drew away from the ledge. 'And now, I am beginning to grow cold – as much from the company as the weather. I should be on my way.'

'Before you go,' Koel said, 'there's just one question I have for you, if you will indulge me?'

Asta shrugged. 'You can ask.'

'You saved my brother's life in Mellerad. He told me what happened. You grabbed his fallen sword and plunged it into the soldier who was threatening him.'

Asta met Koel's gaze. 'Are you wondering if I now regret my actions?'

'No,' Koel shook her head. There was a strange look in her eyes. 'What I'm wondering is how it felt to kill someone. For the first time, I mean.'

Asta held Koel's gaze, without responding, for a moment. Then she smiled sharply. 'I'm a girl from the settlements,' she said. 'What makes you think it was the *first* time I killed someone?'

THE COUNCIL CHAMBER, PALACE OF ARCHENFIELD

'So.' Jared's eyes sought out Axel's across the breadth of the Prince's Table. 'Did they buy it?'

Axel nodded, smiling at his cousin. 'Everything we agreed to before,' he confirmed. 'Your house arrest. The preservation of the key infrastructures of Archenfield. And,' he paused, 'sending you and your sympathisers into exile.'

'And you're certain they'll hold true to their word and still their swords?'

Axel nodded. 'I am,' he said. 'The bloodshed they unleashed, though ferocious, is at an end now. Ven and Henning have done what they came here to do – they have demonstrated their superior military strength, they have claimed first Tanaka and now Archenfield as their first two conquests within the Thousand Territories.' He rose from his seat and walked over to stand at Jared's side. 'But they want a jewel in the crown of Paddenburg's expanding empire. Not a wasteland.' Axel's hand came to rest on Jared's shoulder. 'I know how deeply you feel about the trail of devastation the forces of Paddenburg have left in their wake but, being brutal, it could have been much, much worse.' He squeezed Jared's shoulder. 'And it is at an end now. I promise you that.'

Jared frowned. He wanted to believe Axel. He *did* believe him. But still he was troubled.

'Remember what you said when we met before?' Axel continued, perhaps sensing his discomfort. 'That you expected to return here to find the palace razed to the ground? Well, that hasn't happened, has it? Oh, it's typical of their bully-boy tactics that they would burn the mural and sling an axe at this very table. But, you may rest assured, these are only surface wounds. Now they have what they want' – he paused and smiled – 'now they *think* they have what they want, Archenfield can begin to heal again.'

'With you working from within this new order and me working from beyond the borders?'

Axel nodded. 'Exactly so. Until the time is right to effect the necessary change we both desire.'

Jared let out a sigh. 'They really have no suspicion whatsoever of our alliance?' he pressed.

Axel shook his head sharply. 'None whatsoever. An alliance between the deposed Prince of All Archenfield and the very one who deposed him—?' His finger lightly traced the glimmering letters on the surface of the table, then his eyes returned to Jared. 'Who would ever believe such a thing?'

'Can I really trust you?' Jared found himself asking.

Axel laughed at that. 'Of course not,' he said. 'I'd have thought you'd have learned by now that the smartest way is to trust no one.' His words seemed to echo within the expanse of the Council Chamber.

Jared shook his head. 'Were you always such a cynic?'

'One person's cynic is another's realist,' Axel observed. 'But I suspect that I will never completely win you around to my view of the world. We are cut from a very different cloth, cousin. Which only makes our new and secret alliance all the more potent, don't you think?'

Jared nodded – slowly, cautiously.

'The key thing,' Axel added, 'is that none of your supporters can know about this until you are safely beyond the borders. Then, and only then, can you share our plans with them and start preparations for the next phase.'

Jared felt a wave of nervous energy course through him. He had barely returned from one journey and another was already beginning.

'You should go now,' Axel told him. 'The less time we spend together, the better. I've dealt with one spy at the heart of the Princedom today, but doubtless there are others. Besides, the palace is overrun with purple shirts, in case you hadn't noticed.'

Jared nodded, rising to his feet.

'But before you go, Cousin Jared, there's something I want to say to you. I want you to know that in the few short weeks of your reign, you have proved yourself twice the Prince your brother ever was.'

Jared smiled ruefully at Axel's words and shook his head.

'It's true,' Axel told him, stepping closer. 'I'm sure you

399

became as sick as I did at the intonings of Prince Anders the Golden. But it was all smoke and mirrors. If Anders seemed golden, it was down to those of us around him – myself, your mother and, dare I say it, Logan Wilde?' He paused. 'We moulded your brother like clay. And he allowed himself to be moulded.' Axel was standing shoulder to shoulder with his cousin now, and he smiled at Jared. 'You – in contrast – have, from day one, consistently ignored the advice directed at you from all quarters – well, save perhaps from Asta Peck. And, Cousin Jared, this made you the better Prince.' He placed his hand on Jared's shoulder once more. 'You are your own man,' he said. 'And I respect that. It's one of the few things we have in common. That, and our abiding love for, and commitment to, Archenfield.'

Jared considered his cousin's words, then gently but firmly brushed Axel's hand away. 'If you thought I was a better Prince than Anders, it's a shame you didn't have enough faith in me not to launch a conspiracy against me in the few days I was absent.'

There was vitriol in Jared's voice, but Axel did not flinch. If anything, he seemed amused by his cousin's attack. 'What's done is done. If it's any comfort to you, I did not launch my conspiracy because I lacked faith in you.' He smiled softly. 'I simply saw an opportunity and took it.'

Yes, Jared thought. That makes complete sense. That was how people like Axel and Koel and the Princes of Paddenburg were wired. They saw the opportunities – for power, for promotion, for expansion and glory – and seized them, whatever the collateral damage. The same, though, could be said of his own mother, he supposed, and his dead brother too. Maybe it would serve Jared better to be like them – but he suspected that, even if it was what he wanted, he could never achieve such a metamorphosis.

'Time to go, don't you think?' Axel said, extending his hand. 'Travel safe, cousin.'

Jared reached out and took Axel's hand in his own. 'Look after things while I'm gone,' he said. The words seemed pitifully inadequate, but they were enough.

The two cousins shook hands. Then Prince Jared, deposed ruler of Archenfield, turned towards the door of the Council Chamber and braced himself to make the necessary preparations for his exile.

FORTY-SIX

THE STABLES, PALACE OF ARCHENFIELD

Only a few days before, Jared had come to the stables in the early morning darkness to embark on the mission for alliances; now, he was back again, preparing for a very different journey. Some of his companions were the same: he found the faces of Kai Jagger and Bram Gentle in the crowd. He derived not inconsiderable satisfaction from the fact that of the comrades on his previous expedition, only Hal was now missing. Axel had put a good case for keeping Hal as his own Bodyguard, and Jared had reluctantly agreed, thinking it lent the story of his forced exile greater credence.

The group was enhanced by additional members, starting with his mother and his brother. He had expected high drama from his mother at the thought of leaving the palace, but though her face had initially paled at the idea, she had quickly agreed that it was their only option. He had momentarily contemplated telling her the truth – but decided, on balance, that it was safer to wait until they were far from the palace, in a place of greater safety. When they had crossed the border and regrouped where Rohan's troops had retreated to, Jared would tell the entire company the truth of his covert agreement with Axel and their plans to regain full control of Archenfield.

This morning, Queen Elin's mood seemed stoic as she spoke to Lucas Curzon, another of their comrades, about which of the horses he had assigned to her.

As well as Lucas and Kai, two other erstwhile members of the Twelve were within their ranks – Nova Chastain and, of course, Asta Peck. Jared knew that it had been hard for Asta to bid goodbye to her uncle, but perhaps less hard than it might have been, had their last week together not been marked by deep enmity. Asta had never been in any doubt that she would be riding out in Jared's company and she had tried, in spite of their rift, to persuade Elias to join them. But on this, as on so much else, he had proved intractable.

Jared smiled to see Asta and Nova both settled on their horses, talking like old friends. He was grateful for everything they had done for him – everything they had tried to do to fight his cause. They bore no blame whatsoever for being duped by his duplicitous cousin, Lady Koel. In spite of himself, he felt worried for Koel. He had always had a certain fondness for her. He found it hard indeed to reconcile what he now knew of her manoeuvrings about court with the warm and light-hearted cousin he had always enjoyed spending time with. Who was the real Lady Koel? It did not seem so long ago that he had been giving her advice on how to shoot arrows; now it seemed that she was far more ambitious than he, and that she had always had a keen eye focused right on the centre of her target.

The friendly, almost impossibly handsome face of Lucas Curzon appeared at his side. 'I don't want to rush you, Your Majesty, but everyone is ready now.'

Jared smiled. 'You're not rushing me, Lucas. I'm probably the keenest of anyone to begin this journey.' He paused. 'And you really have no further need to address me as "Your Majesty". Plain Jared will do.'

Lucas shook his head. 'You are still the rightful ruler,' he said. 'So until you expressly command me not to, I intend to address you as "Your Majesty" or "Prince Jared".'

'All right,' Jared said, touched by this affirmation of loyalty.

'Let me help you on to your horse,' Lucas offered. Jared willingly accepted his hand. Within moments, he was back in the saddle of Handrick.

Moments later, Lucas had settled himself on his own mount.

As they began walking the horses out from the shelter of the stables, they felt the first flakes of snow falling upon them.

'I think Archenfield has always looked most beautiful in the snow,' he heard Nova say. Her voice was tinged with the sadness of departure.

'At least,' came his mother's tart riposte, 'the invaders did not do us the insult of coming to bid us farewell.'

'No,' Jared agreed. 'I don't think I could have borne that.'

'Although,' Elin added, 'I still think it was rash of you to disregard Axel's offer of an escort to the borders.'

Jared wrinkled his nose as a snowflake fell on its tip. 'Who needs one of Axel's cronies, when we have the might of Kai and Bram in our company?'

'You hear that, young Bram?' Kai said, his voice as rich and mellifluous as ever. 'Looks like it's down to you and me to repel enemy advances.'

Bram nodded, his cheeks already pink from the frigid air. 'I shall do whatever is asked of me,' he said.

Kai chuckled at his young comrade's unswerving seriousness. 'You always have, Bram Gentle. And I'm sure you always will!'

As they turned the corner into the palace gardens, the talk swiftly died away. It was as if each of them needed to say their own silent farewell to the palace, and as if, too, they were each aware of the need to give one another space to do so.

This is a good company, Jared thought. We will look after one another.

He turned to find Asta now riding alongside him.

'No regrets?' she asked.

'No regrets,' he said, shaking his head. 'I'm only looking forward now.'

She nodded. 'You're nervous, though – admit it. I can see the signs.'

He grinned. 'I should know better than to even try to mask my feelings from you. Of course I'm nervous. Nervous as hell. About any number of things.' He thought of the secret he was keeping from her – from all of his companions. He was getting used to keeping secrets. Still, it did not sit comfortably with Jared to be withholding the truth from Asta and the rest of his company.

Aware of her eyes still on him, he added, 'I shall feel better when I have spoken to Prince Rohan and asked him formally to shelter us while we are in exile.'

Asta nodded. 'From what you have told me, Prince Rohan is a good man and a strong ally of yours. I have no doubt he will grant your request.'

Jared frowned. He thought so. He *hoped* so. He hadn't always been straight with Rohan, but surely his friend would not turn against him now, at this moment of need?

'Whatever lies ahead of us,' Asta said now, 'I know we can get through it together.' She grew suddenly flustered. 'I mean all of us, obviously,' she clarified.

Jared reached out his gloved hand to hers and gave it a

squeeze. 'Thank you,' he said. 'You have a gift for making everything better.'

He wasn't sure if she blushed at that, or if her cheeks were merely reddened from the cold. The snow was falling more thickly now.

Suddenly, they heard the sound of drumming hooves. Eyes turned back towards the sound. Had Axel dispatched an escort, in spite of Jared's specific instructions to the contrary? Or was this some kind of trick? Had the new rulers of Paddenburg let them think they could ride away, when in fact they were to be rounded up and reclaimed as prisoners?

The Prince's company drew their horses to a standstill, allowing the lone rider to catch up. Jared sensed a fatalism within the group – they were all in this together now.

The lone rider was, like the rest of them, clad in a hood and layers of fur to protect against the harsh weather. His horse – for this was definitely a man – was loaded with packages and bags, like theirs. At last, drawing up before them, he drew down his hood and revealed himself.

'Uncle Elias!' Asta exclaimed.

Elias nodded. 'Asta, Prince Jared, Queen Elin, my erstwhile friends and comrades ... I have been a fool, I fear. But I humbly beseech you to let me join your party. I want no more of Archenfield or what it is bound to become.'

Jared could see the tears of relief in Asta's eyes. That was the only answer he needed.

'Good Elias,' he said, 'of course you are welcome to join us. We will ride all the more securely, knowing that we have a medical man in our ranks.'

Elias bowed his head, then drew up his hood. He brought his horse in line with the rest of the company and they resumed their journey through the falling snow.

*

406

Axel stood at the window watching the caravan of exiles making their way across the palace grounds. Snow was falling thickly now and the figures had already become only grey shadows to him. Just before he lost sight of them, Axel could not resist lifting his hand and waving, though of course there was no way they could possibly see him.

'Bye, bye, Prince Jared. Bye, bye, Queen Elin!'

The voice was disturbingly close. Turning, Axel found himself looking in to the amused face of Logan Wilde.

'It's not the best weather for an expedition, now is it?' Logan said, with a shrug. 'But, when push came to shove, I suppose they really had to go.'

'Yes,' Axel agreed, with a nod. And you'll be next, he thought. You might think that you've got your hands on the greasy pole now, just because Prince Ven has a strange fascination with you, but you're on borrowed time, Wilde. I'll find a way to take you out of this picture once and for all. You and your equally ambitious sister. You're not the only one with secret alliances.

He realised that Logan had been watching him. 'What are you thinking about?' the disgraced Poet asked.

Axel shrugged, in no rush whatsoever to answer him. 'Everything. And nothing.'

Logan smiled. 'I know just what you mean,' he said. 'I suppose in our own ways, we have each waited for this day to come. And now that it has, though it is piquant with possibilities, there's also a strange sense that it might all simply be a mirage. Of no more substance or power to endure than this falling snow.'

'Ever the wordsmith,' Axel noted.

Logan smiled again. 'I like words well enough. But I like power more.' He turned to glance over his shoulder.

Axel followed Logan's gaze towards the Prince's Table. It

was a surreal sight, with the axe still buried in its surface, as if wielded by an invisible axeman. And there, in the centre of the table, sat the Prince's Crown; the ancient blue-steel helmet, bound in leather with the golden stag's head rising from the top. Logan must have brought it in with him. Perhaps it was only the shift of light created by the dark skies and driving snow outside the window; perhaps it was something more, but the crown seemed to emit an unearthly blue glow.

Axel found himself – of course he did – drawn towards the crown. Leaving Logan's side, he walked over to the table. His eyes skimmed the glimmering titles of the Council of Twelve – the Bodyguard, the Poet, the Priest, the Woodsman ... two of the Twelve were dead now; several others were in the party of exiles. What was the future of the Twelve? Everything was uncertain.

Axel's eyes moved from the carved names of the Twelve to the crown itself. He reached out his hands towards it but as the tips of his fingers made contact with the cold steel, he heard a loud tutting from over by the window. Glancing back across, he saw Logan, eyes wide, arms folded, shaking his head.

'That's rather presumptuous of you, don't you think?'

Axel frowned. 'I suppose it does beg the question, Logan. Which one of us bastards is now Prince of All Archenfield?'

Logan nodded.

'Well,' Axel said, his fingers cradling the golden antlers. 'Which of us is it? You or I?'

Logan shrugged and, smiling enigmatically, turned his back upon Axel to direct the full focus of his attention towards the thickly falling snow.

THE
ARCHENFIELD
ARCHIVE

THE
SETTLEMENTS
OF ARCHENFIELD

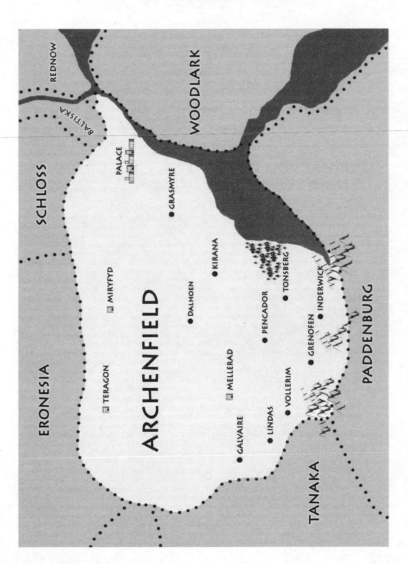

ARCHENFIELD
AND
ITS NEIGHBOUR
TERRITORIES

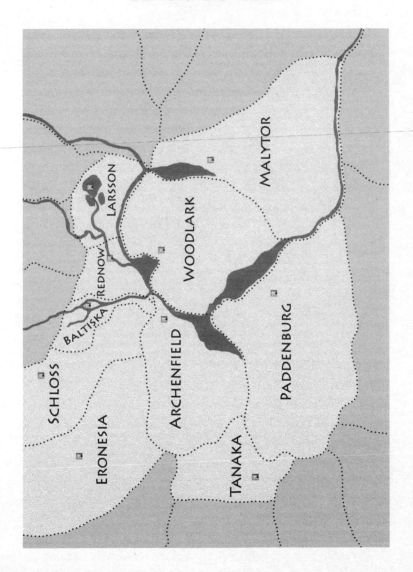

Jared Wynyard
THE PRINCE

Hal Harness
THE
BODYGUARD

Axel Blaxland
THE EDLING

Nova Chastain
THE FALCONER

Asta Peck
THE POET

Elias Peck
THE PHYSICIAN

Father Simeon
THE PRIEST

THE PRINCE
& OFFICERS OF
ARCHENFIELD

Morgan Booth
THE EXECUTIONER

Emelie Sharp
THE BEEKEEPER

Vera Webb
THE COOK

Jonas Drummond
THE WOODSMAN

Lucas Curzon
THE GROOM

Kai Jagger
THE HUNTSMAN

Axel Blaxland
THE CAPTAIN
OF THE GUARD

— Family Tree —

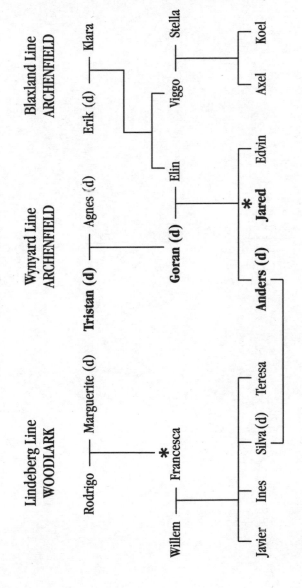

Lindeberg Line
WOODLARK

Wynyard Line
ARCHENFIELD

Blaxland Line
ARCHENFIELD

Rodrigo — Marguerite (d)

Tristan (d) — Agnes (d)

Erik (d) — Klara

* Francesca

Goran (d) — Elin

Viggo — Stella

Willem

Javier   Ines   Silva (d)   Teresa

Anders (d)   *Jared   Edvin

Axel   Koel

* = the current rulers of Archenfield and Woodlark

(d) = deceased

ABOUT THE AUTHOR

Justin Somper is the worldwide bestselling author of the Vampirates sequence, which has been published in twenty-five languages in thirty-five countries. When he isn't writing, he works with other authors as a publicist and trainer. He lives in London with his partner and two energetic dogs. Justin invites you to visit him online at alliesandassassins.com, on Facebook at facebook.com/JustinSomperAuthor, and on Twitter @JustinSomper.